SALVATION'S FIRE

JUSTINA ROBSON

SOLARIS

For Daniel
Thanks for showing me worlds hitherto unknown ☺

PROLOGUE

THE GIRL WAS lost. Everyone was lost at the camp. It was a place for lost things: people, dogs, things carried and loved, things carried and hated, things without homes or names. They were put down there because there was nowhere else to be put down, on a land that nobody had cared about enough to set a spade in or fence around. It wasn't bad land, but it had no particular goodness. Water was far. Trees were sparse. Grass was tough and unlovely to behold. Weed and brambles were endless, hiding the little game. Even the sky was meagre, eked across the hills like a hide stretched too thin which would soon get hard in the rain, and tear, and let everything pour in.

The girl shared a tent with two angry women. They were not relatives but they had a wider kinship that marked them both as Babohendra, the people of the horse. They were further displaced than she was and their semi-circular hoofs, angled legs and furred skins of chestnut and black were foreign enough to be frightening, though none of them had the energy for fright. The Kinslayer's armies had seen to that. All of them were exhausted, worn down to the bones by running. Even after the turn of the seasons had thrice counted them in they were always light sleepers, ready to leave, unable to believe that it was over.

Perhaps it was not over. She wasn't sure. She'd felt him die. A life like that was distinctive, even at a great distance. It had

7

left behind a kind of silence that resonated against all he had touched that still lived. She knew he was a monster, a death-bringer of unmatched carnage, even among his own kind, but she had seen him as a vivid, vibrant exultation of life right until the last moments of his rending. As a life he had been exceptional and the music of the world was less without him. But without his smothering presence she was able to detect other melodies—the brilliant shapes of other Guardians still active—and so she alone of all the sad rabble in that place was completely confident that he was gone, his armies scattered, his plans awry, his destiny reached and story ended.

He had wanted to end her story but he had missed her. She smiled when she thought of this. It was her secret gladness and it gave her the power to endure hunger, thirst, cold and starvation of love. He had lost and she was still alive. But she was alone. Her smile faded then, always, as she knew it. None of these people were her people. Their kind no longer existed upon the earth.

This day, grey and damp, filled with lamenting from one quarter, with glum despair at others, was no different to a hundred other days. The sun had come up, those who were able had gone to hunt and forage, those who were not remained by the smoky little fires and made teas from sticks. A party went out to find out what happened to the last group who had set off to a village some twenty miles distant and not returned. They went armed with sharpened poles, slowly, hoping to be met on the way. Without some kind of trade they were going to die soon in this nothing valley, surrounded by indifferent woodlands, as surely as rabbits in a trap. They had nothing to trade but themselves and a few little trinkets that were precious but of no value to a stranger. There was nothing to be done about it.

She went out of the tent and stood in the mud, watching the other children sit sullenly or poke about with sticks. They didn't like her and she didn't like them. It wasn't personal. They stared at her, sunken eyes that would have been spiteful but now were losing interest and would soon not care. The adults moved around slowly, as if they were under water. They didn't see her. She didn't belong with them. A moment after she had turned away a stone hit her on the head. Probably they were laughing at her, but maybe not. She didn't know, wouldn't give them the satisfaction of looking around to find out. It settled the matter.

She went back into the tent and picked up the rag bundle she used to gather leaves and berries. Heading out past the few log cabins she took the path towards the deeper forest at their backs. They had come this way when they first arrived and she remembered seeing roads.

A sharp jerk on her sleeve stopped her. She looked up. The younger of the two women whose tent she shared was looking, moving her mouth, making a questioning, cross face. Her hoof stamped, betraying her anxiety.

The girl pointed to the woods. Mimed picking, eating.

An expression of exasperation, sadness and concern filled the woman's long features. Her brown eyes were patient, much more so than her hands, which she folded up against the urge to snatch the girl and hold her too tightly. There was an emptiness there, the ghost of someone left behind. The girl knew it and waited until the woman nodded to say she could go. It was all she had to give as a parting gift to the one who had tried to help her, that moment of kindness. There should be so much more, but there wasn't.

She left the camp and moved beyond the briar patches and the glades of wild garlic, the fallen logs where mushrooms came, the boles of familiar trees that were climbable where there might be birds nests and insects within the reach of someone small, light. She knew them all. She touched them as she passed, those slow lives, and felt through their roots across the huge reach of the land to where there were other bright patches, people and their animals. She found a way.

She dropped the rags at some point before it got dark. She drank from a stream and left her fingers in it to go cold because there were fish there, lively and full of brilliance, that lent her a little joy. Once she looked around, looked back. She took a route through the thorn bushes that no larger person could follow, to be sure.

She traced her way safely, guided by the beating hearts of the tiny animals, the darting swiftness of the flies. She avoided humans. She kept to the path of the trees, heading to a spot far away in the West where a brilliant shadow was moving; dark candlelight, the grey, ever-flickering silver gleams of the Wanderer.

CHAPTER ONE

"RIDDLE ME REE, such fancies are free, the cat's in the cream and the bird's on the tree!" Many voices, most of them either intoxicated or excited, the owners full of sweet honey pastries, were united, belting out the words to the old rhyme so enthusiastically that the sound floated all the way across the scattered trestles and decimated feasts to the farthest reaches of the castle grounds. Children playing, dogs barking, infighting amongst various relations, bawdiness and other fine noises of a celebration in its throes circled about the grassy pastures and along the hedgerows.

At Celestaine's family home the number of songs known and sung gustily without the slightest concern for sense or melody always amazed her—joyfully for the most part. But today she was simply grateful that it wasn't another rendition of 'The Blade of Castle Mourn' in which she had a starring role as the warrior who slaughtered a dragon, cut off the Kinslayer's hand and paved the way to human salvation. It would have been unfitting to lie about in a drunken stupor under the blossom-heavy boughs of the cherry orchard and have unwitting relatives find her in the loose embrace of the 'enemy', sharing mead with another 'enemy'. There would have been explaining to do, and shouting about Yorughan scum. There probably still would be. There might be a fight and that would be a pity because she enjoyed a good fight but had now drunk too much to make a showing. The only consolation to the entire tedious day was that finally it was over and she was now free to leave for the open road as she had tried to do three days earlier when Caradwyn had thwarted her. She'd been calling for her horse, her armour, all set to ride off and find out what foolish nonsense Deffo, least useful Guardian, was on about this time (and thank goodness for Deffo, if you could ever say that and mean it, but she did right then, the boredom and the difficulty of being at home already stifling and unbearable) when her cousin had appeared, a spectre of orange and pink silk, blonde braids and rosewater.

Caradwyn was the family beauty. She shared Celestaine's height and "silver-beauty" near-white hair, blue eyes and milk skin, but the resemblance ended abruptly at that point. Celestaine was broad of shoulder, straight and strong, trained for combat and endurance. Caradwyn was willowy at the centre and curvy where it counted. Although in childhood she had loved the outdoors she now considered walking a chore and disliked anything that would disturb her sense of order. Despite this unpromising development she and Celestaine had shared happy childhood moments riding out and canoeing along the river tributaries. What Caradwyn lacked in general gusto she made up for with a powerful imagination. She was the storyteller who had Celestaine spellbound with the lives she invented for them; they were troubadors on the run, they were Guardians helping the poor and driving back the ferocious evil of the underground races (Celestaine knew irony was never going to let her go) and they were heroic princesses, freeing flying horses from evil enchanters, fishing up magical beasts from the dark pools beneath the hanging willows, dreaming of the winged demons of the far north who soared high up between icy mountains on wings feathered with steel. Since then they hadn't seen much of one another. Celestaine had trained for combat and the tough business of every day on the estate, and Caradwyn had travelled to Ilkand as a scholar with her books and scripts to become the master of managing and recording. She took to it with the love of a Cheriveni for numbers and regulation.

They were already distant by the time Celestaine came back, now a person who really was immortalised in song, a hero with a horse. She hadn't even talked to Caradwyn, or anyone, on her return. It was hard to say which had been harder to bear—the adulation and awe or the horror and the revulsion—but on balance it was the revulsion that did her in when Heno and Nedlam were revealed as her companions. Caradwyn hadn't made a tale about that in the good old days.

Heno and Nedlam, as Yorughan, the vanguard and powerhouse of the Kinslayer's elite forces, were the evil enemy from below. Heno was the worst of the worst, a Heart Taker, painted like a devil, a tusked beast, filled with eldritch sorcery. Nedlam was the kind of giant monstress that ate babies. You killed them and left the bodies for the birds. You let them die slow for all the thousands they'd killed. You didn't bring them home. You didn't lay down with them. You didn't offer them home and hearth and heart and feel that of all the people in the world they were your closest friends. Closer even than all who had known you before the war.

So Celestaine had avoided Caradwyn—easy enough given Caradwyn's responsibilities as Fernreame's bookkeeper and estates manager—and then, just as freedom beckoned its crooked finger, there she was, as large as life and twice as sweet, her large, grey eyes bright with the tears that suspected betrayal, those full, curving lips that perfectly pouted in a fully justified hurt.

"You can't go before the wedding!"

Celestaine had opened her mouth and nothing had come out. Fully nothing at all.

She could hear servants in the courtyard without, hauling trestles and benches into place for the wedding of Caradwyn to another newly-returned war hero, Starich the Wolf. He was heir to the titles and privileges of Thistledown; a notable clan.

In addition he was a sufficiently skimpy number of warrior-barons short of the throne of Arven to be in with a shot at it, if he successfully united with Fiddlehead, the clan to which Fernreame belonged. This made him a superlative catch, according to Celestaine's aunt, and a fine fellow according to her uncle, the present Clan head, who couldn't wait to unite the fortunes of both houses and hand it all over to someone else in order that he would finally be free to go fishing.

Celest couldn't wait for Starich to arrive so that their attention would divert onto something they wholeheartedly approved of—something without suspiciously strange frenemies in tow that they must learn to treat nicely instead of beheading. Starich, and not she, could properly occupy the role of the warrior-at-home, thunderously embellishing every tale of battle, relishing feasts, sparring with his fellows and enacting scenes of valor for the amusement of those too old and too young to be sent to fight. Starich wouldn't be grabbing his coat and heading for the hills unless they told him to, not with all that responsibility to weigh him down. They could fawn over him and fuss over Caradwyn and their plans for a rosy future full of ferocious children so that Celest would be able to slip away without further ado.

"I..." she said, but there was nothing. She looked at Caradwyn's face, older now, pale from lack of sunlight, freckled and looking at her with such a longing that was easy to read—only a few days more now of the freedom to be herself, before duty and motherhood came to take the time. She looked exactly as she had looked when she visited years before, hunting out Celest, demanding they continue the adventures of the summer before. But now there would be no more of that. Celest had gone and had one without her. And was now leaving her forever.

"I... wouldn't miss it," she said. "I was just making some preparations. For later."

Caradwyn's despair lightened a little and she gripped

Celestaine's arm firmly, the lie there so plainly to see, the mail freshly oiled and ready. "Good. We must ride out together. I have something I must tell you and you must tell me the truth of everything. I want the whole story." Seeing Celestaine start to demur she shook her firmly, "No! You will not dare deprive me! Celest. Tomorrow. Tomorrow at dawn we ride. Meet me at the stables."

That enthusiasm, that energy, that sense of how much Caradwyn had always liked her—not always returned enough. "Yes," Celestaine said. "All right. At dawn."

"Alone," Caradwyn shook her finger in Celestaine's face. "Nobody else. I want you all to myself."

"Alone." Celest managed a smile.

"I must go see to the chicken man and his money," Caradwyn sighed, rattling the collection of silver keys and trinkets she wore at her belt to mark her as the head of the clan households. "I have missed you. And here you are now. Exactly as I always imagined."

"I'm not what you imagined at all," Celest said, thinking of Heno compared to Caradwyn's suitor and at the same moment realising that she was not at home here, and would never be.

"Yes, you are." In ignorance of Celest's thoughts Caradwyn made a motion of buttoning Celestaine's mouth shut.

Celest shook her head insistently, feeling like a joy-killer.

"You did what we always dreamed of." Caradwyn buttoned Celest to silence more firmly and pointed at her as she walked away, picked up her skirts to hurry off, cast a final smile over her shoulder like a ray of sunlight.

Celest stood, her saddle over her arm, alone in the hall. She felt a thousand years old. Beside her was the old portrait of her dead father which had looked down when two girls had schemed to run the world. Now she was on eye-level. He looked straight at her and she met his gaze and felt she looked in a mirror. Beside him, her mother's wry humor fought with a stern attachment to duty. She was glad they had not lived to see her now. It made things easier.

She'd used to hate adult portraits that looked so stern, so disappointed.

She still hated them.

She sighed and went to tell the others they were staying.

CHAPTER TWO

It WAS TWO days since Deffo had appeared with news of his fellow Guardian, Wanderer.

Celestaine had a cautious trust in Wanderer, which she didn't extend to any of his fellow demigods who had been left by the gods themselves to take care of humankind. Reckoner's transformation into the Kinslayer had pretty much done a hatchet job on a lot of people's trust in them. But Wanderer had given her the sword that could cut through anything. She had cut off the Kinslayer's hand with it, besides killing a dragon. It had allowed her to take him down, along with the others; and now it was gone, buried deep in a rock after breaking against Wall's hammer and flying off. Fate or godly intervention? She didn't care to know. But there was an urgent appeal in Deffo's claim.

"Wanderer's near. He knows where the gods are!"

The Kinslayer had severed the gods from the world. Their temples and their followers were everywhere bereft. Only the Guardians remained. Celest was ambivalent about the gods. A god could have restored wings to the Aethani and not left it to her to attempt the journey in some gesture of reparation she wasn't entirely up to but which had to be done. It had not ended as she had hoped. Some things were not undoable. Maybe the gods were responsible for that impulse to improve and mend that seemed to fill her with the urge to action she felt now. So much had been made ruin and the alternative was to lie in the cherry orchard in a drunken stupor, avoiding people and watching the days pass by unchanged. She couldn't dredge up sufficient self-pity for that.

"But you are going," Deffo said, hanging onto the stable door as a way of half-hiding. "When this is done."

Heno and Nedlam, gathered here under the pretence of looking after the horses, looked meaningfully at her. She fancied there was a twinge of wistfulness in Heno's face, but he was always hard to read. She figured he was getting better at dealing with emotions, but he didn't like to show it.

"We're going. After the wedding. Soon as it's over." She nodded firmly.

"Does that mean I get to sing?" Ralas asked. He was sitting on a hay bale, picking hair out of the horse brush using the iron comb. His movements were slow, pain-filled but executed with great determination and grace. A large ball of horse hair was gathered at his side. "I noticed some rather nice instruments around the place. In the halls. Gathering dust."

"You can have them. And yes. We need musicians. If you want to play, that is. Though you don't have to play 'All Black and Silver Fire He Came'." She named the song he had been working on to celebrate Deffo's musteline heroism in the defeat of Wall—a song fraught with the most expansive lyrics and melodramatic chords, not to mention a role of daring-do which stretched the imagination almost to breaking point. She looked at Ralas with caution. He could be so self-deprecating and sarcastic at times that she wasn't sure he intended to be taken at his word, but he looked cheered. "No 'Castle Mourn'-ing," she added.

"Oh, I think I have to play whatever the bride requests," he said with a smirk and flexed his right hand, looking critically at his long fingers, pale and weak. They were filthy and the nails black with grease from the brushes. "Maybe I could have some new clothes? A bard should not appear as a tramp." He gestured at his rough travelling gear, much of which had not been washed for weeks. "In fact, some of us are in serious need of bathing and grooming." He glanced at the Yoggs.

Nedlam bared her huge teeth in a grin and patted Celestaine's horse, whose hide was gleaming softly in the sunlight coming through the door. She clapped it on the neck, gently, and rested her hand on its withers, managing to make it look small though it was a war-steed and a high one at that. "All finished here. Shiny little horsie. Very nice work."

"He means us," Heno growled, shaking his head as he looked at Celestaine to see how bad it was going to be. There was a strange tension around his eyes, a sombre resignation waiting to be born.

She had honestly not given a thought so far to appearing at a clan gathering with him at her side. With them all looking at her she could see that they were all picturing it, aside from Nedlam who was busy licking a finger and applying it to a streak of mud on her booted knee. Celest looked at Heno, her lover and her most loyal companion. Slate blue of skin, white of hair, tusked, moustached, taller by a foot than any human she had ever known. And Nedlam, eight foot and then some of massive power, topped by a spiked black coxcomb. She had a brief vision of Nedlam in a dress, holding Wall's gigantic hammer with a ribbon tied around its haft, the bloody handprint of a human child on her bodice, laced with the guts of her enemies to join the human and the Yorughan traditional formalwear. She blinked to get rid of it.

Even without that there would be some kind of explanation required. But then, what explanation could she possibly offer?

Hello, everyone. Yes, it's me, Celestaine the Fair, of Fernreame. I know the song says I killed the Kinslayer but really it was a group effort and the people you should thank are these two here. He did breed them in a pit under the earth for the specific purpose of channelling his power to wipe out all humankind but in a turn-up for the books they decided to stick the knife in his back first. So, I know they look like every nightmare you've been having for the last few years but if it hadn't been for them letting me go after I got captured and helping us all to reach the inner sanctum at Nydarrow none of this would ever have happened and you'd all be topsoil by now! Isn't that amazing? And yes, this one that does the death-lightning is here with me. On my arm. We're together. I hope you'll all join us in offering a toast to the bride and groom...

"Maybe it's wiser if we don't go," Heno said. His tone made it clear he was prepared to wait, unhappy about it, but accepting of their place as scum in this scenario—and she hated it, realising only then that she'd just assumed they would all be going, that they were all welcome. They must be welcome, it was only fair after all that had happened, but she knew that her idea of history and the one already making the rounds in the mouths of minstrels and couriers were very different things.

"I'm going to sort it out," she said at the same time. "I'll make it right. But just in case make sure everything is ready to leave at a second's notice." She put her saddle down on the bale beside Ralas.

"What's a wedding?" Nedlam asked suddenly, frowning down at Celestaine, as what had been said ten minutes ago finally reached its destination.

She rode out with Caradwyn the next day after little sleep, wondering how to broach the subject. They took their most common route away from the estate by the river's edge, cantering easily along the green hollow, the stems of flyworts and parsleys breaking as they passed and lending a sharp, herbal scent to the dawn air. This hour and the one before sunset had always seemed the most magical, full of unmanifest desire and the possibility of anything being around the corner. They slowed as they approached the rocky ford and Celestaine started to draw breath but before she could speak Caradwyn turned to her, standing in the stirrups to haul back her spirited grey stallion, her long white-gold braids flying around her shoulders as she expertly wrestled him into a submissive prance.

"Why didn't you tell me you were in love with that Yorughan? How long were you going to wait? Forever? Do you really think so little of me, Celest?" She rolled her eyes. "And now you're giving me the face that says you can't believe I know. I hope you realise that it's not hard to guess. So much sw-sw-sw whispering and glancing and stalwart standing up like a royal trout with a skewer up your arse! And anyway, why else would you be avoiding me?"

Celest reined back, weight lower, hardly moving, her horse instantly responsive from their years of familiarity and battle. "I thought you'd get the same face on you I see everywhere else when they're with me." *They, not him. They. Some kind of new family unit.*

The horses began to pick their way around the boulders and rocks of the shallow river crossing. They let the reins loose.

"I can't say I wasn't surprised, Cel, but not as surprised as when I heard you killed the Kinslayer." She cast a side eye.

"I didn't really do that," Celestaine said, watching Caradwyn's knowing smile. "I was there at the end, but so were a lot of other people."

"I like my version better."

"It isn't true."

"I don't think that's the point of a story."

"Yes, but it's the point of history," Celestaine said evenly, knowing this was only the preamble to what Caradwyn wanted to say next.

"And, since history is being written and you have a starring role, I do think that I can sway matters in your favour for the wedding," Caradwyn said. "I can enforce the peace, until a lot of drink has gone under the bridge. After that I can't vouch for things and I can't speak for Starich or his entourage though I have heard they are many war veterans. So, my proposal is that there is a separate gathering in the orchard for your party. You can do the ceremonial bits, and then join them there. It's not overlooked by the main tents or any of the gardens and it has a clear route to the Ilkand road."

"Ah. I see," Celest said, grateful but also hurt in a way she had not expected. It was minor and she didn't count it worth much. "Thank you. That's very pragmatic."

They had reached the end of the crossing and were gathering themselves up again as the horses stepped out onto the track, one horse to either side, pressed close enough by the overgrowth that their stirrups clashed now and again.

"I wish it would be otherwise," Caradwyn said. "But I don't have that much faith in us all as a collective. Forinthi are progressive and forgiving but they aren't divine. If it were only you and me though then I want you to know I'd be glad if it were a double wedding. I'd never put you aside because of who you choose to love." She reached over and squeezed Celest's hand where it was on the saddle pommel. "Life will take us away from each other but it will never take you from my heart, Celest. This only shows that you are a hero in more ways than merely slaying a mad god. Now, let's ride like the wind! Let's be highwaymen! One more time!" And before Celestaine could react, her heart jammed awkwardly in her throat, Caradwyn had spurred her stallion into a leaping gallop and she was having to dodge huge clods of mud flying up at her face as it showed her a neat pair of iron shoes.

They thundered below the beech stands and the arching banks of the long cutway that ran through the hills south of the estate, the wind in their faces, mud and the whipping lash of branches a strange frenzy, reminiscent to Celestaine of so many other gallops; old ones here in the innocent dawn, and fresher ones across fields of blood, tendrils of tangling bloodweed leaping from the bodies of the newly slain as Tzarkomen necromancers called it forth to poison those fleeing the Kinslayer's ruin. She was so glad that Caradwyn had never been there, so grateful she and her dreamy mind were safe here, and then to her left she saw a flash of metal against the darkness of the woods.

Automatically she was reaching for the Guardian-given sword and found only emptiness under her hand. For a flash she saw the broken, lost blade's entry point to its tomb, a black slash in stone, then recalled her common straight sword, left behind. Her hand didn't pause, travelling to her boot dagger without need of thought. It was in her hand as she sat up, goading her horse faster, nudging to the rear quarter of the grey stallion to push herself between Caradwyn and whoever was in the trees.

The sound of an arrow smacking leaves in flight came to her and she countered her impulse to duck, instead shouting loudly in the war cry that wasn't even a word. The arrow slipped between them with a hiss and vanished silently into the hedgerow on the far side of the track. Caradwyn was turning in the saddle as Celest used the slack of her reins to whack the stallion's rump.

"Go, go!" she screamed after it as she sat back, straight and tall, turning her weight and intent to face the attack. She drove the horse into the woods at the first opportunity, eyes struggling with the sudden darkness, the metal flash locked to a place in her mind. Another arrow came, passing her by a hair's breadth, and she recognised the black fletches on it with a sickening plunge in the gut just before she caught sight of the three Yorughan facing her, one with bow drawn back, one lancer, one with a club. The ragtag of the Kinslayer's armies had broken apart and scattered into warbands that roamed without purpose other than their own survival. They were fractions and free, but without roots or governance their years of living by the sword and being driven to the slaughter continued amok. She could not figure them for anything other than a random crew come to try its luck in the rich farmlands of the Fernreame estates. In these edgewoods they could live for seasons, years even, and use the miles of unclaimed wilds to travel unseen day after day.

Her horse wove left and right, an indirect line that took advantage of cover. Celestaine changed her grip on her dagger to an overhand hold and altered course in a moment, aware of the archer loosing and missing as she lay low to the horse's neck, then sped up to maximum speed to charge them down. The lancer stood to the last moment, braced and ready to skewer the horse with their polearm, its blade sharp—the glinting object that had betrayed them—but the horse was well trained and turned aside on a pin at the penultimate second, leaving Celestaine in only her leather riding gear flying at them, dagger hand scything, going for any good strike. Her impact at shoulder height knocking two of them down. It was a foolish move, suicidal on a battlefield, but here the horse was a liability and without better weapons she had only herself to use.

She felt herself hit them, felt the dagger cut and bite, drag hard so that she had to fight with all her focus to hold onto it but in a second she had lost it anyway, and then she was rolling over and over, fighting to regain her feet and face them. One was down, gurgling its last, the dagger sticking out from a point near its collarbone. The archer was nocking an arrow—the range was point blank, only an idiot could miss her, there was no cover at all. The third, a grizzled war matron with a massive club, was recovering also, reaching for her weapon mere feet from Celestaine's rising face, her tusks bloodied and a grin on her face that reminded Celestaine of Nedlam's bloodthirst. The archer was, beside her, a minor problem.

Celestaine whistled and closed her fingers on earth and leaves. She flung the dirt as hard as she could, jumping to stand as the war matron blinked automatically, snarling contempt, the club rising to her one-handed hold as easily as if it were nothing. Celest stayed low and shoulder-charged the archer with a roar, hoping to put him off his draw. It wouldn't have worked but for a moment that she saw a flicker of recognition in his face.

"Kinslayer's Bane," he said, taken aback, and he did falter: only for a moment, but it was the moment in which she reached him and made her tackle. He was huge and sturdy, but she was heavy and without hesitation. She wrapped her arms around his legs, pulling to the side. He lost his balance, unable to regain it, going over, the bow flung away from him to save it as his hands also went for his knives and sword, fumbling in mid-air as hers also searched, patting over one another in a moment before he hit the ground, trapping her arm beneath him.

"What?" The female Yogg had her club back in its arc, looking at Celestaine as she closed the yard between them, her boot coming down hard on Celestaine's lower leg. It hurt brutally but it didn't break, the tough sole of the boot sliding off her calf, crushing the muscle. "Kinslayer?" She stood, baffled for a moment as to the meaning, or for some other reason that Celest would never discover because at that moment her horse came powering out of the bushes and reared up, its iron-shod forefoot crashing into the woman's skull with the sound of a hardened wooden bowl being broken.

By then the archer was getting up and backing away from her, the sight of his companions' end and her reputation making him fatally indecisive. An arrow with peach and white fletchings sprouted suddenly from the back of his shoulder, followed by another, the point coming right through his torso directly at Celestaine. He looked surprised, as if he wanted to say something to her. He raised his arm, knife falling from his hand to point at her, and then fell on his face, dead.

"Celest! Celest!" Caradwyn was riding at her, bow in hand, a figure of strange colour in the green gloom. "Are you all right?" She slid off her horse and hugged Celestaine hard before standing back to look down at the bodies around them in the little clearing made by all the action.

Celestaine blinked, trying to clear her thoughts and feelings. "Why didn't you tell me you had trouble with warbands?"

Caradwyn's face, flushed pink, eyes bright with fear and excitement, was a picture of startling beauty. Celestaine suddenly envied her, then looked down at the Yorughan. She felt an ugly sensation at killing them, even though they had tried to kill her first. Maybe there was something to have been said and now it wasn't going to be said, but she'd never been the diplomat. She reached out and hugged her cousin with one arm around her shoulders.

"I didn't want to worry you," Caradwyn said, giggling at the foolishness of the sentiment and with an overspill of adrenaline. "I thought it might upset you, given your Heno."

Celestaine nodded slowly. "Just because things look alike doesn't mean they're the same. I think I can handle the notion of bandits, Cara."

Caradwyn nodded. "I'll remember that."

"I thought you were carrying that bow for show."

"I was."

Celestaine looked around them, but there seemed nobody left to say anything. "Let's get out of here." *My Heno*.

"I'll send some men out for the bodies. Tell them to bury them deep here."

Celestaine said, "You've done this before."

"Yes. And I'll do it again. Until they stop."

They rode back in silence.

As they approached the yards they could already hear the hubbub of many voices. Coming through the side gates they found it full of newly arrived wagons and riders. At the centre of the melee a man on horseback was talking to someone standing at his stirrup. He was tall and dark, with long hair and skin the colour of walnut. A braided beard was neat on his jaw and he had the easy presence and power that Celest recognised from seasoned warriors when they weren't in any imminent danger. He looked up as Caradwyn came through the gate and Celest watched her cousin's back straighten with pride. That was him then, Starich the wolf.

"Not quite as large as yours," Caradwyn murmured to Celest, leaning over towards her and crooking her little finger delicately in the shadow of her horse's mane with a cheeky glint in her eye, "but strong in the arm and thick in the head, just the way I like them."

Celestaine found herself laughing though she hadn't expected to. She didn't worry any more about Caradwyn's happiness or her standing. The other warriors riding around the place looked to their leader with a deference she found heartening. Then Starich realised who she was and made a deep bow, head down to the level of his horse's shoulder.

"Kinslayer slayer!" he roared and everyone looked over, not knowing whether they'd laugh or prostrate themselves. Starich grinned as he sat up, though he wasn't mocking, only challenging a little, testing the family makeup in case he was going to be living among enemies within.

Celestaine straightened her back. Then his horse moved and she saw who he'd been talking to—a distinguished older man with a tousled mane of dark hair marked at the temples with thick silvering. He was dressed in a rather new set of tunic and trews made in the Fernreame colours, his hand placed confidently upon the horse's rein as if he were engaging a grandson in a kindly natter, though Starich was no grandson of his.

"Shit," she said under her breath. It was the reinvented sober and serious hero of 'All Black and Silver Fire He Came' himself; Deffo.

*　*　*

THE WEDDING WENT off without a hitch, ceremonies managed, words said, troths pledged and ribbons knotted. Guardians passing themselves off as old men were indulged with songs and a nice seat at a good table. Celestaine did her bit, spoke to various family members in a civil manner, attempted and failed to talk about anything other than the death of the Kinslayer and whether or not Deffo really had delivered the coup de grace.

"I honestly don't recall seeing him there, but it was very confusing," she repeated an infinite number of times, wondering at her own mercy and privately vowing to make him pay because clearly all the interest and the effusive conversation were down to his constant stoking of that particular fire.

Although she was aware of many whispers and rumours flying about things didn't turn bad until much later in the afternoon. As soon as she was able she made her excuses and checked on the whereabouts of the others. Ralas was still strumming and singing near the groom's table, though he was starting to look grey with exhaustion. Deffo was reclining regally amid a cluster of older women, being fed custard tart and mead: she could only imagine what tales he was telling and had to restrain herself from striding over to tip his table and its contents all over him and his doting admirers whilst shouting, "He bit Wall on the ankle!" She took a route that went past the privies and then skirted around through the stables and the rear yard into the orchard.

There she found Heno and Nedlam sharing a feast platter of roast meat and several jugs of wine. Nedlam was lying on her back, mouth covered in grease, chewing a suspiciously long-lasting bit of something that Celestaine sniffed out as ora, a root which was quite poisonous to humans but which Yorughan found deliciously intoxicating. Wall's hammer lay in the crook of her arm, the haft twined with Brigand's Glory flowers in imitation of a bridal stave.

"Riddle-me-ree..." The song, sung from the stables, made her wonder if she'd been followed, but then the place was full of mildly intoxicated servants going about their duties. Everyone had been included in the celebrations. She could just make out the sounds of 'The Blade of Castle Mourn' starting up again from the musicians stationed with the warrior party of Starich's at their pavilions on the Lamb Field. She shook off her worries as Heno stood to greet her and she took the wine flagon and drank a few swallows from it.

"Your onerous duties are done?" He was less drunk than he appeared, dressed for travelling, only his coat on the grass.

"Yes," she hugged him and looked down at Nedlam's idle, grinning face, her eyes dark with drug. "Is she going to be able to move?"

"Married," Nedlam said, fondly patting the hammer. "Wine, meat, celebration! See. We have civil... civil... got good."

"All we have to do is wait for Ralas and we can go," Celestaine said with relief.

But Ralas did not come for some time and by then the wine had gone to her head and made her sleepy. Very sleepy. After a while of sitting, she snuggled against Heno's chest and traced the line of his tusk with her forefinger before twining some of the strands of his silver beard around and around as he snored quietly, the cherry blossom just beginning to snow gently around them. And then it occurred to her that maybe Ralas was too late and she was more tired than she should be for a few glugs of home wine.

She tried to sit up and found it extremely difficult. Her vision kept blurring. Her limbs were slow, as if in water. Her sense of balance wavered. She jabbed Heno sharply, if clumsily. "Hey! Hey! Wake up! We've been p-poisoned!"

"My wife," Nedlam said, grasping the hammer on her second try.

"Heno!" Celestaine thumped him on the chest from her sitting position. Snow was falling faster now and there was a man there, two, no three of them, or six, or three, standing armed with axes. One of them was the priest Starich's retinue had brought so that the wedding could be blessed by the Gracious One, their chosen deity. He was young and blustery, shaking, she thought, as he pointed a finger down at them.

"There they are, as I said! See the ora root has them in its grasp already. Strike now! They are the reason for the gods' turning away from us! These filthy animals from the black pits of Nydarrow are everywhere in this Forinthi hellhole! They have corrupted even the best of us—"

Celestaine felt vaguely that this might mean her as she hauled on a half inch of Heno's moustache and just about tore it out. He woke with a roar of protest and floundered for a second as a fourth, or eighth, human male appeared and said loudly, "Stand back! What is this? Who defiles our celebration?"

Celestaine recognised Starich's voice and then saw a flutter of peach and white beside him and two Caradwyns, both pale and shocked, her deathly pallor suddenly rendered eldritch by a flash of white and blue lightning that went zapping over her head and into the nearest tree, cracking a branch and showering them all with a blizzard of petals.

"No!" Celestaine shoved down Heno's hand as another ball of soft white light began to form in his cupped palm. The magic singed her fingers. She blinked, trying to clear her vision as the priest ranted.

"These Yoggs here have corrupted the Slayer. They are the ones who cut off the gods. They must be sacrificed to appease the Gracious One, here, where is he, that Guardian, the Undefeated. He shall witness our virtue! He shall report back our righteous justice and entreat their return!" There was some scuffling and confusion and in a less portentous tone, "But where has he gone to? He told me. He distinctly told me that Wanderer had news of the gods, knew where they were. Here we can get their attention, bring them to us again. There's so much to do. So much healing and reparation. We can't manage it alone. They must come back. They must."

"Hold your tongue," Starich said. "Have you put ora in all this food? And given it to them?"

"I thought it was safer," the priest said. "Now you can deal fairly with them for their crimes. They are subdued and the Slayer cannot protect them with her misguided sentiments."

Caradwyn cleared her throat and spoke over Starich as he began to speak, "As it is my wedding day I request safe passage for Celestaine and her party across our lands. Until the sun sets."

There was no talk of there not being crimes to answer for or who had done what, Celestaine noted, feeling pain lance across her forehead as she finally managed to get her feet under her and stand up, weaving from side to side. There was only a stony silence and some shuffling as everyone waited for Starich to make his first edict in favour of his priest or his wife.

Into this moment Nedlam chose to get to her feet. There was a visible effort among the warriors not to back off. She towered over them as she rested the head of her hammer on the ground and thumped it once, gently, a thump felt in every boot sole. She looked at the priest. "Kinslayer took them. Far far away." She looked at Celestaine, who struggled to stay upright and found Heno at her side, steadier than she now he was conscious, his fingers tingling on her arm with suppressed fire.

The priest, unable to hold his peace, broke in. "Abominations! Lying, lying filthy abominations! Look at them. Right under our noses. In the woods, in the valleys, creeping up on us in a never-ending tide of death and blood." He pointed his finger at Nedlam. "And this one, she, the mockery of good-women on this day, she—"

Nedlam picked up the hammer and swung it lightly as though swatting a wasp. It hit him in the midriff with a surprisingly soft crump and then he was flying through the air to the side of them all, limbs loose, until his back hit a tree, followed by his head. He slid to the grass and toppled over.

"It Lady Wall to you, son," she said, and held the hammer fast in both colossal hands. Then she looked at Starich with great acuity for someone who had had so much ora.

Celestaine had begun to recover her wits though Heno was holding her up by her elbow on one side. "We'll be going, then," she said.

"Until sunset," Starich managed to get out in his deepest tones, making a short, sharp gesture at his axemen who showed no hesitation in withdrawing. He glanced at Caradwyn with a mixture of feelings, none certain. "Make your goodbyes quickly or they will not reach the border." He spared a look for the priest and added, "He was the son of one of my second aunts and not beloved but even so there will be a lot of—trouble— explaining this. I hear you have a sharp wit. Now would be the moment to show it."

He gave Celestaine a look and shook his head, giving up on it all. "We will preserve your good name in legend, whatever you do with it elsewhere. You are always at home here, though I think it would be wise to let time turn memories fonder before you return." Without waiting for a response the new Lord of Fernreame swept out, muttering to his men.

"Tell Ralas," Celestaine slurred to Caradwyn who was flushed and relieved, but also with a look on her face that Celest knew meant goodbye without saying it. "Thank you, Cara."

"My pleasure," she said and reached out to touch Heno on the arm briefly. "Look after my cousin. She has a short temper and trusts no one."

Heno snorted. "I have my hands full."

Nedlam chuckled. "I take the rest of this root wine?"

"Just leave it if you would, I may need to use it when I find out what befell our priest. I um… may have to clean up two messes with one mop. As it were." And she looked at Celestaine significantly.

"Means 'no'," Heno growled in translation for Nedlam's

benefit as Celestaine bent forwards and threw up, splashing red wine vomit all over the pretty hand-stitched lace of Caradwyn's hems. She paused there, to gather herself and found a dainty kerchief handed to her. She blotted her mouth and nose, cleared her throat and as she felt a little better straightened up again, thoughts swirling. *Oh yes. The dead Yoggs in the wood. How convenient. But this was Deffo's fault. Shooting his mouth off left, right and centre, begging for fame, longing for his moment. Then a weak young man with justified fears got wind of it and heard that silly song and maybe heard about the incident yesterday too. She'd have her own reckoning with Deffo when the time came.*

"Goodbye Celestaine, Heno. Lady Wall." Caradwyn dropped Nedlam a deep curtsey and then, on an impulse, handed over the bridal posy that still swung from a ribbon on her wrist.

Nedlam took it between thumb and forefinger and examined it from a few angles before sniffing it and then handing it to Celestaine. "You have it. You only girl here not married."

When Celestaine looked back Caradwyn was gone. "Let's get out of here."

Afterwards, once they were on the road and making good miles, Celestaine looked but never found the posy and always wondered if she had hallucinated that part of things. The kerchief she had in her pocket, stained forever. So that bit at least had been real.

CHAPTER THREE

"HEY, HEY!" BUKHAM looked around for something light to throw but came up only with an apple which he considered too hard for the task. He had to settle for shaking his fist at the mud-coloured little girl who had snatched beans from the edge of his stall. His shout, he noticed, had also gotten a little less convincing over the last couple of weeks. He stood and watched her from behind the multicoloured piles of his produce.

She scampered quickly to shelter around the other side of the market's stock fence, standing carelessly between the steers as they swished flies in the heat and swung their massive, horned heads. Each head was almost as big as she was. She watched Bukham closely as she popped beans with her thumb and ate them, one, two, three at a time, always three. The long green and purple pods went into the idly chewing mouths of the cattle, one, two, three.

Bukham met her eye as long as was possible, trying to frown, before it became too foolish and the desire to laugh unstoppable. Then he had to turn away and sort out some gourds on the other side of the stand. He'd lately become a good sorter, he noticed, his designs for the vegetables growing more elaborate and impressive as the days of thieving passed. It was strange what god wandered in to teach you and what instruments she found, he thought, and then looked up as his uncle appeared.

Ghurbat was a tall, powerful Oerni whose muscle and

markings set him out as a cut above the ordinary. He looked past Bukham to the cattle pen, scowling as he searched for a glimpse of the bean stealer. "The time's come to send her back. Can't have this going on. Bad for trade to have thieves around."

Bukham looked around, feeling himself as dumb and stupid as one of the steers, as clumsy, as he stalled for time. The pen was empty of little girls. "I do chase her off. She's only tiny, doesn't take much." He turned back and met Ghurbat's flat stare, knowing all he was doing was sealing his fate as the last nephew to inherit the book. He looked, sadly, at Ghurbat's waist where the leatherbound scrips of all their family trade records were wound, thick and prosperous, full of promise. But she was only tiny. And coloured like mud and dung because she was covered in mud and dung. And alone.

It was difficult to imagine what that was like. Bukham was the last of a large, extended family, at least half of whom lived here in the trading post. Someone was always within shouting distance. There was food at someone's house, water organised by the women, a good meal at the end of every day—too good, in fact, because Oerni hated waste even more than thieving and there weren't enough Wayfarers in residence to soak up the surplus. They were all sturdy.

"We could…" he began, meaning to say they could take her in but Ghurbat saw this coming a mile off and put his hand up before Bukham could go on.

"Your kindness does you credit but no. She has people somewhere. She must go back to the Communes. They will take care of her. Blood and trade, she is of their kind."

There was sense to that, Bukham realised. She was no Oerni, much too slight and with that very black hair that matted easily and looked like it was carrying half the twigs and thorns between Taib Post and Caracu in the southern limits of Tzarkand, where she probably came from, before that had been razed by the Kinslayer's armies. What remained of the Caracai were in the tent towns of the Communes, on the unlocked land of the plains, along with the scatterings of every other small peoples who had succumbed to the Eastern assault. The girl had come in one of the Commune's caravans and stayed on when it departed.

"Ehh," Bukham said, as always when he was distressed by the fact of conflict and his inability to confront a family member with whom he disagreed. Ghurbat's patience was ending, he could see by the thinning of his lip and the way the freckled patches across his nose and eyes were darkening. "From a snake to a dragon's jaws, maybe?" He meant that she might have fled even the scanty comfort of the Commune if it had been dangerous for her. He didn't think she would have stayed if she'd had a mother, a father, anyone back there. But he could see that she might stay here if there was trouble back there. Or nothing. Or reminders of the past. From a snake to a dragon's jaws meant he didn't want to send her to the dragon.

Ghurbat wasn't buying it. He had his No Deal face on. "Dragon or not, back she goes. Taib can't afford to keep strays. We trade, we're not a charity. If one stays more will come and we'll end up overrun with them like rats. She goes. You see to it."

"Me?" Bukham was taken aback. "But what about the stall?"

"Your sister can mind it. She needs the practice, in patience if nothing else."

Bukham's heart sank. Tubayu would find managing a produce stall well beneath her capacities. It was the simplest task on the market, requiring only the most basic dealing and gentleness and care in handling the goods. An idiot could do it, and did, as far as Tubayu was concerned. If she had to take it over she'd see it as a punishment and he'd get to pay for that. But he couldn't say any of that and if he had Ghurbat wouldn't care. Uncle had more to say however.

"Murti is going that way tomorrow. He said he would go with you, at least half the way."

Murti was one of the Wayfarers, a priest, notorious for the

length of journeys he undertook. Probably he was the most widely travelled of them all. Certainly he'd gone the farthest from civilisation that they knew of, returning from the deep South beyond Seven Quays after a period of twenty-one years in which everyone at Taib had written him off as obviously dead. They said he'd been at the battle of Bladno and he was the first to have brought them the news from Nydarrow that the Kinslayer was vanquished.

"I…" Bukham began but found he hadn't got an objection ready to go worth the saying. "What if I can't catch her?"

Ghurbat picked up a basket of Mu shoots, coiled pale green and buttery yellow with rich oil, sweet and ripe. "You'll catch her one way or another. You leave tomorrow. Don't forget to tell Tubayu about the stall."

Bukham nodded, already resigned, already failing. He served a customer, his friend Forib, come to get greens and orange pom now that was in season. Two copper scits got a little basketful, though in a week they'd cost two silver pollys or the like, when the weather turned and the mould set in. They exchanged a bit of old market gossip for the sake of something to say, checked their tallies against one another—who had wool for rugs still in stock, how much purple dye was left, did the hole in that van get fixed yet, all small stuff. As he talked Bukham watched over Forib's shoulder.

Behind the cattle pens a long train of dusty travellers, wagons and pack animals had pulled into the halt and begun unloading. He saw Ghurbat striding confidently that way. A Cheriveni arrival was for celebrating. They always had so many fascinating things to show and tell. Normally he would have been itching to start talking to them but now he watched them with a heavy heart, his eyes scanning the open areas between stands for a tiny, angry figure. Yes, angry, he thought. That was right. He didn't see anything but when he said goodbye to Forib and turned back to the fruit side of things his throwing apple had mysteriously vanished.

CHAPTER FOUR

THE GIRL THE refugees had called Kula waited in the shadow of the curtains that hung around the fabric shop. She didn't call herself anything, nor would she have answered to any name. It was clear when people meant her. She could feel their attention like a form of heat.

Her bare toes poked out into the sunlight until she made herself stand on tiptoe. She held her apple in her hand. It had a good, solid shape, a nice feeling, and it was full of life. There were a number of hiding spots around the covered market which were very good, but this one let her watch the most people moving around and since nobody ever looked at the old tapestry that hung before her she felt safe here.

Through the weave she could easily make out the familiar layout of the fresh produce stand, the seed merchant's table full of shallow bowls and the shoe crafter's bench. Many traders came and went and now there were new people she wasn't familiar with coming from the caravan that had just set down. They were eager to see the market and went around in groups, talking all the time. They were mostly small, dark people, favouring blue clothing. They didn't resemble the painted beige and brown giants of the trading post. Most importantly, none of them had the huge forms, strange grey hides and tusks of the killers.

She was waiting for them. She could feel them out there.

Distant, but there. The tendrils of energy that connected them to the web of all life had a very distinctive flavour, especially when it came from those who used magic that was related to the magic her people had once possessed. Once tasted never forgotten.

THEY HAD WASHED over her home in a wave. All the brightness of her family was extinguished quickly. She felt them go out one at a time, fast, like flames quenched by water. For a few days she had eaten the carrots and other things in the root cellar where she was put, but then those roots began to soften and their rot told her that the earth itself had been made poison. It was coming down slowly. She must get out.

Above the ground where her village had stood were only wrecks of the houses, ash and mud. Stinking, foul things were stuck in the mud. After a time she realised they were bodies. A body was not like a root. There was nothing in them left to take. She could not tell which of them had been her mother, her father, her brothers, sisters, aunts, uncles, cousins. She could have, if they had still had enough faces but there was only ruin, blackened, burnt, savaged apart by scavengers while she had been in her hole. There was no mothering, no fathering, no nothing going on. She felt uncertain suddenly about where she stood, who she was, about what to do.

But there was something there, stuck in the mud near the river wash, feeble but alive still. Its heart beat, weakly, erratically, as it clung to life. She followed its light, stumbling, coughing with the terrible smell, the flies everywhere coming at her in waves like water there were so many of them. Their tiny, cold bodies were endless surprises on her skin. They battered at her senselessly, sparkling, brilliant. She felt motes of what she had loved in them, rising to the sky in other forms, but not here, not seeing her any more and her heart was crushed suddenly, and speared, and frozen. She hurried to the life, because anything was better than being alone.

The place that had been the wash, where the shallows of the river spread wide and lapped the shore in a kind of tiny beach was now filth and mud. Amid the objects left there—the forms of the dead and the wreckage of the little pier from which she used to fish—there was a creature, stuck fast.

It was huge. She could see that once the life in it had burned like fires. It was large and had a heavy head which it lifted as she arrived. Its lips moved in speech around thick tusks as it fought against the clothing it wore, trapped beneath it. There was something wrong with its legs. She could see that it couldn't move them. Nothing from its chest down moved. Its breathing was quick and difficult. She realised this was one of the destroyers, left behind for some reason to die here in the mud of the wash while the rest of the warband went on. It lifted a shaky hand, and a fine line of white fire twined around between its fingers. In the ravaged face of the thing she saw the eyes narrow, focusing on her, and tendrils of silver fire came streaking out towards her like hunting dogs.

They were weak. They faded as they stretched. She felt the creature put all its remaining energy into the effort and slowly, surely the silver lines crept up to reach her chest, seeking her heart. The air around them shivered as if trying to brush them off. The tips of the tentacles touched her jerkin and she felt cold and dizzy. She put her hand up and where the silver met her she was burned suddenly, horribly. She snatched it back, the life already gone out of some bit of her and into the thing that reached.

Her throat hurt her as she jumped back. She landed awkwardly on something and fell into the mud. The silver fire rushed at her. She rolled away. Under her burnt hand a hard object shifted and her fingers closed on a rock. In the echo of the silver touch she remembered that this is how the others had gone. Burning, but only for a moment, then the silence. Flies battered her as she spun, vengeful, made of hate.

The rock hit the creature's head. It wasn't a strong enough

throw to kill it but the silver fire went out. A wound opened above one of its eyes and blood trickled. It struggled for breath. Mouth working, working, saying so much.

She got up and walked over to a larger rock, levered and then heaved it out of the mud. The creature's arm and hand flapped about, as though looking for something lost. The fire came again, weaker, moving all around blindly in search of her. She carried her rock closer, watching the fire turn towards her. Within its silvery radiance she could see the creature's essential being, and a piece of her own, as it spent itself in a final desperation. There was almost nothing left in its ruined body, only enough to animate the eyes as she crouched down and looked into them. Big, dark grey, red rimmed and bloodshot, festering with flies at the corners.

They looked at her. The lips worked around the tusks, stuck to the yellowed carvings that marked one of them. Every line of the whirling signs was full of black blood. They seemed to be pictures, but of what she didn't know.

She waited, the fire creeping to her leg, then moved aside out of its reach and hurled the rock onto the thing's face. It fell back, one tusk broken and a piece spinning away as the rock fell aside. The fire sprawled in the air, losing shape. It took two flies, brightened for a moment, then fizzled away.

It took two more blows with the rock's edge, bone crunching, all her effort, before she felt the last of it go. A tiny mote of silver flickered for a moment where she watched for it, right between the monster's eyes, and she quickly reached out with her burnt hand and took it, that piece of her, right back. Then she straightened up and the pain of her hand and the weariness, the hunger, the grief, the rage overtook her and she did nothing to stop them pouring out of her, a fool, as her mother would have said, spending it all for naught on the flies and the mud, tainting the water with it so that downstream some other thing would catch the flavour and be robbed of something, turned to a darker path all unknowing. But she had no wish to stop it even if she had the strength. Let everything die.

But it did not. And eventually she ran out of tears and sobbing, lay empty on the ruined earth and stared at the sky until the sky filled her up to the brim.

She knew later what a fool she was when she had to walk away from that place, alone. She had not even anger to help her feet march or hate to find a direction, though any direction was good enough. She put one foot in front of the other, watching them. She thought of the creature and its strange, ugly face, its unusual magic that was like hers, and not, because it was connected to the same place. It came through the blood from that hidden world. The Tzarkomen's magic was like this too. A source of power that could only find its way through living things—her, or the creature, or the rest of the world. Or it could make the recently dead live, if there was enough of it. That's what the Tzarkomen could do, but not her people. They were a little-known offshoot tribe, whose mastery of it had taken them a different, contemplative path.

The creature could have taken her life, but it would not have known her, it would only have killed her. All that she could have inherited from it—its knowledge, its thoughts, its dreams, the exacting precision of its body and how it was made—she had ignored, from revulsion. Not one bit of it would she touch, even if absorbing its last breath had been her only hope at life. All that she could have inherited from her own people was forever gone, burned like it was worthless, unseen and unknown forever. They could have lived on in her memory, been taken forwards by her, carried by her, transmitted to another life, another time, when a safe place was found. This was their magic. Saving, remembering, restoring, preserving. But her people, the end of centuries of memory and learning, of gentle and exacting preservation, were lost, gone in white fire, as if they had never been.

* * *

BUT NOW SHE was back in a place where there were many people again; kind people, warm-hearted people. Their sweetness was medicine. She hid among their tents and warehouses, finding little nooks in barns and amid the rafters of the drying houses. Because she could tell where they were long before they got near she was able to avoid them quite easily but acquiring food was difficult. They were extremely cautious with that and she didn't like being seen, though it couldn't be helped. Hunger forced her hand, though she knew that this man with the fruits and vegetables would not give her up. She wouldn't have to reveal herself to wandering mages by using her ability to draw life without eating. So she had started stealing from him and was seen, and not caught.

A few hours after the apple, she was starving and hoping to get a little more for the night ahead. When she saw the bowl of smooth, green, oily vegetables, so rich and tasty, placed carelessly at the end of a low row, she knew that they were for her.

A glance at the stall man confirmed it. He was deliberately turning his back, whilst looking over his shoulder now and again. Across the way the other stallholders were attentive to their own business.

She hesitated from her hiding place behind the tapestry. She waited. Time passed and the sun began to go down. The stalls busied as those who'd come in on the last caravan made purchases, their selling done. They lit the lamps and she heard their few musical instruments being tuned up for a little feast, which they held every time a new group came to stay for a day or two. If there was a safe time to go then it was now. She would avoid the obvious dish, try for something easier. She had her exit route to the cattle pen, which was now complicated by new animals milling about. But as she was about to go she saw a strangely dressed woman appear at the fruit stall and appear to examine the bushels.

She was small; wiry, black hair tied up in a fancy heap on her head with long red scarves that fell down in a tail along her back. Leather armour straps were set over other red and brown cloth, binding her from neck to knees and elbows. A fierce amount of pouches and sheaths adorned these straps, all small. She wore a knapsack and her boots were tall. Her face, just visible beneath the hanging scarf at her forehead and above the sweep of the one about her throat, was coloured darkly around the eyes and red at the lips. She had a way of moving that made her seem less than she was. The life in her burned with a ferocity that was only matched by the degree she hid it and made herself seem weak and small somehow with a trick that couldn't be seen.

Kula stared at the woman, fascinated, compelled by the intensity of that burn and the difficulty she had in perceiving it. She didn't know what she was looking at. Not any ordinary woman.

Gold flashed in rings on the newcomer's fingers and about her wrists. It made a soft tinkling as bangles hit one another. She spoke very softly and she held the attention of the young Oerni stallholder effortlessly and completely. He could not look away.

Kula realised her chance was here. She dashed out, quiet, low, seized the bowl of shoots and was stuck fast for a moment, not understanding as she began to panic. The bowl did not move.

Then she felt that it was attached to the stand. It could not move. It was a trap.

The whole stand trembled. Terror gripped her. She found herself staring eye-to-eye with the golden-bangled, fiery woman on the other side of the stall. The gaze that met hers was curious, warm, amused. It saw her as no other had ever seen her. It didn't just see her. It saw the fire, the life, the binding cords of magic. One impeccable eyebrow went up. Kula felt recognised, fresh terror starting in her throat. The stallholder turned, slow, as if he didn't want to see what was going on, because he didn't want to catch her in the act.

Kula let the bowl go, grabbed whatever was next to it: some kind of poms.

There was a commotion suddenly—the large boss man of the place rushing forwards at a jog, a hand on his broad belt to hold his belly down as he came, mouth moving angrily, pointing at Kula.

The fiery woman winked at her and then, with mouth opening in an obvious scream, clutched both hands to her chest and fell down, crashing through the stall's front display, sending colours and shapes flying in all directions before she landed in the dust, convulsing and twitching. Fruits rolled everywhere.

The stallholder turned back to her, agape. The boss man stopped in his tracks to bend down and help.

Kula fled, into the cattle pen, through the beasts, out the other side and among the tents of the visitors. She ran and didn't stop until she reached her outermost hiding place—the abandoned burrow of some long dead creature, shrouded by hanging weeds in a reeking stream bank that backed onto the Post's northern approach. Inside the darkness there she ripped into the poms she had gotten, cramming her mouth, trembling as she ate. When she was done she left the mess behind her and went out on the road, not looking back. She didn't know what it meant. She had seen Wanderer's flame settle down here, at Taib, when she was still at the great distance of the Commune. It was why she came here although she was too shy to go close. If he was here among them it was enough. But now she had seen another Guardian flame in the woman's strange eyes. And she'd been seen.

She felt too frightened. Wanderer was not her Guardian. It was only his light that she had felt secure by. But he had drawn another. She didn't know what it meant. She only felt the lingering touch of the Slayer about that woman's hidden magic, a taint, like a stain, the kind of thing between a mother and a father, between siblings who have been close for long ages and begun to resemble one another. There was only one female Guardian she knew of who fitted this possibility. Most people knew her as a trickster, patron of vagabonds and thieves. She wasn't a proper Guardian because she'd never been given someone to guard. She had no temples though the people of the roads built little shrines to her out of whatever they found at every crossroads, even if it was only a heap of grass. In the war they said she'd gone to Nydarrow and never come out.

The woman had saved her, no doubt. But what for? She didn't want to find out.

CHAPTER FIVE

BUKHAM REALISED HIS little thief was there and his chance was now and that he must do something. But at the very same moment of this revelation the fascinating little woman with the golden bracelets also realised the same thing.

He saw her look over his shoulder and take a breath—to shout out that the girl was there, he thought, to ruin any hope he had left of not having to catch her in an ugly scene. In his mind's eye he saw terror in the little girl's face, screaming, hating him so he was completely thrown when he saw the conspiratorial wink from the woman's large, beautifully painted, dark eye. Then the woman screamed and had a theatrical fainting fit. The stall collapsed. It was a bit overdone but effective, no doubt, there was even twitching and spasming among the crushed berries.

He was so grateful he didn't pause, but leapt over the remains of the counter, scattering apples and poms, sticks of spice and little trays of fragrant leaves. In a burst of yellow good-powder, meant for helping stomachs ruined by eating the Kinslayer's leavings, he bent low to the fallen customer, showing himself heroically involved in helping. At the same time he fervently hoped the little one escaped somehow and his obligations with her.

Uncle Ghurbat was swift on the scene, bringing his box of remedies with him, a moment of two after Aunt Cherti had arrived with smelling salts and Authentic Djinni Waters, which had cost an entire box of dried violet stamens two years back when the last of the glamorous, aethereal Elennae came past, trading their fabulous nostrums. An argument over the twitching body promptly ensued as each insisted their care must be administered first. Bukham was pushed aside as of no interest, his efforts to make sure there was nothing to choke on, no stone too close, all ignored as the physicians went head to head. As he was elbowed away he saw the downed woman cast a quick glance at him through her heavily painted eyelashes and he gave her clear-eyed assessment a helpless shrug. Seeing he was of no use she went back to her twitching, careful to thrash the first dropper of Authentic Djinni Waters firmly away from her face with a well-timed swing of one arm. As Cherti trilled a note of horror and doom Bukham backed off and looked around.

His bunches of barsoon were all over the place. He went towards the cattle pens, searching, and was filled with doubt and a creeping sense of self-loathing as he found nothing. He went around the pen but the ground was churned with prints and it had been dry for days. Two more times he tried but wherever he'd once seen the eyes staring at him there was nothing to find and he knew in his heart she was gone. To his surprise this was worse than the prospect of him trying to return her to the refugees.

By the time he returned to his stand the woman was on her feet, waving away the attentions of his aunt and leaning on his uncle's arm. He went to clean up, doing his best to be ignored, but the dreaded touch on his arm and clearing of his uncle's throat soon stopped him.

"Well?"

"She ran away," Bukham said, pulling the basket that had held the bait off the plank it had been nailed to. "I looked all over, but I couldn't find her. She's gone."

"Who's gone?" The woman who had fainted was standing there too. She had let go of Ghurbat's arm now. Her accent was exotic, strange, he couldn't place it among any of the many tribes and groups he had known. She had a way of speaking that was, in itself, peculiar—a very soft, almost gravelly tone that was absolutely clear to the ear in its meaning and articulation even though it seemed much quieter than the surroundings. He felt uneasy but since he'd nothing to know worth the knowing it seemed no matter to say,

"Some girl that came from the Refugees. Stayed on, hiding out here. Now she's gone."

"Ah, I see."

"You saw her?" Ghurbat asked, turning.

"No, no, I was only curious," the woman said. "It is late. I will go to my tent. Thank you for your kindness."

"Let me walk you there." Ghurbat was at her side in a flash. He turned back to Bukham as an afterthought. "You can pick up Murti and go look for her in the morning. She can't have got far. We have responsibilities, you know, to care for the lost. We are not animals."

Bukham stared after their backs, realising that this speech was really for her benefit and not his. After he had picked up and sorted the stock he packed a basket ready for the morning, counted the tally and found he couldn't account for a set of ready-measured spices arranged in pretty little pouches which his cousin made. Where they had gone he'd no idea but he thought of the slow wink. Well, if she was a thief too she was Ghurbat's problem now. Then he went to tell Tubayu the good news about her job for the morrow.

"You should find her and bring her back here," Tubayu said immediately, once she'd recovered from the notion that she had to debase herself by running the produce stand. "It's not safe. This lot tell me there are bands of Yorughan making forays north, and other bandits."

"But we can't keep her." He knew he was repeating Ghurbat's line, more to test it.

"Of course we can," Tubayu said. "Just one. She never stole anything other than food, did she? Well, then she's not a natural thief. Only hungry."

"All right." Bukham felt better, hearing his own feelings repeated in her words. She always had more conviction than he did and once he heard her he felt convinced too. "But first I have to find her."

"Murti can do it. Don't take too long though. I have other things to do than stack canarops and swish flies. That's for lesser beings."

Murti was in the main tent at Taib, where all visitors were housed. He was with another priest who had come lately down from the north and they were bent together in conversation, cross-legged on the carpets, a little brazier heating their tea and warming some flatcakes. Bukham didn't want to interrupt them but as he entered the room Murti looked up and waved him over with an air of expectation and impatience.

The priest was very old. His skin combined wrinkle markings and weather-wear into something that looked like worn-out boot hide and all that remained of his hair were a few tufts no longer in communication with each other across the bald dome of his head. Their white strands straggled down around his neck or stuck up like the down of a baby bird, directly into the air. His clothing was tough traveller's wear, rougher by far than the pleasantly cut robe and trousers that Bukham had on, and in one glance he had more intensity than Bukham had possessed in his entire life. Bukham was scared of him. He approached, bowed, and sat down where he was directed.

"This is Bukham, son of Oshmet," Murti said to the other priest. "He's just starting out." He beamed confidently and with a kind of pride. Bukham was confused. He thought Murti must have got it wrong. He wasn't going on a journey to start

Wayfaring. He was going on a journey to get the girl and return her to the camp. That was all. It was only a journey. It wasn't a Journey journey.

"Wait. What? I'm not…" but Murti cut him off with a swift wave that turned into a flapping hand that meant he was to pipe down.

"Ah, well, a good time to be moving," the other priest said and Bukham was astounded to discover from the sound of the voice that the wizened husk of a thing, barely Oerni any more and certainly skinnier and more bent than any person should be who was still alive, was a woman. Or had been. Woman seemed the wrong word too. He felt a terrible flustering inside him as he suddenly doubted himself.

"I'm Tillaray, good to meet you, priestling." A hand like a curled rook's claw thrust itself, dark and dusty, from the ragged clothing and made the sign of the Wanderer in a brief manner. Bukham felt amusement and a keen attention on him although Tillaray's face was hidden in wrappings and scarves so that only two gleams like the glint of the moon on a steel blade were briefly visible. The oddness of the name struck him as very un-Oerni but he wasn't about to ask.

"Stifling your curiosity, boy," Tillaray said. "Got to stop. How will you ever learn? On the road you have only yourself to answer to, hm? What's this journey then?"

"I uh… I'm not here to join the priesthood," Bukham said, feeling it needed clearing up quickly before things got any more out of hand.

"Ah," Tillaray said. "I'm sure you think so, however mistaken you are. Pass my tea."

Bukham passed one tepid cup over and then looked at Murti for guidance. "I came to tell you that we don't have to go anywhere. The girl. She's gone. I'm going to look for her and then my sister's going to take her in."

"Oh," Murti said and scowled. He took up his own tea and

tossed it straight in Bukham's face. "Go get your clothes on and get ready to leave." He muttered something about the youth of today under his breath.

Bukham wasn't entirely surprised, although he had started. Priests were notoriously short-tempered and prone to dramatic actions and he wasn't hurt. He felt tea dripping off his nose. He mopped it up with his sleeve. But he did need to make it clear that there wasn't going to be any Journey. "I…"

"Stop talking. We're going to lose her. Go get your things, you can't walk all the way to the coast in those sandals. Your uncle said you'd be ready. What's going on?"

"But…" Bukham began, feeling himself digging in as the dampness of the tea started going cold on him. Why was the old man talking about the coast? What had that to with anything? "I am not a priest. My uncle has played an unkind trick on you. I'm not going anywhere."

"We're leaving in an hour," Murti said. "Moon'll be up then, easy walking. Move your arse."

CHAPTER SIX

THE GODS HAD never been something Celest gave much thought to, until the Kinslayer had raised his armies and set out bent on destroying the human world. Even then, up to and beyond the final battle at Nydarrow, she hadn't cared to muse on their nature, their motives nor what monstrous reasons drove their descendants to madness. She figured that with immortality and massive power came meaningless drivel and stupid whimsy, leavened occasionally by a bit of focused goodwill or malice depending on what decade it was. At least that's what was going on if the last centuries were anything to judge by. Plus there was Deffo, the Undefeated, who had spent the whole of the war disguised as a badger and who was now attempting to curry fame at any price. When he was one of your executors you really had serious problems.

They were sitting at a wayside tavern over the Forinthi border, about twenty leagues from Celest's home: she, Heno, Nedlam and Ralas, clutching the lute that Caradwyn had given him as if its travelling case were a baby. The journey so far had been met with storms which weren't divine in origin but might as well have been since their winds and lashing rain had stopped them almost before they were begun. As a result of the weather the tavern was crowded, muggy and filthy. They got some of the last spaces in the second room which was without a fire but at least allowed Nedlam and Heno to have reason to keep their hoods up. Celest kept her sword ready even so; she knew there were few people outside Fernreame with the patience to figure that some Yorughan might not still be in the service of the Kinslayer and plenty who would hold back only out of fear for their own hides.

She put her own hood back and shouted an order across the room to the server, then fixed the old man who had just taken a seat beside her with a strong glare. He had taken on an affable expression of harmless goodwill and genteel decrepitude, but it was all she could do to keep from strangling him. He was, however, their only contact.

"Deffo, you're sure you know where he's going?"

"Yeah, no, not as such. It was more a general direction and some hunches." He cast her a sweetly helpless, apologetic glance, hand trembling on his staff. What a sweet old granddad.

She scowled at him, water dripping off her hair, down her nose and onto the table top where she leaned over it. Her next words were carefully chosen to keep her rage in check and her purpose clear. She wasn't about to scupper things for the sake of her temper. It could wait. "What did he actually say. Exactly?"

"He said he had an idea what may have been done to cut off the gods and he was going to find out."

"Ye-es, we've done this bit back at Fernreame," she said. She had a good idea that there wasn't going to be any more and she was going to have to continue to hold herself back from killing Deffo for a good long time to come.

Deffo leaned in and spoke sepulchrally to keep their conversation private. "Right, well, he said that there was a way to where they are, maybe, from one of the sacred rings and he thought the Unmentionable One must have used one of these to do what it was that he did."

"What rings?" Nedlam asked, scratching vigorously through her wet, spiky hair, knocking her hood back.

"Those rings of stones that the Oerni priests built ages ago," Deffo said. "You know, giant rocks, on end. Nobody knows how they lifted them. Set them up as marks to the Wayfarer; for Wanderer."

"Oerni very strong?" Nedlam suggested, easing herself onto the uncomfortable trestle in a new position. It creaked under the combined weight of her and Heno, who was sitting quite still.

Celestaine saw a lot of heads, eyes and talk moving in their direction as the other travellers in the room realised they were looking at a couple of Yorughan. She looked up impatiently, hoping they could get to eat before the place erupted.

"No, not particularly," Deffo was saying. "Well-built and powerful, but not strong enough to carry things like that around. They're part of Wanderer's people though. He's their patron, if you like. Or he's like the top priest. I don't really know how they think about it. But the rings and the avenues they marked up are all gateways that Wanderer uses to get to other places. There's a whole travelling thing going on there."

Now Celestaine wished they weren't having this conversation at all. "What other places?"

"Places that only gods can go," Deffo said, looking evasive. "I never used one myself. Not my style. I can't say for sure."

"Places out of this world," Heno suggested quietly. "But in another. That's where the Kinslayer got many things from, including the Heart Takers' power, and the Vathesk."

Celestaine shivered, thinking of the terrible crablike Vathesk and their insatiable hunger. They had been called to serve the Kinslayer's war purpose and their starvation made them mindless; but everything they ate couldn't dampen their hunger, because they could consume but not digest it. Creatures that were unable to die, suspended from their natural habitat: they were insane before she even met the first one or saw them clacking madly as they trampled through the battlefield, shearing and feeding until they were chopped into pieces. Then there were the circles. They were places she'd instinctively avoided, thinking it was better not to tread on someone else's sacred ground without a good reason. Now the news that they were more than attempts at temples made her queasy. Things that could be fought hand to hand she was familiar with: things requiring magic, much less so. And divine guidance, well. She looked at Deffo. "And your plan is?"

"We go check 'em out. One at a time."

"The nearest one's at Hathel Vale," Ralas said with a shudder.

"Then that's where we're going," Celestaine said as their food arrived and was dumped on the table as quickly as possible. Watery gravy and unidentifiable vegetable matter slopped onto the planks as the server retreated, his eyes on Heno as if he expected a fork to the face at any moment. "Let's eat this and get moving."

"I'll just smooth things over with a little rendition..." Ralas said, retrieving his lute from its case. He stood up and staggered around the table, wincing, until he was able to reach the front of it where he leaned in an extravant performance pose which hid most of the others from view behind him. The lute didn't hold its tune in the damp, but he set up boldly, confident in his skill, and the room paid him attention.

Celest wanted to stop him. His suffering was a constant fuel to her urge to mend things and it would never stop because Ralas could never heal, or die for that matter. Extra efforts that taxed him severely were all she could prevent. But she was hungry and Hathel Vale was a journey she didn't plan to make any more comfort stops on. Against her better judgement she let him get on with it and begin 'The Stones of Carrabree', a traditional Forinthi favourite, which she hoped would buy them enough goodwill to get out with their legs intact.

"Maybe travelling through worlds is how he obtained your sword," Heno said, in response to the mention of the circles. Celestaine nodded, and immediately missed the sword itself.

Then she looked up as Heno paused in his laborious chewing and fixed his gaze on the other side of the room.

"Heno?" Nedlam followed the line of his gaze but her sight was blocked by Ralas.

"Later," Heno said, very quietly now so that he seemed to be less muttering than gnawing a bit of gristle. He put his head down to the dish as though it was all delicious and kept his face hidden.

Nedlam scowled. She would have stood up but Ralas was in full swing and it would have thrown him off the table. Also the ceiling was too low and it would have achieved little beyond reminding everyone she was there. Celest peered at the part of the room Heno had scoured but saw only a tall woman in a worn great cloak stuffed into the corner as small as she could go. The feet of a pair of expensive boots stuck out from the ancient woollen hems, tooled with what once would have been gold and was now a few flakes stuck into some embossing. Her face was hidden by the corner's edge. Her hands—dark and elegant—toyed with a breadcrust and a cup.

Ralas launched into the chorus and a few voices joined in. So maybe it wasn't the woman that had spooked Heno but something else, Celest thought. Maybe. She chewed her bread and crunched on a piece of grit, spat it out and felt her tooth with a finger. Still there. One thing that was going right.

After they'd escaped the curiosity of the tavern intact they were riding north, Celestaine and Ralas on their mounts and Heno and Nedlam walking. The rain had abated and become a sullen mist, but the road here had been fortified during the occupation and the footing was fair as long as nobody considered what might have been used as aggregate to get such good drainage. Celest had glimpsed more than one or two pieces of bone and the fragments of Cheriveni armour. Then Nedlam finally said, "So, Heno. What?"

"That woman. Her boots." He turned to Celest to explain, walking by her stirrup. Around his tusks his lips made the words slow and thoughtful. "The Kinslayer had a few lackeys who did odd jobs for him, things he didn't want to do or couldn't get to. They travelled, his couriers and his spies. They're the fixers who stole objects of power and greased palms in the early days, before he'd really got into his stride and didn't need any more help. I saw most of them dead before we left Nydarrow. He killed them early, when their existence was more trouble than it was worth. But some lasted the course. They were the closest things he had to advisors. She was one of them. I'd know those boots anywhere. I saw her outside his sanctum, near the door as we reached it, running away just before that last fight." He meant before he and Nedlam had let in the assassins to kill him.

Celestaine searched her memories of that moment but she only recalled Lathenry beside her—the last moments of his life before the Kinslayer ripped his heart from his chest. She took a breath. "Why would she be here, now?" She looked around for Deffo to start grilling him but he wasn't in sight. She strained from the saddle, peering in all directions and then swore savagely. "Ah, as if I can't guess what's made him run off."

"Tricky," Nedlam said with a huff. She was chewing on the knuckle of the meal's one large bone as she strode along, hammer haft in one hand, the weapon resting on her shoulder, bone in the other hand. She seemed thoroughly content. "That's her name."

"Where'd he go?" Ralas blinked, sure he hadn't missed anyone until now. Deffo had been right there... where he now wasn't.

"Doesn't matter," Celest said. "Stick with the plan."

"I'm still not sure what we're doing," Ralas confessed, trying to wrap himself more comfortably in his cloak, wincing as he moved. His shaking fingers compulsively checked the lute case attached to his saddle.

"Wandering," Celestaine said grimly. "That's how we find the way."

CHAPTER SEVEN

"WANDERING," MURTI SAID with enthusiasm. "That's how we find the way." He gestured at the world north of Taib Post with glee and tugged at Bukham's sleeve. "Onward, onward, ever onward."

Bukham, frowning, took one heavy step and then another. He didn't want to go, especially not with this priest business still all up in the air. He'd looked for his uncle but been unable to find him anywhere. Even his wife didn't know where he was and without Ghurbat he'd never be able to convince Murti that there was a misunderstanding. Fair enough, he'd look for the little one, but after that he was coming home, whatever happened. His sister would kill him if she knew what was going on.

Against Bukham's wishes they hadn't taken a pack lunnox but were instead going with almost nothing. He liked to think this was because it was only a day's outing to look for a little girl with nowhere to go, but a different part of him suspected that Murti considered even what few items he had in his shoulder bag as far too much of a burden for any journey. Since he didn't want a lecture on how nature provided or whatever it was that Murti did on his travels, he said nothing about it.

They made another search for tracks, this time finding a trail that had been wasted on Bukham a day ago and which he still didn't make out now. Murti seemed to have a nose for it. He took them to a small cave dug into a bank and peered in at it through a screen of hanging roots. "Not here," he said. "But she was." He held up a scrap of peel. "Doesn't want to be found now."

"How'd you make that out?" Bukham asked grumpily, curious in spite of himself.

"Because she'd be here if she did. Everything leaves a trail of itself you know. And this feels cold, like a wind you'd turn your face away from. That's how I know." The ancient man shivered, his stooped back straightening for a second before resuming its hunched shape. "You need to pay attention more."

"I'm not a mystic," Bukham said with certainty. "I'm a vegetable trader."

"Well turn your vegetable mind to other things before it's too late." Murti sniffed and flung his scrap of cloak over his shoulder as he peered up at the cloud cover. "No sun. Was she well dressed?"

Bukham thought back. Some ragged kind of dress, he didn't even remember sandals. "No."

"Next time you need to sell more clothes," Murti suggested and began to shuffle back towards the path.

"Dorilia sells the clothes," Bukham said. He heard Murti sigh.

They made their way to the path and then over rough ground to the road which linked Taib with Ilkand Freeport and all points west, and walked until it was light. To either side the land alternated between patches of arable, dotted with farm buildings and tiny villages—or what remained of them after occupation— and dense woodlands. There were thousands of places to wander into, hide or be lost in. Bukham felt his heart sinking with every step. Why hadn't he just grabbed her when he had the chance? Surely it would have been better for her than to face the world alone? Since the war people were mostly kind, but there were always stragglers and loners taking advantage of the weak. What would he do if he found her body in a ditch or a...

Something stinging and sharp hit him around the face. With a start he realised that it was the end of Murti's cloak. The old man was wrapping it back on his shoulder with an offended air as he glared at Bukham. "Stop dreaming! There's work to do. Which way has she gone?"

They were standing at a tiny crossroads where paths from outlying villages had crept up on the main road and attempted to negotiate with it by means of a crude signpost. Bukham floundered about, looking at the ground, his hands, the signpost and the surroundings. He saw, heard and felt absolutely nothing of any use.

"You knew her the best," Murti said patiently. "You have to decide."

Bukham was about to say he didn't know her at all but a glance at Murti's face convinced him that was a very bad idea. He tried to draw up a picture of her in his mind's eye, as she'd been among the cattle, peeking at him. Then he looked back and forth along all the ways. Ahead of them on the main track a group of people were heading in their direction. "Maybe they saw her," he said.

"Let's go, then," Murti sighed another long-suffering sigh and set off at his easy pace which looked like every stride was a struggle but which moved him at a brisk pace. At even higher speeds he fairly bounded but walking made him look like every step was his last. Bukham wondered if it was a front or if he were walking through some terrible secret suffering that didn't show on the surface, because he was so powerful a priest that suffering didn't matter. Or magic was involved somehow. Or prayer.

"You think too much," Murti said, without looking back. "And you don't walk fast enough for a young man. What's the point of dawdling about?"

"I thought we were wandering," Bukham said.

"Wander harder, then," Murti said. "They look like Templars, alas. Can you see from here? Are they wearing blue and gold from Ilkand Temple or the nearly-the-same colours of the Termagents, blast their unimaginative minds?"

Bukham made out various colours, dull but definite. "What are the Terma—"

"Focus. Is it, or isn't it?"

Bukham frowned in concentration. Murti's tone suggested he already knew and was only asking for confirmation. "Yes, it could be."

"Let me do the talking then, if there's talking," Murti said, slowing down to a crawling pace.

"Might be going to the trading post," Bukham said, feeling uneasy. They weren't far away but he wasn't used to meeting people on the road when he was alone, or nearly alone. The Taib moved regularly, north to south, following the rivers, canals and major highways with the flow of the seasons. When it was on the move it was respected and generally left alone by a wide variety of folks although there were raids occasionally. Ilkand Templars he knew of only by reputation and a few official meetings at the port gates when they exerted their customs authority. The Termagents were some kind of offshoot group, but he wasn't sure of the distinction; only that they were somehow more difficult to deal with and more fiercely proud of their god.

In spite of Murti's efforts the two parties met shortly afterwards, the Templars grouped up on their fine horses. Bukham and Murti perching on the grass verge at the edge of the path.

"Greetings," the foremost one said. "Are we far from Taib Post?"

"But a few miles," Murti said. "You'll have a whole day to trade."

"We are not trading," the man replied, hand on his sword hilt. "Have you seen any resembling Tzarkomen on your travels?"

"None," Murti replied. "You're south and east of them a long way, what's left of them. Last I heard they were in retreat to the utmost west of their lands."

The group seemed relieved, Bukham would have sworn, but they only nodded and moved on, having barely spared him a glance. He guessed he looked too Oerni to be of any interest. The Oerni traded and had an honest, simple kindness to them that ruled them out of most considerations in politics or war. That at least was something to be glad about, that they had feuds with nobody.

"Why do you think they're looking for Tzarkomen here?" he asked as they continued their search.

"Probably to kill them," Murti said. "Templars have strong beliefs about the kind of things Tzarkomen do. If they've been seen east of the Ilkand Road the Templars may be crusading to give themselves something to do now they've got no god."

"What do you mean, no god?" Bukham had heard rumours about this but he didn't believe it. Not that he had a god exactly, or a system of belief. Gods were real but the Oerni had no business with them other than through their strange intermediary, Wanderer, but it was more of a guidance and patronage with Wanderer himself, gleaning news of roads and passages, ways in and out of places and markets. It wasn't something relating to the gods themselves.

"The Kinslayer cut the gods off from the world," Murti said. "The first thing he did was figure out how, then he destroyed the means by which he discovered that and then he severed them from this plane. After that he began work on the war proper. Some Templar was the last to hear them, so they say."

"Doesn't that mean Wanderer is cut off too? Are all the Guardians alone now?"

"Those that survive."

This answer seemed very unsatisfactory, but unassailable. Bukham kept looking for little footprints and sometimes he thought he saw them but as they got further and further along the way he began to doubt whether she could have managed to remain ahead of them for so long, but then as more time passed and more miles he started to think they were completely wrong and she could not have got to this point alone and hungry at all. Something must have happened to her. In front of him Murti limped along and showed no signs of stopping. Eventually he said, "Wait I've a stone in my shoe," although he didn't. As he knelt and fussed with it he added, "She can't have come this far."

"Oh," said Murti. "And how do you know this?"

Bukham gestured at the road. "It's been so far. She could have gone anywhere."

"When we wander, we do not wander in the mind. We wander on the ground. What does it mean, to wander?"

"Er... I'm just worried about her. I want to find her and I think we're going the wrong way," Bukham said quickly in an effort to escape. Over the hill to their left where weedy fields were cut among patches of overgrowth he saw a column of smoke rising into the air. It was broad and a mixture of greys. "Look, we can ask over there. There's somewhere."

Murti glanced at it. "That's not what you're looking for."

"I'll just go and ask, it won't take long."

"You're wasting time," the old priest said impatiently but he made no move to stop Bukham who frowned.

"You keep saying these things," he said on his way past, stepping off the track, "but you're not putting up any decent reasons of your own. Wandering; it's just walking about without a purpose. How's that going to find anyone or anything?" He waited for the sharp retort but nothing happened. Murti waved him off.

"Go on, go on, find what you find, I'll wait here. But move like you mean it, it's nearly noon."

All the way over the hill Bukham wondered how the old man knew the girl had kept to the road so far. He couldn't think of a single way to know that. He was struggling with memories of his own tracking, if he'd missed something obvious, and he was still heavily in thought when he walked onto the path into the village and realised that the fire wasn't a hearth but an entire house burning.

Hours later Murti was waiting for him, seated on a boulder at the roadside when he got back. He said nothing but walked with his shoulder close to Bukham's arm as they moved on. Bukham, hands covered in dirt, exhausted, filthy, didn't trust himself to speak. The blood and bodies were fresh, the fire only starting really. Even the dog had been left lying where it fell with its head caved in by something blunt and heavy, like the corner of a shield, or a mace. A girl had been weaving in the yard. The spindle was still in her hand, clutched tightly. Her mother lay in two pieces not far away, a few greens and a basket scattered on her face, as if she were of no more consequence than the dirt. It had taken a long time to bury them all.

He felt certain, beyond all certainty, that the Templars had done this, those they had passed and spoken to with such civility on the road. And he felt certain that Murti knew that was what they were even when he glimpsed them on the hilltop. And he didn't know what to do with a world that had things like this in it, so close to where he'd been living his peaceful life, his quiet stall. He felt that the stall and his people had no answer to this but that they should have, and for the first time ever he felt a deep, terrible shame and a misery so intense that it was as though he was being crushed from the inside. If this could happen today and go unanswered then the world was a ruin and the gods evil and his life was a stupid waste of everything it had taken to get him this far.

The day turned slowly from cloudy to broken sunlight and more heat. They passed a waymarker that told them they had a long way to go to Hathel Vale and even though it seemed impossible Bukham hoped the little one had got much further. He even considered that dying might be better than living on and he'd never had that kind of thought before.

"What were the Templars doing on this path?" he said without realising he was going to say anything. He didn't recognise his own voice, it was so hard and direct.

"They never stir without a purpose," Murti replied. "I expect they were looking for someone. They're from the Freeport, so it's been a long search."

"Were they looking for her?"

"What, our girl? I shouldn't think so. They aren't the sort to give any credence to children, unless she was the child of some high-up lord who was set to inherit or useful for ransom; a pawn in a larger game. But the Ilkand people are fairly pale sorts. You say she was dark."

"Very dark, and a little purple, like a Midnighter plum, with that kind of pale grey bloom where it catches the light, though I think that was ash or dirt."

"Not necessarily," Murti paused, thinking. "Did she have any marks on her face, stripes of colour maybe? What was she wearing?"

"She had some old yellow and orange line on her forehead. She had some kind of dress, but with short leggings underneath. All in grey cloth, the Tzarko kind, with flecks of colour in it."

"'Tis maybe they were looking for her, then," Murti said, muttering it more to himself than Bukham. "That's a Caracu style. They're a branch group of the Tzark. Heretics, of a kind. The Kinslayer did for all of them, the rumour goes. Only a few of them journeyed abroad." He sounded like someone plumbing the depths of old memories, searching for a word. Finally he found it with a small triumph that sounded forlorn and sad. "Deathspeakers, that's what they were called. Ironic because they didn't speak. They only had a signed language." His chattiness failed to mask the loss at the core of what he said.

Bukham swallowed hard against the memory of the massacre at the farm. He knew he would never stop it haunting him and he was angry for that, very angry. It wasn't enough that this had been done; now it lived inside him, changing everything, forever. He was furious, so much so that it made him cold and focused in a way he'd never experienced or known could happen. It frightened him a little. "What's a deathspeaker?"

"They are able to remember the lives of all their ancestors, as if it were their own. They were a living history of all they had ever known of the world, going right back to the start."

At least that seemed less terrible than it had sounded. "So if they were able to remember something the Kinslayer didn't want remembered, then…?"

"Yes, I expect that was it."

Bukham had a very uncomfortable thought. "How would the Templars know she was here? Or that anyone was still alive?"

"Don't jump, lad," the old man said, sighing as it began to spit rain at them out of what seemed to be a fine sky. "They could have come for other reasons. Not every bad thing done is done in the Kinslayer's name. There's plenty happening on other accounts."

Just most of them, Bukham thought, then corrected himself. No, actually the Kinslayer had been only one horror. Everyone who had done anything for him had done it off their own bat. They might have said it was for him, but they'd done it themselves. Because the alternative was a horrible death. Would he also have gone along? He let out a sigh.

"Where did his armies go?"

"They're all over, lad. All over."

"Why didn't they kill us?"

"Because we're priests," Murti said. "Wandering Oerni. No use to anyone dead or alive."

"That could go the other way though?"

"With different people, of course. In that case we're traders though we've nothing to trade and you look like you were dug out of a field so that will be difficult to explain now."

Bukham wanted to blurt out what he'd seen, to ask Murti for an explanation. He wanted it badly, so that he could feel all right, but he knew there was nothing that could make it all right and nothing that could undo it. Something must be done, but he had no idea what to do.

"Do you pray?" he asked, desperately, wondering who they would pray to, even.

"If there's nothing else to do," Murti said. "But mostly I wander off."

"Does it work?"

"Well, it creates a bit of distance is what it does. Distance is a great help."

"I don't see how it helps anybody." Bukham felt that leaving was cowardice, but also he saw the sense of it, that if you had nothing to offer there was no point hanging around.

"It helps me," Murti said.

"I thought priests were supposed to help everyone."

"I expect your uncle told you that. He's a very pragmatic man."

Bukham didn't know what to say to that. He didn't know where the knowledge had come from, but everyone thought that the priests were wandering around doing random acts of something worthwhile, that was the point of them, to find out about distant peoples, to fetch news and to bring credit to the Oerni name. Wasn't it?

"It was a kind thing, to bury them," Murti said as the rain stopped and the sun sparkled on every glistening pebble in the way.

"I couldn't just…"

"I know."

"Is that why you didn't go?"

"No. I didn't go because it doesn't matter."

Bukham's rage exploded out of him. "Doesn't matter? How can you say that? What kind of monster are you? They were killed for nothing. They were good people, innocent people, just living and looking after each other after this bloody war and all that's happened and they died for nothing but some bastard's evil pride and you say it doesn't matter!! What... what..." He was panting so hard, unable to see for tears, his fists clenching and unclenching, not even really facing Murti but the world, the ground, the sky, all of it.

Murti's voice was quiet and unchanged. "I have a girl to find who is alive. Those people were already finished. Nothing I did to their bodies would make any difference to them. But a few hours on the road might make a difference to her."

Bukham in the midst of his agony felt speared by guilt. "And now you're blaming me! You're saying I'm stupid and mean when you were saying I was kind!" He knew it didn't sound like sense but it did make sense to him. And even in the midst of it he knew that he was wrong and the priest was right but he was so hurt that this final knowledge became like a lock, shutting him firmly in the prison of his mistakes.

Finally he managed to say, "Why didn't you say this when it could have changed my mind?"

"Some things are only understood by experience. Actually all things."

"So you let me go off to learn something while she could be dying." Bukham was still furious, but also sinking into a state of despond that seemed to be more powerful than the anger. He groped around, sensing that the anger was more useful and could be some kind of escape from the much worse sensation of futility. "What does that make you?"

"It makes me right," Murti said, still apparently unaffected. "We are Wandering Priests. You Wandered off. It's not my place to call you back from the path. Already you've learned more in a few hours than anything I could tell you in a lifetime."

"That is a convenient load of cant," Bukham said, struggling not to swear more than he already had. Why it was important to maintain politeness and decency in the circumstances he was at a loss to know but it felt better, as if he was winning. "And I'm not a priest. And we're not here to train me, we're here to save a little girl."

Murti said nothing. Bukham waited for the retort or something else but it never came. He was hungry and tired. Everything felt off kilter, broken. "She can't be this far." He wanted to go back to Taib. At least there he could catch up with the Templars but then, what would he do? The Post was a place of amnesty, unless that too was of no importance any more.

To survive the Kinslayer Uncle had taken them far south, to scout new markets, but now Bukham saw that was merely a pretext to get out of the way of trouble. Returning, he'd expected normality as they knew it to resume. But normality was gone.

Murti's silence angered him.

CHAPTER EIGHT

FOR HOURS KULA had struggled to keep moving towards the glow on the hill. It was a blaze of life, but there was more to it than that—a suffusion of magic so powerful that it felt like the flames of the funeral pyres her family had built for the best of their kind, to bring the soulfire that sent a spirit high to the next world. She wondered if maybe some of them had escaped and she decided to try to find them, more sure with every starving, delirious step that this was going to lead her back to them. In her imagination it had already happened so many times, this happy reunion. She felt that she was going home at last after all the long years alone.

Now, after a long climb through thick forest the fire's source was revealed at last. She saw burning but without smoke; orange, yellow and red, even white in places with the heat. Every tree of this part of the forest was on fire and among them the dashing, insane Draeyad spirits of the wood, whose life went on unabated as they burned endlessly, unable to escape even through death. Where she had eagerly rushed to reach and touch them she shrank back now, not daring to. Instead of the happy faces of her family she saw faces of beings lost to an utter madness of agony. In the trees the brilliance was so intense that she couldn't look on it with her eyes. Here was life all right. Life at its most energetic pitch, too high to survive in a body, in flames, but unable to leave. Their pain was unimaginable. The wide-mouthed, screaming faces rushed at her, looking at her, a creature outside their hell but who saw and knew what was happening. They were calling to her to kill them, kill them all. They tried to tear themselves apart in despair but the fire only mended them as soon as they succeeded.

Her dreams of warm hearths, glowing faces, happiness creating all that ferment, died in her. All her hope was gone and in its place a spite sat, contemptuous of her, that she would dare to dream of something like that after all she had already seen. The cruelty of her own illusion hurt her more than anything. She fell to her knees in the dry dirt and fallen needles of the dead wood on the hillside and sat there, ready for death, determined now not to move until it came and she didn't have to feel anything any longer.

She had been there some time when a movement startled her so that before she knew it she was on her face in the hollow behind a fallen trunk, peering through the hole where the wood had rotted through. She could just make out the jerky, struggling shapes of men toiling at a difficult task. Lit by the fiery glow the sweat on their skins stood out like metal in the dusk, for it was night, and they were hurrying, crouching and cowering in the labour as though hoping not to be seen and to get what they were doing done as fast as possible.

What they were doing was hauling a wooden stretcher upon two wheels. A long box was atop it, of the darkest black, yellow firelight casting strange shadows from the ornate carvings that covered its surface. Tendons strained and veins pulsed on the bare necks, arms and backs of the party of five as they wrenched the stretcher this way and that between the trees and over boulders, but it was clear that it wasn't the land causing the problem—they were fit and capable, their red tattoos against their dark skins marked them clearly as warriors of the Tzarkomen, and although slighter than many they were hardly troubled by something so feeble as the stretcher cart.

At first she didn't understand what they were fighting. It was difficult to see through the broken tree but she didn't dare move. She feared Tzarkomen. They had ways with death that she wanted nothing to do with. Their magic could hold her at the gate of death and make her body work for them here until it fell apart, while her spirit fuelled the lethal power of their weapons. But for all the charmed blades and fetishes they carried here it looked like there was an invisible foe that was getting the better of them. For every few steps they managed they had to stop and twist, cowering against the ground, their hands over their ears where their heads were wrapped tightly in bandages. Their bodies shook with the stress of resistance against this force as they ploughed on. When one turned his face to the light, looking for something, she saw the rolling white eyes of madness, the face of an animal in a trap. It looked very like the faces of the screaming spirits.

Then she understood. She was protected because she did not hear but they could hear the screams of the Draeyads, and the closer they got to the boundary where the burning, incandescent land met the dry, dead earth of the surrounding forest the more unbearable it became. The last few strides took them all their effort, shuddering, pushing the stretcher, only to have one of the wheels founder on a stone half buried in dry needles and crack in half. It had come a long way if they had taken it from Tzark. As far as she had come in all her days. She watched them try to catch the stretcher platform as it spilled its heavy contents down onto the ground.

The black box slid off the planks and into the earth with a thud that she felt through her body, as if it weighed an enormous amount more than it ought to. Then the cowering warriors got out picks and shovels and began to dig in the burning ground. The tools caught fire, and their boots where they crossed the boundary. Then they were hopping and running, mouths and eyes wide, foaming. They argued viciously among themselves. One threw down his tools and ran off, hands to his head. The leader cast a spear at his back but it missed and then, with their digging undone and unable to do whatever they had come for—to bury that box, surely—they all broke nerve, save for the leader, and went hurling themselves back down the hillside as fast as they could go.

She felt a little smile on her face. She didn't like Tzarkomen and they looked very silly, even more so that they were the most feared of all and running like rats. But the last one remained, more afraid to leave than to let his task go undone. He went back to digging, focused on the earth just this side of the border. Tears, sweat and his own yelling occupied him as he fought the urge to flee, and so he didn't see the enormous form of the centaur loom out of the inferno. It was one of the largest and most vivid of all the Draeyads imprisoned there—the horse part of it as large as the mightiest war steed, the human part on a scale of an Oerni or a Yorughan. It reared back silently to gather itself and hurled a ball of fire at him, despair and rage focused so powerfully that the impact knocked him off his feet. There was a sudden darkness as the ball seemed not just to hit him but to pass through his skin and vanish inside him as he flew through the air.

He landed right beside the dead trunk that was sheltering her, so close that she could see the terror, the horror in his face as he realised he was seeing his last moments. And the bewilderment too, that always came to those who traded in the death of others so freely. Now she knew he felt life, his life, and all that it could have been. A light came on inside his skin as the soulfire ignited. Instinctively, not knowing she would do it, she put her hand out through the hole in the wood and clasped his wrist in her strongest grasp so that he would not be alone, would know how to die without becoming an instrument of greater powers he didn't want to serve, Those Who Lingered, behind all things.

His head turned and he looked at her in shock, seeing himself gripped by a dead tree, or no, a child of some kind, a grip like that of death itself into which he could run away from the burning and into which he slipped without a thought as the light within him exploded and blew his body apart into fine, powdery ash.

Kula lay in the tree. She could feel the attention, the fixated attention of the creatures in the burning wood. Probably they were angry with her for thwarting their rage but the Tzarkomen was safely dead now and not coming back for anyone. She had sent him into the earth, the greatest of all sanctuaries, which could hold anything. His last moment had been peace, though all she had seen of him as he passed was an endless tide of death: ziggurats running in blood, flesh and bone raw under the burning sky. Children dying. That's what she saw. His own people, falling to blades they had made, one great and endless chain of slaughter. Mothers and fathers had slain their own and then each other until the bodies lay in heaps like strange fruit upon the sand.

She dug her fingers deeper into the dry, fragile ground, burying that vision he had left her with just as they had tried to bury the box; but where they had failed, she succeeded. She willed the earth to take it, and the earth, always merciful, accepted it from her. After a few moments the vision was gone. She was empty and could remember that it had happened, but not feel any of its horror again. This was why she didn't remember the day of the killing at her home, she realised now. Because her mother had bound her in the cellar in a circle of wood and bone, her bare feet on the earth. So she would never remember it, only its shell. She missed her mother then with a fierce grief that no spell could stop, but her body stopped her with a sharp pain.

Her hand was burning. She pulled it back in, splinters of wood coming with her arm. She brushed them off. A white powder of the Tzarkomen was falling now so that a sharp, black shadow of her body lay on the ground when she got up. As she stood she looked towards the fire. The giant centaur was gone. Draeyads of lesser sizes ran mad and threw themselves into the invisible wall of the boundary, trying to tear it down or smash themselves to bits against it. Their efforts were ceaseless.

She looked down at her feet so she didn't have to see them any more. Whatever the box was, it was not alive. But there was something strange about it, a peculiar-not-dead quality of something like a seed, something hidden and waiting for the rain, the sun, the soil to draw it into being. It was shielded from her by the box itself and so she felt it only dimly. She wiped tears off her face with the back of her good hand and moved slowly around the broken tree, her feet leaving a black trail in the pale ash.

The lid of the box had come loose and slid to one side during the fall. She looked at it for a moment and the twisted shapes of the carvings made themselves into tortured animals, faces and limbs, human and not all twining up and out at her as if they longed to escape too, or to drag her in with them. It depended how the burning light fell on them, she saw. It was so hideous she would have left it and gone but for the thing inside. Unlike the box this had no sense of any malice or intention about it. What she was seeing through the gap, she was sure, was bunched cloth and on it the unmistakable shape of a small human hand.

She didn't want to touch the vile box. For a few minutes she searched and eventually found a branch that had enough juice in it to survive a little use. She had to stop and wrap her burnt hand in some cloth from her skirt. That took a long time. She was very slow but determined. It hurt and she was so tired and she saw that she could not stop crying though she didn't feel much of anything, but eventually she was done and able to get the branch into position to lever off the lid completely.

It was heavy but it gave easily, the hinges already broken. With a thud it hit the ground, toppled over and revealed an entire body laid out neatly, dressed in the most astounding finery she had ever seen. Cloths and jewels winked and shone, clean and perfect in every stitch. Only the hands and face of the body were visible but the face was also covered in a thin gauzy veil dotted with pearls and stitched with symbols that the Tzarkomen used for weddings and bindings of all kinds. Through it a female face glimmered in the quaking light.

Kula reached out and touched the veil, cautiously. It felt stiff but nothing happened. She wondered what this could be, a thing that Tzarkomen had and were trying to bury here. They had no use for bodies. They burned the flesh of the dead that they did not eat. The pyres were greasy and oily day and night, the stench half smothered with spices and oils but unmistakable when the wind brought it south to her home. On those days they all remained indoors and only the Shroud went out and about, winnowing. They never had anything good to say about Tzarkomen and aside from adding to their store of factual knowledge they kept none of the newly slain.

This had not been slain, however. That was clear. Without the lid the feeling of potential was so enormous that it made the hairs on Kula's arms and neck rise, it filled her bones with a simmering sense of brimming sweetness and energy so that in spite of everything she smiled. This thing was a font of life, waiting to begin. Nothing that felt this way could be evil. It wasn't the antithesis of that, it was only that it knew nothing of it, knew nothing of anything, was ready... to grow.

She pulled off the ugly veil with its sigils of death and stasis. The face in repose was youthful, smooth, as though carved. A Tzarkomen girl, nearly a woman. She touched it with a fingertip. Once. Twice. The skin was dry and papery but underneath that it was resilient, plump with youth. She felt the chalkiness of the paint on it that had made it perfectly white in the usual tradition for a bride. The expression and the features were serene and lovely with the peaceful sweetness of the innocent.

She was reminded instantly of her mother and all the feelings that she had felt for her.

Then a complete despair came over her and she was as crushed and lonely as she had ever felt. She crawled into the box and lay on the unliving woman, rested her head on the rounded bosom. It was comfortable and with her eyes closed the horrid place receded, vanished to a dim fluttering. She pulled the fineries of the dress around her and closed her eyes, waiting for whatever came. After a while the form under her seemed to soften, or she did. She felt the peacefulness of that face envelop her slowly and sank into it, down and down without resistance. The last thing she was aware of as sleep came was the sensation that loving arms were around her and a loving heart near her and she felt this was the essence of her mother come back somehow from the white fires—not the stern and difficult parts, but the best part, the part that forever and first had loved her and known no other feeling. With a little shiver she relaxed, safe and at home.

CHAPTER NINE

TRICKY WATCHED THE party of the Fernreame Slayer, her Yorughan and her bard vanish slowly as they made headway against the wind and dropped below the hilltop ahead of her. She moved casually to the side of the road, a figure wrapped up against the weather in a heavy oilskin cape, hooded, of no exceptional feature at all save for the boots which, if anyone had been looking at them, could be seen to be fine and strangely undamaged by the mud. She hopped over a few low shrubs and climbed up onto a flat boulder beside the track where a stand of thin trees sheltered her from sight. Next to her the figure of an old man, raggedly dressed, a poor creature of no consequence, shivered.

She turned to him. "So, what news? I couldn't hear anything over the stink of all that drying peasant."

Deffo wrinkled his nose. "They're sold on it. They're off to the hill."

"Wanderer?"

"Might show up. But if he doesn't I can probably explain it." He glanced at her. "Did you make them?"

She reached into her cape and brought out a fine silk purse. Tugging it open she held it up and tipped out a cascade of brown nuggets etched with runes into the palm of her calfskin glove.

Deffo flinched back a little as he looked down at the fingerbones of their dead brother, the Kinslayer. "I suppose you haven't…"

With a flourish of her wrist she cast the bones out before them where they rolled and tumbled before settling in the air, some high, some low, their carved faces dull and lifeless in the light of the coming storm. She studied them intently, reading.

The Undefeated shivered. "What do you…"

He was interrupted again by her, "But seriously! Fuck him."

"What did it say?"

She turned to look him in the eye, her own gaze coming from under a heavy frown. Without looking she snaked her hand out and gathered the bones up in her fist, before dropping them back into the bag and secreting it under her cloak. "Said it's all part of the plan. Whatever you do, you're doing Reckoner's business and that business is still in business, all that kind of thing."

"But he's definitely dead."

"Oh yeah. Definitely. Unless you count living on through events he laid in motion."

They both sat for a moment in a little fug of relief, perhaps a twinge of guilt and a greater sense of anxiety.

After a second or two Deffo said. "You found something, didn't you?"

"There was this mission he had, one he wouldn't share with me other than in name. He was determined to locate *The Book of All Things*. I think it was code for something. I could never get out of him why he was so determined to have it. I tried pressing him but he started to get suspicious of me and that's when he put me on 'research duties' scouring all his stolen junk for relics. Hoo hoo! Happy days!" She chuckled, a covetous sparkle in her eyes which soon vanished as she returned to her story. "Obviously he didn't trust me. Before I went however, I got the impression he wanted to destroy the Book, it was that kind of interest he had. He wanted it gone. It was shortly after that he sent one of his elite legions north. I thought he was making a play for Tzarkand, but later they joined the main force pushing east into the Middle Kingdoms." Tricky paused, an extensive, dramatic pause in which she took out a long stemmed pipe with a curling flourish to its shape and a small bowl delicately carved with flowers. It lit itself, apparently. As a fine curlicue of smoke began to wind up from the bowl, violet on the glum air of the day, a scent of herbs and sweet long afternoons of summer twined into Deffo's nose. There was an unmistakable calm and harmony surrounding them.

He sneezed. "Where'd you get that?"

"I borrowed it from Dr Catt," she said. She didn't puff on the pipe, just held it as if she was in the midst of smoking and continued to talk about the two things. "Number one, the Kinslayer cut a deal with the Tzarkomen, I'm sure of it. And, number two, my informants say that five of them were seen on the road moving south towards Hathel Vale a day ago."

As she spoke the violet smoke shifted, sculpted by unseen fingers into a chiaroscuro illustration of the scene before their eyes. Five male figures in the unmistakable feather and bone-garb of the Tzarkomen elite were jogging a two-wheeled stretcher along a road fanged with tall trees, a moon overhead glowing down to pick out the large container they were hauling and the grim markings that covered its surface. For a moment that image held, then swirled and rearranged itself into the face of a single man. He was painted with the black and white Gorecrow Clan marks, as though a wing shadow crossed his face, but none of the design nor the sharp splinters of bone that poked through his bloody cheeks could hide the fact that he was scared witless, his gaze fixated with a grim determination on something ahead.

The smoke furled away, ordinary again, and beneath the floral notes a sickly twist of putrefying flesh wafted about, and a strange metallic odour. That smell—it was gone almost before it existed but in the split second that it was present it evoked an unmistakable moment in both their lives. The first moment. It was the smell of the gods' forge, their cradle.

"You burned all the bits of him. All. You're sure," Deffo said. It was so difficult to feel secure even with the Reckoner bodily removed from the world. At such a moment, how easy it would have been to be fooled, all one's hopes and fears so close to reality.

"All the bits I could find. Except these." She patted the hidden pouch of bones.

"I think that bears further investigation," Tricky said, pointing at where the smoke image had been.

"Tzarkomen necromasters, scared?" He found it hard to imagine. As long as he wasn't doing the investigating, though, that was the main thing. "I trust you'll be able to discover what's going on."

Tricky shrugged. The pipe had ceased smoking. She put it away. "A good excuse to revisit Fury and get into his tomes. I need something to bring him in return, though. Some trinket to pay with. I'm not exactly his favourite. And by that I mean we are at daggers drawn." A restless and preoccupied look took over her face. She tapped her finger on her chin.

"Look for the book," Deffo said. "Where there are lots of dead there might be treasure."

"I hate grave robbing." She wrinkled her nose. "It's the pits."

"Like your jokes."

"At least I do jokes instead of being one."

"Uncalled for."

"Very called for. Anyway, there is some merit in your suggestion. Let's meet again soon." She jumped down from the boulder and rubbed her bottom vigorously with both hands through the heavy drape of her cloak. "Numb as a politician's sympathies."

"I couldn't have put it better myself."

When she looked up to snipe back he had already gone. She turned towards the road and then sighted off to the West. From a pocket of the cloak she took out a ball of wool of various colours and deftly unwound the end of one black, green and blue speckled line. As soon as she had done so the entire ball lost all the other colours. It jumped out of her hand and rolled about in the grass at her feet like a bit of popping corn on a hot plate, unravelling. Within a few moments it had all come free. The two ends of the yarn found one another and reached out with individual strands, respinning themselves into a single endless line which coiled, reared up and whipped around her, moving faster than the eye could see until she was covered in a loose-knit net. With a whispering sound like feathers brushing across the bone of an old skull the net drew suddenly tight and squeezed her into another shape entirely.

A carrion crow hop-jump-fluttered up onto the boulder and then with a leap took to the air, heavily flapping for a few yards until it got up some momentum before it climbed into the grey skies, circling once before turning to the distant Tzarkona Gate.

CHAPTER TEN

KULA WOKE UP and found herself lying within the dark box wrapped in a soft cloak, alone. A grey daylight was taking over from the fire glow so that she could see sky between the broken spars of wood overhead but that wasn't what grabbed her attention. There was something huge, powerful and very alive close by. A keen sense of self-preservation made her sit bolt upright, clutching the cloak to her. The source of the sensation was immediately apparent. The woman from the box was standing nearby, her back half turned so that Kula could just see her face in profile. The fire shone merrily off the jewels on her dress. She was staring at the burning Draeyads.

As Kula watched she stretched out her right hand and moved it slowly to the invisible barrier that marked the flames' edge. Instantly every mote of flame inside the burning wood leapt along invisible conduits directly to the tips of her fingers. Within seconds the conduits had changed in girth from threads to ropes and then a moment later from ropes to hawsers of roiling fire.

The woman opened her mouth and Kula wondered if she was going to scream and burn but all she did was take one, enormous inward breath. As it concluded, the last spiralling whirls of white, red, orange and yellow zipped along the line of contact to her hand and were gone. The air shivered, like an animal's flank when a fly takes off, and then in place of the

87

burning hell there was only the hillside in the morning wind. The breeze lifted the parched leaves of the trees that were no longer on fire—nor had ever been burned, as the soulfire was a spirit affliction and not of the physical world. They were only weak and exhausted with drought. The grass was crisped to hay, the flowers dead, the stalks straw. Between them the shades of the Draeyads had faded to the near-nothing of ghosts now that they were no longer illumined from within. They held out their limbs and looked; they moved and stretched and danced for joy in the cool wash of the wind that promised, if not rain, heavier clouds. Without bodies they could hold no memory of their suffering and so it was already passed. They were as they had been before the Kinslayer—wild energies arising from the intensity of growth and the richness of the forest, personified by aeons of passing creatures whose minds cast shapes among the fertile swirl of power and who remembered for them.

Seeing their happiness the young woman in the gown exhaled a long, satisfied sigh. She smiled the smile of a job well done and straightened her spine a notch. Then she turned and saw Kula and the smile became radiant, all delight, because it was looking at something beloved.

Kula hurtled into the waiting arms and the woman lifted her up and spun her around and around until her legs flew out and her broken sandal came off. She had never heard a voice, nor would, but she heard this person inside her as clearly as her own senses and knew her name, the name she had gone by when she grew up a Tzarkomen: Lysandra—a sound name. It didn't have a signed form but Kula made one and they spoke briefly with their gestures, repeating until they understood the sign that meant each other's name. Then Lysandra taught her to say her sound-name too. And she learned to say "Kula". Lysandra had many memories of talking words though almost nothing else. She was glad to share her memories of talking words with Kula, though Kula preferred to sign. All this happened within the few moments of their embrace, as naturally as breathing.

At last Kula was set down to regain her balance. Lysandra took her hand and gestured at the hill to show what she had done. Kula nodded fit to make her head fall off. She had woken up Lysandra and Lysandra had made something good out of something awful and it was the best, the very best day.

Lysandra smiled again in pure contentment and Kula saw that her teeth were even, small and very sharp, like a cat's. The irises of her eyes were brown at the edges but gold at the centers, and slitted, also like a cat. She had powerful features, bold and full in the way that Tzarkomen favoured in their notions of beauty. The daylight revealed her clothing to be a vast finery, trains of fabric dragging around in the ash and needles of the floor when they should have graced an occasion that was so fine Kula could not imagine where and what it could be. Just touching some of the panels of the dress gave the feeling that one was touching water, it was so soft. It rang with power and song that she could feel.

Kula gripped Lysandra's hand, to see if any of the fire was somehow left there, but all she could feel was that it had quite gone, somewhere so far she could not reach it. It was not fire any more but its energy was there and Lysandra was bolstered by it, brighter, stronger. She wished her mother were there again and Lysandra looked down on her and squeezed her hand gently because she was that now. She had been nothing, but now she was that.

Kula's stomach growled. The pangs of hunger and thirst returned suddenly. Lysandra straightened and sniffed the breeze like a scouting hound. After a moment she chose a direction and set off without a backward glance at the box or the cavorting Draeyads, her little girl's hand in hers. Together they disappeared into the grey and green vaultings of the forest, although for a long time glints and gleams of fierce gems and gold embroidery could be glimpsed by anyone looking in the right direction.

CHAPTER ELEVEN

THE OLD MAN slowed down to an infuriating pace as they neared the hills of Hathel Vale. Bukham could see the first standing stones at the roadside miles before they reached them with the sun starting to set. He supposed that the girl could have got this far if she'd kept going but why she would do that he couldn't imagine. He'd never been this far from his family and how she would manage it when he was finding it so hard he didn't know. He kept asking himself why she would have bothered; wouldn't she have stopped or looked for something, someone, else to help her? But Murti said nothing, just put his staff out, then his foot, kept on walking. It's not as if he needed the answers telling him, Bukham maintained inwardly, because he could see them for himself, it's just that if Murti said them he'd feel confident that he was right and that they were on the right path whereas now he just felt upset with everything, that it was all out of joint. He didn't want to admit how badly he longed to abandon the search and go home. His uncle would be happy to see him back and the girl was obviously able to fend for herself if she'd got this far. What they were doing was quite unnecessary.

But then he thought of the messy little girl, alone, and, if Murti was right, alone without family in the world, wandering in terror because he had driven her off with his stupid failures to act and stand up to his uncle. He couldn't think of going back without her. But now, with the light going, he started to think that really they should find a place to stop for the night. As he was about to open his mouth to suggest this Murti spoke.

"Nearly there."

"Nearly where?"

"Where we're going."

Bukham's feet were too tired and sore to pursue the point. If it was soon then at least it would soon be over. He felt a renewed surge of shame at wanting to give up and made an effort to copy Murti's easy-going stride. They came around the hillside in the wake of many fresh footprints and a horse's tread and then paused. He saw Murti surveying the rolling woodlands with a contemplative air as though he had all the time in the world to enjoy the view. It was pleasant but nothing special. The avenue of stones marched away through the brush and was soon lost in the tall trees that marched upwards over the next rise. Then he realised.

"Wait. This is Hathel Vale. But where's the fire?"

"Yes, quite," Murti said. "I think we should go find out."

"But…" Bukham began, realising as he said it that there was no point. Murti was already off the road and knee high in thistles and grass, striding as if he was off on a spring jaunt.

Bukham hurried after him, suddenly anxious at leaving the road, taking another detour, another delay.

CHAPTER TWELVE

IT HAD BEEN a few hours on the road, the shapes of the hills slowly giving way to greater, more impressive rises and falls and Celest all the way dreading the appearance of Hathel Vale on the skyline. Red as war, billowing with endless fire, it was a banner of hatred that the Kinslayer had left to remind them all that he had power beyond anyone's ability to stop. Once had it, anyway, before her blade that cut everything had cut off his hand and then in the melee he had proved less than entirely durable. She was still surprised by that.

"Hey," Nedlam said, shifting Lady Wall from one massive shoulder to the other. "There's men and horses up ahead."

Below the brow of the hill in the shadow of the afternoon sun there were indeed three horses. They stood where the road forked, the path to Taib Post some way behind them. Two were mounted, one was horsed but would never ride again. His legs flopped against the beast's side, arms the other way, arse in the air, covered in some kind of blanket. The clothing and the horses marked them out as Ilkand Templars. Celest battened down the last of her hopes for the day. It was clear even from this distance that the riders were arguing.

As they got closer the loud voices carried clear. She consciously slowed down to a crawling pace, Heno at her side and Nedlam at his side all with their ears straining whilst Ralas craned his neck at the back.

"We can't just dump him at the roadside. They'll wonder where we were." This one was grim, practical, resigned.

"But we can't take him back like this, that bloody Termagent'll call justice on the Post and everyone who was at it. The whole point of it was to stop. We had to stop it. We have to." His companion was desperate, on the border of panic. They were so involved with their problem that they hadn't yet noticed Celest's party approaching through the thin veil of the brush between the ways.

"Let's take him back to the farm and leave him there."

"I can't go back there."

"You're coming. I'm not going alone. Someone might see us. We have to make sure it looks like he died there. There's nothing left anyway. Nobody to revenge on, eh? Makes sense."

"Fuck it. Yeah. All right. But… hey, shh, someone's coming." They turned their mounts and sheltered the dead man from the group approaching. They were rigid with tension and only their eyes moved, scanning faces and scowling, hands on their sword hilts. At this range the Temple Ilkand sigils on their cloaks were clearly visible. They surveyed Celestaine and her Fiddlehead livery with quick precision, lingering on her face and the scrappy tendrils of her long hair where it had escaped being tied back and then gone curly in the damp. If they recognised her by description they didn't show it.

Celestaine held up her arm in a friendly hail but didn't speak. She was watching for their reaction to the Yorughan, but they were already so mired in their plot that they didn't respond with any extra signs of aggression. Feeling their riders' upset the horses twisted and stamped, longing to be moving away. Celestaine kept course to pass them, but she knew she must speak—it would have been peculiar not to in the circumstances. One met travellers, one made some effort to discover at least the conditions of the way or another kind of politeness.

"Are you for Ilkand?" It seemed like an innocuous opener, an obvious one.

The one that seemed to have taken the lead nodded, his helm hiding most of his face but not enough of it to conceal the fact that he wasn't keen on chatting.

"How are the roads that way?" she asked.

The man gave an equivocal shrug. "Stay south, and if you've a mind to cross the water you'd be better off taking a ferry from the leemost side. There's some loose monster about."

Against her will Celestaine paused, Heno tense on the far side of the horse, Nedlam easy, her hand flexing on the haft of the hammer although it remained at her shoulder.

Ralas drew alongside. "Is there some trouble?"

"Aye, right will be plenty of it soon," the second, panicky Templar said, his voice steadying.

"Or our heads on pikes at any rate," the first added. "But you're that Fernreame champion what was in on the Slaying, are you not?" He glanced at the company as if to show that he knew who was who. "So if you're looking for a job there may be work in it." He turned away, making for the road towards the Post.

Celestaine nodded and was turning to go when she heard Ralas say cheerily, "So your captain died in glorious battle?"

There was a pause and an awkward halt as they turned to look at one another from mounts headed in opposite directions.

"He was sadly slain during a defence of innocent farm folk from evil bandits." This was said in a tone that brooked no controversy but was, at the same time, so clearly a lie that it was easy to infer that the captain had hardly been on the defending side.

"I wish you a safe journey, then," Ralas said. Celest raised her hand to salute and cautiously spurred her horse forwards. She felt a chance stretching away from her, a chance in which she burned to ask what was going on, and whether these two were alone or in some kind of organised mutiny against the Cleric or whatever went on in Ilkand these days, but she had other business which wasn't headed in that direction.

"Difficult," Nedlam said as they went out of earshot.

Ralas turned in the saddle and looked back. "They're not going towards Ilkand."

"Difficult?" Celest asked.

"Rebelling when there's only two of you," Heno said at her stirrup. "It's difficult. But not impossible." His hand briefly gripped Celest's booted foot and she smiled at him.

"Never thought I'd like a Templar," Nedlam shrugged. "An' I still don't."

They journeyed on in silence, making good time now that the weather had cleared. Some hours later they reached the river and made a turn to the north following the Ilkand Road although it now led through their destination. As they came over the next rise they paused to look. There before them lay the long meandering rollback hills of Hathel Vale with the steady rise of the Wayfarers' sacred hill at its centre, all thick with trees on the crest which they had last seen ablaze. It had burned fit to light the dark for miles. But in this afternoon light it was peacefully, inexplicably, green and brown. The standing stones that marked the edges of the grand Wanderer's Way avenue were visible here and there amid rusty foliage. The hilltop looked withered but there was no trace of fire, ordinary or otherwise.

"What the…?"

"…hells is going on?" Ralas finished for her as they began to descend into the Vale.

Curiosity lent them speed. Within the hour they had reached the base of the central hill and begun to move along its lone ascending path. To their right the avenue of stones was a broad, grassy swath but the track stayed away from it and out of uncertainty they did too. They had been on it only a few minutes when Nedlam flared her nostrils. Her Yorughan nose was deceptively small for its power of detection which far outstripped a human sense of smell.

"Grennish," she said with a nod and a lip curl of disgust. "Others too. Human. On the other side of the hill. They fight. Not too long ago. Blood is fresh. And—" She stretched her neck up, nostrils flaring. "Fruit."

"Fruit?" Ralas eased his back, leaning to the side. "Not the season for that yet round here is it? Another few weeks."

"Fruit," Nedlam said with a nod. "Very ripe. Sweet." She made a small motion of her mouth that said she had tried these and wasn't sure about them. "Burnt flesh," she said, with a more approving grunt.

In the distance further up the hillside Celestaine thought she saw a dark, ragged shape flit between the branches silhouetted against the sky.

"Did that man say monsters were about?" Ralas asked.

"He did, but I think he meant further north where the riverboats dock," Celestaine said.

"Just a suggestion then, as things have changed here—before the war when anyone came on this hill they went by the proper Way. On that path one is a visitor. Every other path, no matter how it seems to take you forwards, always ends up at the road again."

"We are looking for the Wanderer," Heno said. "And it is his way, apparently. Should we not try it?"

Celestaine thought of all the stories she had heard about Draeyad hospitality, none of it charming or sweet. "All right. But be alert. Even if there are no spirits someone's about."

She glanced at the massive rocks of the Wanderer's Way as they passed each one. Some had worn paint on them but most were moss-covered dark granite, lichen-coined, dug into the earth as if they'd been there forever. They were uncarved and bore no marks of any hewing. Hundreds of them laid the trail on either side in two parallel lines that stretched from the hilltop down to the edge of a valley over two miles away. As she had many times in her life she strained to detect some form of magic around them, but there was no sign for her.

Instead she watched Heno, the Heart Taker, whose name came from some form of magic that he did which she had never asked about in any detail. He moved to the centre of the avenue, dwarfed by the rocks, and she sent her horse after him, taking the path that was furthest from any stone. Nedlam, by contrast, as unmagical as Celestaine, stomped cheerfully along to his flank, swatting at flies with a bunch of grass she'd picked. Ralas was humming behind her, a snippet of the Wanderer's Song which had different rhythms for all kinds of places and different words—which were never actual words, she'd realised after years of puzzling; they were deliberately nearly words but not quite words. They, their meaning, their sound, must wander.

She was scanning the woods for signs of devastation and ashes but finding nothing until her gaze snagged on a bright twinkle of something up on the hill. She pressed her horse to a jog and went ahead, carefully, in the middle, until she was level with the glint. Then she dismounted and let the horse amuse itself with the grass while she beat through the bushes to what she'd seen. It was a scrap of fabric, silky and fine as anything her cousin would have worn. A sequin bead had caught the light and shone to her. The colour was dark purple, with pink stitches visible, and there was a vague scent of some kind of incense. Nearby the grass was trampled in a clear path which went down the hill. She noted that but followed it upwards, hearing the others slowly catch her up as she at last made the summit.

Here there was a clearing, where the ground was soft and covered in a deep loam of needles that were all agitated and thrown up. A large wooden box was half buried there and around it were gathered six or seven large, majestic humanoids of different kinds. They were semi-transparent, outlined in the strange pale fire of the spirit world. A green tint suffused them; neither plant nor person, but in between. Then she recognised them, but only from seeing them burn in agony—Draeyads. Behind them stood an even larger figure of a creature she had never seen before. At first glance she'd thought another rider had made it here ahead of her, but as the horse's hefty and very solid chestnut rump turned so that it could face her she realised it wasn't a rider at all, but a centaur.

The young woman part of the centaur was dressed in sturdy leather ranging gear, and what had seemed a saddle was a hefty belt. It strapped to both her midsections at once as a harness which served to carry her gear. In her hand she held a long javelin which slowly levelled itself in Celestaine's direction. Her eyes were a shocking leaf green, her hair corn-gold and as thick and long as her horse tail. She lowered her chin and all of the Draeyads turned with the grace of a leaf in the wind, moving as one to focus on the party as they emerged one by one from the thickets that clogged the old Way.

"Ho, Wanderer," said the centaur in a traditional greeting. She spoke well but her accent was thick and foreign to Celestaine's midlander ears. She didn't recognise it.

"Ho," Celestaine said, freezing by instinct. The stern directness, the sheer force of the Draeyads' attention made her wary. Where they had been as quick and fluid as light itself they were now as still as ancient oak trunks. She had to fight an impulse to draw her sword. "How... I mean... what..."

"Your interest is as ours," the centaur said, the tip of the javelin lifting slightly to a point where it would only carve a furrow out of one of their heads rather than slice them off.

The Draeyads seethed, their auras crackling and whirling around them in tendrils that endlessly wove and separated. One was headed with an owl's face, another was so like a tree it had no features, and a third was part deer and part flower, its eyes the blooms of sun daisies.

"We..." Celestaine began.

"Seek Wanderer," said the tree, lifting a twig hand to gesture at her to come forwards. Its voice came from somewhere deep inside it. "He is near. We also seek to know what is the meaning of this." It pointed down with one finger at the box and as it did so the finger grew and extended. Bright spring green at the tip, it quickly turned brown as it thickened and lengthened until it touched the carved black wood and recoiled slightly. "Is it yours?"

"No... hey!" Ralas was cut off by his own gasp of alarm. Celest felt a sudden shift in the ground at the same moment and without any warning felt the tendrils of roots and shoots from all the plants beside her suddenly whipping themselves around her ankles and wrists. Here was something she did recognise from legend. She hoped it wasn't about to turn into the kind of hospitality that necessitated a long, decaying underground stay.

"We mean no harm," Heno said quickly but he was already being lifted off the ground by the force of the rising growth, his hands imprisoned. A fresh leaf unfolded beside his face and touched the carved tusk at his jaw in curiosity.

"You," the tree said, and the one that was like a bush and a deer came forwards, rustling, ever-connected to the earth and its companions by a twisting swamp mist that shrouded them about the legs. Its daisy eyes blinked slowly, yellow petals folding and unfolding as they came to examine Heno and then Nedlam, who was grunting in an effort to test the bonds and finding herself lashed tighter, her hammer bound to her as if it were part of her body. Ivy had rushed up her neck and now it threatened to go up her nostrils, at which point she stopped and yelled in the language of the Kinslayer's minions, "Sao yorak nor na!" *We are not here to fight.*

"Defiler's creatures. Why should we not feast upon you?" the tree said, its voice coming from a dark slash in the bark where a face should have been as clearly as if spoken by a man, though there was no movement visible.

"They're with me," Celestaine said, feeling vulnerable as the daisy-face deer came and thrust its delicate mossy nose at her. It had small horns which were heavy with leaves, and the prickly bright green balls of unripe chestnuts swung from the branches of these horns in stiff little clusters. As she watched, their outer spines darkened to brown, curled and with a tumble all fell to the ground. The Draeyad moved off to test Ralas, crushing one of the fruits open with its woody hoof. Inside the rind a tiny brown shape Celestaine figured for a nut was revealed but, instead of lying still, it unrolled: the tiniest of hedgehogs. Within a moment or two it had snuffled around the roots that bound her and then vanished under a turned clump of mud.

This was the nature magic that had not stopped the Kinslayer. She was so delighted to see it though the joy sat strangely on her apprehension. She could feel something growing up the length of her greaves beneath the metal armoured shin. At her wrist a thorn pierced her skin and she felt her blood run out over the stems that held her.

"Ow!"

She guessed by the sounds that the same had happened to all of them simultaneously. They were being tested.

A Draeyad that was more earthen than the rest, a kind of fungus grown to some mockery of a fox form, moved around and scuffed at the loose dirt to the edge of the clearing. It was hard to see what was going on but she heard Heno exclaim as the creature worked all its weight to drag something new into view. A stench made her gag as she saw it was a corpse, somewhat bloated and outgassing with a few sullen parps in objection to being disturbed. In spite of its condition it was easily recognisable by its bone and paint markings as having once been a Tzarkomen priest.

"*They* came here," the centaur said accusingly. She pointed at the corpse with her javelin. The point gleamed in a shaft of sunlight and as the flies began to gather one of their thousands came close to the metal tip and was suddenly, briefly, made into a white star before being crisped to nothing. "Who are they?"

"Tzarkomen," Celestaine replied quickly. The centaur's stare demanded elaboration. "Humans who practise necromancy, among other things. I'm not sure what else. I always stayed well away from them. Everyone does. They're secretive. As long as you stay out of their lands they're no bother."

"And if you do go to see them?"

"Probably end up dead," Heno hissed, between his teeth. "They don't wait to ask questions of the living."

The centaur's attention snapped to him. "Why would they bring her?"

"Who?"

"The woman in the box. The one who saved us from the fire."

"I don't know who you're talking about," Heno said, gasping with the effort of breathing in the spread-eagled position he was stuck in. Celestaine could just see him from the corner of her eye, and Ralas on the other side, similarly stretched.

"They know nothing," one of the others said and abruptly all the prisoning branches were withdrawn, and they were free.

"Wait, someone saved you? Where is she?" Celestaine asked, rubbing her wrists as she folded up on the ground for a moment, resting.

The centaur, the only real, solid being among them, looked at Celestaine for a long moment and then she swung her spear point around and pointed in the direction from which they had come, marking a little crushed grass to show where someone had lately passed. "Downhill. They are on the road now."

"They?"

"The child and the woman who ate the fire."

"Who ate the fire?" Ralas asked, a tremble in his voice. "She ate it? Are you sure?"

The centaur turned to look at him, her eyes wide. She nodded. "I am a free spirit. The only one of us to truly walk in this world, the only one of us not bound to her host tree. I serve as the Voice of the Forest. I failed to stop the Kinslayer from burning my kind with the soulfire." She hesitated, but only for an instant, though her face had changed to show deep sadness. "But the woman from the box took it. She ate it all up. But by the time we were ourselves again and I had grown they were gone. That way."

Heno and Nedlam, rubbing their wounds, stared and then glanced at Celestaine for a verdict, although they were all sure of one thing—that they were going to find these people and discover the truth of what had happened here.

"We have to find them," Celestaine said. Because someone who could take that fire like it was nothing and 'eat it all up' was someone who was possibly a bigger deal even than the Guardians, and that wasn't someone who should be going around doing whatever they wanted. A monster? There were so many of those now left behind in the wake of the war. She wished Wanderer were there to give a hint but if he were near then he could find them if he wanted to.

"You're free to go," the centaur said, stepping forwards as the other Draeyads and spirits drew back into the shadows of the trees, vanishing into near invisibility within moments as if swallowed up whole. "I shall accompany you. You may find one who saved us from the fire, but you may not harm her. She is under our protection."

Celestaine weighed it up, and considered her past decisions briefly regarding the inclusion of other people. She doubted that she could decline in any case and if it came to a fight later then she'd deal with it later. "Very well. What shall we call you?"

"Bossy tree horse," Nedlam muttered.

The centaur smiled at one side of her mouth, "Horse it is. They are a noble animal, far superior to all of you in every way."

Celestaine shook her head. "Fine. Horse. Let's go. Heno, you lead, in case they have more magic to use." As she spoke she heard a hissing, rustling noise and felt the earth under her feet tremble. Spinning around she saw the ground swallow up the corpse of the Tzarkomen and reassemble itself over him. Leaves swirled into place until nothing marked that the earth had ever moved. That was Draeyad hospitality right there.

The centaur saw her looking. "It is a kindness, to use the dead wisely to make new beauty."

"He wasn't dead when he got here, was he?" she asked.

The centaur smiled, unruffled. "Who comes uninvited decides their fate. They were tested and found undeserving."

Heno had paused to observe; now he moved a little stiffly, his rangy, powerful form taking a cautious path as he tracked so that he somewhat resembled a heron. Celestaine went after him, leading her horse and Ralas', and Nedlam after her with Ralas hastening in her wake the best he could. Horse the centaur came a stately few paces behind them, making less noise than any.

Now and again Heno paused and handed back his findings: a scrap of lace made out of silk, a silver thread, a ruby the size of a robin's egg, still cased in a cage of golden wires. They all marveled but they didn't pause.

Ralas put the items carefully away in his cloak pockets after an effort to share the viewings with Horse earned him only a frown.

"You are on the brink," Horse said to him as they made their slow way downhill, through thickets and hillocks of reedy grass. "For us the fire. And for you, the edge of death. He was an inventive torturer."

Celestaine listened, trying to figure out what Horse meant. She must be talking about the spell that kept Ralas alive, but never healing.

"Right," Ralas said. "I could put that in a poem but it's a bit crass to make them about yourself."

"But not to make a song about her. Maybe she will find you a way back too," Horse said, as if everything were simple. Perhaps for Draeyads it was, Celestaine thought. They weren't human, you couldn't expect them to be the same. Had their torment been of that kind because only something permanent would work on them—because they had this ability to let the past go as if it had never been? She wanted to learn that trick, and she saw by his face that Ralas did too.

He'd had the chance to take the Kinslayer's crown and use its remaining and much-weakened magic to solve his problems, but he'd cast it aside to keep his pain and weakness rather than touch a device made by the monster. But now it was in him, this little hope, a tiny extra thorn, and with every step it worked itself deeper, exactly as she had felt it when she'd set out to give the Aethani their wings back.

Just when you thought things couldn't get any more difficult to bear, she thought. There was always more.

CHAPTER THIRTEEN

HENO LED THE way steadily, sensing nothing other than a few birds they routed from the shrubs. Within a few minutes they had left the peak and begun to follow the Wanderer's Way more or less, always going downhill in the trail of crushed grasses until at last they emerged from the scrubby bushes onto the road by which they had come. At that point he saw that they had no further need to look.

A few yards off on a grassy bank, a filthy child and a woman in a queen's finery were sitting together, each eating hungrily from fruit and nuts that filled a cloth bag in the queen's lap. The woman was dark and of one of the humans he would have considered Tzarkomen, though he'd never seen any of them dress so outlandishly. She sparkled, bejewelled, and he wondered about that, thinking of Celestaine's cousin. The child was obviously not hers, he thought. It was dark, barely distinguishable as boy or girl—he'd never been good at telling boys and girls apart in humans—and starveling thin, as dark as the darkest bark of the trees in Nydarrow, cast with their same indigo tones, but both matt and pale where the light caught its skin so that it seemed nearly unreal in the afternoon sunlight. The matted hanks of hair festooned the child's head and shoulders, full of twigs, leaves and a fancy diamond pin in the shape of a flower stuck on at an odd angle. It was eating with the ferocity of a wild animal and only the whites of its eyes suddenly showed up as it looked at them. Otherwise it did not move other than to nudge the woman and point a finger.

Heno and the rest emerged one by one from the verge and halted in a line at the road's edge, though only the woman stopped chewing. She leaned over to put the child behind her but it pushed forwards, looking over her arm. It swallowed and Heno found its dark gaze fixed with unerring malice directly upon him with such a focus that he had the sudden sensation that only the two of them were real and everything and everyone else present was an illusion.

He'd been looked at with hatred before but until this moment he'd never experienced another's hate as a strike in the gut, distinctly physical and threatening so that his heart lurched an extra beat and he felt a frisson of fear, so long discarded from his life that its rediscovery was thrilling. He found his hands automatically moving together to the spellcast shape but the child's gaze watched them, knew it, and as if it was a sensitive animal, scared of the light, the power did not come. He was so surprised he just stood and then glanced at the other, for a break from the oddness as much as for help with understanding who they were and what it meant. He was dimly aware of Celestaine going forward, her hand keeping the rest of them back: she cast a concerned glance at him to see what he made of it but he gave the tiniest shrug.

The decorated woman's face was harder to read than the child's. It seemed to have no emotion at all as it watched them, moving from one of them to the next and the next, though it had an intensity and acuity that made every hair on the back of Heno's neck stand up in a way he'd only ever felt beneath an imminent thunderstorm.

They were all stopped in their tracks, even Celestaine in front of him. Only the wind moved, turning the ends of her long, white-blonde hair. The strange woman in the dress was first to move. Never taking her eyes off them she slowly stood up. The bag of fruit tumbled to the ground. Without regard she stepped over it and, lifting her voluminous skirts up with one hand just so that she was able to walk, came towards them, the child behind her, almost entirely hidden. Now that this blocked her sightline to him Heno felt suddenly that he was back in reality, his wits returning. For a moment he had the strange idea that the woman was the child's puppet, not alive at all, but then, as they crossed the broad rutted lane he saw the breathing, the juicy mess the berries had made, the eye-popping wealth of a massive dowry stitched into all the bewitching sigils of what was clearly a wedding dress. His skin prickled. He felt the cold conviction that this was as large a sorcery as he had ever come across and he had witnessed the construction of more than three of the Kinslayer's dragons in Nydarrow's birthing cauls.

Horse had said the woman ate the fire of Hathel Vale. He knew that fire. It was the soulfire, summoned out of another plane by the force of the Kinslayer's will; something only gods and demigods could muster. So this creature, whatever she seemed, may be his equal, or worse. Meanwhile the look on her face was that of an explorer moving into a new land, as though she'd never seen people before and didn't know what they were for. Heno had seen Tzarkomen raise their dead and had cut down many of their zombies and their faces displayed very much the same amazed, witless gawk when they were not stuck in the rictus of their death throes. They never changed, no matter how many pieces they were chopped into. The animation only left them once the necromancer in charge realised they were unresponsive. Then his convictions shrivelled and blew away as the child came back into view.

Ragged and wretched, her smallness was the inverse of his own strength and power. If looks could kill he would have been dust on the wind.

"What...?" began Ralas but Celestaine shushed him.

As Ralas shut his mouth the bride re-fixated on Heno. She

stood, the top of her head level with the top of his shoulder, her face inches from his chest as he remained still, his empty hands falling to his sides. Slowly, as the child clung behind her skirts, the young woman's hand lifted and traced his cheek, the curl of his moustaches, the carvings on his scrimshawed tusk. He didn't move a muscle. Their lives hung on it in a way his thoughts could not grasp.

"Who are you?" The bride whispered it clumsily in the Travellers' patois used throughout the kingdoms, though all the curiosity was on the child's face, not her own. A terrible fear suddenly ran through him as fast as lightning itself: she knew him and he knew her. It wasn't personal, it was deeper than that but there was a truth in it that scratched at the very parts of himself he'd had to bury to survive Nydarrow. He swallowed it all down, hard. Feelings belonged out of sight, in the dark, subterranean, where home had been.

"Heno. Yorughan." He didn't know why he clarified his race. He wasn't sure what she was asking, only that he wanted to have the truth out before she could think of some intuitive way to pry him open, lay everything bare.

"Made by the monster." There was a distinct Tzarkomen accent to her word endings, or he imagined that they held a great menace to his health and everyone else's.

He was quick to clarify. "No. Enslaved by the monster. Never of him. And now free."

Ralas stepped forward with a bow. "One of the liberators of the world, milady…" he said, and got no further as the bride's gaze fell on him and rendered him mute. She looked back up at Heno.

"Heart Taker," she said quietly, as though the words were new and unfamiliar. They all heard it anew in her speaking and they all flinched.

Frowning, she glanced back down at the child who nodded vehemently. Yes. She was turning back, her touching fingers stretching out when there was a sudden thump that made them all jump back. The bride collapsed in a heap of incalculable wealth and Heno caught her, purely on reflex. Nedlam's gauntlet slid off the side of her head and a rounded stone rolled out of it into the dirt of the road.

The child screeched in a high-pitched voice and threw out her hand, open, in Nedlam's direction. Heno saw the big Yorughan suddenly fall to her knees, eyes crossing, overwhelmed. He felt the prickle of fear as his own throat tightened and a sudden exhaustion came to him so that he had to use all his strength to stand and hold the unconscious woman up.

"Stop!" Celestaine cried. "Ralas, Heno, stop everyone!"

As he gasped for air Heno looked at the child but found only fury and relentless, righteous hatred in the black eyes as her gaze darted between them. She looked like he felt when he woke up nights, sweating in the dark, thinking he was going to die for his deeds before the false alarm collapsed into a sadness he could not be rid of until dawn came. He saw that she had lost so much. Thousands of people had. He'd never cared. Now it was hard to see it and as soon as he did see it he felt it and that was much worse. He was almost dizzy. He didn't want it.

As Celestaine gently extended a hand to offer some kind of comfort the girl saw the recognition in Heno's face and her eyes filled with tears. The grip she had exerted on him and on Nedlam vanished. Air rushed into his lungs. Nedlam sat down hard on the ground, panting. Heno felt that in one more moment everything that held him together might be unravelled and then he would confess all he had done: the Aethani mutilation, the countless acts of torture and the things which were clouded in his memory and would never come into focus but had served to cover his skin with the static sparks of magic. But before it could happen—

"Ne'Thuh!" said a deeper, more powerful voice in a kind of whisper and the spear of the centaur came down with a sudden impact in front of the child's feet, making a twanging noise and a burst of light, startling her enough to make her drop back and shrink down into a ball. Ralas and Celestaine shrank away, hiding their faces from the light of the Draeyad's cast.

Horse came pacing forwards, a scowl on her face. She disdained to help Nedlam, who struggled to get back to her feet, gasping for air, and went directly to retrieve her javelin. She smacked Ralas with the side of it and he was suddenly on his arse on the ground, breath coming at last to his purpled face, surprised injustice in his glare. She stabbed the spear into the earth, which held it firmly, and then carefully bent to take the unconscious woman from Heno's treacherous grasp. She carried her a few steps and then with a heavy grunt she put her front knees down on the road, sat down heavily next to the grubby, silently crying child, and looked at Celestaine as their leader.

"This is how you treat people who have saved the Draeyads?" Disgust was in her every tone. Heno resolved himself to stand, face what must be faced.

"No," Celestaine said. She spun to face the Yorughan. "Nedlam, why?"

"She wanted to kill Heno," Nedlam said, on her feet now but leaning down, hands on her hammer haft for support, as though she'd run for miles. "Sorcerers. You have to stop them before they start."

"Child," the centaur said gently. "Do not fear, I am here to serve those who serve the Forest. What say you?" In her arms the woman became suddenly, actively awake, pushing herself free. Heno found himself on bended knee offering his hand for the gods only knew what, though she didn't need him; she had rolled and stood in a moment. The bride crouched, a feral light in her face that was sizing up each one of them in an order to dispatch; and then the child made some noise and immediately she turned, ignoring the centaur as she gathered the small one up into her lap.

Heno found himself close-flanked by the others who had

taken up arms, but now held them loosely in the hopes they weren't needed. He had been flanked before, many times, by battle-hardened colleagues whose interests and his own ran to slaughter and survival. This was new. It somehow baffled him that these, excluding Nedlam, would side with him. His hands remained at his sides to show he meant no harm.

Blood from a cut on the bride's temple dripped down onto the sleeves of woman and child, blooming into red red roses. A small hand went up and touched the spot and as it came away the flow had already slowed and become sticky. A moment later there was no wound at all. Heno and Ralas shared a glance but none of them on Celest's side dared speak in case they broke the peace. After a time the child stopped sniffling and pushed her way out of the bride's embrace. She pointed at Heno and her face lifted regally.

"Kinslayer," said the bride.

Then the child pointed at Nedlam.

"Kinslayer," said the bride.

The child thumped her own chest with her small fist and the woman said, "I speak for this girl, Kula. This girl speaks through me. I am—" She struggled to find the words with the frustration they all knew from trying to speak languages they were new to.

"Tzarkomen," Heno said, gesturing in only the slightest way at the bride to show who he meant.

"Tzarkomen," the bride snarled in a way that clearly indicated what the child thought of Tzarkomen—not much. Then she placed her hand softly on her own chest, "Lysandra. My name. I. Am. *Uht'eltehi*." She clearly struggled to find any other way to translate the last word and failed.

Nedlam scratched her head suddenly, causing them all to jump. "I don't know what *Uht'eltehi* is. *Uht'tlemakli* is big Tzarkomen war sorcerer who leads a legion of zombies. Hard to fight, harder to kill. This kid must be from Caracu. The first legion went there when I was new. Before the war began. They were purple too, purple and darker than the Tzarkis."

The woman said, forcefully, with the first sign that she had a mind of her own, "*Uht'eltehi*."

"And that, my dears, is a very strange thing to say," Ralas interjected, dusting off his clothing unnecessarily. Heno was starting to see it as necessary though. Ralas arranged what could be fixed and he kept his pain in check that way. But Ralas was talking again, "Because *Uht* means extreme-most and *Eltehi* is a word for the other plane that the Tzarkomen claim the spirits wander about on before and after life."

"*Xinmat*," the bride said firmly, bringing both her hands into fists with a swift action and bumping them together, one on another.

"*Xinmat* means 'union' and also 'solid'." Ralas said, testing his jaw to see if it was still working. It seemed to be.

"Lysandra. *Uht'eltehi xinmat*." The bride nodded and added, more softly, "Mama," as she tenderly took the child's hand.

Heno felt himself crack. A fine crack, almost unnoticeable. He was baffled by it. After all he had seen and done, it made no sense.

"That's all very nice, but what are we going to do?" Ralas looked to Celestaine. It had begun to grow dark as they talked and the vale was becoming noticeably cool and damp.

"Let's make camp," she suggested. "We can find out more about where these two are headed and if we stay close to the Avenue then Wanderer can find us." Which sounded like more of a plan than it was but Heno knew she couldn't just let them go. She was ever on the lookout for something that needed mending and here it was, right in her hand.

"I shall create a space in the forest where we may be secure," Horse said, sticking her forelegs out and getting up carefully, spear retrieved. "Follow my trail."

Heno looked at her and shrugged with Nedlam-esque brevity.

Their camping spot was within the lower curve of the Avenue at a place where hazels grew in a natural ring and were overseen by the larger, thicker trunks of bromantain. In the broadleaf canopies a troop of flying squirrels argued furiously before being ousted by the centaur's double stomp of command. A brief hail of tain-nuts and poop pattered down in their wake as Ralas and Nedlam set about making a fire, cautiously watching Horse in case they made a wrong move.

As the heat warmed them and they handed around their food to share the ragged girl seemed to cheer and the icy aloofness with which her 'mama' had held them softened somewhat, although they sat as far from the two Yorughan as they could get and didn't look in their direction. Ralas began to tell a story, a simple one, about the origins of the races, accompanied and dramatised by music on his lute. He was interrupted briefly when Horse gave a cry and hoisted herself across the tiny clearing in a single bound. With surprise Heno saw her target was Nedlam, standing by a tree, her belt knife in her hand.

Horse, of an equal height to Nedlam, furiously snatched a wrist-thick branch away from the Yorughan's grasp. "Do I try to cut off your arms? This is a living tree!"

Nedlam held up her hands. "I wanted to make a toy," she said, pointing with her knife blade at the pair across the fire.

"Then make it out of seasoned old wood or it won't last a week without splitting," Horse snarled and used the point of her javelin to flick a fallen branch up at Nedlam, who caught it easily, a kind of smile around her thick tusks.

"All right, Horsie. Take it easy."

Horse lashed her tail in a swift whisking action of annoyance, but she withdrew and went back to her guardian position near the little girl, Kula.

The rest of them sat down again and Ralas resumed his lengthy story, hoping, Heno saw, to draw the child's interest: but it was the woman who watched Ralas with hawkish attention, her eyes following every movement of his hands as he played and his mouth as he spoke. Her eyes widened whenever he dramatised something with a different voice or expression. She looked like she was devouring him through her gaze. Heno understood the hunger for softer, better things. He glanced at Celestaine.

Nedlam whittled steadily as one by one they talked. Once or twice she tried to ask questions of the girl, but Kula would only stare at them mutely, sometimes looking at her 'mama'. Eventually Ralas sighed and gave up too and put his lute to the side, only to have the young woman immediately reach out and grab it by the neck. Her beaded bracelets jangled and shot the clearing full of reflected colours as she snatched it to herself and gave him a calculating look, to see if he was going to try to stop her. Heno watched covertly, pretended that he had much to do with Celestaine's care of her armour and the horses' saddles.

Ralas sat back, lines of tension and worry all through him as he saw the precious instrument pored over, sniffed, rubbed and flicked. Lysandra tasted the varnish, screwed and unscrewed a peg, twiddled a string, looked into the dark hole behind the strings with one eye, then the other. She rapped its belly with her knuckles, hummed a note some one third higher than the note she strummed and then organised herself so that even with the girl in her lap she made a fair approximation of Ralas' original and expert hold upon it. She copied him relatively well but scowled as her fumblings produced only a series of strange sounds. Then she stopped and sat for a moment, stroked the lute's neck and held it out to Ralas.

"You," she said sadly.

"Thank you," he said and took it carefully back. He tuned it and then played some slow, easy songs as Heno, Celestaine and Nedlam busied themselves with putting away the remains of the food and making ready for the night.

"There's something not right about her," Celestaine said, once they were out of earshot, taking her time with cleaning their knives. Usually she would stab them in the earth and then rub them over but in deference to Horse she was more careful. She paused to grasp Heno's wrist for a moment and he was grateful.

"She is slow," Nedlam said. "New."

"She doesn't like the look of me," Heno murmured, pausing to use a chewed birch twig to clean the ornate carving of his tusks and then the rest of his teeth.

"Nobody does," Nedlam said and he snorted. Fair enough.

"Whose is that child?" Celestaine wondered. "And how have they come to be together?"

"Ask them," Nedlam said, buckling up her pack and looking around them. The light from the evening sky was nearly gone and the forest bulk was a black bulwark against it now, so that they seemed to be in a solid canyon of darkness.

Heno wondered where this would end but he said nothing. Anyone with the power to undo the Kinslayer's work could not be a simple idiot walking the woods—and no simple idiot would be decked out miles from anywhere in a king's ransom. They returned to the fireside. Nedlam tossed her splintered piece of wood into the blaze with a sigh and started slowly on another one.

"What are you making?" Heno asked.

"Worg," Nedlam said, turning the unidentifiable lump of wood over and starting to gouge it with the point of her knife. "But the legs were too fiddly. Now I do snail."

CELESTAINE STUDIED THE group and felt that Horse was right. She didn't like the idea of Horse being right, however, even though it meant that it was likely that Wanderer was involved in setting them up. She hated the idea of being in anyone's control, even if they had meant well. Her alternative was to leave and never look back—however, that was impossible given her curiosity and present company. It would have to wait for another day.

Ralas was plucking quiet, lullaby chords and the centaur was nodding along, though her spear was across her forelegs and she didn't look that sleepy. The atmosphere was as mellow as it was likely to get. Heno remained as still and silent as stone, not wanting to cause trouble. Celestaine took her chance and sat down close beside the guest. She made a show of admiring the fancy cloth and gemstones that adorned it. All along the hems fine stitchwork had been ripped out by thorns and shredded on tree roots. The bulk of the mastery in the thing was tucked around legs and the child as if it was nothing more than a blanket.

"Lysandra," she began, testing the name.

Lysandra looked at her. The centres of her eyes were fathomless dark upon which Celestaine's pale face was reflected back to her as two strange, watery moons.

"I uh... Do you, that is, we were told..." She indicated the centaur with a gesture. "Told that you took the fire?" But her question vanished into the black depths without a sign of meeting anything.

"It is so," Horse's tone cut across the quiet music with a definitive note of offence. "She breathed it in and it was gone."

Celest meanwhile was not done. "Yes, that's not what I... I mean. Why did you...? That is, how did you do that?"

The woman stared at her and her lips moved in a faint copy of what Celestaine had said. They were darkened by some kind of stain, almost cherry black against her dusky skin, that strange colour of ripe plums, dusted with the greyish bloom of autumn. Tzarkomen were dark skinned, or rusty. Celestaine had never seen this tone before. Her hair was done up in a great many intricate braids that were bound in fiendish designs, filled with gold and silver charms beneath a fine veil which had perhaps once gone over her face but which now hung lopsided down her back.

Celestaine turned to Horse. "You don't know who she is?"

"I don't care who she is. Not in the way that you mean. A name, a lineage—what is important about that?" Horse said with a half shrug. "You're upset because you don't know what she is, not who and she already told you all she knows. But what were you all doing here?"

Celestaine said. "We came to the Avenue to make camp here

until our companion meets us. When we saw the fire was gone we wanted to see what had happened."

"Of whom do you speak?"

"A... nobody." Celestaine said and Nedlam snorted.

Horse looked at them steadily for a moment. It was completely dark now, except for the firelight. "I see. Well, I will surely know them if they walk on forest land. Perhaps a hint might assist their efforts to find you?" The centaur spoke pleasantly enough but there was steel in her voice that suggested someone unknown to her might well walk the woods for eternity looking for someone if she chose.

"We seek news of the Wanderer," Heno said, tiring of politeness.

"This is your husband?" Horse asked.

"No!" Celestaine said forcefully, then put her hand out towards Heno's leg and rested it there. "I mean. No, we are not bound in law. We are travelling companions. This is Heno, and the other is Nedlam. I am Celestaine of Fernreame."

"Kinslayer slayer," Horse said, nodding. "This chatterer has mentioned it." Ralas coloured slightly. "Surely it's no accident you arrive at the same time as these two."

"I don't know," Celestaine replied.

"Many things are left over from the war," Horse said with cold accusation. "I expect this is not the first or last of them. He says you gave wings back to the Aethani, after a fashion. Is this your business, then—the cleaning up of the field? Have you come to find another about your work?" She glanced at Lysandra, who was softly stroking the little one's hair.

Cleaning, is that what she was doing? She couldn't help but grin, thinking of how she had rushed from chores to the more interesting material of horse and sword. "Maybe."

The centaur grunted and looked away, blinking slowly like a sleepy cat. She seemed amused. "The girl here, Kula, is deaf," she said. "When she wakes up you must speak only when she looks at you if you want to be heard."

Celestaine found herself blinking in surprise. She would have asked how the centaur knew this but it seemed foolish. She hadn't been paying attention herself or she would have known. At least some of the oddity was explained. "And the woman?"

"I cannot say," Horse said after a moment of thought. "But it is like she doesn't exist, or, did not until she came here."

"Lamps lit but nobody home," Nedlam said with confidence and pleasure at her correct assessment.

"Are there such things as idiot mages?" Celestaine looked at Heno now. She'd never asked to know how his magic worked and he'd never offered to talk of it but now he shook his heavy head.

"No."

Heno watched as the person they'd been talking about, Lysandra, leaned over from where she sat and clasped Celestaine's hand in her own. "Good," she said in her gruff, awkward voice. She seemed to chew the words. "Good. Woman."

"Good grief," said Ralas, frozen between one bar and the next. "She's got a very warped impression of you."

"Thanks," Celestaine said. Her hand was released. Nothing was extended to anyone else.

The moment was broken by a sudden flapping, panicking sound. A quick exploration with a torch revealed the sight of an old man struggling to free himself from a bush. Horse put her spear to his throat.

"Celestaine," he pleaded meekly. "Tell her who I am!"

Celestaine, up on her elbows, peering, grunted. "Horse, this is Deffo, a badger. Deffo, this is a Draeyad, Horse. She doesn't like you."

Horse looked at Celestaine, brow raised as Deffo protested that the badger form was only for theatrical purposes. "But isn't he a Guardian?"

"Trust me," Celestaine said. "Start with total disappointment. That way he can only grow on you."

CHAPTER FOURTEEN

THE FORTRESS OF Nydarrow, the Kinslayer's greatest creation, looked best under glowering cloud cover. Then its fine glass needles pierced the sky and tore it to shreds, lightning surging and striking again and again until the world was shot through with every colour of refracted light amid the thunderous cacophony of celestial rage. But it was no less intimidating on a hazy blue afternoon, Tricky thought, as she approached it and began a wide circle, keeping at least a mile between herself and the outer limits of its span. In the air and beneath the earth tendrils of a more delicate nature, fine as spider silks, stretched out from Nydarrow's heart into the weft of the world. Their lines reached far beyond the mountain dale where the glass spire struck upwards. She would have to hope that there was nobody left now to read the traces from any of the Kinslayer's sensitive threads, set to warn him of all that moved for miles, or perhaps everywhere. She avoided them, delicately, but she suspected they stretched beyond the limits of her perception and that the effort was futile. Nonetheless she made it to the walls, with trepidation.

The last time she had been here she was still very much a part of things. He would never have trusted another Guardian, but she didn't count in that respect. He despised and looked down on her as the runt of the litter. She had been the last to be made and she was left half-baked when the Guardians and whatever impulse had required them were abandoned by the gods. She wasn't even sure that she had been meant to be at all. He had said she was what happened when you left the mixing bowl to rot in the sun after all the good parts had been baked. But that was the kind of thing he said. It remained a fact that what Guardians could do easily she could only manage with great effort. All her magic required the medium of artifice and objects of power.

In herself she was little more than a few principles stitched together in a human form that was itself no prize; small, weak and of no particular interest whichever way you looked at her. The only reason he'd tolerated her involvement was as another of his amusements—she was the eager little sister, trying, always trying so hard to win his approval. He'd delighted in crushing her whenever she thought she'd really made a difference—or at least that was the game she'd gone for as the one most likely to be believed. She'd done it purely to be able to stick around and see what he was doing. It had backfired somewhat, being true enough in its way: she would have served him very well if only he'd given her a moment of care—and she recalled this with bitterness as she scanned the tower of glass, watching for changes. The trouble with Nydarrow in the end was that just as she had miscalculated the effects her play for the Reckoner's confidence would have on her, he had miscalculated the effects his actions would have on *it*. Far beneath the surface he had opened up ways to other places and times and in each he had built Nydarrow using remnants of the divine things that it had been her job to scour from the faces of the world. At some point shortly before his demise Nydarrow had itself baked under strange, distant suns and become, in some way, alive.

This was the extent of her sense of kinship to it and she resented even that, yet she couldn't shake it.

Around the base of the glass spire a dense, mighty forest was grown to maturity. Higher than a cathedral, its creepers and roots festooned the crystal with dark leaves and lustrous, rich flowers the colours of blood and decay. The canopy itself blotted out all inspection from the air though Tricky knew that beneath it lay large pens and holding yards where the armies of the Yorughan and other underdwellers had massed before they marched out. Otherwise there was not much above the ground: only the spire's base with its outlying crops of crystal here and there giving a hint of its structure beneath the surface, and the gate.

She made herself land in a tree several miles away from the tips of Nydarrow's influence, although there was no instinct in her to do anything but put as much distance between herself and it as possible. Cautiously she returned to her human form and wound up her wool, securing it and double checking before she began her progress. Her usual feat was to keep to the shadows. They were easy to employ for the purposes of hiding with only the slightest of tricks, but here that would get her caught faster. Instead she had to move as an ordinary person would, with caution, not too much in the light so that she would lose her darksight, nor too much in the dark that it would rob her daysight, alert for all things. A greater feat was to put herself in a carefree state of being. Fear was a vibration that Nydarrow liked the best. It rattled the web in an unmistakable way. But happiness and simple joy weren't familiar things in this place and they skipped lightly over traps meant for those already in dread. She found herself having to return to these guerrilla tactics she thought she'd left behind; at every moment so sure of being dead that any seconds scraped out of time were a true and delightful reward. Such was Nydarrow's presence after all. It was the place where dying was longed for but seldom reached.

The trees around here grew vast, their roots and branches tangled, sometimes in ways that seemed to embrace but otherwise in a fight for sustenance and space. Little grew beneath them but the hardiest of small plants. The leaf litter was deep and filled with colonies of fungus. Mushrooms and spore pods sprouted abundantly, mostly small but a few with caps higher than her head. Overhead sticky slime mould was rife. Tendrils of goo dripped like syrup down into the empty air or glistened upon the gnarled bark of trunks in rivulets. What animals had lived here were gone or adapted to the thickening atmosphere of loathing and rot which seeped up from Nydarrow's heart. Creatures she could not name oozed in soft curls along branches overhead, camouflaged as they tapped the trees. Elsewhere she did hear the croak of gorecrows but these didn't bother her as much as the sudden change of atmosphere once she reached the border of the fortress and came to the edge of the march.

Tens of thousands had passed along this road daily during the height of the Kinslayer's rule.It was broad, with a smooth, worn floor some several feet lower than the surrounding earth. An avenue of darkness beneath the forest it originated in the marshalling yards of Nydarrow and led out beyond the vale to the major ways leading north and south across the Unredeemed Lands. Now it was full of weeds and stunted saplings. Somewhere out to her right something large was moving without care, snuffing and snorting, pausing itself, then again moving. It seemed like a feeding behaviour to her, so she was not already running for her life.

She studied the path a while, listening, and then she felt about in one of her myriad pockets and took out a tiny scrap of paper, upon which was written a name: on one side it was in the language of the Darhak—demons for want of a better word—and on the other side it was in the language of Oroneshi, spirits that were beyond the reach of mortal things. She was good with languages, which helped a lot with reading stolen tomes or things that couldn't be carried, and she had written this herself so she was sure it was right. This paper she turned so that the Oroneshi side was downmost and placed it upon the road, only for a moment—that was all that was needed.

Far down the lane, just visible, a figure appeared.

"Taedakh," she whispered, to secure its attention on her before something else took it, and ran quickly through the edgewoods towards it, glad.

Taedakh was an old friend. The first friend perhaps, but certainly one that had stayed true, the only one. She needed him to get through the gate. As she approached she saw him taking form in the guise he had used for his role as one of the Kinslayer's guard, a tall and imposing creature with horselike head, massive shoulders, a narrow waist and long legs, also animal rather than human, high at the hocks, his feet like an extended paw at the base. He had no weapons but didn't need them with hands like that, all razor claws. When he opened his mouth to yawn at her in what passed for his smile she saw rows and rows of needle teeth inside the line of shearing blades that ran the length of his mouth. Ragged furs tied on him with string made his clothing and, as usual, they stank, but she ignored that.

"Taedakh," she said again in a whisper as they embraced.

"Little Friend," he said and let her go to peer at her from one large, grey eye on the more attractive side of his head where ratty fur covered the bone up to the rough, beaky edge of his snout. Black and grey feathers on his crest rose a little and then ruffled between his back-facing leaflike ears. "Are we here again?"

Because she had called him on its grounds Taedakh was part of Nydarrow, and this was how she was going to get in, even when she wasn't wanted. "I need to find out about *The Book of All Things*. Do you remember it?"

A clattering ruffle overhead interrupted them, then a sharp series of caws, followed by more flapping and fussing: the crows belonging to the Fortress defences had spotted her. Taedakh lifted himself out of his crouched greeting posture and stretched up to his full ten foot height, head high, letting out a series of coughlike calls in response. The birds in the canopy grumbled and then dispersed.

"The *Book* was destroyed at the outset of the war."

"I need to find out..." she thought, realising she didn't need the thing itself. "I need to know what it was for. Can we go to the Library?"

"We can, but you must obey the rules," Taedakh said, stretching out one massive limb and offering her his hand, of which she held just the outside finger, like a child, so small was she compared to him.

"Hold the hand, do not stray," she said, to give herself resolve as much to prove she knew it. "Do not step off the way. Do not look back. Do not try to see what is hidden. Obey the Guard's instructions."

"Yes. But things have changed here. Even this may not be enough. Must you go?"

He seemed reluctant. She thought of the Kinslayer, his bland face so handsome in an everyday sort of way, his pleasant voice, his kindly manner as he smiled at her to encourage her to stretch herself, find her limits, seek out what was lost in the world and return it to him like a good little dog. She thought of the way her heart had leapt on his every praise. "I must."

They went together, girl and monster, until the yard wall was visible and she could hear the sounds of occupation, but then they turned into the treeline and had to pick a much smaller path. To get his armies out into the upper world the Heart Takers and others had created portals between the depths and the surface. The yards were a small village in their own right up here, but they held nothing of value or use. They were a meeting post and no more. Everything else was kept in caverns far below ground. Without an array of magi there was but one way in and out of Nydarrow on foot, and Taedakh was one of few who could find it because it never wanted to be found. Being of more than one plane himself he had senses to detect the path even when it tried to move beyond the range of mortal sight.

After a time of walking, shouldering through bushes and

letting Taedakh hack away foliage hiding thorns as thick as her wrist, tips red with poisons, they came to a small hillside where a break in the trees let a tiny amount of ragged grasses find enough light to grow up from the heavy soil. These bearded a hole in the side of the hill. It was large enough for a small person to walk into, a cave of sorts, dry underfoot but disappointingly shallow. At the back of this space a passageway that could have easily been mistaken for a bear's winter lair stretched back into the hill before shrinking and becoming less of an invitation, more of a featureless hole. They were cramped up by now and there was no chance to stand side by side. She went in first, single file, while Taedakh shuffled in a duckwalk. Here it was very dark. Although there was nothing to see, the hole held a distinct sense of impending presence. Where they stood the air was too dry to carry much scent but when it came to the nostrils it reeked of putrefaction. A heavy, stickiness suffused the remaining space. Nydarrow wasn't the only place she'd been where the energy was like this, but it was the worst.

"Thanks," she said suddenly and let go of Taedakh's hand, in the same moment pressing the paper to his palm. He disappeared.

It was rude of her. Maybe he'd be angry, but she wasn't risking losing him and anyway, she'd never been good with rules.

The space where he'd been was full of pale vapour for a moment, then it diffused and she was alone. She looked back to the small, ragged mouth of the cave entrance as she secreted the paper and secured it. Every instinct in her told her to run towards it, fast, and never return. But she took out her ball of wool and chose a fine, grey strand. It was very worn and coming loose all over. This would be its last use, she saw, but that couldn't be helped. She knitted it around her fingers as fast as she could.

The hole beside her sighed faintly, and she heard the reverb of a distant sound that must have been very loud at its source but was far, far away; a raucous bellow of pain or rage or despair.

She had lost the art of figuring out which was which long ago. She spun the strand of webbing around herself, twisting in the confined space, brushing her elbows against the dry walls so that a shower of earth fell down and into her eyes and nose but then she was on the floor, on four legs, small, sneezing, her whiskers twitching, claws trembling against the ground.

She ran quickly, keeping her tail high, hugging the wall as she followed the tunnel inwards, around corners, down a slope into a narrowing that was shorter than a man and more slender than most of them. There was a way forwards for a little while, then the floor dropped more sharply and suddenly gave way to a straight drop into blackness. She fell, landed, bounced, rolled, landed, bounced, rolled and then ran on through the lightless upper halls by memory, following the cracks in the floor. There were always times she had come in this way with Taedakh's aid, the way the Kinslayer thought that only he knew. Especially the last time when she had come to undo locks, disrupt charms and bestow thoughts of mutiny to the heads of certain guards and torturers. You could never have got an army in to Nydarrow, but you could make do and bend with what was already there.

Every scamper filled her with rage and sorrow for the old dreams left on this trail—she found herself still longing to rush into the arms of his approval, with the latest cunning scheme, to see his face light up for an instant with something, anything.

In her mind she heard his voice, *"Ah, Little One, what have you brought me?"*

Death, death I've brought you, brother, you filth, you scum, you murderous infidel.

But she had rushed up to his lap, leapt on it and purred under his caress and it had been the best feeling she had ever had. If he'd shown her even an instant of genuine kindness instead of this sickly reward it would have been different.

She heard him speak now as she dashed, tail aloft.

"Did you think you could come back to the place of reckoning

and not have one between us?" It was always hard to know if these things were in her mind or if it were the bones of him speaking, but she knew there was no difference in practice. She would always hear him.

She shook to her marrow, but a mouse always shakes with one twitch or another, so when at last she saw a glimmer of light ahead of her she paused to listen, dreading what she would hear.

The drip of water and silence behind it. The shape of the space was twisted, ugly, with all the agony that had sounded through it. Years of it. It needed music to clear it, banging, smashing, all things that she dare not do here because that would surely draw the attention of the residents in the levels below. As she tiptoed into the old tunnels she found herself weaving through bones still tacky with decayed flesh, piled here and there, everywhere.

She made herself go on, knowing he wasn't there, though it felt as if he could be. The urge to rush out and search, to apologise, to beg forgiveness, to say she was sorry, to stab him through the heart, that was all there still; these undone things that were his pay and her reward. She could feel the pattern of it.

After another few galleries and a teeter along a pipe ending with a leap and scrabble down a massive pillar she came to the vast arch of his private quarters where the water dripped down, one slow relentless *tock, tock, tock* into a single puddle in buckled paving. In the blackness beyond the gang of fighters had finished his final accounting and she, unnoticed in the melee, had crept along the wall and seen herself robbed of the moment she had always dreamed would one day be hers, in which she'd have asked him "Why?" and got an answer of some kind.

Now there was no answer.

Something heavy slid out there in the black. She heard the hand, the fingers dragging it, nails scratching for purchase, forearm trailing, a meaty, heavy, juicy... She knew it could not be that, because he was disposed of, but the mouse shape worked against her as much as it helped. Her terror was intensified to a pitch where she couldn't hear her thoughts any more and lost them entirely. She lost her grip.

Some time later she found herself dashing wildly, propelled by every shadow and movement, bouncing off the walls, her mouth open in a silent scream.

By the time she was too tired to continue and her mind had returned to her, she was shivering in a corner of one of the inner circles of the Gloaming Court, a set of passageways connected at various points by doors, most false and leading nowhere. From the inner ring every one of the lower decks could be accessed by ramp. It was labyrinthine, but she knew it like the back of her hand and navigated each turn with care—*here is sorrow, here is misery, here is despair, here is grief, we turn at emptiness, that's how you know where to turn, when you are worn out to the empty, that is the sign, always.* She had used emotion as her markers or Nydarrow itself had already set them for her to find. The Kinslayer had considered Nydarrow his creation and merely a tool, but like all creations and all tools it had modified its user. She had watched him here, thinking himself the great king of balance, ruling all, while Nydarrow had stealthily extended itself inwards to the depths of his heart.

Yes, he'd had one. Once. Not a great one. They were none of them that valuable. But one. And if not for Nydarrow then maybe...

But this was too late and of no importance now. She was so disappointed in herself to find that even now she wanted to find excuses for him.

She had reached the centre of the Gloaming Court at last, where the walls were illuminated by light-spores and lichens of various hues, parti-colour festivities in the most pale and sickly terms. Here she felt that liminal alive-ness of Nydarrow shift with her presence. What a gift he'd given it, opening it to the passage of entities that existed beyond life. But lovers always give the best gifts, don't they?

The idea made her smile in her twisted way, the way that hurt the scar at the side of her mouth, and she bent her small head under her right foreleg, found the end of the old grey thread and relentlessly pulled it out until she felt it break and suddenly she was there, in the cold near-darkness, in her own form, listening to the fortress breathe.

To her left was the ramp to the beast pens. They held what he had summoned and not been able to categorise in any other way; predators from other worlds. The Vathesk had been there once until they were used and perhaps things still tramped their cells but she wasn't going to find out. She had nowhere to free them to, even supposing they were alive.

Just in front of her the ramp to the Bonehouse was marked by another pile of decomposing bodies that had dried to mummified status. They wouldn't have made a worthwhile addition, had he still been collecting. Swords and shields were tangled up with them, but all of too poor and unmagical a kind to be worth saving. Elsewhere she saw Yorughan tusks splintered as if by huge feet. People had looted all he had gathered, but they hadn't lingered and those that came later, like these, rarely made it out alive. If they found the way in through charms and rites they almost never found the way out. Between the withered limbs of another pile she saw a crystal sphere, fallen and shattered, while another lay just out of reach of a dead man's hand.

A large beetle with an iridescent black carapace and huge, horny pincers crawled out of the corpse pile as she watched and made a neat progress to the next ramp. It vanished around the curve and she followed it, because this way, on the route to the great depths, lay the small room that had been hers. It was little more than a cubby hole filled with paperwork where things that needed reading or decoding were dropped off for her to master and classify.

She had no sooner taken the turn when that roar of misery from the deeps came again, ricocheting over twenty times from various walls before dying out. She looked at the doorway, half open. She pushed the door and it swung silently. The floor was pale ahead. She went on and found that it was all the papers, soggy and ink-stained, bound to the stone with damp, moulds already founding new maps across their surfaces. Someone, or many someones, had been here in her absence to search for things of value. And there, nearly missable, was a distinct footprint in the pulpy sludge. It wasn't human. She didn't recognise its three-toed tread. Echoes of violence came up the long stretch. Screams, perhaps from people, punctuated it and she began to hurry, moving as fast as she dared.

She trod over the footprint and went on, her hopes all dashed at last as she saw the suppurating disaster that had been the library—her grand word for the few books and scrolls that had formed the written collection of artefacts of note. Something had unleashed a lot of water. It was instantly clear that there wasn't a readable thing anywhere. She was forced to admit that her hopes of finding the *Book* or a part of it had been slender. What was good had been looted or was now a medium for slime moulds. The Kinslayer had burned most of what he'd found anyway. Dull anger at the waste of it came as she turned and made her way quickly downwards before her nerve failed her. She had to know what he'd been up to.

Down past the dungeons where Celestaine of Fernreame had been freed by her guard and led to the slaying. Down past the torture chambers, the grey, nameless places where men, women and children had been left to starve to death among the screams of the maimed. Down and down the way ran until its river of degradation fed into the low, stinking black waters of the Ur-march.

Here, in death's distillation, he had made his breach of the world into realms whose energy signatures mirrored the low vibrations of agony and rage he had created here: low because those frequencies attracted bodiless things with the ability to tear holes in the planar fabric through which he could extend his reach for power. This was now a pathway which ran on into the roots of other physical worlds and eventually up and up into other branches of Nydarrow.

She stood in shallow black water over deep black mud in a cave roofed by stalactites. She didn't trust that the mud was a true base. She suspected it was merely the soft vault over a much greater drop whose cold and emptiness was beyond comprehension.

Tricky took out the binding paper scrap again and put it on the water, same side down.

This time Taedakh was of Nydarrow but also of the water and everything the water touched—he was of the many worlds and so he could walk them. Maybe he was from one of them originally, but she didn't know and hadn't asked. That might have led to unpleasant conversations about what he was and whether or not this paper, this word, was a slavery. Without him she couldn't go, and she must go.

"*You won't find it,*" the Kinslayer said.

"I find everything," she whispered.

"We are hunted," Taedakh said, with a tinge of reproach. "Where will you go?"

"Take me to world three," she said at once.

"I do not…"

"You have to," she said, and added, against her will, "Hunted by what?"

"Nydarrow," Taedakh said and bent down on one bony knee to pick her up in his massive hands. His head nearly scraped the lowest stalactites as he brought her inside his shade. "But it is slow."

"I thought you were part of it," she lied, a little, to keep him talking as his wings, invisible in the daylight above, now manifested and shrouded the both of them, blotting out the ugliness of the cavern.

"No," he said, but he didn't offer any more. "Only borrow it, to see with, to hear with, to be here."

Not for the first time she pondered the wisdom of messing about with things she didn't understand but then his wings opened and she sheltered her eyes from the suffusion of greenish light. She was set down. Beyond her boots she saw the stalactites, beneath them. She stood on the black water's surface, but beneath it, what was down was now up. This world she didn't know the name of she had called Versa when she first came here because of this reversal, but that didn't entirely fit. Looking up she saw the vault of the sky was made of stone, beneath it a weak sun shone like a giant, unlikely lantern. Around her the ruins of a city were half buried in drifts of sludge coloured sand. To her left one of the ghosts—tall revenants that looked like rags on the wind—drifted idly, turning about, mindless and at the mercy of the weak breeze. Forgettings, these were, the Kinslayer said—the remains of all that had been known and was lost here. She knew about them: they hungered for knowledge. One of them had prompted the worst turn of Reckoner's actions, though what it had said or done she didn't know. Now she hoped to find one that would trade. The ruins, earlier visits proved, were of Nydarrow in this place, long after it had fallen, for time was reversed also and they were at the end of this world.

The ground trembled a little.

"It sees you," Taedakh said in his voice like the rattle of dead leaves in a corner.

She had her payment ready in her hand—a book of little children's tales she'd collected for a moment like this one, thinking that to bring such things here would change something somewhere for the better, perhaps.

The revenant, dust under rag, bumbled weakly in their direction, forced to take its time by the unhelpful air. She took a step towards it and felt her soles slide on loose stones. She put her handwritten booklet down on the ground and moved back into the shelter of Taedakh's presence.

The revenant surged with a desperate lunge towards the book and from its idle whirligigs a strand of animated dust reached out to touch the cleanly inked parchment. With a whispering noise it rubbed and riffled through the pages. Sound was quieter than she'd expected. In a few seconds there was nothing left of the booklet but dust, sucked and whirled up into the revenant's body. What had been little more than the most vague suggestion of form altered into the approximate shape of a person. A head and a body became distinct though no limbs appeared in the gyre of its lower regions. From the whirling sand and grit and tiny bits of paper a rudimentary mouth formed.

"*The Book of All Things*," she cried, loudly, her words swallowed down the gullet of the vast silence. "What is it? Where is it? What did Reckoner find?" She felt Taedakh's grip at her elbows, ready to flee. The emptiness was so great that no Forgetting could be trusted not to attempt to take everything that they were.

"Once upon a time..." Words spewed in bursts from the mud lips, a grey tongue visible against the background of storming debris. "The dead were remembered. But now they are all dust and bone, dust and bone, bone and gone." There was a pause and the Forgetting drifted closer, stronger against the breeze than it had been, making steady headway in her direction. "The Reckoning can only be made at the end of all things. And none must remember." In the boil of its face images of flowers appeared, then faces—even the Kinslayer, his army, and a book with him, writing itself—all whirled away as soon as they were made. "But one remained." For a split second the mouth was joined by other features, clear and solid. The eyes blinked at her.

Tricky was taken aback. It was the face of the filthy child from Taib Post, whom she had made a scene for, scattering the dimwit stallkeeper's poms. She was so surprised that she made no move as the face suddenly yawned impossibly wide, filled with teeth, pouring the inside to the outside so that a ball of whirling razors was almost upon her, eager to devour her. Only the clap and thunder of Taedakh's wingbeat saved her.

"Thank you," she gasped as she was deposited on her knees on the outside earth, the sun overhead, Nydarrow behind her. The paper was in her hand, the writing back on both sides. She looked up and around her as she caught her breath, blinking in the blinding light as her vision slowly changed from mere shadow and light to reveal a group of Yorughan hunters. Tusked and armed, they were peering at her, their spears pointing her way, bows drawn and knives ready. She held up her free hand as she hid the paper with the other beneath her wet cloak. "I can explain everything."

CHAPTER FIFTEEN

BUKHAM STRUGGLED FORWARDS in the near darkness, getting tangled in brambles as though they wanted to criticise him personally for his lack of faith. By the time he had torn himself free, ripping his trousers in the process, Murti was far ahead, vanishing into a tall stand of witherwills.

As he reached them Bukham heard other voices, surprised ones, and the crackle of a fire. He smelled the scent of bacon frying on a too-hot griddle and seedcakes browning in butterfat. He stepped forwards into a camp of several people, seeing the glint of weapons, eyes and teeth in the growing blue of the twilight. He moved behind Murti, trying to look smaller but he needn't have bothered with the effort. All eyes were on the old man and the woman greeting him at the fireside.

She was tall and well built, of the old human stock of the midlands, blonde haired and battle-suited in mail and leather. A crest of a curled fiddlehead fern adorned her cloak. She was looking at Murti with an expression of delight and relief on her face, as though she had been expecting him a long time. Bukham was so relieved by this moment that it took him a while to register the other faces trained on the scene. There were two Yorughan, tusked and fearsome in their travelling and fighting paint; he didn't meet their eyes. There was an elegant looking young man, slight and well dressed, holding a lute. He moved with the careful stiffness of someone suffering and he tried unsuccessfully to hide the bruised side of his face in his scarf. There was a centaur… He tried not to stare at her because he'd never seen such a thing before but he couldn't help it; she was huge, larger than a human and an ordinary horse together, and a deep chestnut brown with golden hair that was a prized combination in the horses used by farmers up and down the valleys. A spear the size of a sapling was upright in her hand, its blade and tip gleaming. But then, beside her and lying against her huge round barrel of ribs, there was a dark woman in an incredibly ornate gown, jewelled and gilded, her hands ringed, her neck heavy with precious metals and there, in her lap, asleep, her chin shiny with butterfat, was the runaway girl.

It was a sight he could barely take in and he gawped for a good while, all the talk passing him by as the scene imprinted itself on his mind and struggled to find meaning there.

When he came out of his moment of reverie he realised that the attention of the blonde woman, Murti and the Yorughan, the bard and the centaur were all fixed on him, quietly, mildly interested, waiting for something. The crackle of the twigs in the fire were all he could hear. He searched back to see if he could recall anyone asking him a question and looked at Murti for help.

"They want to know are you going with them," Murti said after another terrifying moment of calm. He was smiling and he looked amused, so Bukham knew that they had already said what they were doing and where, but he had missed it and now he recalled nothing at all. For a second or two he felt the crippling humiliation that had always paralysed him in front of his uncle, but then something of the day's horror and weariness came up through him and he lost his patience with himself.

"I'm sorry, I was looking at… her," he said. "I don't know how we came here or who you are, or where you're going. My uncle told me to be sure she was safe—" He had been going to say "safely away" but stopped because he didn't want it to reflect badly on Taib Post. "Safe."

"We are going north, to the Dharhak Waste," the Yorughan male with the carved tusks and the fearsome appearance was speaking. He was not in favour of north, it seemed by his growling statement and scowl, but his determination was clear. "We are going to the Veiled Ice, to discover what has happened to the gods."

"Well, I... uhh, I'd have to ask about that," Bukham said. "I never was north of Ilkand Freeport. I don't know anything about ice and my cousin is minding the stall for me and if she has to keep it on for more than a couple of days I think she'll be very angry with me."

"I'm going," Murti said cheerfully.

Bukham did a double take. "You can't go. You're old. The north's no place for old men. Everyone says so. Besides, the world's in a terrible state. You should stick to the regular roads or... whatever you do."

There was something about the way they were looking at him that made him think a joke was on him.

"You won't go with your own godling?" the centaur said finally, eyes wide.

"Yeah, you go home, boy," the other Yorughan said, grinning. He thought it was a female, but clearly that was madness and he must be wrong.

"Godling?" Now he really was lost.

"You worship the Wanderer, don't you?" the man with the lute asked, eyes twinkling.

"I... it's not so much worship, because he's only a Guardian. It's more a sort of life-philosophy."

The lute man burst out laughing, "Oh I like this one! Let's keep him."

The blonde woman grinned and frowned at the same time. Snickers let him know the Yorughan were amused. Only the strange woman—rather lovely—in her incredible dress was looking straight at him without an expression. The intensity of her gaze was unnerving. He felt suddenly hot all over and wished he were tiny, as he felt, not the big, capable creature he looked like. "I didn't mean..."

"No matter," Murti was saying, chuckling, patting him on the arm. "I was a little mean, I suppose, not to mention it."

"Mention what?"

"This is Wanderer," the blonde woman said and then she pointed at herself, "Celest of Fernreame, that's Heno," she gestured at the male Yorughan who bowed his head. "The bard is Ralas and there's Nedlam." The other giant gave him a cheeky nod upwards as if greeting an equal, which really threw him. She was definitely female. He looked at the centaur.

"I am the Voice of the Forest. Called Horse, for now," the centaur said.

"And we have no idea who these are," Ralas waved at the woman in the tattered finery and the child, "Their names are Kula and Lysandra, but apparently they have taken away the Kinslayer's fire from the vale."

Bukham felt his mouth trying to work, except it didn't know what it was going to say. He looked at Murti, searching his face that was familiar but suddenly new in his sight. "You are *the* Wanderer?"

"Someone has to be," Murti shrugged. "Now, to business. Have you got any dinner about you? We've been on the road all day."

Celest nodded. "Unless Nedlam ate it all."

"You insult my soldier's heart," Nedlam said, opening up the pot which had cooked their food an hour before. "I take only my share. There is enough for a small bowl each."

She and Heno set it out for them and Bukham found himself seated at the fireside, eating, which was good because it occupied him without him having to say anything or think very much.

He looked at the sleeping girl and let himself feel the immense relief he'd longed for since they set out on their walk. She was safe, at least as safe as she could be. And then it crept on him, the notion that there was nowhere truly safe that was outside the span of the vegetable stall, and even that was uncertain if he were honest. He had not been very honest with himself, secure in the caravan, protected by the special nature of the traders' reputation and the need for their presence. Surely they would have fallen to the Kinslayer's armies if only Uncle had not had the foresight to roam ahead of them, always avoiding their passage. Did this mean that they were cowards? Did it mean that they ought now to have more obligation to those less fortunate? A travelling trader relied on the needs and curiosities of those they met on the road and in return for safe passage they relayed messages, offered good deals and hospitality. It was the Wanderer's Way. Did his obligation somehow stop now? If it did, what was he doing here—the Wanderer himself—making plans with these strange people? What did it mean that the girl had found a mother in this most unlikely woman. Why was she wearing the wealth of a nation with such carelessness, as though it were rags? Why was she here? How could either of them have anything to do with the Kinslayer's fire? He stopped eating, appetite lost.

The woman and the child he had buried earlier in the day were suddenly there with him. He could feel their ghosts at his side. He realised, as he looked over the flames at the living woman stroking the girl's hair, that the spirits of the unknown people would always be with him and somehow, though he'd never known them, he loved them and they were his family. Further away the dead man stood, watching, waiting for him to make things right, to explain, to show a way forwards on the road because they didn't know where to go, these lost things.

The woman Lysandra looked at him looking at her through the flames. She looked slightly to the side, as if she could see them too. "T'sk," she said to him and gave the slightest of nods.

He looked around. All of them seemed surprised she had spoken.

"What did she say?" Bukham didn't know the language at all, which was strange for traders knew nearly all the languages spoken on the ways of their countries.

"It's Tzarkish," Ralas said, sounding puzzled. He too was looking between them. "It means 'kin'."

"Well, if you're family then you come with us." Nedlam said.

"I thought we'd be going home," Bukham said, not daring to make a comment on what was going on.

"Home?" Murti sounded cheerful. "Home is wherever you are, no?"

No, Bukham wanted to say, *it's where the trading post is*. But because this was apparently a Guardian he didn't say anything, just nodded, because how could he disagree? "We've come too far to go back," he heard himself saying—one of the platitudes of the traders, said so often it meant nearly nothing. Now it struck him with the force of a blow.

Tzarkish—he'd not known that because there was no trading with the deathly ones. Even if he'd wanted to, none of them ever undertook any transactions with people outside their own. Maybe it explained at least why she could see the dead but the rumours about Tzark were the least comforting stories he'd ever heard. She was very pretty. It seemed wrong for things like that to be true of pretty people.

He sighed. He was a fool and knew it. Then he wondered if the girl ought to be with her. And the dress. It wasn't right. But they looked right together. He rubbed his hands together where the backs of them were patterned in pale brown, chestnut, ochre and nightshade, just as his own mother's were. They were of an Oerni colouring that was most commonplace and it had always made him comfortable, that sensation of belonging to a larger band than others.

"Then it's decided," the blonde, Celestaine, was declaring. "We go north to the thinning point."

"I don't want to get ahead of things but what will you do even if you find them?" Ralas asked, putting his musical instrument away, wrapped carefully, in a carrying case. He looked at Murti and his gaze was deceptively mild.

An uneasy moment stole through the group. Bukham could watch its passage through the individual faces—only the centaur and the one called Lysandra showed no concern. They looked towards Wanderer for an answer but he didn't give it—it came instead from a new voice that cut confidently through the darkness.

"We're going to get some answers."

As they all turned, rising, startled, hands going to weapons the voice added, "Sit down. I'm not here to make trouble."

And then a short woman stood with them; not emerging from the brush and striding in but just as if she'd been there all along unnoticed. She was next to Murti and gave him a cursory nod as she settled down next to the fire, her heavy cloak wrapped around her, hands outstretched to the flames for some heat. Beneath the hem her boots poked out, gold and silver buckles and embossing on them in the shape of leaves and birds.

"Another one," Horse said, her eyebrow raised, hand relaxing a little on the haft of her spear.

She seemed very cold, Bukham thought, because the night was quite mild, not even damp for the time of year. If she got any closer to the fire she'd be in it. Her face in the yellow light was haggard, but young. She wasn't interested in him. She glanced only at the girl, once, fleetingly, and then fixed her stare into the flames, rubbing her hands.

"Then if it's not trouble, what do you want?" Celestaine asked.

"I've got something to tell you," the woman said. Then she spotted Bukham's bowl. "Is that left over?"

He passed it around to her and she fell to eating like a starving dog, entirely absorbed for the couple of minutes it took while they waited and Lysandra fell asleep against the centaur's belly. The newcomer licked the bowl clean and then the spoon, and put them aside before she said, "You might be walking into a trap."

"What makes you think so?" Celestaine said, sitting down beside Heno.

"Yes, go on, Tricky. Tell them. It's safe enough, not like we've much choice is it?" Murti added giving a rather fond glance at to the newcomer who had started to look a bit familiar to Bukham, though he'd never seen anyone pick her teeth with a silver toothpick before.

"Because I've just come from Nydarrow," she said, and spat something into the embers near her feet. "And he spoke to me." She rolled her eyes as there was a general alarm rushing through them all, leading to hands reaching for weapons and clenched jaws. "Nah, nah. Not like this," she made her thumb and fingers into a yapping mouth. "In here," she tapped her head. "He always spoke to me like that even when he was alive, and that's how I knew when to see him and when to avoid him so, maybe, I get you, maybe it's not him, but it sounds like him, yes? And it always knows what he was doing. It's like a kind of spying. Or maybe fearing. Hard to say. But it's saved my butt too many times to mention so it'll do for me." She paused to flick the toothpick around her molars. "So what's her story?" She pointed at Lysandra. "Runaway is she? From..." and then she paused and her animated little face went very still and pale. "Wait a second. Where did you find her?"

"On the hill," Nedlam said, watching carefully. Bukham could see her weighing up this new person and not quite liking her.

The little woman got up suddenly and turned about, scanning the dark sky. She revolved twice and then she said, "Where's the godforsaken fire, then?" in a tone of absolute amazement.

"Funny you should mention that," Ralas murmured. His

hand had left the lute case and was straying in the direction of his dagger.

She noticed the movement and looked irritated. "Put that hedgehog sticker away. Like you could beat me in any kind of fight." Her head went up and suddenly Bukham saw her, the dark, mysterious woman who had taken his fruit and given it to the girl days ago at Taib. He opened his mouth, drawing breath, and she turned to him faultlessly and said, "Shut it, before the moths fly in." Without pause she turned to Murti as she sat down again in a little huff. "You're not seriously taking him anywhere are you? He can barely manage an applecart."

"He's very good at minding the applecart," Murti said, with a mild reproof in his tone. "You, on the other hand, talk too much when you're nervous."

"Yeah well, I just realised what she is," she said, gesturing to Lysandra with a sigh. "I just can't figure out what that is," she said, and nodded towards Horse, "or that..." and then she looked at Kula. "Or why they are together."

"Well..." began Ralas but she waved at him with such effortless disdain that she shut him up.

"No, don't tell me, I'll get there."

Bukham found Murti patting his hand amiably. "She loves a puzzle."

"While you're thinking on it," Celestaine interrupted, "what is she?" She indicated Lysandra.

"Kinslayer's Bride," Tricky replied.

There was a moment of contemplative alarm.

"But..." said Heno.

"What?" said Nedlam.

"Oh dear," said Ralas.

"You have to be joking," said Celestaine.

"Ah, I thought as much," said Murti.

The fire slumped on itself, sending a shower of sparks high into the air.

"Why were you in Nydarrow?" Celestaine asked into the anxious quiet.

"I was looking for things," Tricky said.

"You were always his lapdog," Heno said suddenly. "The lady in green. Always doing his work."

"Yeah, well, how else was I going to find a way to stop him if I didn't know everything he was doing?" Tricky said as if his accusation had no interest for her. "You were his executioners, torturers, labourers and general dogsbodies, speaking of dogs. I suppose you think it was some kind of accident that you were on that duty when she appeared," and she jerked her thumb at Celestaine.

"Are you saying that you…" Ralas began but was imperiously waved off again.

"I'm not saying it," Tricky said as if the entire conversation was annoying her while Heno bristled and Nedlam started stabbing the embers with a stick. "Ah ha! I've got it. This Draeyad is here because the fire is out. This girl just wandered here when it was still burning. This mazagal is here because they tried to get rid of it in the fire but it didn't burn for some reason and so the girl found it and now it is hers. The Draeyad is protecting her in thanks. That's it, isn't it? Tell me I'm right." She looked immensely puckish and pleased with herself.

"That's am—" Ralas began but Celestaine was already talking across him.

"What's a mazagal?" she said.

"Oh, it's a special creation made by necromancers where they put several spirits into one body to create a being with extra abilities, usually because they want to send it back and forth between the realms of the living and the dead."

They all looked at Lysandra, snoring slightly as her head lolled against the round ribs of the centaur, Kula safely nestled in her lax embrace. In the firelight they looked exactly like any ordinary mother and child, peacefully resting after a long day.

"Dead and evil?" Nedlam asked after a moment.

"No," Tricky said. "Even Reckoner wasn't... well, he wasn't until later but I think he'd been across too many borders, went too far and something, in one of those places, kind of changed him. You know that's why they make mazagals."

"If she's going to excuse that bastard I'm leaving," Ralas declared firmly.

"Nobody is excusing anything," Murti said. "But there is some truth there. Before he was the Kinslayer he was the Reckoner and he wasn't always as you knew him."

"My heart bleeds for your loss," Ralas said coldly. "Meanwhile, what is this mazagal thing now? Is it dangerous?"

"They are made with a purpose," Tricky said, fishing around in her pockets for something. "So they are always kind of... what's the word... on the lookout for doing that thing that they have to do. But they're usually bound to the sorcerer that made them. There's something that makes them serve. I don't know. I'm thinking she was the price that the Tzarkomen wanted to pay to stop him wiping them out and for some reason he was willing to take it. Which is weird because he was well beyond deals at that point."

"I remember," Celestaine said coolly.

"Yeah, yah," Tricky yawned. She had found what she was hunting for—a stick of birch—and began chewing on it vigorously, talking in between gnawings. "So, whose idea was it to go look for the gods?"

"It was Deffo," Murti said.

"Wait, no. He said it was you," Celestaine retorted. "He said that you had found a clue about how to reach them."

"Did he?" Murti scratched his head and shrugged.

Tricky was watching them both like a hunting cat. She settled on Celestaine, "So, what? You just heard the clarion call of glory and went trotting off without a thought?"

"No!" Celestaine said firmly. "Maybe. What's your point?"

Tricky waved her chewed stick at them, pointing at each in turn. "My point is that something... is afoot here."

"You see meanings where none exist," Murti objected. "You're always paranoid."

"Kind of a given where the dear old gods are concerned," Tricky said, unrepentant. She fixed her gaze on Bukham, to his surprise. He'd been so fixated on following what everyone else was saying and doing he'd almost forgotten that he existed. "You," she said, stabbing in his direction with the twig before jabbing it back in her face and fussing around, speaking with her mouth full of improvised toothbrush. "Yo're un bit of it I don' un'nerstand. You don' fit."

Bukham said, "I only came because my uncle made me."

There was a pause.

Tricky rolled her eyes. "Great. A wild card that's a mummy's boy." She looked at Murti. "Where do you find them? No, don't answer me, it was rhetorical. I know where you found him. We all found him." She chewed the stick, grilling Bukham, then Murti, then Kula with her gaze. "Three's the charm, eh?" She spat into the fire and listened to the hiss of sizzling spit with her head cocked. "Even fire agrees. So, that's cooked."

Murti watched her with paternal amusement as she sighed, replaced the remains of the twig into her pocket and stood up with vigour. "So, I need to see for myself. Where is it? Up the hill there? No, don't get up, you all look like you need some rest. Bags under your eyes could hold a dragon's hoard. Know what I'm saying? I remember where the fire was well enough."

"You should," muttered Heno, audibly. "You were there when it started."

"Yeah, funny story about that, but it'll have to wait." She turned with purpose and took one stride and then, even though the firelight reached a good four or five steps she was gone from sight. A few seconds later there was a rustle, a crack and a couple of sharp curses about damned boots, stupid invisibility charm, and then quiet returned.

"Ah, that's how I know her," the centaur said in her mellifluous alto, breaking the strange spell they had found themselves under. "She was the one who held his cloak."

CHAPTER SIXTEEN

KULA WOKE UP to the smell of something delicious mid-toast and the smoke of a wood fire. Beneath her cheek the soft form of her mother's chest was steadily breathing and under her outflung hand the ribcage of the centaur was rumbling in a way that she thought funny, though the funny didn't make it near her face. She opened one eye cautiously, then the other. It was dawn. The figures she remembered from the night before were busy breaking camp. A skillet was over the campfire and the fat stallholder was bent over it intently, watching bubbles pop in the top of pancakes, a machete held aloft, ready to flip them over.

To his left the pale woman and the two monster people were busy in conversation as they polished and attended various weapons. She kept a long gaze on the painted tusker but he seemed engrossed in what he was doing, softened by his association with the warrior at his side, and none of them were paying attention to her. Carefully she pulled her hand off the centaur's side and moved a bit to show that she was awake. A sense of disquiet and urgency kept colouring them all, but she thought it was different for each one of them.

Her mother sighed and went to get up. Kula stuck close. She was able to hear a little, through her mother, and as she concentrated this ability grew. She wasn't used to listening

151

but she thought it must be useful and her mother was still not awake, not properly. She was only a little bit aware and she had almost no understanding of what was going on, so Kula had to lead her out to the security of some bushes to make water and show her how to manage the clothes, then back to the camp to get something to eat. She didn't have to have the food herself but she knew how not eating made these people suspicious and anyway, the smell was very good. It had been that smell, among others, which had brought her out of the fields to Taib Post in the first place.

She accepted two cakes from the stallholder, who gave her a well-meaning smile, a weary look that she knew meant she'd caused him trouble. She handed one on to Lysandra, shuffling the hot things in her fingers and trying not to laugh when Lysandra copied her as if it was an important part of the process. She copied the laugh too. Kula pulled a piece off her cake and popped it in her mouth. Lysandra mirrored her and then Lysandra's eyes widened in surprise and she started grinning as she was eating and then she leapt up with joy and jumped around as Kula wanted to do but hadn't, making noises of appreciation that startled everyone and pointing at her mouth and holding up the cake and shaking it as if it were the totem of a mighty spirit. The sun was just rising and it caught all the jewels in her hair and on her dress so that for a time she was a gyrating dancer of brilliant colour, graceless and exuberant, like a peculiar bird.

Eventually she spun to a halt and toppled down, sitting, smacking her lips and making much of the cake. When her eyes met Kula's gaze they were so full of life and fiery joy that Kula felt her heart catch it too. She had been right. Her mother was not gone, she had only been missing for a while and now they had found one another again. She smiled and ate her cake, filled with happiness.

CHAPTER SEVENTEEN

As THE BREAKFAST was being made and served Ralas had noticed the strange, dark little woman come down through the trees from the hill summit. He paused and his heart skipped a beat with a strange lurch compounded of guilt and excitement, making him scowl. Quickly he flipped to another page of his journal, away from the sketch he'd been making in an effort to capture the peculiar qualities of her appearance, so beguiling at certain angles and so hard at others. It was quite impossible and he had the smeared chalk of his efforts all over his fingers.

He closed the leather bindings on second thoughts, and cleaned his hands on his ink rag, pretending great care over it as he peered through his ragged fringes to watch her strut—yes that was definitely the word for her gait. She was swinging a bag on long cords back and forth and walked right into the middle of breakfast with an air of satisfaction, picking a cake off the skillet with finger and thumb and juggling it as the big, gentle giant, Bukham, chided her and impotently waved his machete. In turn he got a reproachful thump off Nedlam who didn't enjoy sharp things being wafted around her shoulders.

"Mind your manners, boy," she grunted. "I've killed men for giving bad haircuts before now." She ran a hand through her inch-cropped hair, forking it stiffly into spikes and guffawed briefly. In fact, the atmosphere was incredibly pleasant all around and Ralas found himself smiling. He was still smiling when Celestaine caught his eye and raised her brow as if to say, "Oh yes? What's up with you?"

He quickly stared at his boots and heard her chuckle again. His face was not his friend again, it seemed, giving everything away. He brought a few verses of something he was working on to mind but was cut off his train of thought by the return of the centaur. In the light of morning she was astoundingly large, her horse parts mighty, her hoofs revealed now not to be single but tripartite, with something that looked very much like a spur at her heels, hidden by the heavy long feathers of hair that shrouded her from just below the knees. Something that large shouldn't be able to move so quietly through thick woodland as she did.

She was staring at him too: no, he was staring at her. He sighed and shrugged and she made a horselike expression of equanimity, furred ears flicking one forward one back, and tossed him an apple. He fumbled the catch with his pain-stiffened arm and watched it bounce off his thumb. Then he then fell off the rock he was seated on as he tried to grab it and heard Tricky snicker. For a few moments he lay in the grass, and then decided the sky was quite nice to look at and took a bite of the apple. It was only just the start of the season but it was sweet and good, not even a worm hole. His back ached and his legs and hands were their usual ruinously awful selves, but for a few minutes he could pretend that things were quite nice.

That reverie was broken by Celestaine's command voice saying with disbelief, "You've done what?"

"Negotiated with the Draeyads for the box she came in," Tricky said, through a mouthful.

Ralas stretched his hearing as far as he could, holding the chewed apple against his teeth quietly.

"And it's where?" Celestaine sounded confused.

"In here." A patting sound of hand on pocket, or something like that.

"How's it fit in there?" That was Nedlam.

"I could tell you, but then I'd have to kill you," Tricky replied airily. "Point is, it's covered in writing and I think I know the very people who could read it, thereby telling all of us exactly what's going on here. Knowledge is power, and power is power and you're about to take a strange, powerful thing to a strange, powerful place so don't you think you should cut me a little slack. I am helping you."

"Yes, but why?" Celestaine said with all the puzzlement and distrust that Ralas wanted to feel but didn't. Instead he felt a balmy, charmed kind of feeling that boded very ill. He made a couple of quick chews and swallowed.

"Reasons," Tricky said. "Like yours no doubt. And his. And hers. You know. Reasons."

"You're a Guardian," said Heno, "but what is your calling? Tricks are not a guardian kind of a thing."

"What would you know? It is so a thing. In fact, I'm not a Guardian. I'm more of a go-between, freelancer operative. Specialist. In a broad sense."

"Where's Deffo got to?" Celestaine.

"He's looking at boats on the river. For when you'll need them to get to the Freeport. He's good with boats. Not much else. But boats, he's good at. Or any other kind of general escape vessel. You're best keeping him moderately terrified if you want him to be any use but I'd've thought you were well aware of that by now. Speaking of, what's your interest in all this god business?"

Ralas had never heard Celestaine short for a reply before but now he felt a distinct gap in which he imagined her composing herself and putting her chin down as she re-asserted some authority. But instead she said, "I can't sit around at home. I'm in the way. I need something difficult and dangerous to do."

"Yeah, got to keep busy, eh?" Tricky said. "I heard you got the wings back for those birdy people. Not much you could do there but nice try. And that is why I am helping you. I've got my own paybacks and we share a common set of needs and businesses, as you might say. You want to see what happened to the gods. I want to see that too." There was a definite edge to her voice which reminded Ralas of a steel for sharpening blades.

"All right," Celestaine said, in the way that meant she'd go along with it but not an inch further than she had to. "So, where are you taking the box?"

"Catt and Fisher's of course," Tricky said. "And I'll need someone with me for—well, I'll need someone with me since me and the old Fish don't quite see eye-to-eye. I'll take him. He's not doing anything for you."

Heno laughed and Ralas felt his ears go hot. He took a bite of the apple and let the noise of his own chewing drown out whatever else was being said as he wondered if there was some chance that there was more interest in him than simply the need of a stooge for whatever she had planned, if she wanted his company specifically for reasons. He wasn't sure if he hoped that was true or not. He did. But then again, she was obviously terrible trouble in any imaginable sphere. It occurred to him that maybe he ought to voice an opinion about it all and not lie there like a dumb ox being traded at the market but then again as soon as he got up the world would go back to the business of being unpleasantly real and in need of painful actions and he was enjoying it from the position of not really bothering. Left alone he would have stayed there all morning, turning over little dreams and phrases, fitting them into a story of his own liking and a tune that suited.

"It's up to him," Celestaine said with extra volume, so he took it as his cue and sat up.

Everyone was looking at him.

"I…" He hadn't actually had any plans but now it seemed like he should be making an objection so that he didn't look like a complete fool, but his only sense of a future event beckoning was the possibility of re-starting the Festival that bards had attended in the autumn at Cinquetann Riverport and since the start of the war that had been out of the question, and was now only slightly a question since he had lost track of everyone he knew and was afraid to find out their fates. "I can always go there and leave some messages. I was going to anyway. It's a good place. Everyone goes there. We can rejoin you at Ilkand. If that's still where you're going to get the boat north. I mean I can rejoin you. There."

He kept his attention on the small woman though he looked straight at Celestaine. Beside her Heno was doing the slow blink he did whenever someone talked very fast. Celestaine herself had a curious look and she gave a sideways glance at Tricky. "All right. I was just thinking it might be better to try to hide these two—" she indicated Lysandra and Kula. "Rather than drag them around the countryside.

"I don't think you should let them out of your sight," Murti said, belching after one too many pancakes. "I certainly won't." His voice was mild but his resolve unwavering.

"Fine. Then let's get moving." Celestaine looked at Horse. "Are you coming or will you turn back at the edge of the trees?"

"I am coming with you. We wish to see the evolution of this matter and also the Forest itself has been destroyed in large part; by the war and by people wherever they go. Now that I am free to walk again it is my duty to repair and replace, seed and nurture, to keep the Forest connected as one. I will go with you to the coast. Ilkand fell more than once and every time the armies destroyed more. It will be a good place to start again."

Lysandra, hands slimy with butterfat, lips gleaming, glanced up from where she was attempting to clean Kula's hands on some broad leaves. "Me go. Me see too. We. We see." At her side the girl kept her head down, frowning as if she was concentrating though her hands weren't moving. Ralas felt a shiver run over his arms.

Those standing shared a look that acknowledged they hadn't

known she could talk. Tricky stood up slowly, joining in, and said quietly. "See, the girl is her sorcerer. She can't hear. But the mazagal can hear. She's teaching it." She snickered and tossed back her curly black hair. "Now we need to get that fortune off her before she has ideas about it herself. This expedition isn't going to come cheap."

Lysandra stood with a swift, elegant movement that startled all of them. Ralas felt his hand go for his dagger hilt automatically. She pulled hard at a diamond secured to her skirt and ripped it clear of the embroidery. She held it out and then with a swift flick tossed it to Celestaine. "Take. I pay. Pay all."

Celestaine swiped it out of the air and looked down at the jewel in her palm for a moment. She held it up in her fingertips and they were all briefly dazzled by the brilliance of rays shooting from its many facets. "Most people's homes are worth less than this stone."

"Nobody has any use for rocks right now," Tricky said. "But there's enough small ones to use in trade. Keep the big ones for other things. I'll have a few. Scholarship of the kind I need doesn't come cheap."

Celestaine tossed the diamond to Ralas after one more lingering look. "Here you go. Now you've got a job."

Ralas caught the thing this time and stashed it inside the leather pouch he kept hanging around his neck for valuables. "Diamond carrier?"

"There must be a rhyme for it somewhere." She smiled and then they set about helping to detach the wealth from the wedding dress, dividing it up and at the same time careful of Kula's insistence that the dress itself not be harmed. It was a long task and the sun was high by the time that the last coil of golden wire had been wound and stowed. A certain disquiet had overtaken them as the magnitude of what they were to carry sank home, and the possible disaster that being found in possession of such things might bring.

They did all they could to distribute and hide what they had. A lot of sewing was needed, at which none of them were adept, and this took another few hours in which Bukham, who didn't want to carry any but was made to sew coins into his hems, cooked another round of cakes and some dried fish. By the time the moment came to set off they were all sad to leave, except Celestaine who was anxious for movement and Tricky who had got restless because of having to remain still for any length of time. They made perfunctory farewells in the tradition, Ralas thought, of those who didn't want to dwell on the prospect of finality in any shape or form. He slung his lute over his shoulder, checked his boots, and then left the clearing, glancing back to see that the only traces they had been there was a ring of crushed grass and the fresh earth where they had buried the fire.

"Come on, Plucky," Tricky said impatiently. "Long way to the shops from here."

"Ralas," Ralas said mildly, matching his stride in her footsteps. "Are you truly called Tricky as your actual name?"

"None of us have actual names," she said, with bitterness. "So what does it matter?"

"You can have any name, then. Wanderer has a name."

"Wanderer has many names, none of them mean anything. Does yours mean something special, Plucky? Is it better than Plucky?"

"From your lips nothing is better than Plucky." He was astounded he'd actually said that. It more or less slipped out without a thought and he found himself suddenly face to face with her as she spun around in her tracks. Her gaze was snappy and sharp.

"Don't try to charm me. I don't charm."

Her upturned face was warmly lit by the rising sun. There was something twisted about her features—he could see them beneath the glamour spell's veil of beauty, and somehow the combination of the veil and the mismatched shapes beneath was breathtaking; he felt he could see a secret at the heart of the world. The songs had it all wrong. Love wasn't blind. It was revelation.

"And don't get all mushy. I don't look like this anyway." She turned and was striding off again on the narrow trail, boots leaving no mark at all in the shallow mud.

He followed, bringing to mind a love song that he'd always felt entirely ridiculous until now. He felt foolish and indescribable. He started to whistle, without realising what he was doing. A moment later she joined in, providing the little-known descant to the song of a fine man's fortune lost in the pursuit of a careless witch.

They were still on the second verse of it when they came out of the tree cover and onto the road. From the direction that the others had taken, north, came distant but distinctive sounds of fighting. He hesitated, "Should we?"

"Nay, they've got it," Tricky said with a dismissive wave of her hand. "Anyway, what're you going to do, scream very loudly and hit them with that lute? It's a Principal Verduchine. You'd be wasting it on them."

"You know about lutes?" He hurried to keep up with her, more off guard than ever.

"I know about value," she said firmly. "I know quality when I see it and I know who likes that kind of thing."

Abruptly he felt concerned and tugged the lute's strap to be sure it was still there.

"Don't worry, Plucky," she chuckled and gave him a wink over her shoulder. "I've got lots of jewels to get through before I get to that." Her stride was deceptively swift and he had to stifle a lot of aches and stabs from his permanently broken toes to keep up. He was soon so out of breath that he forgot the distress vibrating through the voices behind them, a timbre of rage and desperation that he'd come to know as well as his own heartbeat since the war began: people with nothing to lose finding they had some spite left after all.

CHAPTER EIGHTEEN

THEY WERE ATTACKED as their way out of the forest cleared into a path. Men came out of the trees on either side of the road, hollering. A net was thrown at Horse though it fell across her back and caught on nothing.

They circled immediately to shelter the woman and child and with a surprised shiver Celestaine heard the crackle of Heno's magic in the air. Then she was too busy facing screaming ragers with their weapons all upraised and rushing like kids towards a wooden target. That told her they were no army, nor army men, but they had the fury on them and she parried and shoved with precision to get them aside, her blade harrying for minor injuries to slow and give them second thoughts. She both regretted and did not miss the magical blade she once had. It would have killed them all in moments and leave no space for thought at all.

Nedlam had no such compunctions. Lady Wall was out and swinging in wide arcs, a man and his friend soon following her suggestions, flying for strides through the air before landing, the crump of the hammerhead connecting matched by the crumpling sound of their bodies meeting the ground.

The haft and end of Horse's polearm whirled, thumped. The business end sliced once, twice. But then their brief success turned for a moment as another few came rushing from the cover and these ones bore their weapons with intent. They were once soldiers who had waited for the unskilled of the band to soften up and test the targets. Now they knew their business and a grim determination fuelled their movements.

Celestaine let hers come, circling a little, until her shoulder banged into Horse's rump. She heard the snap and sizzle of Heno's charge cut the air and then a scream of agony that far outmatched any cries that had gone before. This, instead of cutting the enemy's mettle, fired them. They pressed the assault and she found herself sword to sword with an old pro, wily and light, who knew when to wait and when to strike. Her Forinthi swordmaster's skills were the only thing to preserve her against his intelligence. Behind her she felt the thump and slide of another net landing on Horse and the centaur made a snort and yell of rage as her polearm was fouled in it.

More came, non-fighters, laden with things that looked like spades and forks, slow and anxious as they looked for something to do that wouldn't get them killed. So far they had been short on killing, Celestaine thought, and changed her grip and her stance. She heard Nedlam bellow and the unkind, brutal sound of Lady Wall striking a head; the noise was curious, sodden, surprisingly light. From within the circle of them she heard crying but it was hard to say who was making it: she'd have put money on the market trader.

She stepped forwards and slammed her shield—a recent acquisition from home—into the man in front of her, roared, "Enough! Put down your arms or you will die here!" She hated to fight those without a chance and these had little of it, but she was prepared to back her threat all the same.

There was a pause and she found herself looking at her attacker more closely, seeing he was not the leader but looking towards someone for a sign, a hopeful slackness in his face as blood ran from his broken nose. The bloodlust she enjoyed feeling slumped inside her, disappointed as he backed off a step, then another. He was scowling as if his thoughts were confounded.

Then for no apparent reason he stumbled and went down on one knee. She heard Heno's grunt of surprise just as she was feeling it too. Behind her Horse wrenched off the net and flung it violently back in the face of two young women near her, the point of her spear wavering at knee height, slicing up the grass there in case there was some doubt about her will to use it.

"All right," one of the soldiers who had faced Horse said, defeated and agitated, gruff with command. "Stand down. They are not for the taking today and we can afford no more."

The attackers put up their arms and backed off to regroup, some bending to take care of the wounded or examine the dead. There was some wailing of disappointment as survivors discovered someone lost and Celestaine realised how young most of them were under their general coating of filth and disarray. She sheathed her sword carefully and re-hung her shield at the ready on her back as she watched over everyone else's recovery. Though they had minor cuts and bruises none of them were much hurt. Kula was safe, cowed under Lysandra's bent body, Bukham the trader huddled close to them; only Heno and Murti looking about with composure, Horse snarling with anger, Nedlam content to swing her weapons and grin her threats as she made a circle of them, pushing the bandits away to a distance. Beside her when she stopped, their leader was barely up to her shoulder and slight, even for a human.

"We should kill 'em all," Nedlam said, matter-of-fact. "Bandits no good for anyone."

"We are not bandits. We're refugees," the leader said coldly, trying not to cower and mostly succeeding as he faced up to Nedlam's dismissal. "From you. You should know. Filth."

Nedlam's face remained impassive.

"Filth that saved the day back in Nydarrow," Celestaine replied, walking around, stepping over the one Nedlam had killed. "These Yorughan were there at the end, and they were against the Kinslayer. Back off. We are done with war but we can bring it back if you insist."

How many more times will I tell that story? Will it wear out its power one day?

"He doesn't want it," a woman near the middle of their group blurted before any other had a chance to respond. Ragged and worn, she must have been Celestaine's own age but life had treated her much more unkindly and she gave off an air of despair that couldn't hold back any longer. "None of us want it, but we go here, we go there, nobody lets us stop or stay, nobody offers anything, we have to fight real bandits off but they take everything. We came here because the fire went out. We thought nobody would be here. There must have been a great peace happen here. We'd be safe." Her accent was soft but distinctively southern with its lilting vowels.

She must have been on the road for a long time to be so exhausted, Celestaine thought, but she didn't like the look of the fighters in the group; they were still out for blood if it was possible. They had been ruined by war and they would ruin anyone now in the notion that it would repair their pain by levelling all fates to the same agony. Reckoning had no end to it. The thought made her feel like she was made of mud, without feeling; she left her sword elevated and ready.

Nedlam and Horse were holding them off to the flanks, and Heno's magical threat held the rear, but their respect was temporary. They looked around shiftily from one to another, seeking a spark back to action when their own hesitation let things hang. She agreed with Nedlam. They were better clearing up, not leaving them to carry their rage, but Horse stepped forwards.

"The depth of the vale is not for you. You may pass through the rest of the forests and remain there unharmed, but only those of pleasant intent may remain."

From behind her the figure of Lysandra, astonishing, boldly coloured, stepped forwards, Kula at her skirts. She moved carefully past the end of Horse's javelin to where the apparent leader of the band stood, sword and machete in hand, grim and glowering. Celestaine wanted to speak but her throat was caught between warning and wanting to see what was happening here. There was a strange lightness to Lysandra, utterly without guile or sense, walking up to him, ignoring his weapons. Kula came with her, a tiny shadow. She couldn't see Lysandra's face from where she stood, but she saw the man's arms tense as he re-gripped his blades, his chin dipping in warning, body bracing for action.

"Don't be afraid," Lysandra said in the clear, fresh tone of someone without care. Her clothing shone like flowers against the muddy green and brown of the woodland. She embraced the stranger and laid her head against the bloodied leather of his chest. "It's all right. We are people meeting in the woods and it is safe."

Nedlam's face was a picture of quizzical disbelief. She licked around her short tusk in anticipation. Horse's spear point raised suddenly, sweeping a curve to point at the sky until the end thudded to the ground beside her hoof. There was a heartbeat of time in which the sense of balance swung wildly, Celestaine felt, watching the expression on the man's face, Lysandra's closed eyes and peaceful cheek, the intense focus of the child at her side, fist clutched in silk skirting, leaning forwards as though her will was a lever with which she could shift the world.

"I..." said the leader, staggering slightly in an effort not to bear Lysandra's touch.

Celestaine found herself longing for him to give up, to give in, to let it go and relax. She wanted to see someone do it so she'd know better how to do it later and she felt compassion for them, but also she felt almost no hope—that Lysandra was speaking out of a misguided love and faith that had never understood loss and destruction, that she was foolish and ridiculous. Then she saw they were all foolish and ridiculous. People meeting in the woods, with no trouble, making trouble. A glimpse of something longed for and not understood hung there, this promise of a possible future. And then with a violent shake the man brought down his fist at Lysandra's unprotected head.

"What witchery is this?" he was bellowing and then he was on his back on the ground, Lysandra was moving to one side, her arm out to shield Kula, as though they had taken a mis-step in a complicated dance. Then he stopped thrashing and lay still and looked at the sky. The sword and machete flopped to the grass one by one as his hands went slack. "Blue. Clouds."

"You've murdered him!" shrieked one of the women, half-hidden in the trees. "Gaballan is murdered!"

"Shut up," said another. "He's not dead."

A brief scuffle that had broken out near Nedlam was ended with two decisive thunks of her club and whimpering. They gathered around to see what had happened to the undead man. Celestaine saw Kula tug at Lysandra's skirt and bring them both back into the shadow of Horse as attention fell away from them. She saw the group of refugees slowly emerging and crowding up and took the moment to signal that they should go. Beside Horse the tall, bulky shape of Bukham was staring open-mouthed at the scene. She cuffed him on the shoulder as Murti said, "Hey, time to go."

Bukham looked at her with a dazed expression, his skewbald features waxy and idiotic with shock. "I don't..."

"We'll talk later," Celestaine said. "Right now we need to move." She felt irritated by his imbecility. This was going to be like herding cattle all the way. Nobody could afford to be on the roads who wasn't prepared. Somehow she would have to make them prepared. "Nedlam, take the rear. Heno, you go forwards. Horse, you can take the child on your back. We must be quick for a time."

Horse made no quarrel and within a moment or two both Kula and Lysandra were riding. She put Bukham at their side and Murti just ahead of him with strict instructions that the old man was not to fall behind. Once they had cleared the woodlands and were moving towards more open ground she jogged forwards to Heno's side. "What did you make of that?"

"I don't know," he said. "Kula did something."

"We'll have to watch them." Celestaine muttered, uneasy because dealing with this felt way beyond her experience. She went back along the line to Nedlam. "Any sign of trouble?"

"They didn't follow us," Nedlam said, striding easily under the weight of Lady Wall, resting it on her shoulder. "What did Heno say?"

"Said we're in deep shit," Celestaine said. She looked to where Murti's bent back and bandied legs were making easy work of the road. She felt out of her depth, longing for action to relieve the anxiety of it, dreading the same thing because there were too few of them with any experience to manage a more serious assault than a half-starved, disorganised rabble. And then her mind returned to Lysandra, riding happily, staring about her at everything with delight, and she shivered.

KULA LIKED RIDING on the back of Horse; she was warm and furry and she walked with confidence. Lysandra's joy in the world was infectious, even though the people on the road had nearly ruined everything as they always did. Even being the most kind towards them never worked. They were too far gone and they were too needy. When some of them would have been nice the others would spoil it. Children and women would pay for it. Those who weren't themselves already full of the plague of horrors were the first to be turned on, with hatred. She wished them dead, but she could not do it. She had thought, once, how wonderful it would be to replace them with silence. Here was a chance, but something about them made it too difficult. She had felt that she, not they, would die. She would have asked her mother but this mother didn't know the answer to that and neither did any of the others.

She turned the lead refugee soldier's memories over and over, watching them rise and fall. They were full of violence done to him and by him. He'd lived a long time compared to her and most of what he had known was painful to him and, when she paused to study it, to her. She knew these pains very well. She hadn't wanted Lysandra to see them because it would spoil her but she couldn't restrain all her own memories when she saw his. His ran in his actions, in his eyes, in the rat-running panics of his brain. She couldn't kill him, but she could take the memories away.

It had been a favour to remove all that from him, all the way back as far as it went, starting with some male faces, some blows, some agony in a dark place. Lately, towards the end, the faces of the big ugly grey ones came up again and again. She could see that these were not the same big uglies as the ones travelling with her now, but they were definitely the same kind. The ones with the lightning stars and the carvings in their massive teeth—they were often there.

She looked at his uglies compared to the one she had taken in the river mud. It had remembered a lot of killing. It had ended all she had known without knowing even for a moment what it was doing. Kill and destroy, that was all it had meant to do. But for it too there were these distant times in a dark hole that felt like love and belonging, purpose and curiosity. They had not always been what they became, but she understood that what they had become must end so that it was not passed on. If they would not end it themselves, then she would have to find a way.

At the next time they made a stop she pretended she must get a drink and took a skin of water from their supplies. She stood and drank from her hand, though she took nothing in but breathed the memories out and let them run through her fingers. Before the water streams had struck the ground they had dissolved everything into a jumble that was nothing more than moments and soon these would be gone too, soaked into the soil, consumed by the roots and converted into other lives that were much slower and so different they would have no infectious force at all.

She felt much better without them. She practised the names of the others as she rode, whispering them under her breath until she felt they were right. She didn't understand anything they were saying but she knew names and her mother was getting a better grasp of everything all the time. Heno. Nedlam. Celestaine. Horse. Bukham. Murti. The Undefeated.

Murti was strange. He had a life that went all over the place, even into other bodies in other places. She'd never seen anything like him before.

Then there had been the dark woman with the apple. Joy, she was called, small and bright, the one who had forgotten something. Tricky, she'd said she was, but that wasn't her real name. She wasn't human. She wasn't a demigod. She was Joy. Kula had no other word for what she was.

Then there was that man with the vibrating box of strings. Ralas. He'd been funny. She had liked him.

Bukham was funny too, but now he was sad all the time. She caught him looking at her and knew she had caused some of it although many other threads tied him to other people and places. The thread that led to her however, this he had followed and now he wanted to go home but the old man had caught him. He was a fisher, that old man. He was a net. She didn't mess with that as she didn't want to be caught.

BUKHAM TRUDGED AS much as he was able given the pace they were going. He wasn't sure who he was trying to impress with it but all he could think of was how angry Uncle was going to be when he found out that Bukham wasn't coming back. And his cousin. She would take the stall. She would ruin the trade because she always gave away free things and didn't know that not every herb was worth the same. She had no idea about spices either. And she had no idea about how to handle all the fruits and vegetables correctly so they looked their best and didn't bruise. Some had to be kept warm, others cool. Some must be dry, others moist. She would put them all together and in two days there would be a heap of mush.

Thinking of mush made him think of soil and digging and his hands hurt with the feel of the spade and then his body hurt with the soft thump of earth landing on a newly dead body, a newly dead face that had, that morning, been glad to be alive with no sense of what was coming. So he looked at the little girl and tried to imagine that at least he'd helped one. One. Strange little thing and seemed to have been alone.

She smiled at him warily. He tried to smile back but tore his gaze quickly away, feeling his face do it all wrong. He wanted to cry but he didn't. He wanted his mother but she was gone. He wanted to go away from everywhere but it seemed that this was already what was happening.

In front of him the old man bounded along while the shock of the morning's events was frozen in him. They had killed someone. Now that someone was a face down to the earth. And another had faced up to the sky. This was not how business was done. This was not how things should be. You couldn't simply leave it all hastily, like criminals, and rush off. There were responsibilities to take care of.

But when he thought he'd ask the blonde woman what was going on her expression made him think better of it. She looked like someone who executed responsibilities. He could have turned and left of course, at any time, just gone home himself. He knew the way. But even though he thought about it every other minute, he didn't go. His body wouldn't turn around and take him. He was afraid to, but also he wanted to see where they were going. Going itself was horrible but it had a promise in it that returning didn't have. It had graves in it, and lies, he felt, but still he was going.

Behind him he heard the huge monstress with the cudgel whistling a basic but cheery tune. He looked back at her and she grinned at him so that he was amazed by the size and yellowness of her tusks. His people were big but Yorughan were tough and rocky with it. He'd never seen an army like her on the march. He couldn't imagine standing against even one of her. She had a simplicity about her that promised insufficient imagination for mercy. But in the story told of Celestaine something like mercy, opportunity and other inclinations of rebellion had come Nedlam's way and she'd taken them and so now they were not at war. Such a turn of tides boggled him, and then he tripped on a root in the road and went flat on his face, burning with embarrassment. The Yorughan laughed and picked him up by the back of his jerkin, letting his feet dangle before she set him back on them. "Mind out," she said.

He hurried back to Horse's side and busied himself with worrying about how they were to get enough supplies for everyone. They were at the end of the meagre load this morning, he noticed. Hopefully as they got closer to the Freeport there would be some chances to trade. He remembered more than ten little settlements that the Post swung past each year and cheered up at the prospect of being able to show his usefulness, given what had happened in the fight. He stayed close to the girl and Lysandra, feeling fraternal and not missing his cousin or his uncle or aunts or any of the many familiar faces of Taib.

Around Lysandra's ankles he saw the bright red fabric of her underdress, muddy and torn, and the threads where gemstones had been plucked away. He thought of the fire of the Draeyads, soul-burning, fire in another world, and then he looked at her ordinary ankle and her foot in its ornate sandal, scraped of gold and the blue metal named Tarenid, the trader's curse, so-called because a desire to own a coin or ring of it was the death of many and as soon as one had it luck turned away. But it had been everywhere. The Binder's Burden, Uncle had said it was, because they used it to shackle prisoners who were masters of any kind of art beyond the ordinary, to prevent their escape.

She'd been covered in it, in little sigils, scales, threads. All undone now.

Lysandra hung onto the strap of Horse's bandolier as she rode, drinking in everything with boundless interest. Kula lolled in front of her, braiding the centaur's long hair with a ribbon of bright fabric, pulling it out, doing it again.

They passed onwards, a steady procession of the outlandish. Travellers on the road stared or gave them a wide berth and Bukham's unease grew. He watched Murti hurdling along with his game leg, he watched the stride and brace of the Heart Taker that led them, the blonde captain that was their leader, and he wondered at the strangeness they must seem to others. He looked at his mottled hands, with nothing to hold but thin air.

CHAPTER NINETEEN

THE ROUTE TO the river was mostly a matter of taking the road, then a tiny fork that led East once you reached Pauper's Bridge, but even that was too much for Celestaine's nerve after she saw the second rider make them from a point near the horizon, then ride off quickly back the way they had come. They may not be wanted for themselves in particular but the centaur plus the Yorughan might be too much of a talking point somewhere, and her general unease about minding the non-combatants started to take an ugly turn towards dread. Riding with warriors with only their skins to worry about was easy compared to this, and it could only get worse as they came to more populated areas.

Once they had paused for a rest beyond noon she took them away from the obvious route and on a line that ought to bring them to the riverbank by nightfall, south of the Islets Dock. The lands between them and their goal were hunting country, sparsely wooded with many thickets, rocky slopes and broad rolling hills. There were few settlements and nothing notable. As soon as they were out of sight of the road she felt better. But they had only been going a half hour when Heno whistled from the front of the line.

She moved up and fell into step with him.

"Look," he pointed at the ground. There were many prints of people and animals, the ruts of some wheels that had passed across their way, moving in the same general direction.

She studied them for a moment. "These are only a day or two old. They've gone, anyway. Looks like two carts."

"Going quick," he said and she found she had to agree. The gaps between strides, the depth and angle of the divots all said the same. She kept their course and was glad when it deviated from the fleeing trackway, but as they crested a hill and began to descend between two scrubby strips of woodland she felt the hair on her neck prickle and then smelled something burnt as the wind came their way from the north. The woods looked suddenly like a canyon but to alter course would only take them miles out of the way and it was getting late. The river was down one more and one more again small valley by her reckoning. They could easily make it in an hour. If they made it at all.

"Go look," she said to Heno. "I will keep on this way. Rejoin as soon as you can."

He nodded and swung off to their left, his stride lengthening out into the true Yorughan fast march that was almost the running speed of an average human. Within a few moments he had vanished into the shadows beneath the trees.

"Where is he going?" asked Horse.

"Scouting," Celestaine replied, trying to sound light about it so she didn't scare the little one. "We'll go on to the river."

The centaur, a creature of few words, said nothing. On her back Kula yawned. Bukham, the trader, asked, "What's he looking for? Do you think there's trouble?"

"I don't like to be surprised," Celestaine said. "But no trouble."

"If he's not here won't we struggle if someone, you know, if they come like this morning?"

"No," Celestaine said. "We've got Nedlam. And I haven't lost the use of my arms yet."

"What happened to that man, though, that wasn't either of you," he continued, not taking any hint to let it drop so that she fizzed with annoyance, and the urge to hit him ran suddenly through her in a way that meant she had to wait before she spoke again.

"He had a change of heart, that's all that matters. If he hadn't then they'd all be dead by now. Is that a better outcome for you?"

"But how do you know they'd be dead and not us? You don't know that. I mean, to start with it wasn't like we were all winning straight out. It looked quite outnumbered. In a way."

"Quiet," Nedlam growled from the back of the line, though her voice had a carry to it that suggested large bears had been in mind when she was made. "You talk too much."

Celestaine was grateful when he did stop, though she heard him muttering to Murti afterwards. She didn't want to explain that it was actually harder not to kill them. She and her friends were a warband, when you came down to it. If they hadn't got a job to do, they'd be a lot of trouble themselves. The itch that had made her take to the road in the first place was gone now, but it would be back after a week on her arse in a chair. Now, on the other hand, she was full of herself and alive in a way that she knew would never come without some danger and some difficulty. Her only problem was that she wasn't sure any more whether she was to protect Lysandra and Kula from others or the rest of the world from them. She had a strange feeling it was the latter and that Wanderer had known this from the start; why else would he put a flea in Deffo's ear? And why would Deffo, most keen of all not to see battle, be so delighted to recruit her? Not that she'd seen much of him since the bush incident... not that...

She became aware of a figure walking on a parallel course to them which trotted forwards as soon as she noticed it, huffing and bent over like an old man on his last legs—the sickly twin to Murti's able vigor.

"Hullo, Deffo."

"Avast. Doing well. Came to tell you I've got a boat but you're too far south. It can't come to the banks down here, they're too shallow and reedy. You'll have a time getting bogged down. Need to make it a bit north and then it's all good."

"I'll turn once we reach Lampwold Chase. We can stay on the hillside."

"Good. Good good good. Just, close to the treeline."

"The chase is open land, easy to cross. What's wrong with it?" She had a sinking sensation that almost instantly became anger. "Deffo, what are you not telling me?"

"Nothing. Nothing. Probably nothing. Let's keep a good jog up. Doing nicely." He kept up with them at the back, last but Nedlam.

Celestaine sighed and her hands automatically checked her sword and daggers. The afternoon was pleasant, but it had become grey and misty and visibility was shortening all the time. They reached the end of the woodland on the right and beyond it she saw only grassy and rocky hillocks rising slowly into the murk. The sun was a flat disc in a flat sky. As she glanced at it there was a flicker, as though a large leaf had blown past it high in the air and blotted it out for a moment. She looked again. Nothing.

They walked on. After a few more minutes Heno returned at a jog. He gave Deffo a scornful glance and then said.

"I found the carts. Broken, burned. Couple of dead men, all burned, no weapons. Oxen and those long-leg goat things, lunnoxes—nothing left, only blood. Lots of scorching. Looks like about ten people including at least one child escaped. Headed to the road and up that way. Dropped a few things."

"Deffo?" She turned accusingly, but there was nobody there. Of course there wasn't. "Dammit." She thought for a moment. "Burned like your magic?"

Heno shook his heavy head. "Burned like fire."

She felt a draught of air against her cheek, cool and light with mist.

"Analysis?" Because she had to ask. Even though she knew of only one thing that flew and used fire and ate large ground animals she was fairly sure that the five dragons the Kinslayer had concocted were dead. Vermarod the Invincible had died by her hand at Bladno and was now a wayside tavern called the Skull Cup. Another had joined a Kelicerati colony and was out of the dragon business for all intents and purposes. She remembered the parasitic grubs that had replaced its eye with a shudder of revulsion. Other monsters had roamed the world before and after, of course, but it was rare to see one near the Middle Kingdoms, of any kind. Bounty hunting had taken them all to adorn the walls of wealthy patrons.

Heno shrugged. "Better take cover."

"I don't think there is any," she replied. The woods were a death trap, even when damp; the open land doubly so. They were miles short of the river and even if they did reach it, bogs notwithstanding, there was nothing about a riverboat that was easier to defend. The mist made it impossible to see—but that went both ways, she thought, wondering. She turned back to walk beside Horse and ask her advice only to find her scanning the skies, tulip ears wobbling all around at the sides of her head, spear already hefted for casting in her hand. Lysandra and Kula were on foot, walking behind her with Murti and Bukham, Nedlam walking backwards to be a set of eyes facing the way they came but keeping the pace even as they went downslope into the scrubland of the valley.

"What is it?" Celestaine called up to the centaur.

"Some kind of Ur-beast," she said, using the word for the first creations that had come into the world, when it was new. "It is not hungry, just curious."

A little of the tension went out of Celestaine's shoulders. "We need to get away from it."

"Big hunting territory," Horse said. "You will not avoid it any time soon."

"Is it going to attack us?"

"Depends if we go close to the nest."

Suddenly Celest found herself with a small girl attached to one leg. She looked down at Kula, halted in place by the light weight, the tight grip and the intent look in the child's face, eyes like dark saucers beaming up at her with excitement and more animation than she'd ever shown. "Not now," Celestaine began to say, realising it was useless, wondering how to deal with a deaf child, when Lysandra came forward and took Kula's hand. Kula abandoned Celestaine promptly and gazed trustingly up at Lysandra. Lysandra looked Celestaine in the eye and said in faultless Traveller, "She can see it. She wants to lead the way."

A whoosh of air interrupted them. Splatters of water struck Celestaine's cheek and forehead. The tip of a leathery, part-feathered wing, black and brown, sliced down from the cloud bank and cut a short swathe through the mist overhead before it slid upwards into the grey. Two slow whirls of fog spiralled in its wake. Celestaine wiped her face off with her fingers. A faint scent of charred meat came in on the breeze and her stomach growled. *You'll lead it here in a minute*, Ralas would have said, but he wasn't here.

That thing had to be huge, as far as she counted sizes anyway. She looked down at Kula, dancing with eagerness in a way that seemed completely at odds with the circumstances but it was that which convinced her. "Lead on."

"Can you eat 'em?" Nedlam wondered aloud, obviously following Celestaine's gut thoughts.

"The meat of the Utbeast is poisonous to man," Horse said. "And most things, except other Utbeast."

Nedlam snorted in disappointment. "Are you one?"

"I suppose I am," Horse said.

Nedlam shook her head. "Lot of steak on there," and she gave Horse's rump a friendly open-handed whack.

"The hide must be valuable though," Bukham said, tentatively, fear causing him to stammer slightly. "And the er... teeth and bones and whatnot. For souvenirs and medicine and that."

"I used to hunt men for sport," Horse said in a pointed note of protest and a mild warning. "I can start again anytime."

"We are not hunting it," Celestaine said although now that they had started the subject she wondered if that wasn't exactly what they should do. She was watching Kula skipping along at the front of the line, performing a strange leaping jig that at first she'd thought was part of the tracking but later realised was simply playful. Lysandra strode behind her with the free and easy gait of someone in blithe ignorance of just about everything.

We might have to hunt it, she thought, considering that was the only thing left to do if it was already eating livestock and burning people.

They saw the fin-like wingtip again many times over the next hour. It circled them in a way that Celestaine could have sworn was teasing. The whirlpools of mist were greeted by leaps from Kula, her hands outstretched, arms like wings, dipping and curling, Lysandra swooping around her in a perfect mirror. Their faces were gleeful. Sometimes they snarled in passing, pretending to be wild dogs, but only as a joke. The entire thing took place in silence. The *thunka thunka* of Horse's triple-hooves, the patter of their feet and the clink of metal bits of gear were the only muffled sounds.

"Am I the only one who doesn't know what's going on?" Bukham said from behind her after about ten minutes had passed and the game had subsided into ordinary walking again.

"Nope," Celestaine replied.

"Is that some kind of—creature?"

"Yep."

"Is it a dr—"

"Don't say it," Celestaine said, interrupting before he could get the word out.

"We should kill it," Nedlam said, closer than expected, trying to whisper ineffectively. "It will bring a bounty or at least goodwill. I can do it."

They did need it. People couldn't eat diamonds but they would like anyone who saved them from becoming monster food.

"I'm leaving it for now," she said and gestured at the woman and girl. "They seem to like it." She wanted to know what Kula was doing before she made any rash decisions.

"They like it now," Bukham said. "But later, when it's hungry. Then what?"

Celestaine turned sharply and he almost walked into her, as she'd planned. "You talk too much."

"Yes but it's a dragon and it'll eat us sooner or later. Ned's right. It's got to go."

Celestaine unclipped the scabbard and took out her sword, held it to him hilt first. "Go on, then. Have at it."

"No, no, I can't, I…" Bukham looked about, pleadingly, but only Murti's chuckle answered. "If this mist lifts we've had it though," he said, more plaintively. "Haven't we?"

"Maybe," Celestaine said. She let the sword slide back into place with some reluctance but she had no plans other than a vague notion that the Draeyad might be able to spell her spear into taking it out of the air. On the ground they had some kind of chance, although nothing that could pierce a dragon's skin with the possible exception of Horse's spear. She was hoping that better land would turn up, but at that point a consistent squelching that had been getting steadily more present underfoot became the outskirts of a bog, limed in green and with mud thick enough to sink over the ankle. They had reached the river. She took a bearing and decided they must head further north, and was just about to announce it when she found Kula standing before her, hands on her hips, glaring up at her. Lysandra paced up behind her, silently, her hems dragging in the mud.

"Yes?"

Kula was fidgeting again, making gestures that Celestaine suddenly realised weren't the jabbings of an angry child but the jabbings of an angry child who was using a very fast and clever way of talking—to Lysandra, in silence. Because she was deaf. And apparently Celestaine was slow off the mark but now she glanced up at Lysandra for a translation and saw a look of tender, maternal care on the young face as it inclined to Kula. One which quickly became cool and business-like as it moved to her.

"She says it heard you. Because you want to hunt it, it will go away."

"It talked to you?"

Some more fast handwork.

"No talking. Understanding. Heard you on the inside."

"But—if you can talk to it then, ask it where it came from?"

The girl's stare became a little contemptuous.

"She already did. It said it came from the hole in the world."

"And where's that?"

A shrug. Like, who cares about that kind of thing? As if it mattered.

"I think it might matter." Murti had come up behind her while they were talking. She felt startled and angry.

"Are you reading minds now too? Is everyone suddenly able to do it but me?"

He looked up at her for a moment from his stooped position. The mist had made strange dew on his rough beard and the straggly ends of his hair. Behind him the bulky figure of Bukham looked like a clay golem made of two muds, louring in the gloom. "I wander. But you're right. It matters a lot. If there is such a thing we might avoid the necessity of a long journey."

"Just—" Celestaine paused to look about the skies in which nothing figured but the gloaming fog. "Just what is going on here? First you say we're off to find the gods and we have to go far to reach some place but you're short on detail and suddenly this dragon business and fires and Draeyads is making me very keen on the details. I'm not going a step further until you tell me what's on your mind. Wherever it's been. Is going. You know what I mean."

"It's not far to this boat…"

Celestaine turned neatly on her heel and punched Deffo firmly on the jaw, mid-sentence. "Stop sneaking around."

Nedlam guffawed with a sound like a bear coughing. Deffo went over like a felled tree and lay looking up at the barren clouds.

Celestaine straightened, eased her fist. "No more godly fannying around. Now you're here. Now you're not. It's as far to this boat as it is to the moon until I get some answers."

Murti sighed. "I feared that it would come to this but I never thought it would happen so soon."

"What would happen?" Celestaine felt that her head would soon burst from the inside if she had to restrain herself much more. She'd run with the Guardians a few times, that was true, and it had all flowed nicely in the simple necessity of stopping the Kinslayer, but now that was done with all of their goals seemed far muddier and less noble in comparison and she wasn't about to get tangled in bad business. There had been a lot of that. She rubbed her forehead, thinking of the Aethani as Deffo said quietly from his spot on the ground,

"What he did to the gods has made the structure of the world a bit leaky. Stuff seeps through. S'why we need to go see what he did and undo it, or fix it, or fill it in, or whatever it is. Find the gods, find the problem, fix it."

"That sounds… like a good thing?" Celestaine asked, looking to the two of them, rubbing the knuckles of her punching hand gently with her fingertips.

"It's more a case of a necessary thing. Mending." Wanderer said. "Otherwise there'll be a lot more wandering going on and not of a kind that is going to help anyone. Things out of their places, stranded, causing havoc. You've seen it. Need I go on?"

She thought of the Vathesk. Immortal beings from another world, ever-eating, never sated, insane. He need not go on. "I want the world to go back to being stable and a place where people can live in peace. Somehow." She said it aloud, centering herself on that. It had always been her goal, one which she realised as time went on that was possibly only ever to be a dream. A twinge of an emptiness she had been staving off for years pulled at her. She turned to look for Heno and found him standing patiently, watching the whole group of them very closely with his keen eye for the turn of a head or a heart. He glanced at her and nodded.

"We have much to make up for. It's all right to spend a lifetime trying to fix broken things. The world can be remade better than before." He nodded to her and she knew that he was referring to his own past, a butcher, a breaker of beautiful things. No longer.

Her sense of purpose abruptly returned.

She looked down at Kula who was watching her with an expression remarkably akin to Heno's. "What do you recommend, if we want to find this hole?"

The girl turned and pointed north north-west. She flickered her rapid hand signs to Lysandra.

"It is too hard to tell you how to get there because she has not seen the land, but she can see the hole. North, beyond this land's edge."

Celestaine went to Deffo and offered him her hand. She didn't feel like reconciliation but she didn't need it, she realised. "Let's find this boat, then."

"You will say this time how I was helpful, won't you? This time you will say I got it right. They will make a song about this most heroic journey."

"Boat," Celestaine said. "Before something from another world makes us its dinner."

CHAPTER TWENTY

THE SHOP OF Messrs Catt and Fisher was located in Cinquetann Riverport. It was in the wrong direction for the rest of the party but Tricky was able to get them there in double quick time, using Pond Hopper's Drop, a trinket that the Kinslayer had never missed and which had served her admirably well since she'd found it in a shipment of valuables looted out of some Grennish place or other. She'd been in charge of the museum and the armoury at the time, an oversight of the kind anyone only made once, but once was enough.

The Drop was a phial of murky green water and persuading Ralas to take a drop of it was more than she could have stomached what with all the questions that were bound to flow and then the even worse lengthy explanations of how you could move from any watery stop to any other watery stop. Being a Guardian, or demi-Guardian probably helped, she figured, as the phial itself had been wrapped in an alchemist's vellum containing many painstaking notes that ended with a volley of epithets and damnations about its inefficacy so virulent that they had made her eyes water. For her it had worked a treat, however. She had a way with making things work.

So instead of telling him, she'd gone to some great lengths making mint tea at their rest stop and popped a drop in there. From then on all she had to do was be sure to hold his hand.

That had proved harder to engineer, so she'd had to add some wine into the mix. After that it had been a doddle to encourage him to think of some roistering old marching tunes and then sing along as they went. The day was damp and rainy and sure enough within an hour she'd found a muddy puddle of suitable size. From there on it had been a simple matter to be sure to grip his hand and swing his arm in time to the music in such a way that he simply followed her as she jumped into it.

Then they fell through the world and came out with a massive explosion of water, weeds, mud and leaves from a little fishing hole just the eastern side of the riverport town.

Both of them were quite dry, although Tricky had to remove a medium-sized trout from her hood. She watched Ralas closely as he spluttered with surprise, standing in a braced position as if he expected the world to tip him off it when he wasn't vigilant. He was still mostly drunk and she wondered if she could pass off the entire thing as a wine-induced hallucination rather than magery when he turned and threw up suddenly into the long grass beside the pond.

Across the water she saw an old man, Cheriveni by dress with his regular blue tunic and matching trousers, his neat and ever-so pragmatic wide hems and edged pockets: but he was much too ragged for public consumption at any civilised spot. He sat watching them, fishing pole in hand, his jaw slack.

"What ho, squire!" she called merrily in her best weaving voice, meant to mend any social break. "Sorry, sorry!"

She tossed him the trout, which flapped vigorously in objection, but it merely slapped him around the cheeks and then dropped back into the grass at his feet before flipping itself into the dark water.

"Useless old duffer," she muttered, angry that her effort was wasted. People were terrible fools most of the time, in her experience, and while this could be made amusing it was now only annoying. She grabbed Ralas' hand most firmly as his retching stopped and hauled him with her as fast as she could make him go. He felt like skin and bones in her grip, something only a few days short of being scrying material, and she had to bite down on the surge of guilt that came with that comparison. A dead brother who deserved it was one thing, but Ralas hadn't deserved what had happened to him. Fortunately there were bushes close by into which she made sure they disappeared before the old man could get his wits about him. The painful slap of brambles across the face had her saying sharply to Ralas. "Snap out of it, man." And she was herself snapped out of it.

"What. What," Ralas was saying and she began to regret everything she had ever said or done that had brought her to this point.

"You're a terrible soak," she said, covering her lies with more lies which were completely irrelevant as the magic that held him outside death and beyond healing had no effect on regular alcohol intake. She hoped her bluster would act as a smokescreen as well as annoy him out of putting two and two together and figuring she'd conned him. "Drinking all the way. I expect you've even forgotten what day it is and now I have to fish you out of a pond because you can't even walk straight. And you call yourself a friend."

"But, but..." Ralas staggered a little, trying to tug himself free of her but in a way that suggested his heart wasn't really in it.

"There must have been something in the wine," she added, wondering if he really was going to fall for it. "You can't trust anything the clans trade, they're always thinking they can get one over on you. That Forinthi woman definitely looked suspicious to me."

"Forin... do you mean Celestaine? She's the last person to trade... actually she's the last person to have wine. Also, I don't drink. I was only pretending to so that you'd stop pestering me."

He was too sober and in a minute, he was going to start asking questions and then they'd never get on. She took a leap out of logic and sailed far beyond it. "I'll forgive you the terrible things you said about my mother, but you need to make more of an effort. Honestly, you're a burden. Don't you want them to succeed? Who knows what terrors they're already facing if this really is the Kinslayer's unfinished business?" And with that medley she had given it her best obfuscating shot. "There's an inn up the way here. We need to clean up and get organised. This is Cheriveni territory and we need to get in and get out quick. They write everything down, the little pests."

"Anyarrgh," he seemed to be saying, holding his head as if holding it together. "You... can't go there."

She hauled on his arm, setting off at a smart pace so he had to spend all his focus on staying upright. "Don't worry, so sweet of you to think of it but really I have all the right paperwork. Let's just keep going so we can get changed. We've nearly made it. And you could apologise. It was all very hurtful."

The magic of the phial, or the pond water perhaps, had not agreed with him and he was unable to muster a response other than to stumble along with her. His bony arm felt too much like a stick in her hand so she let go of it and went for sleeve instead, of which there was far more than she expected. Nonetheless she was able to keep up a good degree of fishwifery all the way to the small inn, at which point she turned rapidly very convivial and comforting for the benefit of the family who owned it and to whom she was known as a regular, friendly little travelling tailor. They were so pleased to see her that the oddness of her companion and his starveling condition didn't bother them in the slightest once she had explained his bruised face and hobble as the result of single-handedly fighting off a gang of ruffians in the woods and the prospect of a musical evening even had them offering the best room and a hot bath.

Tricky arranged for Ralas to get the bath first and sent for new clothes for him while she chatted and mended a few items here and there which the family had put by in case of her return.

When he came to find her at the fireside of the small receiving room he found her changed into a small, neat red-headed young woman with a freckled face and a snub nose, one hand thrust into a large woollen sock, the other darning neatly across the wooden shape of the egg she held in place. Two others of similar age were close by, folding laundry or forgetting to whilst she regaled them with some story about Rezmire, the southern limit of the known world which may or may not still exist depending on how the war had gone.

To Ralas she didn't look the same, she didn't sound the same, but it was indisputably her, just as the dark seductress, the rogue and the drunken singer were all her. She gave him a look that told him to play along or else, and then introduced him as her cousin and said they were off to the Riverport to look for new buttons and for him, a wife. That gave rise to a lot of giggling and, standing there with his hair wet and in his newly acquired clothing, with a body that would never be healthy, he felt quite foolish for a moment. He was an idiot for even going this far with the burden of his condition which he could never put down and certainly would never impose on someone else. But then, someone like her couldn't possibly be serious about someone like him and clearly she was only using him for some reason that had yet to clarify.

That noted he pulled himself together. Two could play any game. He straightened up and made an affable grin of the kind he offered at the start of every ham performance, said, "She's having you on. It's we who are to be wed."

Her face in that moment was priceless in its genuine surprise, perhaps a hint of respect, that quirky eyebrow she had lifting so far up her forehead it was almost in her hairline, and he felt his heart lift and soar with a streak of sweetness in its wake that boded very ill for him indeed. He almost forgot to add, "Isn't that right, darling?" and to smile at her with a smile that was filled with what he found to be genuine adoration. The thought came to him that he was a dead man who could only lose this fresh stupidity, and the irony made him laugh.

The innkeeper's girls took it for lightness of heart and immediately began a flurry of nuptial chatter that swept all the rest of the day's business temporarily out the window. They didn't escape the excitement of preparations for a celebration dinner for another two hours. By the time they were on the way to the town they had fabricated two not entirely separate histories in which they met in the war, were battlefield sweethearts, attempted to be married but were thwarted by an invasion and had recently met again after months of searching. As neither of them had living relatives they were to wed in the nearest place where they could find a suitable minister. That had been a mistake, Tricky reluctantly thought, as the innkeeper's wife had been only too happy to inform them that the Gracious One Hospice had lately reopened itself as a place of ministry and healing both and as her niece was an understudy there, she would be delighted to make all the arrangements.

Ralas limped along at Tricky's side as they walked in an embattled silence. "I never insulted your mother."

"You insulted someone's mother." Tricky waved him off. "At some point. It's certain."

"What magic was that which you…" He had to pause and smile as they came around a corner and found themselves face to face with a woman coming the other way, a knapsack on her back and a heavy bag in her hand. Behind her the town gates rose, scaffolded but steady, against the sky. Guards were patrolling along the parts of the wall which had been restored.

"It was one of the lesser charms of Luciba the Lazy," Tricky said as though these were common knowledge and of no account. "She never looked the same twice. Bad gambling habit and a terrible loser but she was never arrested and had six husbands all in the same town. Now look. I'm going to do the talking. You stretch your repertoire and do the standing around looking like a tough guy."

Ralas was taken aback. "A cripple with a lute?"

"Any musician that plays like you do has to be pretty tough." She shrugged with a careless manner that made her seem winsomely vulnerable beneath a hard-won streetwise exterior.

"Plays like... what do you mean?" He felt insulted to the core, even as he noted her acting abilities were a little on the nose somehow, as if she had something genuine to hide.

"You know. All sincere ballads and things. Glory songs. Nothing funny. You need more... funny in your act. Like the Far... like bawdy songs. Songs for the common folk."

"What would you know about my 'act'?" For a second he'd been sure she was going to name the 'Farmers of Doubty', the song he had sung to the Kinslayer just before he was killed for the first time, but she couldn't know about that. Bawdy hadn't really done well for him.

She tutted. "Do you know 'Cenella the Vampire's Paramour'?"

"I... is that a drinking song?" He would have bet a day without pain on the fact that he knew mostly every song that was hummed and bowdlerized and badly remembered between any two points on the map but this one didn't ring a bell.

"It's more of a post-drinking song. He lived to suck blood and she lived to... The point is it's very funny."

"You'll have to teach me. But bawdy and roisterous," he said, annoyed with how much he was trying to impress her, "I can do that."

"Good. Find ones with happy endings. People want to feel there's some hope left." She was fiddling with things in her pockets, he could see, looking preoccupied.

As they neared the gate the number of people increased and the road became hemmed in with huts and shelters that had been built in the last few months as refugees gathered at the portside, hoping for news and lingering, still too fearful to attempt returning to wherever they had come from and finding comfort in numbers.

They joined the group of people gathering for entry, and Tricky took out a small scroll from one pocket and undid the ribbon. She kept her travelling hood up, pushed back enough to show her face but also to keep it shaded.

Ralas, in his sensible blue blending-in attire, felt nervous. The Cheriveni were sticklers for protocol, something which set his teeth on edge. In his youth he'd been had up by their magistrates for a failure to present the correct licences for performance within the city limits. Those were days when he'd thought it was a fine life to carry on as a street entertainer, before the war had got close enough to him that he could ignore it no longer. Being here was the strangest sensation for those days seemed very close but also untouchably far away. Memory was like that, it comforted, reliving old feelings, and then it hurt as the present compared to them and fell down flat on its face. In every person nearby he saw the same, resigned expression of expected disappointment, though this could have had something to do with the pedantry of the gate watch, whose lips moved steadily as they read everyone's papers.

One woman caught his eye unintentionally and was captured by the shocking bruising of his face, lingering with a moment of alarm that sent her looking all around and down the road for potential attackers even though she was next in line and the wall was policed by a steadily marching patrol who showed no care. He passed a few moments looking at all the Oerni faces around him from various trading families, thinking of Bukham and wondering how he was getting along.

Meanwhile Tricky shuffled around and attempted some information-gathering small talk. When she turned back to him she opened her gloved palm and showed him some worn leather thongs with wooden rings on, a charm made from a mouse's foot and two copper scits. She shook her head in disgust.

"These people have nothing."

A moment and a few gliding moves later and she had replaced

the treasures in their allocated pouches and pockets, or at least that was what he assumed she was doing. Then it was their turn at the gate and the guard poring over their scroll, holding it three inches from her face.

Behind him he heard a muttering of surprises, quickly suppressed to levels below official eavesdropping, but he distinctly caught a woman whispering, "Look it I found inna pocket! A polly." A flurry of "me too" followed and the air of despond was replaced by a subtle, silent mixture of glee and alarm, the luck astonishment and happiness vying with terror at the inexplicability of it all.

Tricky, eyes fixed on the guards, had a curl to her mouth that was full of satisfaction. She caught him staring at her as they were pushed through the wicket gate and sent on to the open road into the town. "Polly pockets. It's a good game, hm?"

He nodded, genuinely surprised and briefly feeling something he could hardly name because it had been so long since he felt it: "It's a great game." Joy.

The broad, muddy road led from the gate and then rapidly branched out. Tricky took them past the Hospice. "Let's get the state of play, eh?" she said, as they neared the structure. Ruined by Heart Taker white fire, the stonework of the original building was still silvered and shattered, but within it a more modest wooden structure had been erected and painted in white and gold. The Gracious One Hospice was back in business. Ralas wondered what they'd make of him, was tempted to go ask, just in case there was someone who could offer him hope—but then again, it was more likely to get him killed if they discovered he was without remedy. They passed it, moving through places where much hard labour had made homes nearly grand again, the colours of the footmen and servants washed and bright against the awnings and bustle of the market streets. A terrible aching clawed at his heart and the lute banged his bony spine. As if she read his mind he found Tricky touching his arm in a conspiratorial fashion.

They passed a man playing spoons and a woman twanging a simple harp made from a broom and a barrel. They were doing a fair version of 'All The Fair Lads of Kheri', and he longed to pitch up and join in, but his broken feet and his sore face told him it wasn't a good idea.

They passed food stalls and alcoves filled with tiny tea stands where people of all sizes and shapes bent close to each other to hear business and make deals under the guard of the general hubbub. Rats scampered through the rubbish and they were nearly barged over by a gang of children, each with two sticks— one sharp and pointed, the other heavy and bearing dangling rat bodies tied by the tails—as they chased these down with single-minded lust.

"Good to see the nippers doing something fun and productive," he ventured.

"Indeed," she said and turned into a much less crowded street where scaffolding was up against one in three buildings. Their destination was a small but tidy and notably whole house near the middle. He looked up and read the freshly painted lettering on the sign. *Catt & Fisher, apothecaries, physicians, notaries of law, layers of note, dealers in the unusual.*

"I'll do the talking," she said. "You just keep an eye on everything and let me know if you see anything untoward."

"I know them," he said. "Untoward is their middle name."

She cocked her head. "You know them?"

"Met them at…"

"Not now." She put her finger to his lips. "Haven't got time and don't want to get caught talking here. Thing is that Fishy and I have a little bit of history and I need you there to act as a bodyguard."

"Me? You need someone like Nedlam, surely?"

"No no. She's a violence lodestone. Bringing her would be like asking for it. But you, they'll never do anything to you. I mean, look at you. You just stay quiet and pay attention and if I should happen to hand you anything while we're in there keep hold of it."

"Aw, you're not going to steal—"

She had her finger up against his mouth again. "Not now," she said, and opened the door.

A bell tinkled as they came into a room that managed to be both cluttered and dim, making him pause to adjust for safety's sake amid low hanging bunches of herbage while Tricky slipped onwards like a smoothly sailing boat towards a glass countertop. Behind it a tall, old man with a face made grizzly by black stubble that contrasted nicely with his greying hair was fiddling with something laid out in bits on a cloth. All around him shelves were full of objects so diverse Ralas could not have said what most of them were. In spite of the shabbiness of most of them, there wasn't a speck of dust anywhere.

The old man looked up, his long face lengthening as his chin dropped briefly. An air of caution made him straighten up and widen his eyes as his hands quickly rolled up the mat and its knickknacks and stowed them quickly out of sight beneath the counter. His gaze never wavered from Tricky's face and he swallowed a couple of times. "Ah. It's you."

"Delighted to see you too, Fishy," she said as the man sidled out swiftly and went to the door, sticking his head out to check the street before closing it, shooting the bolt and putting his back to it. "Catt about? I've got some interesting items I need an appraisal on. And by some I mean one."

Ralas put his scarf down from his face and peered more closely through the glass counter. "Is that an Oerni whistling pipe?"

"Indeed it is, young man," Fisher said. "Wait. I know your face. That black eye is most distinct—you're the Slayer's bard." He peered at Ralas as though inspecting something for value. "How did you come to be in her—" he nodded at Tricky, "—possession?"

"I'm not actually a possession," Ralas began but was interrupted.

"Fishy." Tricky tapped her nails on the counter-top impatiently as Fisher came back from the door and began to slide the window blinds down one at a time. "I've brought him to ensure fair play. You've met him and clearly you trust him. I need a disinterested man of judgement involved. Such is the quality of the item."

"Such is the risk of it, you mean," Fisher said. "And not forgetting the fact I vowed to kill you next time I saw you. So more of a witness. Though who he's going to tattle to I don't know. The Slayer, perhaps?" He gave her a withering look and Ralas felt queasy. During this talk Fisher had been moving towards to the back of the shop where another door was ajar to a dark hallway. He called through this with an effort not to sound urgent. "Catt! Catty! She's ba-ack."

"Who?"

"Yer mother!" Tricky called loudly enough to be heard on the street and laughed. "Favourite aunt. Love of your life. Bringer of all the lovely gifties. Director of Treasure Central."

There was a brief silence. Fisher looked up through a thick bush of eyebrow, his broad nostrils flaring. He glared at Tricky. "You're only on remand because I can smell what you've got."

"Proof positive, I think, that there need be no bad blood over the loss of that special item."

His gaze became darker and Ralas thought the counter and various of the loose objects around the room shook slightly. "Only if you're giving it away and I doubt that." There was a brief pause. "Do you still have it?"

Tricky grinned. "You're not having it and neither is anyone else."

Some of the tension between them seemed to lessen. At that moment footsteps shuffled behind the door and it opened to reveal a second old man, slightly shorter and more rounded than the first, his jeweller's lenses set high on his forehead holding back a shock of near white hair, his expression as affably concerned as Fisher's was acid with disapproval.

He glanced at them and then held out his arms in a dramatic display of welcome. "Oh, madam mischief, what fell wind has blown you back into our fortunate lives? And Ralas, the singer of fate, nightingale of Nydarrow. A rare privilege indeed, I feel. How very unusual to see the two of you conspiring together in our humble domicile, I do hope that you were not followed here by unkind men keen on pressing home their lawsuits against your light-fingered appreciation of certain heirlooms as per your last visit?" And with this he cast a meaningful look at Tricky, who was standing with her hand on her hip, grinning at him.

"Hey Catty," she said. "How's the old hock shop?"

"Let's do this in the back," Fisher said and made a gesture at Catt to shoo him back and usher them both through at once.

The room at the back was smaller and curated with exacting care. It was quite full from floor to ceiling with labelled boxes and shelves groaning with the clutter of a huge number of small objects. Strings and pulleys held rolls of cloth and bulging sacks up close to the rafters. Bits of taxidermy in various states of repair twirled idly in the draft as the door was closed. Dry and warped, a stuffed parac bared its huge rodent teeth in a yellow rictus, defiantly resistant to any semblance of life but determined to carry on regardless. Ralas knew how it felt.

He heard Fisher muttering about artefacts of making as Catt returned to his carved throne—a seat with eagle talon feet which twitched as he and Tricky made their entrance, and then reached out covetously to grip the rug the chair was set upon, as though they fully expected it to be stolen out from under them.

"I know you're sore about the thing," Tricky said, taking a long breath as both the Doctors eyed her with deep suspicion from their position side by side. "I know I promised it to you, Fu-Fisher. But this thing I've got now is just as good. Well, nearly. It's probably as good. It definitely held something that's just as good. But it needs expert eyes on it to be sure. And in return for your esteemed and very valuable help here I'm willing to part with it. By my honour."

"Ha!" Fisher barked. "Let's see it and believe it later once you're long gone."

"Now then," Catt put out a hand and gently touched Fisher on the arm. "Patience. Although, my dear, you do owe us a very large sum of money for the destruction of property, trespass with violence and representation of your good self in the Cherivell Court system by the esteemed lawyers you see before you." He reached over to the table at his side where inkwells, pens and papers were scattered in vast piles and, with delicate precision, used thumb and forefinger to extract a leaf of paper from near the bottom of one pile. It was long and filled with rows of numbers and lines of minute writing. "Your bill, if I may." He presented it to her with a little flourish of pride in his work. "Oh, and here at the bottom, the extra for the laundering of Fisher's second best pair of trews. I'm not charging you for the smashed Egg of Foreboding Visions although I think you'll find there's precedent for that. It did break after you left but it was definitely stressed beyond endurance by events surrounding your presence and I would think it deeply generous if you would consider making an offer for, let's say, half its value in the current market."

"Yeah, thanks." Tricky snatched the paper, screwed it up one-handed and stuffed it down the front of her shirt. "So." She pushed her hood back and withdrew from her cloak a tiny bundle of unpleasant looking sackcloth. "Get your multifarious whatsits in order, and put up some wards," she said. "I've got artefact stuff to unload."

Catt was leaning so far forwards he was nearly tumbling out of his chair. "Isn't that the Wrap of..."

"It is. So push the furniture back as well, because this thing is big." She backed up and Ralas went with her, right to the bookshelf behind him.

"Wait, wait good lady!" Dr Catt exclaimed, holding out a hand to forestall her undoing the parcel. "I must admit a slight sense of unease at what may be about to transpire. We have, it is true, held several objects of considerable power at our shop before but..."

"But me no buts," she said, although she stayed her hand as Dr Fisher worked hard to push the huge chair back to the wall, dragging the rug with it, Catt still in position. "I know very well what you've got squirreled away and as a fellow collector of antiquities and interests I'm telling you that you have to see this and you have to see it now. As a gesture of goodwill just for taking a looksie, I will be paying you a substantial sum, to whit—" and she slipped from her glove a large ruby which Ralas recognised as being from the dress of Lysandra. It had been on the bodice, over the heart, and aside from its remarkable size it shone with an inner fire that twisted and twirled idly, strong enough to lend a scarlet glow to the lower angles of both their faces.

Dr Catt was out of the throne like a shot, his self-satisfied face suddenly there over her hand, his lenses flapping down as he flicked them into place. "I didn't think there were any of these left in existence. See, Fishy! A serpent's eye."

"A serpent's eye indeed," Fisher said, reaching out and then pausing to look up at Tricky. They shared a glance that spoke volumes and Ralas didn't need to know the details to see that the death wish was off the table now and something reluctant and allegiant had taken its place.

"May I?" Dr Catt asked, looking plaintively up at Tricky without lifting his head, eyes at their maximum swivel as though he couldn't bear to remove himself from the jewel's allure.

"At your own risk," she nodded.

Dr Catt held out a hand towards Fisher. "Glove."

"Is that a good thing ruby or a bad thing ruby?" Ralas asked, not certain he wanted the answer but feeling left out.

"It's an eye from the time before men, when creatures made of gemstones ruled the under-crust of the world and dragons fought over whatever was left on top," Fisher said, using both hands to fit a kidskin glove precisely over the fingers and thumb of Dr Catt's outstretched hand. Then he cast his gaze more circumspectly over Ralas and a slight twitch betrayed his unease.

"What does it do?" Ralas asked as Dr Catt held the stone between thumb and forefinger and leant back. He held it up to the light from a brightly glowing sphere which lit the room and which Ralas had assumed to be a lamp, but which was now revealed to be simply a ball of light without a tether.

"Watches," Fisher and Tricky said at the same time, then glanced at each other with a lift of the nose. Fisher continued. "It watches until a time is right, and then it makes the way for something to happen." He held up his hand and waggled it like a fish swimming or a snake slithering. "Depends on how it's used and who by."

Catt slowly brought the stone down and pushed his lenses back until they sat high on his brow. He looked solemnly at Tricky. "Where did you find this?"

"Charm's gone, huh?"

"Whatever it was set to look for it has seen done. Nothing left in it. It's ready for another spell, should one ever find a mage capable and willing to risk their neck on it." His nose twitched at the end and he folded the stone carefully into his fist. "This is really just the fee?"

"If you can do some reading for me."

"So—you have…"

Tricky held up her hand to forestall him and fixed him with a direct stare. "I have the whole damn snake."

"A moment, if you would." Dr Catt beckoned to Fisher and they went into a huddle as far away as they could get, which wasn't far. Tricky made a big show of looking in any other direction, tapping her foot and changing her weight from one leg to the other. Ralas could not even hear them whispering, only see their cramped gestures and emphatic head motions. After a minute or two they straightened up and turned.

"Gentlemen," she said and then with a flourish threw the object in her hand forward, allowing it to unwrap its own bindings on the way. They both had to step back smartly, flattening themselves to the wall, as most of the remaining floor space was suddenly taken up by the black, ugly shape of the lidless coffin. Whatever they'd been discussing died into the silent moment that followed.

Ralas stared. Magic was always there in so many places, small and great, but seeing this scale of it at work robbed him of words. He was almost frightened of Tricky in that moment. She was so casual with it.

"We need the help of Zivalah," Catt said after a while had passed. "Go get her, would you, Fishy?"

Dr Fisher showed no inclination to move, but he cleared his throat and a few seconds later he slid past the box and hurried out of the door. The latch clicked and the key turned at his back. Dr Catt fumbled behind him along his workbench and there was an audible click. A hum filled the air, quiet but insistent and he relaxed, reaching out his gloved fingers to run them over the box's rim and then over some of its heavily embossed carving. "My my. This is true ebony, hardened in dragonfire."

"I want to know what it all means," Tricky said, pointedly ignoring any reverence that might have been going around. "Every word, glyph and pictogram."

"Old Tzarkish," Catt said, confident. "The written form that goes back to the first humans. That's why we've gone for the local expert. Zivalah does tattoos now but she was apparently quite a matriarch back in the day."

Tricky balled up the old scrap of sackcloth and tucked it in one of her pockets. "How long is it going to take?"

Catt stood back, lips pursed forwards in a universal gesture of assessment on a task of great difficulty. "I don't know." Then he glanced up. "I thought you knew Tzarkish?"

"I know enough of it not to want to risk reading something that's not meant for my eyes," she said, tapping the box with one finger. "They have a way with traps and mind bombs that I don't care to risk my sanity over."

"But we do?" Catt put his heavy hand over his heart. "I'm affronted. I thought we were friends."

"The whole snake," Tricky said, unmoved. "Hm?"

"I'd have to see it, of course," Dr Catt said.

Ralas realised that the serpent's eye was gone from Catt's hand. He must have put it away, he thought.

Tricky nodded, and then they heard the return of footsteps outside, in a great hurry. The latch popped at the same moment as the key turned in the lock and Fisher burst into the room, breathless, a look of surprise and concern in his face. "She's gone. Left town."

"What? When did this happen?" Catt frowned, his hands clenching into fists.

"Just now, apparently," Fisher said, looking at the box and then at Tricky with clear misgiving. "Where did you get that?"

"Hathel Vale," she said. "Where the fire has gone out. Now, are you going to read this or am I going to take my snake elsewhere?"

"As if there was an elsewhere," Dr Catt said, drawing himself up to his full height and looking faintly green with the effort. "We shall read it. Come back later."

"No, thanks," she said. "We have a lot of appointments far away very soon. Come on, I know you can read it, traps or no."

"Meaning you think these traps are for…"

"Sure, whatever," she breezed on, waving a hand in the manner of a queen dismissing a minion. "Don't say the word and don't think the thought. You, as ordinary men of

Cherivell," she gave Fisher a long, significant look and a pause, "well-educated but so far without any divine intervention, you're going to be all right with it. Probably. For a Guardian it would be dangerous. But it'd be pretty unlikely the Remaker of Bones and the Gravewife have much of an interest in small-town market lawyers. Apothecaries. Bankers. I forget, what is it exactly that you do?"

Ralas couldn't miss the condescension of the last part but although he didn't feel what threat it might hold something had impressed the doctors: they gave each other a nod and Catt began to slowly circle the box, head to the side, studying. Fisher stood back, surveying with what looked like one eye half shut and the other fully shut. Tricky took out a tiny dagger the size of a finger from her sleeve and removed her gloves, carefully using the point to clean her nails.

"Here's the start, Catty," Fisher said after about a minute. Catt moved around the box to join him and they fussed with their lenses, moving, studying, conferring and moving on at very brief intervals. "You do the reading. I'll write it down."

Fisher wrote Catt's pontifications down on a slate, adding alternatives and interpretations, rubbing them out with the ball of his thumb very thoroughly once each one was puzzled through. Ralas and Tricky watched them work. Talking seemed sacrilegious so Ralas said nothing. After a while Tricky went out and returned with teas and griddlecakes. Ralas would have dozed off if not for the constant aching of his bones. At last the two men stopped, exhausted and pale with effort.

Catt cleared his throat and patted his chest gently. "The casket you see before you is the holding maze of the greatest creation of the Tzarkomen necromancers, into which they have poured, literally, their heart's blood."

"Ten thousand women, girls and babies, slain and raised in one form. Almost an entire people sacrificed to create a single being of unsurpassed capacities," Fisher said quietly, head down, hands composed, rubbing his chalky fingertips together.

Catt nodded eagerly, his enthusiasm for potency overrunning. "A creature intended for a great purpose beyond the realms of…"

Tricky held up her hand. "Just the facts, gentlemen please."

"The being in this box was charmed with the serpent jewels to become bound to him and to serve his purposes—whatever they were. There is a sub-clause, of a kind, which prevents it from turning on its people of origin hidden right down at the bottom of the head end and disguised as a prayer. At least they had some circumspection."

"Godly puppet," Fisher said, looking grey with fatigue. "But… why on earth would they give him such a…"

"To get him to leave them alone," Ralas suggested. "Because not even death can stop him." He looked at Tricky. "It can stop him, can't it. If he's the one who's dead?"

Dr Catt broke in. "Where is she? Did you get this from her?" He held up the red gem.

"Don't know and yes."

"So then she's bound to someone already." Catt sighed, deflating somewhat, pushing away his scrying lens so that he could rub his sore eyes. "If not him, then who?"

"Don't know, doesn't matter," Tricky said briskly. "Good job. Here's your snake." She was suddenly brandishing a beautiful jewelled strap composed of a good number of the scintillating stones from Lysandra's dress, twined together with the golden wire that had bound them in their original positions. As she modelled it for them, draping it across her own arm, it moved of its own accord in a soft, unmistakable ripple as though a long-lost memory was attempting to reconnect it with the world of the living.

Catt leaped backwards, or tried to. Instead he crashed heavily against the bench, gasping for air. "Can't stand snakes!"

She tore it in two and put the halves on the workbench where they twitched but otherwise remained suitably mineralised.

"Only to prove the puissance," she said. "Thanks. See you later."

"Wait, where are you going?" Fisher asked, working a handkerchief across his brow. He gestured vaguely at the box. "Take it with you. Please." There was more than appeal in his gaze as he looked at her. Ralas read there something much more important.

"Pleasure, darling," Tricky said, "I have to see some Tzarkomen about a dog anyway." She reached out with her scrap of rag as though she were going to use it to take a hot iron from a fire. A second later she was wrapping the thimble-sized black casket up and a second after that it had vanished about her person somewhere. For the life of him Ralas could not have said what she'd done with it but the look of relief on Fisher's face was matched only by the wistful sadness in Catt's.

"We could put it in a Vat of Holding, Fishy," he began but a look from his friend quieted him. "Ah, no. Maybe not. Perhaps it's best that way as you say."

Within moments Ralas and Tricky were both outside in the street again. The bell tinkled merrily at their backs. In its aftermath they could just hear Catt's voice complaining about snakes and devious vixens from the nether pits of hell. He sounded very pleased with himself.

"Mission accomplished. Family feud laid to rest. I think it's time to get a commemorative tattoo," Tricky said, straightening her cloak and tossing her head so that her dark red hair flowed out into the breeze. "This way."

"Wait. What?" Ralas set off after her, struggling to keep up as she set off to the markets at a pace. He wasn't sure what he'd witnessed. He recalled a vague notion that Doctor Fisher was not a Cheriveni antiquities dealer or a lawyer, but the Guardian Fury, but he couldn't for the life of him remember where he'd picked that up from. It was as though some veil was drawn over it. As soon as it occurred to him it darted away again and he was filled with doubt.

CHAPTER TWENTY-ONE

"ARE YOU SURE she's gone?" Catt waited as Fisher held the seashell to his ear and balanced the tip of it against the wall closest to the street.

"Gone," Fisher said, taking the shell down and replacing it on the high shelf over the workbench.

They both of them leaned on the workbench for support and then Fisher reached underneath it and pulled out a little chest. He placed it on the bench and opened it. A gentle radiance of rosy gold filled the room as they both looked down on the Diadem of the Forinthi, which had once adorned the crown that Wall had taken from the Kinslayer. The gem in its midpoint had a similar glow to the eye of the serpent which Catt now held up towards it, but there was no mistaking the fact that the god-given blessings it was capable of were gone. Even so, its history and its possible restoration made it the most valuable object of their entire collection. As one they sighed, and then Catt lovingly wrapped it up and put it away. He set out the jewels that Tricky had left behind.

"I do believe that it may be time to dust off the Sheep Chariot," Catt said.

"Where there's a will there's a relative?"

"This created woman must have had many interesting Tzarkomen relatives, probably all dead. They may have the other half of that snake. Or knowledge of its whereabouts. Finding so many pieces of it does hint at a great ability with detection I had never heretofore expected of them."

There was a knock at the door and someone called in, "Oi! Are you available for makin' a bill of sale? Hello?"

They ignored it.

"Do you think she gave us half deliberately?" Fisher asked, nearly hypnotised by the sway of movement inside the gemstones. These had once been part of a celestial being, maybe even the one that the Forinthi jewel had come from and there remained the chance that if they found every single part of it, they could put it together again. Minus one small segment, of course, otherwise said being may not find itself fully content with remaining in the little Cherivell shop not-on-display. One part was miraculous. But the whole thing...

The light danced over Doctor Fisher's long, solemn features like sunlight through water and gave him the illusion of a certain underwater fluidity.

"I'm reasonably sure she did, so that's more or less an invitation from the gods themselves, is it not?" Doctor Catt said, polishing a facet here and there with a fine cloth he drew from his pocket.

"And the labyrinth in Nydarrow?"

It was as though Catt hadn't even heard him. "I think you must head for Tzark. I shall brave the barrows and warrens of the Wretched Darkness and any salivating serpentine sorceries within. *The Book of All Things* is out there too and we cannot leave such things to the vagaries of the illiterati. You must obtain it before there is a disaster. Yes. It would be a terrible thing if it fell into the wrong hands."

Fisher looked at him in surprise. "We're splitting up?"

"Needs must, Fishy. Think on. There are already at least three Guardians abroad with similar destinations in mind. You read the left hand side of that coffer. It was very specific that the *Book* is beyond the Tzarkona Gate, in the south, in the forbidden place. Imagine—" He stood back and sketched the scene out in thin air with his hands as though he could already see and hold the precious item. His face was alight. "*The Book of All Things*; the past, the present and the future all within its leaves. What a firenight storytime that could make, eh Fishy? And what insights, what clues to the location of so many more treasures of the ancients! There would be nothing we could not find!" He closed the imaginary book reverently and set it aside on the desk, giving it a pat. Then his tone turned business-like and sharp as though he were ready to debate against the finest scholars in open court. "Now, let's see what I can take with me. Hand down the inventory."

Fisher took up an actual old ledger from the shelf nearby and opened it by one of its many ribbons. "Grey, for the most powerful items." He tapped his finger on the page where plenty of space was still left between the neatly ruled margins.

Catt surveyed the page listing their premium items with satisfaction. "Capital. No end to the ambiguity of power, is there? Let's start with the Endless Satchel."

CHAPTER TWENTY-TWO

TRICKY WAITED IMPATIENTLY for Ralas at the end of the market's busiest thoroughfare. "Come on, you can do better."

"Tell that to my feet," Ralas said, puffing with effort and the pain of rushing his boots over the cobblestones. He glanced up to see her clocking two strolling guardsmen and took advantage of the time it took them to enjoy a moment of respite before he was bundled off past the wooden stands of fresh produce and bleeding, fly-swarmed meats—which were uncomfortably reminiscent of several parts of his anatomy—to an alcove of fortune tellers. A Grennishman like a scrawny spiderish dwarf, thick in the middle but long and spindly in the arm, looked up hopefully as they came in, then quickly clomped a bowl down over his divining snails and pretended to be busily occupied with something on his seat. Tricky gestured at the empty chair beside his stall.

"Where is she?"

The Grennishman looked with one set of eyes, then the other set on the side of his head. His single antenna bent itself in a leisurely arc and scratched his head. He shrugged, moving some runestones quietly about with his other limb. A hasty movement and some swearing made all three of them dart a look to the back of the painted tenting behind the chair and then in almost the same moment Tricky had hurdled the chair and punctured the canvas wall, dragging a dagger-blade through it and stepping through the new hole to grab someone on the other side.

"No, no no! I no know anything!" came a voice struggling to pronounce words and doing a bad job of it. It was female, but on the lower, rougher end of the scale, with a burr that suggested smoking. "Please you let me go. I must to go home."

"Don't hurt her!" cried the Grennishman almost in the same instant, reaching under its table to produce a slender knife that it waved furiously in Ralas' face. "Thieves! Bandits!"

Ralas backed away, his hands in the air, wondering what he was expected to do. A look around revealed thunderous faces peering from several alcoves and a bustle in the larger street suggested that guards were going to be soon on the way. He looked back, nervously, to find himself alone, no signs of Tricky and only the empty flaps of the shredded tent blowing open in the breeze to reveal a collection of small boxes upturned, bright coloured pigments scattered on the ground and no sign of anyone. "I… uh…" he said and then with a sense of desperation, seeing a large Oerni woman with a wooden cudgel coming around the side of the cheiromancer's door, dodged around the chair and thrust himself through the canvas gap.

On the other side ran a common lane that linked the fortune tellers to the stalls behind them via a shared avenue filled with crates and boxes. From his left a man with a sledgehammer was coming out of the back of a small smithy so without thinking Ralas turned the other way and ran, seeing by the marks of bright pink and dots of blue powders scattered here and there that he was probably going the right way. His conviction was confirmed when he ran around the corner at the end of the lane and, instead of coming out between the stands into the square, he went around the same corner, again, and was enveloped for a moment in complete darkness.

When light returned he found himself inside the smoky bar-room of a minuscule tavern, his head almost knocking on a low beam, his boots on boards and straw instead of the road's paving. Someone was puffing cherry and rum tobacco. A hubbub of apparently distant clinking, drinking and chatter managed to be at once far away and filling up his ears with a fug of sound that blotted out every other conversation in the room.

Before him stood Tricky, panting, and with her the taller and more miserable figure of someone he supposed was Zivalah, a middle-aged Tzarkomen, with more bones in her hair and amulets around her neck and arms than he'd ever seen anyone wear. Despite the crowds and the noise they seemed to be in a tiny envelope of calm all their own.

"I not ever go back," Zivalah was saying insistently, adding several sharp gestures. Her dark skin was pocked with scars and tattooed everywhere with designs that led the eye one way, then another. He recognised the twisting, turning lines that doubled back and ended abruptly as something he'd seen before. Across her eyes a broad white stripe of paint stood out, applied with apparent carelessness in a single splash, so bright that the rest of her, besides her eyes, seemed almost to vanish into a shadow.

Tricky glanced at him. "Welcome to the Inn At The End Of The World. Always only a corner away."

Ralas tried to see the other patrons but no matter how he stared they remained out of focus, merely shapes that suggested pirates and soldiers, ladies in strange clothing, the long legs and beaked head of a Hegula dipping down from an unlikely height beneath the roof. Their conversations folded in on one another, no word distinguishable.

At one end of the room there was the suggestion of a bar. He longed for the ability to drink something strong but then Zivalah caught sight of him and the tremor of anxiety that had made her quake beneath Tricky's insistence turned to a stillness so profound she could have been turned to stone. Her expression of irritation and fear changed to open puzzlement and then she stretched out a hand and made a sign in front of him. He felt a distinctive flicker of electrical energy ripple across his skin. It hurt him where his wounds remained but was gone before he could do more than gasp.

"You are not alive." And just like that her difficulty with diction and trouble finding words was gone. She straightened up and put back her shoulders, glanced at Tricky and then stepped forward to examine him more closely. "But you are. Not by Tzarkomen sorcery. By some other means." She looked at Tricky with a fresh curiosity giving her animation an almost friendly air. "Is this your trouble, Darkness?"

"Not really," Tricky said, "He's more of an ongoing issue, although any news is always appreciated."

Zivalah circled him, her study growing more intense. "I have not seen this before. Tzarkomen raised many, many friends and foes but only in the ordinary way. All of them empty vessels."

"Well aware of those, thank you," Ralas said, turning so that she couldn't get behind him. Her stance had become a little predatory. "Definitely not one of those."

"Very different," she agreed. "It is like… like the life in you is undying, but something stops it always. A heart," she held out her hand, palm up, and then stabbed down with the index finger of her other hand right into the centre of it. "Pinned down. It goes right through you. You are Kinslayer's making, hm?"

"Yes," Ralas said. "If all you are referring to is my living situation. The rest of me has nothing to do with him, thankfully."

"I want to know about the Book and the mazagal that your lot made for Re… for the Kinslayer," Tricky said.

"Ahya! That." The Tzarkomen slumped back to her hangdog look and covered her face with inkstained hands. She had long nails, clawlike, sharpened to points and painted black. They dug into her forehead and she was crying as she said, "This is why I will never go back. It is not an ordinary mazagal. It is a Zafiid. A collector. Like the *Book*. But the *Book* was taken. He took it all. After the Tzarkomen now living die there will be no

214

more art. It dies with us. They made it so that he would not destroy us but without the *Book* we are nothing anyway. Just another set of people with a sad story and no power to do more than make little charms. The *Book* is gone. The dead will fall. Only the Zafiid remains."

Ralas didn't understand the distinctions she was making but her misery convinced him that what she claimed had truth in it.

"But he died before he took possession of it," Tricky said.

"It cannot be undone," Zivalah said and her fingernails had dug into her skin deeply enough to draw blood. "All my sisters died for nothing. Nothing. My daughters. My mother. You don't understand. I left them there to carry away the burden." She took her hands down. Tears of white streaked her cheeks.

Ralas watched blood run down her forehead, over her thick, whitened brows and into the creases around her eyes. She blinked and it became a film of pink across the whites, a paler sheen across the dark iris.

"We always send one daughter away," she said. "One to tell, to remember. We always save one. But she has to go and not return. She carries the death guilt with her, so that the Gravewife and the Remaker are clean. She will die in the wilderness and not come back again. This was my duty. But the Zafiid is lost, an empty vessel. We had hoped, maybe, it would become powerful enough to collect him. But now it was for nothing." As she had been speaking the misery and the fear had seeped out of her and with the last words her knees folded and she sat down heavily on her heels and then slumped over to one hip, hands loose in her lap, her face gone slack with loss.

"Maybe," Tricky said quietly, "if we could find this *Book*…"

Zivalah gave the merest shake of her head. "You don't understand. The *Book* was lost at the start of the war. That's why we made her. Because he had proved we couldn't stand against him."

"Where was it last?"

"Caracu, near Ghevera, in the south," Zivalah said. "But you won't find it." She turned her face to Tricky. "End it, Darkness. Friend of the Lost. End it for me now? I have years left to bear this alone. End it." She reached out for Tricky's hands, cowed and pleading.

Tricky stepped back. "How can I get into Tzark, to the labyrinth?"

"They will never let you in to it. Maybe. If you offered them something new." And she looked at Ralas in a way he didn't like at all which reminded him of examination tables and cold, sharp metal edges. "It would intrigue them to consider new methods of handling death. But by now they are a lost people. It may be they won't care for anything at all."

"Never mind." There was a faraway look about Tricky that suggested to Ralas her quicksilver mind had already taken another path. She strode around them both to go to the bar, passing through the blurred veil into the distance abruptly. When he tried to follow Ralas found himself rebuffed, walking on the spot, a feeling like heavy cobwebs about his face and hands, and tangling his feet. He stepped back, feeling stupid and awkward, glanced at Zivalah who was still staring at him intently through her self-inflicted crimson facemask.

"Do you know any songs?" he asked, trying to fill the tiny space and its silence.

"Songs carry memory, we do not need them. The blood is our memory. We sound out the tones to bring it forward. That is all the singing we do."

Ralas blinked.

"Here you are, drink this," Tricky said, returned, holding out a wooden cup filled with something dark and faintly steaming.

"It will finish me?"

"Definitely will do the job," Tricky said as Ralas looked on, appalled. "Come on. We have to disappoint some burghers about a wedding."

He wanted to resist but her grip on his arm was strong and the world was already spinning around them. By the time Zivalah had drunk all the contents of the cup and flung it away from her they were back in the market and the cup was clattering down on the stone cobbles and rolling under the harness-maker's bench. A moment later Zivalah was walking back towards her stand as though nothing had happened. Ralas waited, and waited, feeling Tricky tug impatiently at his sleeve. "You didn't kill her." He felt baffled by his own bafflement, that the lack of violent death was now so unexpected in him that this surprised him.

She sighed, but briefly. "In a way I did. That was Furny's Mnemtastic Tincture, a speciality of the house. One drinks it to forget. So now she's forgotten she was the scapegoat, and everything associated with it. All she knows is that she must not return to Tzark. Not that I think that's going to be much of an issue as I doubt there's much left to return to. It was a mystery for the world before the war and it's still one now. The only people going into those lands are bandits and chancers, zealots wanting to finish off the undead, possibly a few unwary refugees, maybe the odd expeditionary party on behalf of wealthy entrepreneurs, but most of them won't be coming back. Dead Tzarkish things are still fairly undead."

He looked at her, and saw her again, anew, a committed missionary with a goal of great weight on her shoulders. He wondered that he hadn't noticed it before. It was the kind of thing you noticed about Celestaine almost immediately. Being around Tricky was like having a strange blindness: her ever-changing ways were a storm around a core he wasn't sure he'd ever glimpsed and he was humbled because all the Guardians he had met, bland and terrible by turn, had never seemed this close to the divine. All the same, he would welcome a break from terror and undead things didn't sound like that. "Please tell me that's not where we're going."

She held onto his arm, a conspirator, a sweetheart consoling a suitor as she let him down. "I'd like to."

"You'd like to go?"

"I'd like to tell you that. But if it helps then we're not going straight away. First I have to get back to Nydarrow and check a few things. Don't worry. We won't be there long."

"To... Ny..." She was hustling him away again as alarmed shoppers had begun to look at them and take an interest. It was good because he wasn't sure he wanted to hear any more.

They were halfway back to the gate before she started speaking again. "I'm concerned that the business the Forinthi champion and my weaselly brother are all fired up about is not all it seems. I..." She paused in preoccupation of thought and a couple of the many, incessantly present guardsmen almost walked into them.

"Mind your manners!" one barked, adjusting his cloak and giving his halberd a slight shake. "Stay on the left for the gate, keep moving at a sensible pace or you can pay us five scits for every dawdle and two pollys for waiving the non-buyer's licence for leaving without a purchase. Town isn't rebuilding itself." He and his partner both gave identical sharp nods to emphasise the point.

"Sorry, sorry," Tricky said, sounding distinctly unlike herself, but hustled Ralas forwards, half carrying him with her grasp on his arm, and then they were off again. As soon as they had cleared the officials at the gate and paid the exit duty and the safe-streets voluntary donation they passed into the world in which they were old sweethearts, fabricating stories of a past that never was to explain their wedding, and then its delay. "We'll just put them off a bit," Tricky said as though this, and not the other dark quest, was her real goal in the world, of the utmost importance. "Better than a blow to the hopes. We'll go for an engagement celebration. Everyone wins."

Ralas managed, "It makes me nervous when people say that. But anyway, if we do that won't we be actually engaged? I mean is it real or is it pretend?"

She hugged his arm and drew him close to her side and he fancied he felt a touch of affection through her coats and leather harness filled with knives and potions and the thick wadding on her fencing arm. "You're a wise one, bard. Not easy to fool you. Let's just say that there can be some fun and leave it at that. Or are you one of the Gracious One's devotees?" She looked up at him quizzically.

"I'm not," he said. "I was always more of the opportunist, depending on whichever god seemed to have the most benefits for musicians and that depends on where you are."

"Exactly! Wise," Tricky said with enthusiasm and cuddled his arm to her as they went so that even though it hurt abominably, he didn't let out a single squeak of protest.

But once they had wound their way out of the surroundings of the town and had come to the thicketed lane which led to the Inn she let go, folded her arms and pushed her hood back and spoke into the air in front of her although she meant it for him. "You know, there's a labyrinth on that box that matches one inside Nydarrow, well, not exactly but close enough. Like brothers, hm? But not like twins. I knew as soon as I saw it that they must be connected. I've been to the one in Nydarrow..."

"What? When were you there?"

She took a breath and a careful step onward, measuring now. "I've been many times there, but most recently a day ago. I was looking for some news on a thing called the *Book*, which is also referenced on the Zafiid's casket. Interesting how those two old scallies failed to mention it, isn't it? I knew Fishy wouldn't. He'd try to keep that knowledge to the two of them so that they can go loot for themselves and I get to chase off after that scapegoat. Fishy's tight. If he'd made it more worth her while she'd have properly got out of town and not just tried to hide among the bins. Sometimes I can't believe how predictable he is. If I hadn't scared the poop out of him by threatening to leave the labyrinth right there in the shop he'd have not mentioned anything useful." She didn't seem to care that she was carrying it with her all the time but Ralas was getting a little bit of the hang of how she worked now and he sensed that this was a bait he was meant to take to stop him mentioning the horrid suspicion which had begun to form in his mind. He stood still.

"You were there. You were there with the Kinslayer in Nydarrow."

"The *Book*," she said with determination. "The *Book* is not an actual book, I think. It is a reference to something else. But the labyrinth is a place I suspect we ought not to go, and by we, I mean everyone living and by go, I mean..."

"You were there when I was there."

She took another breath, chin down in a kind of nod, the kind that teachers give when they are forced to divulge an unhappy fact. "I may have been there, at that time."

"Did you know?"

She finally lost patience with all the calming breaths and the measured strides and spun into his path, her pointed chin firmly down, her gaze scowling. "Trust me, you do not want to follow this line of thought! No profit is to be found there. Did I know you were locked in that cell, keeping his attention, fouling his dreams, measuring his ambitions and finding them pathetic, challenging his soul to its own reckoning and finding him wanting, eating at his sanity night and day, paying with your life over and over again like the joke coin on the end of the elastic string? Were you keeping him occupied whilst others went about their shady business in the distant background, buying their chances with your suffering? I may have known such a thing. Must we go on?"

He thought about it. She was there. She knew. She saw. She with the spells and the trinkets of magic and the ways and means to get out of trouble. She knew. He had not been saved, not then. She had not saved him. She had let him stay. "No. No need to go on."

"Excellent choice. Then, Ralas Dunwin of Forinth, scion of the noble but minor house of Parsleymaine, bard to the courts and friend of the Slayer, tell me again, how did we meet?"

He repeated his lines in a stunned monotone. "It was during the celebrations after the slaying of Vermarod. I had been with the army and you were with the retinue as a maker and mender and a stitcher of wounds under the auspice of Doctor Panthedreon, who shall never gainsay you as he died shortly afterward of the dragon's venom spit. We were in the hospital, you as a nurse, me to take the final notes of the dying and the record of the dead."

"And your present wounds?"

"An unlucky meeting with brigands upon the road here two days hence. They wanted your silks and your virtue and I gave an excellent account of myself. We are less the silks but not the virtue."

"It's a good story, I think we can still improve it if we think hard."

"It is a good story," he said and hung his head. Stories. She was all stories.

She saw him and her voice was bitter as she spoke, "Sometimes we must make a better story than the truth and believe that. This is how the world is made anew."

He would have thought her the most callous person in the world at that moment were it not for the fact that he could see her face was wet and turned up to the sky and her voice full of so many new beginnings that there was no end to them.

CHAPTER TWENTY-THREE

FISHER PUT UP the shrouds, transforming the little shop into an abandoned building, rank with webs and filth, a suggestion of rat gnawing on the few bits of old counter and bench left long ago. An air of damp and neglect sank down over the place. "I always hate doing this," he said. "One day it will be real, won't it?"

"Don't think of that," Catt said gently, patting Fisher on the arm. "Think of it bright and full with the best of the new collection, the *Book* for me to read, the snake in the hearth, burning with jewelfire through any night of cold. We will have cosy feet."

"I hope so," Fisher said, closing the door behind them and pocketing the key. They turned and went in different directions, one on foot, striding out with a staff. He covered the ground deceptively fast. The other climbed up onto an ornate chariot and took the reins of his heavily-horned rams and gave them a little shake. "Hup, boys," he said, quietly. "Hup hup." And the sheep pulled and the chariot, much taller than they were and with a semblance of being really far too large for them, rolled quietly over the stones and was a cause of much merriment all the way to the gate for there was no dignity in sheep, apparently.

CHAPTER TWENTY-FOUR

BUKHAM SAT ON the prow of the Shelliac ferry and watched the slow passage of the banks. They were moving through hills crowded with woody vegetation, not large enough to be a forest, not small enough to be much else. Here and there where the river curved, broad mud and sand banks stretched down to the water in crescents, pockmarked by the hooves and paws of animals coming to drink. The mist of earlier in the afternoon had passed off and the strip of sky above them was clear. Multiple globes of midges whirled around beneath every overhanging bough. Bukham was plaiting a fistful of long reeds together to make a whisk to keep them off as he kept watch.

Bukham liked the Shelliac, even though they were somewhat hard to look at with their mouths full of moving fur-like strands and their multifaceted eyes which never blinked and shone like fancy buttons. The Shelliac and the Oerni shared a fondness for Wanderer as their Guardian of choice, so Murti was now deep in conversation with them and Horse, who was forced to take her place at the only point she was secure, amidships, near the back of the boat.

Beside him one of the small Shelliac women was squatting, demonstrating how they had taught their otters to do different tasks in the water. She was distinguished from the men only by the upper part of her dress which covered the part Bukham found hardest to look at on any of them because, through their tough, shell-like skin, their hearts and other organs were visible. It made him feel almost sick with vulnerability on their behalf although he was by far the less armoured. The lower half of this particular woman's body was swathed in a practical skirt which all Shelliac wore, embroidered with clan sign and little pictograms of moments from their lives. Her otter was sleek and well-fed, skimming easily on its back as it watched for her signal. She told it to check the bottom of the boat for clearance on the riverbed and it flipped and was gone in an instant, leaving only rings on the water. At Bukham's other side Kula quivered with excitement and thumped the deck with her hand. She could seemingly hardly contain her excitement at seeing the otters work. Lysandra peered over her shoulder. Of Deffo and Celestaine there was no sign and he guessed they were napping below.

The Shelliac were a quiet, efficient background on their boat. They communicated by sign and whistles, a language in which he was fluent thanks to some mutually beneficial trade alliances between Taib and several of the Shelliac clans. This particular one was of the highest cadre, with an ancient lineage whose history was painted in every detail upon its panels and stanchions. With the most favourable routes on the widest passages they had the means to build a grand boat. It was broader than most and boasted a welcoming space for passengers besides its cargo holds. Even the resident otters wore barding of coloured leathers and necklaces of shell and half-pollys. They had their own cubbies on the deck for when they were not fishing, checking the waterways for dangers or maintaining the underwater sections of the craft. They became acquainted as the boat passed smoothly along midstream using only the current to make its way towards Ilkand.

Once the business niceties were over the Shelliac sign and chatter was less reassuring as they told Bukham in detail of the river-dragon's wrecking of large parts of the country all around them. He had translated for the others.

"Sounds like one of the many warbeasts let loose to roam," Celestaine had said but the Shelliac seemed doubtful. They showed where they had placed harpoons on the boat and where there was a water butt with multiple buckets available for putting out fires. Over its gunwales the boat had been cladded in temporary defences. The wooden sides of this armouring were solid, slitted for arrows and charred in places. At first they hadn't wanted to go to shore when they saw Deffo signalling them from the bank, but they had sent a reluctant patriarch over to see if there was a negotiation worth the risk and the story of their narrow escape from the beast had secured them a place, though the jewels Celestaine offered didn't hurt any either.

Only Lysandra and Kula remained oblivious. Bukham's gladness for their safety had begun to pass into a mild panic at the thought of their imminent danger. The boat was not so short that he couldn't hear enough words coming towards him about the terrible happenings at the Freeport. Phrases about Templars clashing, city burghers, tradesmen in riot, a host of horrors descending unexpectedly from the south west, suspected at first to be a plague of some kind of bat left over from the Kinslayer's cache but turning out to be more like malicious leaves blown on a wind of their own sorcery. Monsters were one thing but bodiless entities were worse. Of all the things to end their reign, it was a snowstorm coming in off the sea that finished the plague: the melting flakes stuck to their filmlike bodies and the water melted them into a nasty sludge. Apparently, fish and rats liked to eat it though everyone had lost the taste for fish for a couple of days, and the rats had a brief surge in fortune. Then, however the talk returned to dragonish matters: where it was, what it was doing, why it was there, how to get rid of it, the fact it didn't much like a sharp pointy thing brandished in its face, though fire was no deterrent. They were not sure if fire attracted it.

Bukham made sure to watch carefully but it was Lysandra who was worrying him—she was so much sharper today than she had been yesterday and so much more alert this afternoon than this morning, although the others were too wrapped up in their own business to notice. Now she and Kula were busy at the prow, making the otter cots more luxurious and learning how to offer treats, as if there was no trouble in the world.

"Mind if I join you?" It was Heno. There was hardly room for another big body on the planking at the ship's side but Bukham shuffled over and the boat tilted very slightly as the big, grey form of the Yorughan sat down. He folded his long, dark coat around him so it didn't drag into the water. They were riding very low thanks to the extra passengers and the armouring that had been hastily applied to the deck roofs. Water passed by only inches from their feet.

He felt nervous. Heno had a lined, canny face with a heavy battering ram of a forehead and tusks which made him seem doubly beastlike. In addition he had the fabled magic, and Bukham wanted nothing to do with that. It frightened him but he was too big to show it. He tried to console himself by remembering Taib Post and that it was still there, but then he didn't know if it was there or not. Celestaine liked Heno. He tried to stick that notion to the person sitting beside him. He found he trusted Celestaine.

Out on the water some expanding rings showed where trout were surfacing and he put down his spear and reached instead for the small fishing pole that had been secured beside him to a slot in the hull. He brought in the line, attached a lure, and twitched it out over the water in their direction. The ferry was moving slowly, almost silent except for the steady wash of wavelets from the tiller oar. There was a chance of a fish.

Heno watched him closely. "This is the fishing?"

"Mmn," Bukham nodded. Without thinking he held out the rod and Heno took it. There was an awkwardness to the movement, quickly covered. "The boat is doing the work. After we pass, pull in the line and we can cast it again."

He made some show of looking up and around to make it clear that he was doing his job on watch, but there was no sign of any flying horrors or wisps of smoke. The river was broad and they were skilfully weaving down between fast flowing currents, far out of reach of the banks. It was peaceful. Only the bite of the midges spoiled an idyllic journey. That and what lay at the end. He liked Ilkand but he was terrified of Templars, especially the Termagent Phylactery whose strict codes cast suspicion on everything they saw. Thinking about them made him more glad to be with the Yoggs, strangely enough, as if they would be his allies when the Termagent discovered something they didn't like about him and selected him for sentencing and death. He pushed the image away and concentrated on helping Heno attach bait from the pot. They cast a few times, one then the other, until Bukham was sure that Heno could feel the play of the line. "If it catches, give it a good yank. Either you will free it from the weeds or get the fish hooked on. Either's good."

Heno grunted and they both watched the greenish water.

"You never fished before?"

"We lived in the mines, mostly," Heno said. "No fishing there. No sky. No rivers."

"No soft beds, no nights under the stars, no sun, no wind, no nothing." It was Nedlam, who had come up behind them, very quietly for a woman of such scale. She had a slingshot in one hand and was turning over a few stones in the other. She glanced at Bukham and his face became hot.

"You have a lot of catching up to do," he said, carefully, in case they took offence at being so close to someone soft who had done nothing in the war but drop the price of grain when he should have put it up for scarcity. Up close their scars were terrible to see—they had them everywhere. Bukham had only one, on his foot, from stepping on a cowbite thorn when he was little.

"You never had a weapon in your hands?" Nedlam asked, scratching her nose with a finger before gesturing out before them at a low hanging branch. "Think you can hit that?" She held out the sling.

"I... no... it will disturb the fish," Bukham said, but then had a thought. "May I borrow it?"

He took it from her and dropped a few bits of old bread from the bait pot into the cup and then briefly whirred the sling around before releasing one end. The bread pellets flew out over the gloom beneath the shade of the overarching trees where Heno's fishing line was slowly being dragged behind them. Within moments the surface of the water rippled and then suddenly there was splashing and vigorous movement. Heno yanked the line with a sudden, almost girlish, exclamation of surprise.

"A fish! Did I get it?"

"Let me help with the line..." Bukham was reaching, reeling. Heno was gripping the rod as if it was the last straw in a fearsome ocean and he unable to swim.

"Ooh," Nedlam said, stepping forwards to see what was happening.

The combined weight of the three of them concentrated in one spot caused the boat to dip a little—only a fraction because she was a big vessel and well loaded—but it was enough for Bukham who was already off balance, and who dare not grab onto Heno or Nedlam. His foot slid off the side and then he was falling into the river, rotating, his last sight two comically surprised grey and white faces gawping at him like giant fishes, a tiny fish flapping between them on a thin line.

After that there was coughing and flailing and the sad memory that it had been a long time since his boyhood on the banks of the Tularesi during which there had been something of a large mass gain and a skill loss. But his skin felt the cool grip of the river and his leg hairs twitched with old memories of the currents and somehow he kicked to the surface without bashing his head on the hull to find a huge grey hand reaching down for his wrist.

Nedlam lifted him out of the water with one arm and he laid on the boards of the deck coughing and flapping, the little fish beside him in the same spasms of life searching for breath. The Yorughan were laughing and he heard the conversation had died and others were merry behind him. He reached out and found the fish, took it off the hook. It wriggled but he had its measure. In his hand it was like liquid metal. He held it up towards Heno as he sat up.

"Your call. Eat it or throw it back."

A rainbow of colour flashed on the trout's side, its scales bright, its eye glaring.

"No eating Bukbuk here. He cooks good," Nedlam said, clapping Bukham's shoulder with a force that almost had him over the side again.

Everyone was laughing. Even the little one had her head out of the otter cabin to goggle at him. Lysandra stared, mouth half open, looking like any young mother, if she had lately been at a fancy human ball and run away through the woods for a week to live feral by her wits.

Heno stared at the fish. He stared, and licked his tusks, and then he grinned. "Throw it back," he said.

"Ahh!" Kula said and jumped with joy, clicking her fingers together. It was the first time he had ever heard her voice try to say something. It was raspy and high pitched and raw but its delight was clear.

Bukham tossed it. The fish landed with a rich plop in the swirling current and was lost to sight immediately.

After that even Lysandra smiled and there was a brief sense of oneness among the crew, even the Shelliac, bound by that moment of the fish's fate under the falling sun. Bukham, pulling off his wet shirt to dry it, saw Murti nodding quietly.

Later as they were watching the river, halberd at hand in case of dragons, he said to Bukham, "You see, only a holy man can do such a thing as has been done. You have united disunited things."

"Keep your ambitions," Bukham replied, but without any of the resentment he'd had before. "I'm just a fool who sells vegetables and I don't even have any of them." A strange happiness had engulfed him and he wanted it to stay.

Dusk had started to come on and a mist had begun to form as the air cooled. Their progress remained stately within the river's broad meander. Fisherbirds darted into the water and out again, catching rising moth larvae as they came up to feed in the shadows. Aboard the ferry he could smell dinner on the make and hear voices, quiet. Murti was lost in thought, or asleep, as the water rippled nearby and a few bubbles rose to the top and burst one after the other.

Bukham found he was watching those bubbles. They made a line of steady progress and then he realised why it was odd. They matched the boat's speed and position. He was suddenly aware of how close Murti was to the edge of the boat as he lay carelessly in his half-sleep, and moved, halberd tightly gripped, gunwale held fast for safety, to position himself as a guard for anything rising from the water.

Horse called from the boat's centre at the same moment, his name or something like it, her voice a warning note that went through him from head to toe although it was quiet, barely above the plash of the ripples against the hull. Right in front of him the water domed upwards for a moment and he saw the curling foil of a large fin and the silvered flash of a large, sinuous body rolling away beneath them at an angle that would take it beneath the boat. He grabbed the old man's ankle, dragging him backwards to the safety of the centre. Murti woke up and flailed about in protest.

The Shelliac were pushing past him, the rudimentary nature of their faces become quite blank with anxiety as they scouted, javelins and harpoons in hand. They swarmed over the boat, their unblinking, faceted gaze on the furls and strands of the river. They were talking about dragons again and poling the craft over into the fastest part of the current. Celestaine came up, buckling her breastplate on, but was beaten to a view by the shadowy slip of Kula, one moment not there, the next hanging out over the water to stretch her thin fingers down into the flow.

Bukham released Murti and shouted at her before remembering it could do no good. He threw himself flat in an effort to reach her before anything could pull her over the side.

KULA FELT THE beast much more clearly when she touched the water. It had an age beyond most she'd encountered. When she'd first sensed its slow circling of them she'd been afraid but her curiosity had drawn her closer and closer to the water's edge. When the big man fell in she'd been terrified for a second but surprised more than anything. His face was so funny as he tumbled over that she couldn't help laughing. The splash he made had caused the creature to come closer, though it was used to boats and especially this kind. It came to taste the newcomer, as she came closer now to discover more about it.

She was fairly certain that it wasn't Bukham that it cared for. It was drawn to the deeper, more complex flavours of Wanderer's dark flame and the weak pulses of the Undefeated's signature. Now it was hunting the source of that rare scent which stirred ancient memories inside it, but weakly. It searched to remember something that had happened generations past, to river creatures that had swum and hunted here before the ages of men.

Kula told it that humans didn't see these things. They were so blind that they thought this creature was the same as the one that had flown in the air earlier that day but this was only a river beast. She warned it off as it turned in the muddy depths and felt a sluggish notion stir within it as the otters came to see what she was doing, whiskers tickling her cheek.

Though the idea was slow the giant dragon-fish was not. It skimmed away across a bed full of stones and silt, heading upstream to put distance between itself and the dangerous, predatory things-from-above. In its wake it left her the memory of the winged one. It was downriver a way and had built a nest there. The dragonfish knew to keep away from it.

She was about to turn and look for her mother to discuss it when she was seized. Everything she'd been thinking and her quietness was lost in a sudden, violent surge of rage and struggle. Then she realised it was Bukham holding her and that she was being set down. She whirled and glared at him, rubbing her arms where she'd been grabbed. Beside her the otters chittered crossly and one bit him on the ankle.

He yelped in pain and was making apologetic gestures and pointing at the water. She scowled and told him he didn't know what he was talking about, but then, seeing how baffled he was and that he didn't understand her signs anyway, she sighed and shook her fist at him. He'd intended to save her, but that didn't make her feel better.

He pulled a sad face, very sad. She smiled and then he smiled back. She helped him to dress the otter bite with some salve from Celestaine's pack and then she took her otter friends to visit Horse, who was all by herself at the back of the boat swishing midges off Lysandra as she dozed on Horse's broad back.

Kula loved Horse. Vast and strange, wild and ancient, she was. She was before Kula and the people. She was almost before everything, just like the dragon that Kula wanted to talk to her about. There were traces of memory so old in her that touching them made Kula feel that she could see almost to the beginning of things. She was the opposite of Kula herself, in whom nothing stuck. Horse was an old, old book and Kula was a blank page. Kula knew that this is why she could see as she did, as far as she did, as completely. Because nothing stuck. She remembered that she had been part of a people, in a place, her family, her life and that between them there was not a single thing from the origins of the world that had not been remembered, but for her it had already faded to the point that it was like a distant dream. Now there was only the one the others called Lysandra, her mother. She knew they had a journey to go on, for a reason. Horse was coming because of the reason so it must be important and if it was important to Horse then she ought to make sure there was no trouble. The dragon was a big trouble.

She sneaked up on the centaur who was pointedly looking the other way and pulled her hair.

"What little bat is that?" asked Horse, looking the other way as Kula hopped over her broad back, waking Lysandra. Kula heard her as clearly as if she had spoken, though not in words, and flapped her arms and fingers like bat wings as she went for another tug.

"What little bug is that?"

They played on, Kula talking about the dragon, as at the boat's foredeck the others ate the evening meal and talked so serious, full of memories. They carried the past like stone in their faces and hearts because they couldn't let it go. She felt sad for them. They were difficult to be around. Even when it was peaceful they couldn't stop. She undid them a little, loosened a few things here and there, explained to the Shelliac and the otters that the dragon was ahead of them still, not far away.

BUKHAM SPENT THE evening swatting biting flies and fighting an urge to slip away and go home. The Shelliac lit smoky torches and handed out cool pachi fruit, stowed carefully enough to keep it cool and sweet as they made a show of talking emphatically it in hugely exaggerated gestures like a travelling theatre group—*what a shame such good fruit would all go to waste because of a dragon. The land hereabouts was already wasted and the people driven off by the thing. Plus with the*

Kinslayer's armies now devolved to roving bands of witless thugs it was too much to suffer a monster when the boat was full of legendary monster-slaying figures. Surely, for the sake of the good fruit and the safety of law-abiding, peaceful folk, the mighty warriors could get up off their arses and take a punt at dislodging the thing before it spawned.

Finally, just as he thought he was about to leap up and go it was Nedlam beside him who moved first. Only understanding a bit of what they said but all of what they meant, she threw down the last rind into the slop bucket and snapped, "Fine. Fine. I will do it. I will get the beast!" just to shut them up and because Heno's fish had been put back and now there was only fruit to eat and she was grumpy. Bukham slumped with relief. He wouldn't have known what to do after the standing up bit.

"You're the salt of the earth," Celestaine said, approvingly and as a preamble to some plan or other but a plan she never got to. A second later she looked as shocked as Bukham felt to find herself hauled up by the front of her jerkin, an inch from Nedlam's blunt nose. He felt a sudden palpable menace, the barge far too small and confined.

"Ned," he said quietly. "She didn't mean it literally. Let go. She was saying thank you." He put his hand out and touched Nedlam's arm, the muscle there as solid as rock.

He felt her quiver and then she said decisively, "I only salted it because I had to, not because I wanted to!"

The declaration was loud and after it the silence was intense, broken only by the relentless lap of water against the boat. Nedlam herself looked surprised. She let go slowly and dusted off Celestaine, holding out her hands to show she was sorry. Bukham patted Nedlam on the back.

"It's a saying. It means *good*," Celestaine said, relaxing back cautiously, a what-the-hell expression on her face. "What's the matter, Ned? You're never upset."

"How can it mean good?" Nedlam said quietly. She glared at

Heno as if it were his fault, her voice full of hurt. "Tell your woman to keep a straight mouth. Who says things like that and it's good?" She pushed her way around the group and out of the door onto the deck. Bukham heard her boots on the gangplank and then the splash of her walking onto the islet's swampy sanctuary. A second later a bestial roar of rage and misery split the evening's froggy murk and the otters came rushing in, hurtling around in wet, muddy streaks until they found their cots.

The air was so tense even Kula didn't move a muscle. The Shelliac looked thunderous, and frightened, their gaze flitting between Heno and Celestaine as they tried to decide which of them was the more dangerous, waiting for some kind of retribution to fall, a doom they had expected, betrayal already trying to leak into their expressions, fingers slowly moving towards weapons.

"You people are such weak materials." From the darkness behind Horse's massive bulk a smallish figure in a multi-coloured dress stood up and turned to face them. In the dimness of the night and the oil lamps they could see her only by the reflection on her eyes and the whiteness of her teeth. "No wonder he came to kill you all. And still, it didn't do a bit of good to you."

"What would you know?" Deffo said, from his position in the most inaccessible corner, but he was suddenly cramped out of style by the addition of everyone else as they gave a lot of space to Horse and the woman standing beside her: Lysandra.

Bukham couldn't believe what he was hearing. That Lysandra spoke wasn't entirely new. That she had an opinion of her own was unexpected. That it was this condemnation was devastating. He felt crushed. As Kula's mother, Lysandra had been so caring, so joyful, dutiful he would have said. As she stood now, her words had seemed to destroy all of that. She was siding with the Kinslayer. How could it be that anyone would have a good thing to say about him and, above all, that it should be this? How could she dare say it, knowing what they thought and how they felt and what had happened? He felt scared of her and scared for her at the same time, his limbs urging him to run away before things turned bad, as they surely must any second now.

Celestaine's hand was on the hilt of her sword. Heno was frozen, staring as if he could discover the truth by concentration.

"So much killing and still we kill it kill it kill it and salt the earth," she said to the Shelliac trade-patriarch. She was contemptuous, and angry, Bukham thought; a contained anger that was coming out in a considered way. She was disappointed.

"Monsters kill people," Celestaine said firmly. "What other way is there? They don't talk."

"Yes, the talking," Lysandra said. "Very successful. But even your greatest friend can't survive the beast ahead, nor any of you. It is time-lost, like Horse here. An army won't dispatch it. But don't worry. You—" she turned to the Shelliac leader and swept him up and down with a scathing gaze. "I will get the terrible, terrifying dragon out of the way." She turned to look at those of her own company and bowed her head once, then walked out, down the plank and onto the islet.

"Oh dear," said Murti with that glee of his that Bukham was starting to dislike even more as it presaged trouble.

"What the ever-living fuck?" Celestaine said, looking at the space Lysandra had stood in.

Bukham rubbed his palms against his tunic but there was no getting the damp and discomfort off them. He looked at Murti. "Now how good a priest am I?"

"Not everything's about you," Murti said impatiently as Heno got up and passed him on his way down the gangplank. Celestaine followed him. Bukham looked back and saw Horse holding a sleeping Kula in her arms. Well, at least that was all right, he thought as he found himself alone by the firepit. Beside him one of the Shelliac, internal lights pulsating rapidly, signalled to him—what? What was that? Who was this strange person they had brought to endanger the boat?

He tried to explain but a commotion of voices from the islet cut him short. Without hesitation he hurried with the crew to go see for himself what was going on.

He found everyone, even Deffo, lining up on the islet's shallow beachline. Nedlam, resolute with her hammer over her shoulder, was apart, a few feet into the water. Lysandra was much further out on the sandbar where it reached into midstream. The water, lit by the moon, broke around her ankles and tugged at the trailing hems of her gown. She had one arm upraised and was looking directly up into the moon's large face. Clouds scudded across the stars in rags, brief blots on the broad V of the sky that was visible to them between the sharp rise of the land on either side.

A breeze rippled their hair and clothing. Against the rush of the water in its uneven bed, the sound of leaves sighing, filled their ears to the brim, heightening the fear in Bukham because he hated the wind and the way it masked all other, much more important sound. Their sense of expectation rose, rose, then began to subside, but Lysandra remained still and so they waited.

Down in the sharp point of the V something flitted across the visible stars moving from left to right. Bukham felt the air cold all over his back, aware of its exposure, his height, the space at the back of his head where the shirt hung off his neck. He found Murti nudging him with a grunt, the old man's thinner form looking even more like a bag of bones than usual.

"I feel we are about to get our arses kicked," he muttered.

"You're enjoying this," Bukham realised.

"Who doesn't love a good turnabout?"

Celestaine turned and looked back at them. "Where's Deffo?" She spotted him then, standing close to the boat and almost invisible in its moonshadow. She turned back scowling to face whatever was coming towards them.

A giant bird with a long, whip-like tail flew over the river's course. Its silhouette seemed feathered, elongated, the tail trailing a vertical diamond which Bukham recognised suddenly as the downward fin that had cut through the clouds earlier on in the day. Compared to the size of the creature itself, the fin was large.

Then with a speed and suddenness that surprised them all there it was, landing in the river's shallows with a small splash of white water, just ahead of Lysandra's station. The long wings folded down and it used the knuckles as forelimbs. The brilliance of the moon made all shadows as black as the abyss. The thing was a collection of mismatched, ugly angles to Bukham, a nightmare with two vividly glowing red eyes. He wanted to run but nobody else was leaving. Streamers of blackness seemed to ripple off the creature, and Bukham could feel a vibration in the tissues just beneath his skin as if it were emitting a constant, inaudible tone.

It wasn't a dragon. He realised that now. He knew them by story: huge, bejewelled, ancient, venomous—the list of their features was as long as it was unlikely.

A commotion broke out among the Shelliac, a clank and clattering and subdued but urgent whistles. The thock of a bow being shot startled Bukham even as the hiss of the arrow and its splash into riverwater was already there with him. He stepped back and found himself treading on Heno's foot. He moved aside and stood shoulder to shoulder with the Yorughan.

The creature made a complaining, stuttering sort of sound ending on a hiss and Lysandra turned around with a violent gesture. "You will not shoot it!"

The beast sprang back into the air and the downdraft washed over them in a strange, dry stink of things they couldn't name or place, animal but at the same time alien in a way that Bukham felt give even his bones pause for concern. They all must have felt it because there was a moment of near panic as the thing went sailing overhead and then on, down the river towards the shallow bend and beyond in the direction of the Port.

Lysandra spun around, her hands in fists, arms straight at her side as she came towards them. Bukham took a few steps back.

"What did you do that for?" She pointed at the archer, a Shelliac with shortbow drawn, a harpoon arrow in place. "Why? Why?" She was angry and as she came at them there was a sense of presence about her that went far beyond the ordinary, as though her every step pulled something unseen and terrible behind her so that you could feel the ripples of it spreading out from her in a gigantic train.

"What the hell?" Nedlam was there, moving forwards, putting herself firmly in all their way.

Lysandra stopped as she reached Ned and threw up her hands in the air in a gesture of exasperation. "Now it has gone back to its nest."

The Shelliac captain broke in to say they would not be going anywhere until the beast was dispatched and all danger to the countryside removed.

"I hardly think you're going to turn around with a full load and take it back where it came from," Celestaine replied. "And now we've all seen it's some kind of big wyvixen. It's not a dragon, not any of the Kinslayer's creatures, it's just a monster from the wilds upset by the war. There were plenty of them in the wars to the south. It's just an outlier. We'll sort it out in the morning." She sounded like she was making a pitch rather than stating a fact. Bukham didn't buy it. He believed Lysandra, who stood alone, having left a sleeping Kula with Horse.

Neither Celest nor the captain seemed to notice that where Lysandra stood at the shore her feet were surrounded by white water, bubbling and popping as if it were on the boil although it didn't look right for that. Still, it was bad in Bukham's eyes, like the bottom of a non-existent waterfall. Then he thought that perhaps Celestaine did know because she went to intercept the Shelliac and make a foray across the islet with them in the throes of planning a hunt in quite a loud voice. Silently Nedlam and Heno fell in to back up her reassertion of leadership. He was left with Murti and Deffo in the van and that suddenly felt bad.

He watched Deffo cast a long, thoughtful look at Lysandra and then decide that it wasn't his problem. They shared a glance and Bukham gave a sheepish shrug. Deffo tried to sidle up to Murti who was already walking back to the boat but Murti ignored him; although it looked like he was just too quick, his old man shuffle one step ahead of the other old man shuffle. Bukham, alone, looked at Lysandra reluctantly.

The water was calming down. She had folded her skinny arms across her chest and her chin was down. She looked thoughtful but not angry and came forwards the last few steps out of the river to dig her toes into the sandy mud. After a moment or two this distracted her completely and he watched her loosen her arms and look down, then pause and start to play, dabbing marks with her feet that filled quickly with water and became tiny, five-toe mirrors in the steady moonlight.

"Is that what you really think he was doing?" He had no idea he was going to ask it until he did. "The Kinslayer came to kill us all because we were too weak? That we failed the gods' plan? Was that part of the plan all along, to make us stand up to him?" He didn't expect an answer but he was surprised.

"I wanted to make you all stop." Lysandra caught Bukham's eye and smiled. Then she passed them and went back aboard the ferry. "I wanted to make you think differently about what has happened. Stop attacking everything. Doesn't the dragon have the right to the land, as much as you?"

Bukham swallowed. "I don't know. It's very dangerous. I think that when something is dangerous you plan to be rid of it."

She seemed to think about this as she stirred the mud and sand with her toe. "Yes. I am confused about this because I have no fear of it. Thank you. Even so, I will not let you kill it. I will find another way. Kula would not see it die. She would like it to eat everyone who did not help, who is not kind, who cannot escape their—what is this thing that stops you all? Their...?"

Bukham thought of his uncle, their careful progress, their

lack of action. But they had kept trade going, they had supplied the people as best they could, and fighters twice as much. They didn't fight but they had done their part. Someone had to supply. But Uncle had said Kula must go. What did he do that for? "I don't know," he said, because he wasn't sure that Uncle's actions could be put down to anything other than simple impatience in the end.

He found Lysandra studying him, a smile on her face, slight but definite. "It's all right. She doesn't want it to eat you." Then she passed him by and went up into the boat and on her way past she whispered, "But something will be eaten."

In the morning his worst fears were realised. After the briefest of breakfasts in the dawn the Shelliac set themselves up with gear—harpoons, nets, torches—and poled off from the islet while the mist was still clinging to the banks. Celestaine, Heno and Nedlam, always ready, remained on watch. Lysandra and Kula came up on deck. The boat moved with steady progress around a long curve and then back the other way, the river broadening. Either side the woodland proved too thick to show any signs of habitation but on the third bend they came to the pathetic remains of a wooden jetty, and the Shelliac insisted that it had been a fishing spot and trading point until the dragon had taken over this whole stretch of the waters. Bukham recognised the tone. It was grievances aired to fuel the fire of a fight.

Then came the sight of the midstream island they were expecting and a hush fell, broken only by the scrape of a pole as it fended them off a mudbank below the waterline. The only movement on board suddenly was Kula playing with the otters. She had made some little balls out of knotted rag and gleaned some dried fish from the supplies and they were racing about in pursuit of one or the other at a great rate, oblivious to the interests of the adults on board. Lysandra was nearby, sitting quietly, and it felt to Bukham like they were cruising to the end of the world. He wiped his sweaty hands down his clothes, feeling how dirty they were, how tired he was, how frightened he was feeling for no reason other than that they were approaching the hunt of a monster and there was something off about everything, like a tilt that would see them all sliding helplessly into an abyss...

The quiet was broken by the hunting splash of a fishermartin plunging down from one of the trees overhanging the river near them and vanishing into the frog-rich depths. Then quiet again. They drew alongside the first island.

The soft plash of the poles, the ripples of the water, the breaking slurp of wavelet on shingle—no animal sounds at all. They slid past its mud shore, ferns trailing in the water like tiny green fingers feathering the current. Beside them, black feathers.

Half hidden by the deep grass the 'dragon' lay in a motionless lump, its true size clear in the bleak grey light. Skinny claws and awkward joints were piled like discarded wood. Its head, long and ugly by any standard, lay with the wide, toothy beak half open, sifting the water without tasting. The eyes were blank and dry. It was quite unmistakably dead.

The ferry was brought to a halt, grounded and two Shelliac sent to investigate. Morosely the others gathered at the railside to look down on the proceedings. They prodded the beast with poles until its stiffened carcass rocked. At the edge of the group Lysandra and Kula looked on, their faces impassive. Bukham saw Heno watching them both with all his attention. Lysandra sighed but all the anger and menace of the previous evening was nowhere to be seen. Heno nudged Celestaine and she turned to look at them too. Words were exchanged too low for Bukham to hear. He watched the tall, blonde warrior scratch her head and then she was calling for them to go. For the Shelliac's part it seemed they were satisfied with the outcome. They forayed into the island interior and there was some sound of crushing—eggs were broken, a nest trampled it turned out—before they returned to loot the corpse for feathers and claws, bone and teeth. Then they were back aboard and casting off, all the talk about what could have happened—had it died of old age or was it too far from home, all that kind of speculation that could never be answered and left a lingering unease in its wake.

Later, as they sat and played a game of chase and fetch with the otters, Bukham saw Kula quietly stroking a small black feather as though consoling a little animal. He didn't interrupt her but she looked up directly into his face and smiled a small, sad smile before putting the feather away in her vest pocket. Lysandra helped the Shelliac with their food preparations and later took a pole to learn how to angle the boat at the right points to take advantage of the current. There was a new kind of purpose to her, he thought, something keen and sharp as a knife point that hadn't existed before. Where she had passively followed and peacefully accepted whatever happened, now she was alert. She didn't speak or attempt to initiate anything. She just paid attention and as the day passed she wove herself silently and seamlessly into whatever went on around her.

He was sitting with Horse, weaving a basket to pass the time, when he overheard Heno and Celestaine talking. They must have been outside on the gunwales.

"You're sure it was Lysandra?"

"I saw the girl at the front of the boat. The mother was away in the night," Heno said, barely audible as more than a low grumble.

Horse was also listening, her tall ears twitching.

"And you saw magic?"

"I felt it," he said.

They moved along out of earshot. Lysandra and Kula had killed the dragon after all they had said? He didn't understand. And how could they have done it? What did it mean?

A holler a few moments later put them within sight of the Freeport.

CHAPTER TWENTY-FIVE

An OLDER MAN, tall, with a blue-grey stubble of a beard and a sharp, intellectual eye, watched the boat turn towards the Ilkand Locks. He had a staff by his side which he leaned on, resting in the shade. After the barge had gone he straightened up and turned. There was a brief glow from the staff in his hand and he took a purposeful step towards the river.

The step ended with Dr Fisher standing on the muddy bank beside the ravaged body of the dead river dragon. He set the Staff of Striding aside and took out a large, beautifully polished magnifying glass from his dainty leather satchel. Crouching down, he used a twig to poke about among the few remaining feathers and the large, unpleasant pile of innards. After a time he got up and eased his back, leaving the flies and beetles to get back to business on rendering it all down.

"Natural causes, Catty," he murmured, as if his companion were at his side and in conversation with him. "Looted and left." There was a pause as he considered. "Yes, I agree, I should get to Tzarkona Gate. But why would it drop dead so conveniently? Well, all right all right, don't get your earwax rattled, I'm going." He took up his staff and turned his nose up to the wind, sniffing and changing the direction of his nose until something told him that was the right way, then strode off and vanished from the scene.

He came back a moment later and picked up the little silk bag for the looking glass from where it had fallen on blood-soaked mud, tutted and then sighed and strode off again.

CHAPTER TWENTY-SIX

THEY TRAVELLED ALONG the hidden threads of the world, Ralas joined to Tricky by their hands, woven together at the fingers, matched at the palm where the lines of their lives surged and ran. It was nothing like his first experience of magic seizing him, through the splash in the water, using an element to translate instantly from one point to another. Although she warned him she was about to use another trick, showed him the spindle and the reel, talking him through the strange simplicity of casting the line, when she seized him the moment was as different from his previous life as stone from air. For one thing all the pain went away.

It was like he became music itself. The two of them were tiny complexities of constant themes and motifs, whirling in a living, dynamic throng, mastered by a single mighty composer into a symphony that was so vast it was beyond his understanding. They travelled on the melody of Tricky's line, searching for its resolution at the one point in the universe where the cadence came to a natural close. All around them the whirling dance of the world paced itself to the beat of time, to the harmony and discord of its billion parts, and he was a part of it, a song of his own, brief but essential.

And he was once again standing on the kind support of the earth, his companion's hand in his, the air full of dark smoke, tears pouring from his bruised and battered eyes. The pain was back. He hurt and they seemed to be facing a totem pole made up of half-rotted corpses. They stank to the heavens but they were beautiful, incredible. He could just hear the traces of their tale. He waited another second, another, as she turned to him, mouth opening to speak. He waited for the music to leave him and longing for it never to leave him. It left slowly and he felt his tears trying in the hot breeze.

"It's music," he mumbled to her, a gibbering fool. "Music!"

She smiled and nodded, tears on her face too. "Yes." She pulled a silk kerchief out of her coat and dabbed his eyes and chin with it before scrubbing her own face dry. "And here we are in the dissonant chords, mate, on the trail of one who kept the score. So let's be careful."

The totem pole stank. It was swarmed black with flies. A whiff of it and a few cold little bodies battering around him soon had him back to his ordinary senses. "What's this?"

"It's a border marker of the Tzarkomen," Tricky said. "Beyond ye shall not go and all that. Means we're in the right place. Come on."

The right place was a thickly wooded grove in a land of rough rocky terrain, sandy soil and boulders. Rolling hills and steep scarps alternated with dips of forest. There was no such thing as a clear sightline or an unimpeded view in any direction. It would have been hard to drive any army through this land, but then, maybe they weren't coming in at it from the same angle. In any case it was hard to walk on, even without the promise of a lingering and excruciating death.

Tricky took a bearing on their direction every few hundred yards and adjusted her path accordingly. They came across trails now and again—overgrown—but she avoided these. Every so often she paused for a long sniff at the breeze. The fetor of rotting flesh was here and there, and above them spirals of black birds circled in stacks, but lazily, as though merely keeping an eye on things they couldn't be bothered to own. Ralas had spent only a little time at the undead front during the war. He expected an onslaught of the things he had seen there but aside from the odd twig snap that could be put down to something else there was no sound of anything on the move except themselves.

As the day grew older a gentle but insistent heat began to collect beneath the trees. They followed the course of a dry stream for a mile and then came to a rivulet that trickled through an acreage of mud that had been trampled into pocks and craters, then baked and cracked. Here were the footprints of many Yorughan, and the bones of Yorughan, with dry flesh baked on. A couple of vultures hopped about and flapped off as they approached, heavy, barely able to lift themselves off the ground. The breeze sighed through the dry leaves.

"This is the main trackway from the south," Tricky said as they paused there. She turned around, her dark hair like smoke on the wind. Ralas eased his aching feet.

"If you have such strong magic, why can't it get us closer to wherever we're going?"

"Because I don't know what I'm looking for. Exactly. I don't know exactly. We come in quietly, we look around. And there are some charms and shiz stopping me doing that. They're not known as the world's greatest sorcerers for nothing."

"But nothing's happened. I mean. We saw a totem pole."

"Fetish pole, but all right."

"We saw a fetish pole."

"And it saw us."

"What?"

"The pole saw us, marked us, watched us all the way. It has eyes in the sky."

Ralas squinted upwards. "Those are just vultures."

"Vultures with eyes in their heads. They've watched us come in. We have made it to the place they want us to see."

"I'm sorry. They want us to see what now? Who is they? There's nobody here." Ralas eased his back and fought for clarity against the tide of her apparently obvious statements.

"The Tzarkomen are dead," she said. "But they are here, they are left in these things and their will is here, and they know what we have come for."

"This *Book* thing?"

"Yes."

"You think they'll let you have it?"

"Well, we've got this far," she said.

She led the way forwards across the mud, between tall rushes trying to regrow, through a field of yellow and white bone laid like old sticks in the grass. Ralas looked as closely as he could, minding his footing around the sharp, broken ends of the long bones where they'd been cracked open and the marrows looted. Here and there weapons stuck up through the wispy, dried remnants of last year's seeding plants. A shield on its back provided a rainwater puddle that had dried almost to the last drop, heavy with a harvest of large red and black snails. The second wadi they reached held an entire torso, preserved by the black coat it was still wearing. Though the hands were missing and the ribcage had been thoroughly plundered, the neck and skull remained intact, the rest of the body mired in the dried earth. Ralas recognised the coat as being like Heno's Heart Taker badge of office. This one had its arm outstretched as if reaching for them, or pushing them away. Both, he felt as they neared it and stepped around its summons.

Beyond this was a meadow clearing and the burnt remains of what had once been a sizeable collection of huts. All the roofs were gone but the mud structures of the bases were still there, blackened and crumbling. There were no bodies here. As they stepped onto the ground of the village he felt the air change from a numb emptiness to something quite different and he stopped, automatically, looking up at Tricky who had ascended to the top of a few remaining steps at the side of one home to get a better view.

A kind of whisper floated past him, a voice heard from a great distance, blurred by wind and time. He felt his face brushed by a faint breeze that otherwise did not exist. He wanted badly to ask a question but dare not break the quiet with his voice in case he broke something else. Somewhere in another house a hollow object fell and rolled, clearly audible as it clattered against wooden boards. He saw a movement at the corner of his eye and when he looked the faintest outline of a figure was there at the broken-down doorway of a large structure, hesitant, crouched, as if hiding. Even as he looked it was already gone.

Another, sharper movement made him half whirl, off balance. Something small but distinctly dark, like a shadow, had darted between the buildings and the loose brush and trees of the edgewood.

"Soul hunters," Tricky said, coming down and joining him to his relief. "We don't have long. Well. I don't. You're probably good. Let's find this thing."

"What thing? What hunters?"

She began to lead him swiftly between the homes, taking an inventory of each as fast as she was able, looking intently for something. "Soul hunters are old demons, summoned by sorcerers to guard places or objects from interference by the living. They don't have any mind, as such, and they don't have any bodies. They are hungry for life itself, connected to the realm of the dead—it's not the dead but let's call it that. They will take anything they can get, but they're bound here, so they can't go outside the circle which I am guessing is set at the limit of the houses judging by the fact that…"

"Nothing in here is alive." Ralas finished.

"Yes. Now they're hunting us. Well, me. I don't think they can do much with you but it's worth finding out."

Ralas wasn't convinced. He looked up.

The dark shadow slipped through a window and behind a distant mound. A second one crossed its path, moving forwards and vanishing as he watched, seemingly evaporating into the sunlight between the walls. Again the voices came, blown on a wind in another plane, past his ears. Howling and crying, rage and despair—he might not know the words but the song of war was always the same.

"I'm looking for a ghost," she said. "There..." and she pointed over two broken-down spars through the skeletal frame of a minor home, filled with a rubble of broken pottery and heaps of mouldering cloth.

The faintest shapes of a figure bending down to cover something, then looking up, hands clutched to its chest, then turning to flee—he saw it like a dream of shapes in smoke, a thing of light and shade that could easily be missed in the broken cloud lighting that swept across them as the afternoon weather began to turn. The figure was female, the head large with some kind of scarf on it, he thought. As it faded away, leaving the place, its shape took form again and repeated the whole sequence of movements exactly, rushing, hesitant with fear, determined—all this he could see simply by the way it moved, and then it was gone. And back. Again, it planted its secret, tamped it down, turned to scatter or throw something over, fled. And again.

Tricky showed none of the fear he felt. She rushed over to the spot, Ralas close behind her.

The ghost faded away as they reached the building and stepped through a gap in the wooden frame to stand where it had been. The space it had filled held only dust motes, agitated by their arrival. Where it had been closing something there was a trap door yawning open in the floor. In the thick dust, not quite obliterated by their own footfalls, a set of child-sized footprints led out of the hole.

Tricky was fishing around in the pockets of her long coat.

She fumbled and then pulled out a circle of glass, rimmed with bronze, and stuck it into Ralas' hands, gripping his fingers for a moment. He found himself looking to her eyes and foolishly had a vision of the two of them standing at an altar, the glass a posy, the words of the missed and lied-about wedding waiting behind his lips.

"I gotta go," she was saying. "You look through this and tell me who's there. All right?"

At the end of the small room they were in, a darkness moved, swift, passing through a stool and table as if they weren't there. It looked small, humanoid, but the head was too long, the fingers too long and too sharply ended, stretching out like needles—

The hands on the glass with his became soft and feathered. With a clapping frenzy a large crow darted upwards between the last rafters and flapped away heavily into the sky, leaving him alone with the shadow thing, the glass in his hands and a stupid look on his face as he realised she'd abandoned him. Left for dead, he thought, and just had time to see the dark shadow gather itself and pounce.

Five talons tore through him from left to right, large enough to cut him into six pieces, had they cut flesh; but they were jagged and caught and tore at something else. He felt it stretch and catch, his body ready to fall as it had fallen so often, all necessary powers taken from it—but then something even more peculiar happened. The talons snagged. The attack stopped. It would not go. His metaphysics defeated it.

There was a pause in the tearing; a surprise, he felt, and then it let go and he was right back where he had been before, undamaged, the glass held up before him giving him a perfect window into another world as the creature that had hunted him sped past. All round the window he saw nothing, not even a disturbance in the dust, but as it turned to look at him through the glass he saw something with thousands of eyes; a vast, multiply-split jaw, festooned in teeth, shrouded in a kind of living darkness that pulsed into tentacular life and as quickly became smoky tendrils of in-substance that ballooned and drifted to the movement of vast and invisible tides. The thing's body boiled with these, as though it was made of ropes and vesicles without a bone. He felt its hunger. He was always hungry too.

Now that the moment had passed and he was unharmed, relatively speaking, he looked around. There was no sign of it. In that distant building the clattering object clattered again, as if struck in anger.

Then the world behind the glass changed again and the ghost he had seen was suddenly there, fully fleshed and solid. She still moved through him, as if he didn't exist, but now he could see her—she had the dark, plum-coloured skin with grey/white tones that Kula had. Her face was painted with an intricate pattern he realised must be a tattoo, in white and red inks. It made her look like a fox. Her arms and hands were marked in the same way, with a million tiny lines. As she bent over she was dropping a child down into the hold in the ground, holding her by her upper arms, then letting go and saying something into the hole. Then without a pause she was closing the trap door and pulling over it a long rug covered in half-finished baskets so that in a single instant it seemed there was nothing there beneath. Then she ran.

As he turned the glass to see where she went the hut was solid again, the door a white rectangle blocked by her body, then showing the running forms of other shapes, grey, black and huge. He saw her cut down by a huge Yorughan sword a moment before he had the presence of mind to put the glass down.

That Kula was the survivor of a massacre, that's what it meant. But why this was important? He thought they were looking for a book. He looked into the hole but nothing in him wanted to investigate it. He probably should. If there was a book around it would be in there.

Then he saw movement in the hole, a black-against-black shiver of anticipation, and he almost put up the glass but instead he held it close against his side and went out into the stuttering daylight, winding his way to the central gathering point where he supposed she might fly in again, or at least where he could easily see the sky.

The centre of the village was a rondel which had been sunk into the ground, leaving a broad circle with stepped seating around it. All that was left of it was the earthwork, sandy and overgrown with weeds. People were standing there, arrayed on the tiers. As he came around the corner of a hut and saw the circle they turned to look at him. They were of medium height and all dressed in robes of dark colours. Their skins were a variety of tones and colours from deep purple through all the brown and ochre families up to a pale slate grey. Some had staves, topped with bones or feather fetishes. Others held nothing. Those closest to him were armoured with bone chokers and bracers, their front and back covered in plates made from scapulae other, flat bits of skeleton from a variety of creatures. One or two had helms of the skulls of monstrous things or gigantic, long-beaked birds. All were tattooed with the red and white marks he'd seen on the ghost. All were silent, motionless, as if they'd always been there. An air of patience and waiting hung about them, a flatness that left Ralas unable to be properly afraid. That and he was tired of fear. He wasn't even what he should be afraid of among the spirits.

He looked through the glass at them. They were exactly the same seen through its revealing lens, although some had auras of a blueish light around them, concentrated on their heads and shoulders. These were also the least decorated of the group, and the most central—the ones he would have said were the leaders. He put the glass down, relieved at least to see no hideous invisibles displayed in it. From the sky a sharp caw announced Tricky's return. A big black bird thumped down onto the rondel's centre point and when it landed and straightened up from its crouch it was already booted and growing, feathers to coat, beak to face; in a single liquid movement the last Guardian appeared. It was only in this moment he dared admit to himself that's what she was and it was a very different thing to know than to suspect. He felt nervous and underprepared.

The ghosts didn't look surprised. Ralas moved cautiously to meet her and they watched him until he was at her side. The central figure, the most plain in comparison to his fellows, moved forwards one step towards her and spoke in the traders' tongue.

"You have come by the long road. You looked for the *Book*, like the Kinslayer."

"For your part in it," she said. "I came by the long road. You gave him the *Book*."

"We gave him a book," the old man said, composed. "And the lives of all our people." He turned and bowed his head briefly in Ralas' direction. "And now you bring us a gift for the dead."

"W-what now?" Ralas asked her but she waved to shut him up.

"I have questions," she said. "About this." With a flourish she produced the tiny bag which he'd last seen in Dr Catt's offices and without hesitation spilled out the entire massive shape of the black box onto the ground. It came out tumbling and the lid slid off it, revealing the empty finery of the interior. A silken pillow rolled out and came to a halt at his feet.

Now Tricky had her hands on her hips like she meant business. "What have you got to say about it?"

As one, as if they were one person, they all had flinched backwards as the box appeared, shuddered as the lid fell, leaned in to peer inside it and watched with fixity as the pillow rolled away and settled on Ralas' feet like an errant cat come home. Swift, dark forms flitted from hut to hut behind them, up on the eaves, down in the shadows of the walls. The silence was unearthly. The air around the box shivered.

"The Reckoner is dead," the Tzarkomen said at last. "Our bargain is done."

Tricky seemed very dissatisfied. She faced up to him as if to a bad shopkeeper. "You never mentioned this. You never said anything about any books." Ralas realised she knew him, from a long time back. Yet one more thing she never mentioned.

"*The Book of All Things* is gone, that's all you need to know. You will never find it."

"Ah yes. But my question isn't *where* it is, Zafiko, my question is *what* is it? What was it for? Why did he want it?"

The leader gestured around at the village. "You have seen him take what he wanted of us. We and a few others are all that remain of an entire people. We defied him at the last, when we had already spent all in his service, and he repaid us most fully for our disagreements. The Heart Takers consumed the dead."

"What is it that you made?"

"Where is she?" he said, and pointed down at the box. "The Kinslayer was dead before she was complete."

"Well, mixed news. Your botched efforts to hide her in the demonfire went astray as your Death Hunters couldn't survive it long enough to dump her. She was found and now she's out and about."

There was no outward sign of reaction, but Ralas saw the telltale shimmers of the soul hunters stealing down from the houses towards the circle. They were almost invisible, like a heat haze. As they moved he noticed that without seeming to move at all the circle of Tzarkomen had closed around them, so that they were now in the middle of a completed ring. He didn't know anything about sorcery but everyone knew the meaning of a magical ring. It was the shape of the unassailable fortress.

"We thought that the Bride would satisfy him and leave us at least enough to survive on."

"Yeah like that's the whole story. Come on. Spill it. I need to know what fresh horror you've unleashed now it's all gone wrong. Was there more? Is there something special about her that the Kinslayer asked for, some way that she's still doing his bidding?"

Tricky's focus never left the leader's placid face. They might have been talking in a town square on any day of the year were it not for the fact that more and more figures kept joining them. Wherever he looked the people on the tiers of the ring stood silent and still, but when he looked one way he wasn't looking another and as he turned this way and that their ranks were filling all the time, one and another, then more, and more, each one of them dressed and tattooed like the rest; short, tall, young, old, of every age and size and kind they arrived, garbed for war and for peace, their gaze solid and unwavering, every focus upon him.

If Tricky noticed this she gave no sign.

"Let us talk first about what you have there," the leader said, pointing at Ralas.

"I was hoping we could trade information," Tricky said. "This is something that the Kinslayer made. I tell you about this and you tell me about the Bride."

The old man studied Ralas for a moment. "In olden times, when the Tzarkomen first began to weave with the darkness, we thought that there was such a thing as death. We pressed where others feared to go. But we did not find death. We found other planes of being, different to this one, through which living things could pass. We never found the land of death, or its gods and goddesses. There is no such thing. There is only being, and nothingness, of which nothing can be spoken or known. We turned from studying the world to studying that which is not. The mystery was—how shall something become nothing, and how shall nothing become something and live and breathe? And the answer to that is memory. To move into life there must be memory, and to move out of life there must be forgetting."

He walked down the last step and around the box to Ralas.

They were of equal height, one in sandals, one in boots. "You are locked here by a memory, fixed by Heart Taker fire. I can fix you, if you like. I can tell you how they did it. Even they won't know, because they are fools who have no idea what they do." He smiled, a smile full of black and broken teeth.

Ralas shook his head quickly. "It won't... Could you maybe, reverse it the other way so I don't have to die?" He couldn't help feeling a flicker of hope, quickly crushing it as the chief showed no sign of agreement.

"You've seen the undead, as you call them? My army?"

"All our soldiers you raised against us," Ralas confirmed, swallowing nervously. Now the ranks of the undead around them, the spirits present, were filled. Un-alive might have been a better term, Ralas thought. The arena was so thick with Tzarkomen that there was no space between them anymore. They occupied the rondel and the space between it and the huts and they crowded thickly between the houses, and inside them, rank on rank of the standing, silent witnesses, breathless as the wind alone stirred the hanging tendrils of their hair and the rags of their clothing. It could have been all of them who had ever been.

He stuttered, "I remember thousands of them. Our friends, fighting for the Reckoner. We had to burn them..."

"Fire destroys the memory," the old man told him gently, patting him on the arm as if to console him, though he felt no touch. "Nothing can stand against it. It is the element of forgetting. Remember that, when you have had enough."

"But they weren't like me," Ralas said, suddenly struck by a fresh horror. "Were they?"

"No," said the sorcerer. "They did not remember themselves. Only the body's memory was active. The mind has its own fires of course, its own hunters—I believe you have seen these already. Once we discovered the truth of how the world works we used them to police our borders and keep our secrets. Such knowledge could surely be used for great ill by those who had not earned it through generations of suffering and loss. But he wanted it for himself, of course. He came for the army but he stayed for the power to open the ways to the other realms. Which is when she appeared…" He lifted a hand in Tricky's direction as he returned, completing a circuit of the fallen coffin. "To offer us a bargain. A deathly curse, and an end to him, her guarantee. And so he is ended but too late. We had already made our own path. The book, as you see, is gone forever."

"But the ways are still open in Nydarrow," Tricky said. "I was there. You didn't close them off."

"To put ourselves beyond his reach and the book as well, we had to go before him. Once he had disconnected the gods it was clear he wouldn't stop for a few warlocks. Time was not on our side but we played it to our advantage when we refused to hand over what we knew. The *Book* was here—it was the people of this place. He massacred them all. And so he destroyed the very thing he needed to maintain his control of the Overworld. And we made the Bride, to ensure he could take no other path. Her secret purpose was to ensure he would never find this way. It was in her but he never looked in others, he only saw them as means to ends, not ends in themselves. So that was our plan. In doing so we spent all we had left. All."

The wind sighed and then Ralas and Tricky stood alone in an empty circle. Above them on the hillock a dry shadow flickered.

"Not all. I've seen her. The lost girl! Kula!" Tricky shouted into the emptiness. "Isn't she the *Book* then? Is it her? Now?" She spun in place, looked at Ralas with a stricken face. "I don't believe it," she said. "There must be some left further north. No way was that woman back in Cinquetann the last of her kind. And Kula. And Lysandra. But… maybe they're not dead. Maybe they only crossed over."

She was struck at that moment by a shivering, splintering ruction in the air which seemed to spring up from the ground and surround her in less than a second. Ralas could do nothing as she screamed and tried to change form but the soul hunters, whatever they were, had got their fangs well in. Through the glass, he saw them rend and tear, pulling out something like a sticky blue-white taffy from her and sucking it in through their gaping mouths. Above the glass she writhed and buckled on the floor, defending from invisible horrors, weakening with every move. He smashed at the things with the glass, not knowing what else to do, a desperate kind of horror in him making him feel something he hadn't felt in a long time—terror that someone else was going to die. Rage made him strike harder and the glass connected with a nebulous head so that for an instant he saw through a large, glaring yellow eye, through its black slit into a distant, icy sky full of stars and the trembling filigrees of light that were the ghosts of dead suns.

There was a noise like a shlooping in-suck of mud, the kind made when someone pulls a foot out of deep river silt with a mighty effort and the stuff takes a deep breath of water and air in return. The eye, followed by the creature, was sucked into the glass. At least that's what Ralas thought had happened. It looked like it had been swallowed up, was being turned inside out and somehow boiled at the same time. The vision was so repellent and surprising that he jumped back, lifting the heavy disc for another blow when two shadows fled out from the edges of his vision.

Tricky was gone.

Only her long, heavy coat was left, lying on the ground.

Shaking with fatigue and his usual weaknesses back in force now the action had passed he bent over slowly, sadly, to pick it over, thinking maybe it was one of her little ways, that she had hidden herself in the lining or beneath it somehow. She wasn't really gone. Couldn't be gone. She was a Guardian, well, kind of a Guardian. Besides, he was going to marry her and although that was a joke, really, it wasn't a joke either at the same time and his anger became misery suddenly as he saw that this was only a coat after all.

He turned the glass over but now it stubbornly showed only a somewhat bent version of the world he could already see, with its empty grass, its sandy, bone-stubbled ground, its burned huts and its old coat. After a moment of despair he bent down and picked up the coat.

A scrap of paper fell out of it and feathered down onto the earth. There was some kind of strange marking on it in a language, he supposed, but one he had never seen before. He picked it up, turned it over. It seemed to have been torn from a larger tome, and the marking was charcoal, but that was all. It didn't do anything.

He put the coat on, missing her terribly. It was a bit too small across the shoulders, even though he was no prize-fighter, but it fitted as long as he didn't try to do it up. The big sleeves and the skirting no doubt looked ridiculous on him but it was the easiest way to carry it. He tried to see if the glass would go into one of the big outer pockets and it slipped easily inside, without making the coat any heavier, oddly. He tried it again. Outside the coat, a heavy lump of glass. Inside the coat, nothing. He looked inside the lapels. There were many pockets here, each one edged in a distinctive colour of embroidery. Carefully he poked the note into one of them so that it couldn't fall out again. Seeing that it couldn't have fallen in the first place made him wonder if it was an accident it had been out at all. He tried some more pockets and found all kinds of tiny tat—thimbles and wool and a little packet of needles and some regular string in a roll. In another place, old candies in a paper bag and a blown glass phial with what looked like dried ink in it. Under the right arm he found a throwing axe so large that by the time he pulled out the haft he didn't have the strength to free the blade. That went back in. Under the left arm there were some daggers and what seemed to be a very large variety of weapon hilts, each connected to blades which came out of the pocket without slicing it and went back in without clattering against their many fellows. When he let these go the lining of the coat remained smooth and in every way fitted with the tailored waist that had given its mistress such a charming outline.

He was turning around, wondering what to do, still sad and uncertain if he could really begin to think of her as gone or dead—surely not—when he saw she had used a finger to write a word in the soft earth, well, three letters.

N Y D it said. There was an arrow next to it, pointing the way. It pointed south.

He looked, to be sure. Very sure. But all the delaying didn't change the message.

She was telling him he had to find her at Nydarrow. There wasn't even a river down that way called Nyd that he could have persuaded himself was the destination. The place he had been tortured and where he was made into an undying, ever-agonised wreck, forever living in a feeble state. The place he hated most, if hate were even a thing he could manage now.

He started walking. He had all the time in the world to refine what it was he was trying to think about fear, well, at least he had a few days always supposing he didn't run into more trouble and on the plus side as he had no need to eat or drink or stop for a rest it was, assailants aside, going to be fairly straightforward. Then he thought about Tricky, and what might be happening to her, with the creatures from the Overworld, in some terrible pit, but over, because it was higher up, and he started to hurry and tripped up on a dried up yellow tibia sticking out of the worn earth by the side of the path. It stubbed his broken toes very nicely so that he sat down suddenly in pain to wait until the stupidity and the agony had worn off. As he did so his gaze crossed the abandoned meeting circle and met the ruined hut where he had found the hidden cellar. In a shimmer of heat-haze a young woman was standing there.

She was a ghost—he could see right through her.

He glanced around but all the others were gone, without trace.

He looked back and she waved at him, hesitantly, leaning forward to peer at him through time. He thought there was the trace of a smile about her and he felt a conviction that this was Kula's mother.

As soon as he thought that, the image of her broke up and blew away on the breeze. At the edge of the village one of the black dog-things which had taken Tricky now howled a sound of utter loneliness and despair from a very human throat.

He felt the weight of the lute's case suddenly on his shoulder.

He went back to the circle and tuned the strings. Then he sang to the empty round, a simple song from his childhood that people sang whenever anyone had to make journey— the going song, he thought of it, though it didn't have a name. Now as he sang it he realised for the first time that it wasn't about going, but returning and he sang it for the people who had lived there who had thought they were not returning, but going, so that they could stop a madman whose bargains they had sought and suffered by.

The run of the river is a merry run
We bowl and wind along

A shadow slunk out of a burned woodpile and sat down barely visible in the long, dry grass.

The sound of the wave is a lonely sound
But the ocean is naught but a song

Another shadow slipped along through the weeds and lay down by the curve of a brown, broken skull.

Be sung, be rung, be run and round
Come first and last to the end

He was singing it for her, so she could hear it, to tell her he was on his way.

We turn and dance in the light of the sun
I'll see you again, my friend.

He was alone with the wind and the sunlight. By the woodpile and the skull empty air stirred and sifted its handfuls of nothing. He had sung it for himself, so he was able to go—a song for the dead. And it had worked. He felt better.

As he picked his way clear of the place he watched every footfall and this time he didn't make any mistakes.

was pleased that Horse was going. It was one more person less to get in the way of any manoeuvre he would have to make in

CHAPTER TWENTY-SEVEN

HORSE MADE HER departure from the ferry early, a mile before the port. She suddenly heaved up to standing while they were packing their bags and sharpening their blades and announced she must get out. The Shelliac, fearful of having a crazed centaur aboard the boat and concerned for the reaction at the Port authority, were quick to pole to the nearest available bank and put out the boarding planks.

"I will begin my work on the hills above the city," she explained, shouldering her shield and picking up her javelin. "I will be heading west along the cliffs to the barren hills. I'm sorry I can't go with you." She looked down at Kula and smiled softly.

Kula was not surprised. She'd watched Horse's connection to the forest gradually dwindle as they went further from it. Even before the centaur said anything she knew that there was no way she could stray beyond the reach of roots and the soft webs of fungi that stretched the limits of the Draeyad's perception beyond the woodlands to the edges of the saltwater shore. It was better Horse leave now, while she was strong.

Kula wasn't sure about Murti but she was sure that she didn't like Deffo, who was never about unless it was a meal time. Murti was easy to see. Deffo snuck around, in and out of sight, and he was pleased that Horse was going. It was one more person less to get in the way of any manoeuvres he would have to make in his one-step-ahead of whatever was going on style of planning. Anxiety about the mission had meant that his watching for any mischance had been focused very sharply on Lysandra the last couple of days and now Kula felt he was fishing about for ideas as to what to do about her, how to control her, how to get her to listen to him. This she must thwart.

As Horse stepped regally off the ferry and onto the bank Deffo was there to watch her go and make sure she was really leaving. Even Celestaine was relieved, though mostly because she couldn't think of a way to shepherd the centaur safely through the hubbub of the Freeport. Since nobody had seen one lately she would have created so much trouble for them that this problem had occupied Celest, Heno and Nedlam all the way here from the island. Now they were watching the problem walk out of their lives and a great relief was on them. Kula was sad though. Horse had been such a warm, comforting presence. She had vowed to come back and see her as soon as whatever business they were being dragged around on was done. As the centaur turned to wave at her she found herself in tears, but sort of glad at the same time. She didn't want Horse hurt and the steady, approaching roar of the port promised a chaos that was filled with danger. As they poled off into deep water she watched the figure of her friend receding and becoming smaller and she wished they weren't going.

It never occurred to her that she could object and not go herself. Lysandra had told her that she felt a sense of purpose in going with Murti on his journey and Kula was now a part of Lysandra, under her wing; where one went the other must. She wanted to be a good daughter. She felt kinship to the lost family even though they were forgotten and even though they had deliberately hidden her and cut her off so she could never remember them. They must have had a reason and as long as she lived they weren't entirely gone from the world. What they had been could find its way again through whatever she did until she had to leave and maybe by then there would be others and other ways forward. Their presence was so strong she was sometimes stretched to imagine that they had been ended in any way at all. Only the pitying looks of the adults reminded her that it must be so.

She stroked the black feather of the creature from the river. She remembered it very well. It lived within her. She could feel its sleeping weight, a soft, single-down brush of awareness waiting for her to find a place to let it free again and she reassured it that she would, as soon as it was safe and away from where stupid people could harm it. Then they were all arranging themselves for the end of their voyage, emerging on deck, clothed, packed, armoured—which for her and Lysandra meant no change at all as they had only ever had the clothes they stood up in.

Just prior to their arrival at the Freeport Celestaine took her aside and handed her a share of the jewels they had taken off Lysandra's dress. Kula was impressed by being given the same share as everyone else and hid it inside a deep pouch of her belt which she was sure was secure, her faith in the tall, blonde warrior bolstered by a fresh responsibility to her. Lysandra didn't have a pocket so they paused to sew her one, concealed by the dress's still-magnificent extravagance of skirt. What the others did with their share she didn't know, but she did see Nedlam biting on some gold wire and holding it up to the light to see if there really was such a thing as a metal you could just chomp into shape. When it moulded to the contours of her jagged teeth she chuckled and wound it around one of her jutting tusks. She saw Kula looking at her and winked.

"We'll see who comes get that, eh?" she said and looked very pleased with herself.

As well as loot, they were divided up into two groups. Murti, Kula, Lysandra and Bukham were to obtain the food and clothing they would need for a journey into colder weather— quite a short journey, Murti insisted.

"We're going to Galdinnion Island. It is a two-day sail or so, around the whirlponds, and then it will be a day or more to hike the Wayfarers' road all the way to the northern circle on the glacier."

Kula didn't know what that meant but it sounded grand. It gave her the courage to face the Freeport itself, which she didn't really want to because even from the outskirts she could see Ilkand was a big place, built both around the river mouth and up on the overlooking hills. It reminded her of the camps and their crowded strangeness full of despair and hunger. The only plus side to it was that Deffo and the others would be about a separate business finding a ship so she didn't have to keep an eye on what he was doing.

At last it was time to say goodbye to the otters. They came up with a trout and deposited it in a sly, proud manner on her foot, scattering water from their whiskers and chirping as the Shelliac whistled them back to their cots. Kula picked up the fish and held it with a finger through the gills like she saw the Shelliac do and gave them a shy wave. They all waved, to her great surprise, and seeing them smile at her made such a sudden tender feeling that she had to rub tears off against Lysandra's sleeve on the way down the planks to the docks.

Once aground and with a mission to the marketplace Bukham soon had them organised with himself at the front and Murti bringing up the rear. Celestaine dealt with some long and tedious business involving guards and identifications and a lot of talking that made people bored and long in the face. Kula waited it out with patience, watching other people come and go, her hand firmly in Lysandra's grasp as both of them stood amazed by the sheer variety of all that was to be seen in such a small area. It felt as if it was raining with people of all different sizes, colours and customs. On the headland above them a tall silver tower stood. The sight of it made Kula shiver. She tugged Lysandra's hand and drew her attention to it.

"Powerful dead things," Lysandra signed to her, confirming her senses. "Not going there."

There were many worse threats than some empty tower though. People with dragonish looks and scales, people with peculiar oily skins and clothing like beetle bits, people with all kinds of decorations and armours, clothing and weapons. Things that may be weapons or agricultural implements or both being carted away in stacks next to firewood and cages full of small animals. Everything was strange. Everyone was peculiar to her. She saw no faces like hers and Lysandra's anywhere, and the group she'd been in, which had seemed only people, now felt like it was more than people. They were stared at. People recognised Celestaine with mixed feelings, but mostly saluted; they saw things in Heno and Nedlam to hate and fear; they welcomed the Shelliac; they tipped their hats politely to Murti and Bukham; they looked long at her and at Lysandra, with narrowed eyes, thinking things that Kula could see weren't very pleasant. She returned their stares and made them break the gaze first but inside she felt as if she wanted to cry and this made her angry and the anger, first hot, was almost instantly cold and hardened to a shell. This was like the camp again and she would have to put on her armour inside to make it through.

She felt Lysandra copy her in that way she had of always knowing exactly what Kula was doing. Lysandra made a noise of surprise in the discovery. She asked Kula—do these people really hate us?

"Fear us," Kula said with the hand speech. "That's our edge."

"Our edge?"

"Some people have a sword made of metal. Some people have edges in other ways. Fear is the best edge for control but it cuts off one from another completely."

"So, they hate?"

"No. Hate binds. Fear separates. Combined they are a trap." Kula didn't know how to say what she wanted to say, but

Lysandra could feel how it worked. Kula felt her surge with brightness, as she always did when she was learning new things. Every time it happened the brightness lasted longer, spread further. She understood what Kula saw but also through their connection Kula could see what Lysandra saw. Lysandra could do a task or use an insight better, further, faster, once she had mastered it. She could connect it to everything and see how it fit. Kula relied on her now for gaining the bigger picture of things. So it was in a few moments that she felt a shift in her perception of the Freeport and its people. They were no longer things divided up by their looks into incomprehensible groups of strange and unknowable freaks. They became things divided up by their behaviour and their motives. In that they were all equal. Her sense of people vanishing and being replaced with hostile creatures she didn't understand shifted. They became an influx of ordinary beings like herself, moving in a single sea of circumstances and moments, easy to understand, easy to see.

She squeezed Lysandra's hand. This was much better. Now everyone was the same and she didn't have to be afraid.

Ahead of them the big, slow-moving hulk of Bukham was moving forward, trailing the warrior group in through the dockyard gates on the roads that led into the port's heart, his head up and his purpose clear. He was like a different person to the sombre, brooding figure that had sat on the ferry. Now he was like she remembered him at the trading post, big and full of confidence and charm.

They agreed a meeting point and time and then the two huge Yorughan and the smaller warrior between them vanished into the crowd, trailed at a short distance by the anxious figure of Deffo who attempted to walk tall as if he owned the place and Celest was merely his bodyguard, but somehow managed to give a distinct impression of both limping and slouching in the most craven way. A guard went behind them, to help them reach some important place which they clearly already knew how to reach by themselves. Kula scowled but she was being moved in a current heading in a different direction. For a moment she felt a clear sense of danger, that they would not meet again.

CELESTAINE WAS HEADED to meet with Governor Adondra, to make a formal greeting and to ask her advice about gaining passage on a trustworthy vessel. The delicate ins-and-outs of politics could have shifted the weight of influence enormously even in the few months since she'd last been here and she didn't hold out much hope for figuring it all out by trial and error, at least not in any timescale that would be useful. Adondra had dished her a sharp but useful lesson in presuming to know anything about port business and she felt a certain desire to make amends for what had happened on that visit, when the Archimandrite had heard the gods' farewell and Adondra had seen the prospects of her town full of refugees go from mere survival enforced by religious zealots to something with a much larger potential for expansion—the future looked more interesting but the difficulty of her position between an enlightened Temple and a seething mass of human interests far beneath that had been expanded a hundredfold. Celest was hoping that some of Lysandra's wealth was going to help with whatever was now going on. And hoping they would not all be put to the stake again.

This time, instead of getting an audience by trading on her power as a Slayer she petitioned in the usual way and lubricated the process with just enough gold that would seem auspicious but not so much it would cause undue suspicion—as if coming into the city accompanied by two Tzarkomen wouldn't do that, but they were mild, shopping-only Tzarkomen, not even tattooed with the markings of the necromancy, and they were with an Oerni trader and a Wayfarer priest. A more harmless bunch there couldn't be.

"How long d'you think before we're arrested?" Nedlam

asked from behind Celest's right shoulder as they waited in the yards of the Governor's mansion. They were already attracting plenty of attention.

"Not this time," Heno said with confidence.

"Wait, don't we know that guy?" Celestaine pointed to a stake placed high on the walls overlooking the yard. Upon it was a head. Although it was discoloured and puffy its death-snarl of surprised disgust was still in place.

Nedlam shrugged—her eyesight was not that good at very long range, but Heno sighed.

"The Templars we saw before Hathel Vale."

"Yeah, he's the dead one that was on the horse," Celestaine agreed. "And you said you liked them."

"They had a dead Templar with them, it was difficult not to like them, as any Templar dead is obviously a good thing, even if the others remained alive," he objected. "But now that looks a lot like Termaghent Phylanstery justice to me. Perhaps even they can do right sometimes."

"Maybe we should skip this and go to the dockhouses at the sea end of things," Nedlam said. "No need to bother the Governor. She doesn't like you anyway."

"Bit late for that," Celestaine replied. Through the milling people a man with the Templar and City surcoat on was coming purposefully towards them, accompanied by guards trying to look like they weren't out for an arrest and failing.

"Fernreame," the official said carefully, assessing the Yoggs with an eye that was pretending not to notice that they were Yoggs at all. "If you would accompany us. The Archimandrite would be pleased so see you now."

"I only wanted to pass on my good wishes to the Governor and ask her advice on a minor matter," Celestaine said as they were casually surrounded. She deliberately took her hand off her sword hilt.

"You have a way of precipitating major change and that is

not welcomed today," the man said. "Please attend."

With a sigh Celestaine fell into line and followed him into the mansion, Heno and Nedlam behind her, making her think of innocent hounds following their master into a ridiculous position of danger without any idea of what they were doing, which wasn't true but it felt true.

They were ushered into a major room where Celestaine recognised Adondra, and was in turn recognised with a glower. The Governor was seated behind a large and imposing desk. She sat behind one end and behind the other, the figure of a much weakened and aged Archimandrite was upon an upholstered throne. A woman with the kind of grimly practical haircut that smacked of self-loathing stood rigidly upright beside him, wearing the pale wool robes of some variety of abnegating low-ranking priest. She was so clean and exacting and the Archimandrite's gaze so dreamy and vacuous that Celestaine had no trouble placing who was the power at that end of the table.

"To what do we owe the pleasure of another delegation from the house of heroes?" Adondra asked, but she was more weary than the last time they had met and she lacked bite.

"I came to ask your advice about safe passage to Galdinnion Island in the Golden Isles. Who takes ships that way and are there any disputes that I might fall foul of."

"Really? That seems so unlikely, and yet... I feel there's more. Go on. What is the purpose of this monumental quest. You have saved the Aetherni and now you are going to save someone else lost in a terrible place without hope except you and your crew of one-time genocidal maniacs?"

Celestaine looked at the discomfiting, flat gaze of the dark-eyed priest and then at Adondra, surviving on sarcasm alone these days. She decided to chuck some truth under the wagon. "Yes. You know me so well. I am off to seek my fortunes and discover what has happened to the gods."

Heno made a disappointed noise, as you might make if you had just seen someone score a magnificently unanticipated own-goal.

The Archimandrite sat forward, awake suddenly. "You're going to find the gods? What a lovely idea. But I must tell you they are very far away and have said they can't come back. If you find them, you will not come back either. On the other hand, I rather like the sound of that."

"I..." Celestaine began but was cut short.

The very serious looking priest with the bad haircut who had been looking at Celestaine without affection broke in. "Do you have any idea how difficult it is maintaining the peace and the rule of law now that being a Templar means enforcing a godless generosity on all and sundry?"

"Does it mean putting the heads of bad soldiers on pikes?" Celestaine hazarded.

"That is one of its less appetising results," the priest said. "I am Carzel, the Archimandrite's moral advisor. It falls to me to judge what kindness means, in any particular dispute. And there are many disputes. Almost as many new ones about kindness as there are old ones about vengeance and robbery and whose land is it. Now we must deal with all the imaginary slights of unkindness in words, deeds and thoughts. And all the omissions of words, deeds and thoughts, whose absence cuts a hole in the hearts of the pure." If it was possible to kill people with contempt via enunciation Carzel would have been guilty of multiple counts of genocide.

"People are very touchy," the Archimandrite said in a mellow manner, and Adondra rolled her eyes in search of patience, as if it was stored under her forehead.

"Those displayed on the poles have been slow to come to the new teachings of the Temple. They don't give up god easy around here," Carzel said. "Which is why, Slayer, I think it would be best that you take the swiftest ship to the Golden Shore and be very prudent about returning, especially if you were to, let us say, inadvertently bring some lost beings with you."

"You don't want the gods back?" Celestaine asked and the whole room sucked in a breath between its collective teeth.

"Heaven forfend, I have never said and never will say such a thing," Carzel stated flatly and with loud, clear diction. She looked fit to spit a tack. "I say that I would not want to see you involved in such a thing."

Adondra leaned forwards, composing her hands. "You want a Drake ship. There's a captain in town I suspect of smuggling ora root among his trades and other materials of similar properties so he won't be averse to paying passengers. Vakloz is his name. He taxes me and I want to tax him, especially on his 'secret' imports. I think you and he would get along very well. I believe he has connections on the Golden Coast that reach well inland and as far as the Islands of the Guloss Archipelago which is where you are headed. There is no end of territory out there in need of great heroism and mighty deeds. You can find him near the docks at the house of his mistress, the Lady Demadell."

Celestaine glanced at Carzel who was drawing one finger slowly across her throat as the Archimandrite smiled and tapped his toes to some unheard music. Her gaze was flat and its meaning crystal clear. But to be sure she said, "Whatever you do, don't bring anything back with you. Customs would take a dim view of anything they can't quantify. We have lately appointed a young man of great ambition from Cherivell and he has firm views on paperwork. We however are very grateful— very grateful—for the gods' final words. And we will do our utmost to see them carried through. People who fail to do so are clearly lacking in the most basic piety and will have to be regrettably detained or made examples of. Since the new rules have come into place the benefits to commerce and daily life in this city have been immense. I hope I'm being as clear as possible."

"Better not come back at all, really," the Archimandrite said dreamily. "Although if you could send them a message with our best wishes I would really appreciate that."

Celestaine was dumbfounded. She hadn't expected them not to want the gods back at all but it seemed that this is what was being said, or not being said. She'd been ready to fend off all kinds of demands and arguments, all kinds of pleading and hope, every situation under the sun, except this one.

"Pop along," Adondra added. "There's a good girl."

Celestaine stepped forwards and put her hand down on the table with a loud clack. When she withdrew it several gemstones lay there, winking and glowing in the lamplight and shooting the odd rainbow ray thanks to a sudden shaft of late sun. She gathered her wits. "We do apologise for troubling you. I hope that this goes some way to assisting with city business."

Carzel leaned forwards and picked out two gems, pushing the third towards Adondra. She looked at them, and then handed one back to Celestaine. "I will see that this goes to help the needy. Those are the people the Temple works for now. We are devoted to service and good works in honour of the departed gods and their final, very clear and explicit wish."

"Be kind to each other!" the Archimandrite said, raising his hand and pointing at the sky with a beatific grin before lapsing back into a blissful doze.

Celestaine blinked. Had these people really gone all out for a godless world of service in such a short time? Even if it was enforced by draconian rule, was that so bad? She hesitated, then gave the spare gem to Adondra. "It's for whatever is needed."

Adondra took both jewels on her side of the desk and pocketed them. "Your good works are noted. Well, I'd like to be snarky about your generosity but there's so much to be built that I won't. Feel free to come and go as you please. Especially go. The longer you stick around the more people will think about Guardians and gods again. The Widow Demadell has a very good table I hear, and she likes to start at dusk. There. Is that enough niceness to satisfy you?"

"I just wanted…" Celestaine felt Heno kick her ankle. "Yes. Thank you."

They were escorted out. In the narrow hall Carzel caught up with them and snagged Celestaine's arm. "Listen, Slayer. It's not that we're not all grateful but I'm just going to put this out there for you to think about. 'Be kind.' In your experience is that the sort of thing that the gods who left here, and left the Guardians, you know, like Wall and the Kinslayer—d'you think that 'be kind' is what they would choose for their lasting legacy? D'you think that's really who he heard through Cinnabran's skull? I'm just saying. Think about it." She put her finger on her nose and then pointed at Celestaine and then at the Yoggs, one at a time. She gave them the thumbs up sign plus a very exaggerated wink and then spun back into the state room.

"So—she's saying they weren't kind," Nedlam said.

"Yes," Heno said.

"Why is everyone talking like they aren't saying what they're saying all the time?" Nedlam scowled.

"In case the gods are listening, or someone with an axe and a grudge," Celestaine said, thinking about it with a growing sense of unease and complicity. "The last two much more likely than the first."

"It does my head in," Ned said and shifted her hammer to the other shoulder.

Another delegation of quarrelling Cheriveni were already filing in two by two. The corridor smelled of too much perfume and nervous farts. Before the door closed they heard Adondra's voice and the rap of her gavel calling them to order.

"What's happening?" Celestaine asked them as they came back outside into the yard. She felt as if she had been summoned to see her mother for a dressing down and while she was all right with falling slowly out of favour as time passed, not able to trade on old glory, she was deeply irritated by the way they resented her when she had come, well, to be kind. A grinding sensation in her stomach made her wonder if she were right about kindness and doing the right thing. Amkulyah's people— that had been better than terrible, when she had done all she could to return the wings. Hadn't it? And here she was, not expecting thanks, but this all felt very unnecessarily resentful. She looked up at the kindly severed head of the unreformed Templar on its pike. "It's just like before, only... very slightly different. Is everyone mad?"

"Dunno," Nedlam said, "but she said something about dinner at the Widow's house. Do you think they can cook like Bukham?" She licked her tusks.

"I think that went as well as you could have hoped," Heno said, clearly having hoped it wouldn't happen at all. "They said we could have a ship. They didn't ask for explanations. They even told us where to get one."

"But I gave them a fortune," Celestaine said, still puzzled.

Heno put his hand on her shoulder as they walked out of the building. "At least they didn't ask where it came from. Smarter than that. But also, smart enough to wonder if someone's coming to find you for it, you not being in possession of a mighty fortune all by yourself and having a reputation for killing things," he said and shifted his shoulders uneasily inside his long dark coat. "Let's get moving while we're lucky. That priest might already be sending a word to this Widow about getting rid of us permanently."

The grinding sensation eased. Heno was right, Celestaine realised. She'd been so focused on thinking of what she might do for the best she hadn't thought about what could happen for the worst. "All right," she said. She felt quite back to herself; positive, focused, all because of danger's thrill and it occurred to her for a moment, that all her works may in fact be aimed right at creating these situations, so she could be what she was, free to move without second guesses. It was a fleeting thought and it flitted fast, swept away by necessity. "But first we need to find the others."

BUKHAM WAS STANDING in the low roofed room that was Rofuel's Ilkand Bank, his mouth half open as he looked at the table where the ruby he had placed down was being examined by a series of experts in a deathly silence. He was awed by the order, the precision, the books and the sense of authority of the place.

There were actual walled vaults, with iron barred doors guarded by uniformed men bearing pikes and axes. There were scales of different sizes—some for coins, some for grain, some for raw metal nuggets—all of them in use, their arms tipping lazily one way, then another before the contents of a pan were bagged and labelled, then carried away by small men in a different uniform to the guards, but similar, cloth jerkins instead of leather over mail, their hands neat and clean, inked in places, their hair tied back or cut short and orderly. He felt a little bewildered, but in a good way. He was following what they were all doing and had realised that a bank was an amazing thing.

At Taib Post the wealth was kept by individuals and regulated by the honesty of their relationships with the matriarchs. It was all rather vague and only the patriarch had a clue as to what the totals might be at any one time. Here there was an incredible order and an exacting system of valuation. Bukham had become expert at understanding the value of a vegetable at any point in the year—depending what it was, its condition, its scarcity and its popularity. He had considered the future value of vegetables only as far as his sense of the weather's consistency ran. He fondly remembered the day he had understood how money worked, and how he could translate the value of a coirib bean into the value of crabapples directly through copper scits.

Here in the bank they were not only able to say what his jewel was worth in terms of scits and pollys but in terms of anything at all, and any combination of things—they had a ledger, continually adjusted by their reviews of supply and demand. Here, at the bank, he saw them talk in terms of things called futures and the values of land and buildings as collateral. He saw them chat over ten ways to consider lending and whether interest was robbery and how to tailor loans carefully to any kind of customer, whatever they thought about interest.

He was so absorbed in this incredible expansion to his repertoire of trading techniques that as he watched his jewel turned he lost track of Lysandra and Kula, thinking them paying attention like he was. It was only when Murti tugged on his sleeve and murmured, "I think we've lost some of our party," that he looked up and realised they were nowhere to be seen.

THEY HAD BEEN bored as soon as they entered the bank with its quiet and order and had gone out the doors to wait in the much more interesting street. At first they had walked up and down, looking at the windows—Kula had never seen a glassed window before and they amused themselves pulling faces at their reflection until a woman came out yelling and chased them away with a broom. A few doors down a delightful smell revealed a bakery and they went inside, watched other people hand over coins for what they wanted and then looked over what they had in their pockets. Lysandra could only find a ring with a green stone in it which looked like it was close to the copper and silver coins. She held that out when their turn came.

Outside in the warm afternoon sun they sat together on a bit of grass at a corner where four streets somehow turned into five streets and tried to share a pie so large that even with a huge chunk in both hands for each of them there was still most of it left. The pie was meats in a fruit-rich, thick sludge of a gravy, and so good that they stuffed themselves, smiling at the people who paused to stare at them and point and laugh. When some ragged little children turned up they gave them pie and Lysandra also broke up the crusts and handed this out to passing rats, who ran off at first as they were used to fleeing for their lives but then, sensing a moment of rare fortune, stayed to gorge themselves and leap for new treats. Lysandra soon discovered that a rat would jump very high, even somersault, if there was a piece of beefy pastry in it for them, and that they would also run up her arms and sit on her head or hide in her pockets. Soon there was quite a crowd.

"Here, what's going on?" A small, filthy man in leathers pushed his way to the front. At the sound and sight of him the children fled, laughing and shrieking, shouting things as they went. He was Ilkand stock, with a grubby Temple badge stuck upside down to his jerkin. "Stand back, I've vermin to collect. Get up there and stand away." He had a net on a stick and a long rod with a sharp, poking end much stained with mud and gore. There was also a wriggling sack on his back and he had a smell which gave him all the room he wanted far faster than his vocal demands. He peered suspiciously at Lysandra.

"Soft in the head, eh?"

She smiled and held out to him the last chunk of the pie which had been resting on her knee. It was as big as two hands. A gob of the filling dropped out of it and landed on the ground, immediately seized on by three rats who had been investigating the bizarre tangles and lengths of her skirting.

The ratcatcher's eyes bulged, torn between two conflicting imperatives.

"An entire Hunter's Bludgeon," a woman said from the crowd with great envy. "An' they've eat the whole thing. Enough for a family of five."

"What's she wearing though?" asked another. "She must be a lady."

"Not any lady behaves like that," said a man with disgust.

Lysandra got up suddenly with a single motion, like a doll being lifted by strings. She held out the pie to the ratcatcher as rats sped in all directions, causing a few bystanders to squeal as their feet were dashed over. "Well, perhaps they should," she said in a pleasant tone.

He took the pie silently and brought it to his mouth as if he expected it to explode with rats but it was clean enough and there was no room for a rat. In a moment he was too busy eating to bother with anything else, although he looked this way and that with ferocious intent, as if marking every scurrying body's whereabouts for later.

Lysandra bent to wipe her hands in the grass and to flick a crumb of pastry off Kula's chin. "We need winter clothes," she said, bringing her hand up with gems in it. A particularly large grey rat was still riding on her shoulder, sitting on its hind legs, hands composed in cleaning its whiskers, ears perked. Lysandra addressed everyone, "Where do we buy those?"

"I know!" A young woman stepped forwards quickly and beckoned. She was dressed in handsome leather gear with a brown knitted scarf around her head and neck through which long, dark hair came in uneven tufts. Her belt had a dagger and a purse on it and she wasn't as dirty as many who were grumbling now the street was blocked. "Kifti Fulp's Furs and Leathers. It's not fancy but it's really well made. And she has some Ystachi working for her. They do the best light mail underlays. Are you going far?" As she moved in closer to Lysandra she hissed quietly, "You need to get moving, words are all over town by now that a rich madwoman is handing out jewels for nothing. Let's go. Quickly!"

Lysandra took the arm she was offered and Kula picked up her other hand. Suddenly there was a loud screeching beside them that made everyone jump. A boy who had tried to pick Kula's pockets as she was watching their new friend was leaping around with a rat attached to his gloved finger. It let go as he waved it about and used his shoulder as a springboard to dive back onto the girl's dress and scurry back down where it had come from. Kula turned and thumbed her nose at him as he yelled about being bitten. He had a knife out in his hand in an instant but a squeaking at his feet made him pause as rats appeared and seethed in a mass suddenly, surging towards him in an arrow shaped wave, whiskers angrily raised over yellowed teeth. He turned and fled as the ratcatcher, still chewing, started to flail around with his net in a big show of determination that captured not a single beast.

Meanwhile a small but fixated entourage was trailing them. Downstreet and upstreet they went at a barely respectable distance. Their new friend took them past streets of modest homes, along the paths where canals were thick with narrowboats overhung by tottering tenements and vast warehouses. They went along narrow ginnels between fenced gardens and wealthy estates, crossed several broad squares with riverside moorings attached where day sailboats and dainty yachts were moored alongside splendid merchantmen and then across the great arch of the Temple Bridge with shops all the way along its length and a tiny temple at the peak, draped in flowers and messages that travellers left to name and search for people lost in the war. Every step brought a new gawker. At last they went up the winding tailor's ways, through the bolt market, the retinue gathering mass from retters and linenmakers, buttoneers and lacemakers, spinners, carders and tanners until they reached the furriers' store at the end with its heavy, iron-studded door. Then Lysandra, Kula and their new friend who introduced herself as Mags Broadaxe of the Ilkand Broadaxes, (smiths and ironwrights, do call in if you need any metalwork doing or are in want of weapons), went inside beneath the heavy wooden plate marked with various runes and letters declaringthem welcome to Fulp's Skins and Hides in several languages, all misspelled and, in one case, offensively so.

Inside the shop Mags carefully closed the door and clicked her fingers in the face of a staring shop boy. "Fetch the Mistress!"

Lysandra looked about. "Mags," she said. "How does shopping work?"

KULA STOOD, AMAZED as the women talked over her head. She had never thought there were this many animals in the entire world. Every wall and surface was covered in piles of fur, leather and scale. Some of it massive. The walls held entire suits of clothing made from these things in various sizes and there were open chests filled with knapsacks and harnesses, gleaming with buckles and studs. Everywhere she looked there were finely made things she didn't even have a name for.

The entourage gathered outside to look through the open shutters. A disgusting reek of boiling leather from the vats in the back yards wafted around them, causing a few to abandon the post while the more tenacious pressed inward at the door to get a better view. At the back various officials and guards craned their necks and pushed people around for lollygagging and other unprosecutable offences against the public wayfares.

IT WAS THIS sea of backs and the back of heads that Bukham found when he finally tracked them down, Murti and the ratcatcher chatting behind him all the way. There was no way to get closer and although he was tall and imposing as an Oerni, taller than most, nobody was bothered about giving him a special view, so he had to crane and peer until Lysandra and Kula emerged from the door. They, he noticed, got a kind of hopeful avenue opening before them which let them out.

They were wearing long, fur-lined coats and carrying heavy packages wrapped tightly and bound up with cord. Without a second thought Lysandra dumped these into Bukham's arms and then looked around, casually picking at her teeth with a forefinger. She seemed satisfied that her work was done.

"Where've you been?" he asked, not sure it was going to be answered as so far—and he only noticed this now—everyone had always talked about and around Lysandra and the girl, and never to them. They hadn't expected her to understand or answer, because when they first met her she had shown no ability or interest in doing so. But here she was, in a white arctic fur coat that couldn't have been handed over for nothing. With nearly a shop's worth of heavy, oiled and treated gear that weighed enough for a good few people.

She glanced at him, "Shop'n". She was looking at him as if he was a bit slow. Her gaze roved around, searching for a new interest. She smiled vaguely at Murti and tapped the top of the corded bundle, pointing at him to show she'd got him something.

"This man says…" Bukham began, turning for support to the ratcatcher only to find he was gone. "You were…" He looked at the number of people following his every word raptly. "Did you spend everything?"

"Mmn," Lysandra continued to fuss with a recalcitrant piece of something in her molars.

"But…" Bukham felt weak, physically weak. The wealth. The value. He didn't know how to explain it to her. He wondered what Celestaine was doing and where she was but in that he didn't have to wonder long because he heard her shout them from the corner and turned to see Nedlam giving him a wave.

"Lysandra, is this a friend of yours?"

He turned back and found a small human woman looking up at him. He looked at Lysandra and back at the woman who held out her hand.

"Broadaxe," she said. "Mags Broadaxe, of the Ilkand Broadaxes."

"Bukham of the Taib Gathering," he replied automatically, shaking her hand.

"We thought you were never coming back," she said, as if she knew him. "Your caravan still wandering?"

"We are, although we have been..." He was cut off by Celestaine's arrival. The two Yoggs had got most of the street traffic plastered to the shop walls on either side, making a show of looking anywhere but at them.

"Hey, Bukham," Celestaine said, affecting not to notice Heno's coat was clearing the area on its own because of the way it marked him out as a Heart Taker, only the truly drama-loving able to stay within earshot of them now. "Who's your pal?" She smiled at Broadaxe and bent down to greet Kula and offer her some kind of sweets which the girl took shyly but with distinct gratitude.

"Broadaxe," said the woman and they shook hands in some complicated way that made them both laugh. "Ironwork and swords. Fine weapon you have there, Slayer."

"It'll do," Celestaine grinned. "Got all the coats already, Buk? Fast work."

He was about to explain what had happened when a carriage came along the lane at a fair speed, drawn by a dashing pair of lunnox whose beards and foot feathers flowed like white water around them as they pranced. They drew a small buggy with two large wheels and a towering canopy of purple silk beneath which a lady in emerald green and mink was seated and wasted no time departing as it drew level with Celestaine.

"You must be the Fernreame Champion. Celestaine the Fair!" The woman had a powerful voice, strongly Ilkand accented and with the plush tones of someone used to getting their way. "My dear, how splendid to see someone of your stature and experience at one of our finest institutions."

Bukham remembered to close his mouth as he surveyed this extra person. She was tall and well-built, strength and flesh combined in a way that had an authority of its own, like the great cattle of the Demri Plains. She had dark hair, curled and combed in lush coils that lay heavily over the deep emerald green of her fine, fur trimmed coat. Mink frothed daintily in veiling an immensely impressive bosom and extended the breadth of her hips below her corseted waist. Her skirts were almost as thickly pleated as Lysandra's dress.

"Permit me to introduce myself," she said. "I am Vantari Demadell. The Governor has appraised me of your arrival in our delightful city and mentioned your need of a vessel." Her gaze swept them all up, like a civilising broom, and under her appraisal Bukham felt himself taller, better, surprised at his own agreeability as though he had always been a fine fellow and only now noticed it. Heno and Nedlam straightened. Celestaine's chin lifted. Lysandra smiled vaguely, Kula giggled. Murti cleared his throat and went pink about the ears. Bukham saw Deffo sidling out of the crowd and edging forwards though he wasn't spared a look.

"In the light of the great generosity shown to the citizens here I would like to extend my hospitality and the use of my connections in obtaining a vessel and crew for your occasion. Please, when you are ready, do join me at my home. I will leave my servant with you. He will show you the way. Good day, Ms Broadaxe."

She didn't wait for a response but used the gangway given to Lysandra to sweep majestically back to the carriage, not a second glance at the Yoggs or Bukham, as if she saw their like every day. Her presence allowed the bystanders to come closer, and the tension in the air lifted.

Bukham looked around. Nedlam was grinning, for some reason.

"Care to explain?" Celestaine asked, looking at Bukham, curiosity in every line of her face. She peered at Murti. "Is this your doing?"

Murti shrugged and held out his empty hands. "Things fall in place when the time is right."

Celestaine's nose twitched. "If you're on homily time then we are in trouble. I think things fall in place when the Governor can't wait to see the back of you. Bukham?"

"I was in the bank," he said. "But they couldn't change the money because they didn't have enough so... she, they, came out and..."

"Got the things," Lysandra said, successfully flicking a piece of fibrous vegetation off the end of her finger into the road now that she'd got it out of her teeth. She patted the parcel Bukham was holding. "All there."

"But I think she spent all the money," Bukham murmured to Celestaine as quietly as he could. "On a pie and some coats."

Celestaine glanced around Lysandra to where Kula had got into a game of jacks with some local children, all of them crouching in the dirt in complete focus as the adults around them went on with whatever boring things they were doing. They were betting coloured pebbles. She was using diamonds and pearls. "I see?"

Lysandra frowned. "I did. I bought a bakery and a leather shop and an ironwrights."

"What?" Bukham said.

Lysandra took a deep breath with an air of fortifying herself for a difficult explanation to the mentally challenged. "I bought a bakery. All the people will run it just as before and deal with all of the things, but now every time we come here, we can have pie. And I bought a leather shop, so we can all have clothes and a smithy, so we can get metal things. Not just once. Always. Mags told me how the things work. She will be running my metalworks."

"But what about the profits?" Bukham said, with the keen sense that the day was escaping him. It had started out quite well, but now it was definitely outpacing him.

"I can't be doing with any of that," Lysandra said. "I've no time for it. But as long as these people can manage I can get pie, clothes and whatevers. Now we will go buy a ship. Then we will have everything. Demadell knows a lot about ships if she speaks true. I will give her this coloured rock of no use at all and I will have a ship." She grinned and her teeth were shockingly white against her plum coloured lips. Her gaze left no doubt that she was using simplified terms for Bukham's benefit.

"But how... a few days ago you..."

"I was with you in the bank," she said. "And in a minute I saw everyone was so busy trying to change the stone for coins and papers and gold and people's goodwill and badwill. That's all right for you and your money. But I don't care about it. So I got the things. I thought it would save you a job."

"...he said you had given them an emerald ring for a pie," Bukham said.

"How many pies make a ring?" she asked and Murti started laughing so hard he had to hang onto his knees.

"A... lot?" Bukham suggested.

"Yes, I think a lot of pies," Lysandra said and looked away from him, dismissing him kindly but firmly. He felt himself in his place and it was not where he thought it had been. He was supposed to be shepherding the mentally unsuited and now he was being organised by... he didn't know what she was but the cautious way that Celestaine trod around her suddenly started to make more sense. "But you didn't know anything about trade yesterday," he persisted, not sure why he had to have answers but he did.

Lysandra glanced at him. "Yesterday." She seemed lost in thought. "It was so long ago."

There was enough distance in her gaze that it might have been an aeon ago. The sight of it made Bukham shiver. He watched her crouch down and gently tap Kula on the shoulder to get her attention. Kula left the pearls and diamonds on the ground, got up, a filthy piece of ribbon twirling about her fingers, and put her hand in Lysandra's hand, ready to go.

"We're off to see the Widow?" Nedlam said hopefully. "The one with the table."

"I would never have picked you to want to live the high life," Celestaine said to her, nodding and casting suspicious glances at Murti, who was intent on retying his sandal and showed no sign of even hearing the conversation.

"Heh," Nedlam chuckled. "No harm in having a little taste of it though. You: show us the way!" She pointed at a man in grey livery, so quiet and still that he could have been a statue until this activated him.

He bowed and made a beckoning gesture. Nedlam picked up Lady Wall and gave a grin of satisfaction, Deffo just behind her, leaving Bukham to carry the purchases all by himself.

THE ENTOURAGE FOLLOWED the servant, and them, all the way through the town. By the time they reached their destination at a three-storey house overlooking the waterfront, the news of a Slayer who had brought wealth and patronage was on every other tongue within the walls. It had to compete with a story about a rat-charming witch who had conjured an infinite amount of pie from thin air and a child who would change pearls for stone. As Celestaine and her party were being welcomed as honoured guests of the Lady Widow Demadell, Governor Adondra was closing the last hearing of the day and listening to a fifth rendition of these tales with the strong, almost unbearable urge to slam her face onto the sturdy wooden table in front of her.

"Shall I send for her?" the Guard Captain of the Temple asked, wringing a glove in his hands as he felt the tension.

"No, no, don't do anything to impede a speedy exit," Adondra said. "And think of something that will discourage everyone within a hundred miles of coming here to seek their fortune. We have enough bother with those who are already present." She glared at the deputation in front of her from the ferry service that ran between Ilkand and the strings of little islands that swung out to the Westerly Ocean. They were thrilled with the stories and pleased to see someone as important as the Governor and the Archimadrite with their problem but as she studied them more closely their worry and discomfort made her irritation with Celestaine began to fade and turn into a fond memory. She rapped her gavel upon the board and nodded to the Captain to begin.

"It's about this hole in the world," he said, awkward with having to say things he expected not to be believed. His hoarse, damaged voice was careful on each word. "I don't think exactly that the sea is draining into it. But. There's definitely things coming out of it."

"Where is it?" Adondra said. "Is it a threat to Ilkand?"

"It's out to the West of Varkadia Mountain, the one that's always spoutin'. Big. Like the biggest whirlpool you've ever seen and it turns, but slow. It's not water turning. It's more like something inside the water. Below. And on the shore nearest to it, on the Varkady shores, we found this. It was among the wreckage of a big ship."

He placed a signet ring on the table, respectfully.

Adondra picked it up. It bore the clear mark of Ilkand and the crest of Captain Neveth. "The *Moon Runner*," she said. "The ship that the Kinslayer stole." It was their largest and most well-made craft, a ship intended for crossing oceans and discovering worlds in order to bring most of them back in the hold.

"Aye," said the Captain. "Matchwood now. Varkadians have been all over it, and their animals, so there's no bodies to speak of."

Adondra sighed. "Thank you, Captain Voran. I will convey the news to the families of the lost. You will be compensated for your find."

"But what about the hole?" he asked and she met his gaze steadily.

It occurred to her that here was the stone for two birds. Maybe fortune was turning her way, she thought. "Mark its location on a chart and have it sent to this address with my note," Adondra said and signalled for parchment and a quill. Under her breath she muttered, "If this doesn't get rid of her then nothing will."

The Archimandrite watched her with a comfortable expression. "The island is far away."

"Far enough," she agreed. "We will be sure to send no ships that way and lose almost nothing. Those who choose to go for the sake of adventure and discovery will do so at their own account. Voran, if you would keep me informed of any changes of state the hole may make the city would be glad to pay you for the trouble. In the meantime, your silence on the matter would be appreciated. Until we have more information."

"Yes'm," he said and took the paper she handed him. "I'll do it right away."

When he had gone Adondra turned to Carzel and the Archimandrite. "You are not to speak of this. Are we agreed?"

"What if she doesn't return?" Carzel asked.

"She will," Adondra said. "Those whom the gods wish to destroy they first make run a very long chain of errands into terrible dangers, and one dragon and one demigod slaughter is hardly a chain. There has to be a third link for that. She'll be back."

"Mmn," the Archimandrite murmured reprovingly as he got up, leaning on Carzel, "I don't think our gods would do anything like that to someone. Not very kind. In fact it sounds very much like spiteful envy to me."

The gavel hit the table smartly. "Anyway, the day's business is adjourned," Adondra said. She paused, and sighed. "I suppose we could give her supplies."

"Yes, I think that would be the least we could offer," the Archimandrite said. "If we wanted to stay on the right side of things. Not to mention there is the hole that needs fixing."

Adondra looked at him with caution. "What things? You mean you. And the Temple."

"I mean the things," he said. "All the things." From a doze

of negligent beaititude he was suddenly wide awake. There was such a presence about him, such a certainty—and she knew he wasn't talking about gods. If there were more things about than gods, guardians and Ilkand city's populations she didn't want to know about them at that moment. Put it down to an old man's fancy.

She closed her mouth in an uneasy line. "Well we'll give her supplies and a ship if that tosspot Vakloz decides he can't be bothered."

CHAPTER TWENTY-EIGHT

DEFFO MET FURY, or Dr Fisher as he was known to everyone besides the other Guardians, on the headland overlooking Ilkand Bay. He hadn't wanted to but Fury had insisted and since Deffo didn't like being followed everywhere by a noisome parakeet constantly asking him, "Where's da trouble? Where's da trouble, squire, eh?" he had discreetly withdrawn from the party as they walked through the market and made his way up here, following the flapping, multi-coloured invention of Duke Timoran all the way. The parakeet was meant to be for lords and ladies who enjoyed new and exciting means of rapid communications in setting up their various intrigues but, like the brass mechanical army, it had suffered a lot from local weather conditions and was now only fit for annoying someone to the point of madness until they did whatever it had been told to ask them to do or found a way of permanently disposing of it.

Deffo had swatted it with his walking stick, but it was too quick for him and after a houseman in livery had tossed him two scits, thinking him a refugee doing a busking act, he'd given up that effort and done as he was told.

"What do you want?" he asked the taller and more distinguished Fury. Fury had a certain short tempered, hawkish nature that didn't abide Deffo gladly and he was longing to be out of there and into a pleasant evening anywhere else.

"I want to know what you know about this Tzark business," Fury said. The parakeet, now that its duty was done, had returned to his shoulder and switched itself off with a distinct spanging noise. He removed it and placed it back in his satchel. "Tricky must have seen you. And here you are. Who are those women and where are they taking them?"

"I don't know and we are all going with Wanderer to see the gods again. Why didn't you ask him, anyway?"

"Asking you is always more rewarding," Fury said. "And he has a way of not giving the answers. Did Tricky say she wanted to reconnect them with the world?"

"No." Deffo paused. "Did she say that to you?"

"No," Fury said. "Isn't it strange that there are Tzarkomen abroad with you and Tricky had a Tzarkomen coffer with her the other day. But she's not here and they are."

"It's strange that you spend your life working in a dusty shop pretending to be human but I didn't bring that up," Deffo said, resentfully. "Each to their own. I should think you'd find more answers in Tzarkand."

"The shop is not dusty," Fury said. He paused, watching the gulls and gannets wheel over the port, the cloud coming in across the sea on a breeze of chill and damp. "She's up to something, but for the life of me I can't figure it out."

"Tricky?"

"Who else? And if I find out you knew and it endangers my existence in my clean and beautiful shop then we will meet again."

"Why would I know anything?"

Fury looked at him. He smiled, although it was very much a baring of his long, slightly yellowed teeth. "Go along now. Before they miss you."

CHAPTER TWENTY-NINE

THE WIDOW DEMADELL owned one of the finest houses in Ilkand. It was set back from the harbour partway up a hill in a many-terraced splendour of mingled gardens and small buildings, from whence it commanded many excellent views of both the town and the sea. A certain grandeur of vision had given it a torchlit hall capable of hosting over a hundred guests in a prime position, lower than but certainly on nodding terms with the Temple on the opposite cliff.

The walk up to it wound through fragrant bushes and alternately attempted to amaze and delight as it offered glimpses into secluded bowers followed by the sharp, windswept vastness of the sky, land and waves. It was almost impossible to get Lysandra, Kula and Nedlam more than ten yards without a game of halt, stare, explore. Bukham had started to feel churlish by halfway up as he chivvied them along. He wanted to appear urbane and sophisticated but inside he was joining in every laugh as they discovered another hidden stone table set with sculpted stone jugs and fruits or gawped at a breath-taking expanse of the sun going down in orange splendour behind the mage's spire. Gulls shrieked and wheeled high overhead and they could see smaller and fatter birds skimming the waves far below. It gave plenty of time for both him and Celestaine to reconsider the wisdom of accepting an invitation without the forethought of bathing and dressing accordingly, especially when they forgot to consider whether or not they would be the only guests. He had memories of the finer parts of trading life and they didn't include greeting people in the same sweaty, stained things you'd been travelling in for days. These people perfumed the air with sixteen kinds of bushberry flowers. It seemed unlikely they'd be keen on street people, but their fears went unrealised as they were ushered to the open hall and were greeted by the sight of all the guests wearing nearly identical garments, even Lady Demadell herself, who was cunningly outfitted with a half-armour and linens beneath an artfully muddied cape.

She swept it back gracefully to reveal a short sword and a dagger in her belt as she came to greet them in person, Celestaine first, then the rest. "Slayer, honoured voyagers, how thrilling to have you. Please, no standing on ceremonies, let the feasting commence!" She flourished her hand and the gathered worthies, of every kind, including some he didn't even know the names of, immediately fell to plundering the tables and filling up the benches. Bukham was gazing, stupefied with surprise at the honours, at the planes of her majestic bust, and found himself suddenly wondering what had happened to Tricky, and poor, wrecked Ralas. So piercing was his guilt for them missing out on this that he stepped aside and asked Heno if there had been any signs.

But Heno was looking across the hall at someone steadily making his way towards them through the crowd. Bukham followed his gaze. The two of them towered over most of the guests but this man was shorter by the same margin, though he seemed to be not only short but entirely scaled down one level. He was wiry and dressed exactly as Bukham had always imagined sea captains, in sturdy thigh boots, tight trews and a short overkilt of heavy oilcloth panels hinged together with mail. His shirt and doublet were wrapped about by double bandoliers upon which a variety of weapons and pockets and tools were neatly hung, their leather as black and supple as only lifetimes of steady use could make them. He had a skirted overcoat in red, black and purple which was his only extravagance besides a waxed moustache and neat, pointed beard. His silver-white hair was half braided and hung down his back to his waist. Three heavy plaits that hung over his shoulder bore an array of trinkets, rings and beads, finished with feathers and, on the largest, an owl skull with a black beak.

Heno was staring at him strangely, even more than the appearance warranted, Bukham thought. Celestaine noticed Heno's fixation too and stepped in front of him just as the man reached them and the faint scaling on the sides of his face became apparent in the flickering torchlight.

"No need for defences, Slayer," the man said in a choppy kind of way, as though biting through every word of the Kandir and then devouring it. "News of your presence here travels fast. I am Vakloz, Captain of the *Snakeheart*. We sail out of Ystachi waters and bear Ystachi flags though we are free traders. My Lady Demadell informs me you want to sail to the edge of the Wanderer's Ice Road on Galladion Isle."

He barely came up to Celestaine's shoulder. Bukham was aware of Kula tugging urgently at Lysandra's hand as they all gathered to see. Around them the socialites of Ilkand, those who were scraping together society from war's leavings, craned to hear as the Lady joined them. It wasn't her gaze that the Captain's locked with, however, but that of the stooping, twice-his-height Murti.

"Hello, old friend," he said. "What brings you to this neck of the woods?"

"Mysteries," Murti said, and smiled before Celestaine cut him off smoothly.

"We are seeking to restore some old relics from pre-War days to their rightful owners," she said, with a smoothness that Ralas might have been proud of.

"Reparations?" the Captain looked surprised. "Well, you're the only ones I've seen so far."

"And retributions," Heno added. "Where required."

"Indeed, and what have you to be venging, friend?" There was a distinct iciness to the Captain's tone.

The Lady put her hand on his arm gently for a moment and something passed between them before she let go.

"A lifetime in the mines and the cells," Nedlam said. "So, the usual. And yourself?"

"Five ships and crews. Some in the drink. Some went to the life-forges."

At the mention of these things the Lady became paler and her lips thinned.

Celestaine frowned. "Life forges?"

But before anyone could explain they were interrupted by a slim boy wearing the Lady's livery who came dashing up with a note sealed in the Governor's wax and signet. The Lady noted it and then with a curious look passed it to Celestaine. "It appears this is for you."

Celestaine broke the seal and unrolled the letter. They could all see that it was a map, and rather a fine one, which had been lately annotated and a key attached to it with bearings. A compass was included which slid out of place and would have fallen to the floor had the Captain not darted forward and caught it, bringing it up in surprise before his face.

"Ystachi-made. What have you there?"

Celestaine held it open and they peered at it. "It's a map of the ocean to the North. But someone's drawn on it—a route from Ilkand that leads to the Ice, but then follows… What is this circle?" She angled it so that Captain Vakloz could see but he didn't need to. Even upside down he had already noted the essentials.

"It's the whirlpool," he said. "The hole in the world, as they call it since it opened up. When the Kinslayer came through here, when he took my ships. That's where he went. Some over the ice and some towards the archipelago. They sank there, all hands lost. The crews of his on the ice set up the forges and well, that's where he made his dragons."

"How did it get to Bladno from there, then?" she asked.

"More than one hole," the Captain said.

"Wait, you mean under the earth?"

"And the ocean," he said. "Yes. And he had ways of connecting places that didn't pass through the world in between. The life forges are down there."

Celestaine let the map roll up. "How do you know so much about it?"

"Because I was on board when the last ship went down and I came back, through the ice."

For a torchlit feast the hall had gone mightily quiet.

"More drinks! We have fables to tell!" Lady Demadell commanded and at her gesture some musicians gathered in a corner struck up a fresh tune. She turned to Celestaine. "One can share a story with a Slayer one would not bother to trouble lesser minds with. Your map shows what the sailors have known for ages but had not told until lately."

"Why now?" Celestaine asked, reaching to a passing tray for the largest cup of wine she could see. She watched Lysandra and Kula help themselves.

"Because you're here, my dear. Nobody dares the wrath and curses of the Varkadians, nor the galleys of the Ystachi, and the hole requires a venture into regions both claim as their own. Much as they live in terror of the whirlpool they have a more pragmatic vision when it comes to their mortality above the waves. But you have killed the beast at Bladno and you have brought an end to the Kinslayer himself. Rumour has it that you have given wings to the wingless and here is proof that you have become allies with the most scurvy and terrifying of souls," she said and glanced warmly at Heno and Nedlam.

"Not to mention your most generous, wild companions," this time the glance went to Lysandra who was drinking wine like it was going out of fashion, both hands on either side of a small jug, oblivious. "Surely you see where this is going?"

"I'm here to clean up the mess..." Celestaine said, wonderingly, feeling an appalled expression settle on her face. "That's what everyone thinks. That I'm the cleaner."

"Was heroism ever anything else?" Lady Demadell asked. "And seldom has it ever come in such a well favoured and generous package as yourself."

Celestaine reached out suddenly, dropping the map to grasp the Lady's arm, gently but firmly as she spoke in a whisper of absolute conviction, "I do not want to be sung about, talked about, or considered anybody's doer of great deeds. Do you—"

She was cut off by Lysandra coming up for air, one hand sweeping across her mouth before she declared loudly and in perfect Ilkand-Kandir. "Lies. She loves cleaning. And besides, that's where we're anyway going."

All eyes turned to her, as if they hadn't been longing to anyway.

"And who might you be, my dear?" the Lady asked, her gaze roving over the tattered threads on Lysandra's dress where it was clear that some decorations had lately been snipped away.

Lysandra finished her drink, wiped her mouth on her sleeve and tossed her cup aside. "I'm Lysandra. The Kinslayer's Bride."

CHAPTER THIRTY

AT FIRST WALKING to Nydarrow seemed like it was the only thing to do. It was painful and it was far, but it was possible for Ralas. He was glad to leave the Tzarkomen's bereft world with its flitting ghosts, like a constant shiver at the edges of vision. They ended once he'd passed the marker post of skulls and so he figured that's what it had been. He didn't know for sure and he didn't care to know. On his back he carried the lute and in his arms he carried Tricky's coat because it was too hot to wear two. Sundown came quickly as he measured his way in steps, moving with a slight rhythm, like a phrase made of footsteps, talking to the way, asking it how it was going, how far, how long.

Dusk came and the answer was clear. Too long. He had made a few erratic miles. She had been swallowed whole by... well, by something he didn't understand—and if his only way to find her was to reach Nydarrow he had days of marching ahead at an army's fattened, whip-lashed pace. He had a dead bard's pace. It could be a week. He could go astray and it be more. The only bonus to being in this landscape—full of small valleys, full of trees, thick with an absence of people—was that only the geography was giving him trouble. And then the geology decided it would give him some more. His foot struck a large rock, concealed cunningly in the open, and he tripped up and went arse over tit down the steep hill he'd been trying to carefully negotiate in the vague idea that at the bottom was either a little track that led to the north road or a river full of midges that also, eventually, led to the river that led past the north road.

He clutched the coat reflexively and endured the battering by counting how many things he struck on the way past. Grass, stone, small tree, bigger tree, thorny bush, thistle... and there we are, there was a river. Call it a stream. Muddy rivulet. Rocky-bedded thread of deceptively cold mountain dew. Whatever it was it was wet and full of hard and painful reminders that he was easily broken. He waited for an arm to straighten and for an ankle to remodel itself before pulling himself up and onto the hillside. He was soaked but remarkably Tricky's coat seemed dry. It shed a few drops of water which ran off it like diamonds. The piece of paper had fallen out of the un-fall-outable pocket and landed on the muddy scrape that passed for a bank. Rat feet had marked it and showed the way to a remarkable number of holes, he saw as he bent to retrieve it. The last daylight glowed fiercely orange in the west as he reached, seeing, or thinking that he saw the lettering on the note shivering and changing...

A thing surged upwards out of the raw gravel and muck, causing it to burst open and fountain about, scattering in bits everywhere. He lost the paper in the deluge of earth pattering down on his head and hands. He glimpsed, through the cage of his fingers, a humanoid thing, black in the twilight, glistening on hard surfaces; clawed hands, chitinous plating, a long, ugly head like the painted skull of a horse, teeth, a long tongue flickering out to taste the air in a whiplash of slime. He waited for the inevitable pain and brutality, not braced because that never helped, only delayed and prolonged matters.

He was still waiting ten seconds later, and ten after that. He took his hands down from his face. The thing stood there, folded in storklike angles into a resting state. He didn't see eyes—the face if there was one was covered by a shield of translucent grey which reflected the sun's dying light in soft lines of gold and pink. Beneath it something slid. The tongue came out again, not so much this time, like it had gathered all it needed and was only checking for updates.

When it continued not moving he stood up straight, clutching the coat to him, reminded of his childhood ragdoll with a sudden sharp pang in a bit of him he'd thought long since gone. Up and down the gully only the water moved, undeterred, around the creature's legs. If he hadn't seen its arrival he could have mistaken it for a dead tree in the near-darkness—well, if he didn't count the tongue. He felt that somehow it was linked to the paper and looked about again for the note but there was no sign of it anywhere. As he moved the creature moved too, startling him even as he realised it was mirroring his own actions.

What unnerved him the most about it was the clear sense that it could not have come out of a hole in the ground because now there was no hole visible and because it was far too big for the amount of upheaval it had caused. The impression he was left with in his unmagical senses was one of it emerging simultaneously from below the actual earth and from nowhere. Or off the paper and the mud slinging was accidental damage when it exploded into being.

"I... er..." He found himself talking and stopped almost instantly as it reached out one arm towards him—slowly, cautiously.

He stood, freezing and wet, and made himself stay as the limb extended and a clawed appendage reached out, fingerlike and tentacular at once, its tip revealed by the expiring daylight to be reshaping itself from the hardness of a claw to the nub-end of a finger. It gently tapped the collar of the coat he was holding. Twice. There was a careful patience to it, a kindness, that made him feel it wasn't here to hunt and slay, but to do something else.

"It's her coat," he babbled. "Her coat. Your paper was in it. Something like a ghost or a shadow dog took her underground.

Under," he pointed down with an exaggerated gesture, understanding that where she'd gone and where it had come from could easily be the same place. "She left a note saying I ought to go to, or was it that she had gone to? Anyway, to Nydarrow. Nydarrow. I have to take her the coat. I have to save her from—" But he didn't dare say "you" and even if he'd wanted to he couldn't have because at that moment the thing which had been so patient and treelike became faster than thought.

He was grasped in a net of rapidly hardening tentacles which sprang from the palm of its hand and gripped in towards its knobbly, awkward body. It hissed and warbled, the sounds very like speech although they were coming from nothing like a human mouth. "Take you there," he heard and then they were enveloped in a kind of breath-ripping cold and darkness he'd never experienced before, in which he was convinced he had instantly dissolved like a mote of salt in water.

The symphony of the universe reverberated within him again and for an instant he saw it one more joyful time but before he could make anything of it the protective grasp of the creature was unravelling. He wished it wouldn't but there was no protection that would work in any case. They were at Nydarrow and all he had to do now was go into its guts, find Tricky and get out.

He looked around. Everything was grey, vague. He was standing on a kind of fine sand. He felt insubstantial and that a light breeze could destroy him and on reflex reached out to grasp the creature's arm. It was solid and hot, hotter than a moment ago but he held it and gasped his way through the next few painful seconds.

"This place," Taedakh said as he had to take a pause for a few moments, "is where I am from. When the Kinslayer made you, he brought a part of you here and then kept most of you put. You cannot come here and survive, but also, you cannot leave here. The magic of the Heart Takers is one of separations. They found a way to bind you in both places, through your body."

He said, "It's death."

"It is not death," Taedakh corrected him with more than a trace of annoyance. "It is my home. The gods made the first hole that connected this place to your world during their joyous creation of your Guardians and in so doing began its end times. The necromancers made many more of them, without noticing at all; hundreds and thousands of tiny holes. And the Kinslayer more still, though he punched with greater intent to draw energy for his magics. None of you did anything to contain what came back the other way. Our life, if you will call it that, is a delicate balance of finely tuned vibrations, most of which was destroyed by the time you were born and most of us with it. The holes allowed order from this world to leak in as the energy that was taken leaked out, and so things that ought to have dissolved remained intact and because they were bodiless and without mind they are constantly driven to seek their original forms. They accrete energy, disrupt the fabric, destroy us merely in passing on their way to search for a route back into your existence. Their struggles amplify the dissonance and the holes expand accordingly in cycle which is ever-speeding to the point where this world and yours will slowly undo each other, order into disorder and so on, until there is only a fragment storm of this sand: a structure of emptiness, without meaning. Together you and I will find your lost companion with our memory of her. Make a song. Music is an incredible power to order. Make an order that defines you against undoing and which makes her seem most real. The dogs are hunting."

Ralas almost missed the last line, he was so busy trying to understand. He fumbled the coat, dropped it, went to pick it up off the sandy floor as he reached for the case at the same time but his hand never found it. He was grabbed instead by a sharp, acidic tendril of pure pain at the wrist which sent a shattering, terrible thrum up his much-mended arm. He screamed reflexively. Taedakh lunged over him and the grip vanished. He turned to—

"Do not look for that thing," Taedakh said with finality. It handed him the lute case. "Play."

"But I..." He was curious, in a grievously foolish way, but since he couldn't die he didn't see what harm it would do. At the last moment however, he found he didn't do it. He took out the lute and began to play the first song that came into his head when he thought of Tricky. After a second he realised with embarrassment that it was a slightly cleaned-up version of 'Three Farmers of Doubty' and not something he would ever, ever have chosen if he'd had a minute to think about it.

Immediately the path firmed, shape and form appearing out of nowhere, and Taedakh picked up their pace again, head lolling from side to side as it divined the way. Ralas had started to tire. His fingers, his arms, the coat he'd recovered dragging. He was sore with playing now and lack of practice made him fumble the notes here and there. They turned and he was sure they had been there before. Even in the song he had lost track of what verse he was in. His feet ached, his back was a bent rod. He began to lose sight of everything in a softly blowing hail of sand.

"Tell me about her," Taedakh said. "Quickly. Tell me everything." The urgency in its tone made him frightened. It had grown as they went. In one stride it covered enough ground for ten of his, hop-picking its way like an ungainly crane through the grey world where all that existed was a thinning strip of rock-strewn path, turning around and back and down, earth falling away on either side of it into a dark that seethed. He was dragged with it as though attached by an invisible cord, the sand abrading everything, filling the lute until it became nearly silent.

"I can't," he said. "I don't know anything about her. She's always lying. Or not lying but not telling the truth. Her hair... curls... at the ends." The vibration in his arm felt like a running current flowing out of him and as it did so his thoughts began to jumble. He started babbling in a panic, "It's dark. I used to think it was black but really it's more like a very dark red, you know like that wine the Kelicerati value so highly, the legendary one made from the envenomed blood of living prey combined with the juice of the shadeberry; a single thimbleful is enough to kill an octilant but it makes the Kelicerati have visions and enables them to see far away to other bands or what are they called, a group of Kelicerati? Is it a host? A brawl? No, too disorganised." He was so busy naming thoughts to try to pin them down that he had stopped playing, and found that he was plucking the same string over and over again, barely moving.

"A skitter," said a voice from the grey haze in front of him, beginning to resolve into a form he had started to think he would never see again. "A skitter of Kelicerati. Quick, pass me my coat."

Ralas watched as her hand was the first thing to take shape, fingers emerging from a general hand, then the nails, a little broken and grubby beneath their chipped paint thanks to the journeying, then the soft ochre colour of her skin coming in over the strange grey of Vadakh's primal substance like sunlight moving across a statue. Movement of the fingers triggered the appearance of fine lines at the knuckles, then a texture of the skin and suddenly it was her hand, in its fullest, attached to an arm that stretched backward into the nearly-nothing ghost form of something that might have been a woman or a man.

He held out the coat, almost falling down with exhaustion. The hand took it and in doing so brushed his fingers. An electric sensation of cool running flowed out of him and into her. The rest of her stepped free from the fog and with both hands she gripped the coat at the collar and swirled it around to put it on her—but the coat spanned suddenly more than her small body. Its sweeping wing was cast over and around Ralas too, and around and over the towering stick insect that Taedakh had become. It spun him around as his knees gave way and beneath its flowing hem for a moment he glimpsed behind him and saw the light of it shine off her face and the points of her daggers, the gold of her rings. It was only a split second, not enough to understand it, only enough to save it for later. Then the coat was around them and the mass of Vadakh rushed around them as it closed. He heard a violent banging and saw the brilliant white flash of firecrackers, smelled the harsh sulphur of their smoke as it cut the air in half.

The coat lifted off and Tricky shrugged it onto her shoulders. "You did well. You remembered me," she said, looking herself over and then reaching down to help him back to his feet. She was smiling.

THEY STOOD IN the murky dank filth of Nydarrow's dungeon lanes but it was a vast improvement to Ralas with its solid, dependable, everyday horror. He never thought he could have been grateful to be back inside his old cell but the sweet relief of solid floors and massive iron bars which couldn't be thought out of existence was so enormous that he clutched the cold metal and hugged them to him for a second.

"Steady on," Tricky said, eyeing him. "She's not that into you."

He realised they were back to business as usual and let go, easing back into his pains and aches. The two of them were alone, no sign of Taedakh or any hint that there could be another reality. The air held a fetid odour of rot and fermentation so thick it was almost edible. In the feeble light of the globs of glowing, snot-like secretions on the lichens which festooned the walls, they both looked like animated corpses. Echoing around them a constant threnody of shrieks, hoots and rumblings made a background soup of inhuman noise: the rumble of a sinister and hungry jungle.

The delight was quickly wearing off.

"Where's Taedakh?" Tricky asked, patting her pockets. "Do you have the paper?"

"I lost it," Ralas confessed as a cold breeze swept briefly over them. It bore a sulphurous stench and a hint of barbecued flesh. "Back in Tzark near the border."

Her shoulders slumped. "Well, I suppose I'd outplayed him anyway. He was due for a rest. In that case the only way out of here is going to be in disguise." She slipped a hand into one of the jacket's inner linings. "We'd better be something everything else fears. Our scent won't change but I think that'll hardly be noticeable." She produced a silver half disk, rather like a coin that had been clipped, but it was unmarked and completely smooth. The flatter side was thick and the rounded edge was thin and sharp. "Elder Dragonscale," she said. "Prismatic magic."

Ralas touched it. The surface was as smooth as glass and mirrored. "What's it do?"

"By itself, not a lot, but with the Galick's Mirror, which is a mindsight mirror, it will change how we appear, as long as I am awake—" She held up a small bamboo hoop, covered with what looked like a piece of skin, stretched out so thinly it was translucent. Red and blue veins in it seemed to pulse and he didn't look closely enough to see if they really were doing that.

"Better give it some water," she said and looked around, eventually finding a puddle of liquid at the edge of one cell door. She dipped the skin into it and when she brought it up the pulse had quickened. "Nice. Now. You have the scale on you and I will operate the mirror."

It had, he saw, two ribbons attached to it with hairclips that she put in place so the horrible disk was over her forehead. Immediately it welded itself to her skin, a grisly diadem. She seemed unconcerned as a fresh surge of red lines trailed like new rivers through its damp webbing and tucked the shiny scale into Ralas' hand. "Put it somewhere you can't drop it."

He thought a bit and went to put it in the lute case only to find it was gone. "My lute!"

"Did you leave it in Vadakh?"

"I... I must have dropped it when I fell over under your coat," he said, miserable beyond measure. "I... yes."

"That could actually be useful."

"You wouldn't be saying that if it was your lute!" he complained, heartbroken in a way he hadn't expected and angry because that sudden hurt blindsided him. He remembered now, there had been the drop and slide of the case strap slipping off his shoulder and down his arm. He shoved the scale into his shirtfront where it ended up at his waist so he couldn't lose it. His belt was tight, helping to hold his guts together, and there was no danger of it falling through.

"I might say it and I'd definitely have left it because it would be one way of finding a route back into the damned place and you never know when you need one of those." She tossed her hair back. "Now, be careful because you're going to feel as if you're actually the thing you're pretending to be in terms of, you know, arms and legs and whatnot, and I'm thinking you definitely won't be able to talk."

"Couldn't we just jump in a puddle or something?" he asked hopefully, suddenly much more keen on yet more magic compared to a few minutes ago.

"Used up all those spells," she said. "It's been a very expensive trip."

"We'll never catch up with the others," he said. "We've come the wrong direction."

"We were never going to," she replied airily but she was cut off by a screaming shrill from behind her and then the sound of running, so fast it took Ralas' breath away just to hear it. A dark shape came through the end of the hall arch and pounded towards them. It stood up from an all-fours position at the last second and he realised that Taedakh was there. He was smaller than his towering form, barely the size of Ralas, but obviously stronger. He held a bulky, rounded shape over one 'shoulder' and set this down as he arrived so that it rolled through the muck and sat up of its own accord, coughing and blinking. It was Dr Catt.

He got up, holding the strap of a large satchel that was around his shoulder as if it were a rope to hold him into life. "I may have tripped a few of the place's defences," he said in that half-bumbling way that made Tricky's teeth grind. "It's been quite an exploration. Tell me, my dear, if that festering gallery two levels up was the library. Was it?"

"Yeah," Tricky said. She had her hands on her hips and was looking at him without a lot of love lost, Ralas felt. "What's it to you?"

"I came merely to see if there were any forgotten little items being used as cutlery and so forth, by the Yoggs, you know, and while I was looking about I came upon… ah… oh!"

The satchel, which had been trembling—and Ralas had thought trembling with Dr Catt's entirely plausible sense of mortal terror—suddenly exploded at both sides of the cover flap and a brief torrent of small dark forms came scurrying out. They rolled and bounced, balls of blackness that looked both furry and not entirely corporeal, and darted about his feet, tumbling up against Taedakh and even against Ralas' own feet. He could feel them popping and rolling over him as lightly as dust bunnies, which was strange because he was wearing boots and really should have felt nothing. It was as though they almost passed through him a little bit.

"Ah, no! My dears. My little ones. Back you come!" Dr Catt made a valiant effort to pounce upon the things but they darted nimbly out of the reach of his fingers and circled, gathering and spreading in rapid waves. Ralas kept fancying he saw tiny paws and flashes of tail and whisker but these were only suggestions, rather like the ones that Taedakh had when you looked at him—suggestions of tree and rock, scale and case, skin and features—but when you looked with your direct focus that suggestion became unfocused, blurred and lost. When he didn't look at these things they were small, round mice with very long whiskers. They may have had holes for eyes. When he did look at them they were a misty ball, larger, but indefinite. They were a sort of rodent, or a little predatory warm creature, furry, for certain. Their hands were infinitely delicate. They could have made clockworks for gnats with those exquisite fingers and thumbs.

"You took the vholes," Tricky said with anger and disappointment.

"They were his bookkeepers," Dr Catt said with a helpless neediness—the weakness of the collector in the presence of a unique find, as if anyone would have done it in his place.

"I trust you still understand they were not here of their own free will," she said. "And now look, you've used something on them. What was it?"

"A little nip and fizzle, some sleepy herbs that work so well on rats. Nothing they won't soon recover from. But they were so hard to get into the bag, you see…" He stopped because her hands were at his collar, twisting it hard into his neck, her face almost touching his.

"Stupid, greedy old man!" she hissed. "Do you ever care what you've done? No. You don't care. Did you know I could read that damned box? But you thought you would fool me, didn't you?"

"I… knew you would be safe enough. It's your nature."

"And what about him?" She jerked her head in Ralas' direction.

"But he's, my dear, he's already quite dead. There could be no trouble for him." He peered at her forehead. "My goodness. The Mirror of…"

A screeching sound, claw on glass, dividing. She dropped him and as she let go the creatures all turned as one and rushed towards Taedakh, onto his feet and up his legs as they climbed him like a tree and gathered in a mantle upon his shoulders; a mantle that winked with hundreds of glimmerless eyes.

"Why didn't you go for the sceptre?" she spat with fury at Dr

Catt. "Can't you even manage to get *greed* right?"

Ralas didn't understand but he saw the satchel swing with something short and heavy inside it as Catt re-established his hold and his footing.

"How little you reckon with my abilities. One might think you had sent me here on purpose," Catt said, puffing and clutching his chest for a moment.

"If one weren't pursued by ghedkhani one might give some time to that thought," she agreed, reaching for Ralas' hand. "Time for a game of dare."

Something screeching, creaking, picking its way on the tips of needle-sharp points came clacking around the corner at the end of the hall. It moved like a spider, a body suspended in the middle of many-jointed legs, but with a long tongue-like neck emerging here and there from it in thick, muscular outgrowths of rippling bristle. Each 'neck' ended in a mouth filled with tiny teeth. There were no visible eyes or ears. Instead its attention showed when the necks all craned in the same direction, mouths gasping for a taste of air.

"What are those?" Ralas asked as more of the things appeared, one walking the low arched roof as though it were another floor.

"Like Vathesk," Tricky said, "only much faster." She did something with her mirror.

Ralas was suddenly taller, thinner, made of something tough. Taedakh let out a sound of surprise and the eyes of the vholes winked on and off. Ralas found himself looking at another Taedakh, only smaller and leaner, on all fours like he was, like the shadow dogs that had taken Tricky to Vadakh. Only Dr Catt was left unchanged but he was reaching into his bag and then—just like that—he vanished.

The things at the end of the hall paused.

"While they're confused," Tricky said and Ralas felt a pull as if she had tugged on an invisible skin that he had and then he went running after her, thrilled above all to find that his human pains were gone even if his spine was bent and his arms too long, his head front heavy with bony jaws. Quills and poisons burst from his back. A miasma that was both scent and toxin spread around him. They were plague on legs. One touch would be fatal to anything of his own world and things of many others. Things all over this place had been touched by that darkness, and died of its creeping claim. Now their bodies called to him to come and take them home.

They ran for the surface levels, three monsters and one invisible collector of ancient heirlooms, faster on his feet than any ordinary man thanks to the iron rod in his left hand, pulsing with the energy of shackled, distant suns; their faint gravity his faithful horses, he their ungainly plough.

Tricky knew the way very well. Ralas remembered only snatches of it from strange angles, having been dragged and carried in various manners through it. Whilst it had been in use Nydarrow was immaculate, for a place made to be uncomfortable, efficient, full of the marching steps and well-shod determination of thousands of Yogg soldiers and miners. The Kinslayer himself had glided along avenues of perfectly laid rock with the anguish and misery of hundreds set out to either side for his amusement. It had nothing on what had happened to it since his death. Ralas felt he'd really missed a trick.

The place was teeming. Monsters from far and wide had been carted in and dumped in various places for purposes that had been long forgotten, but someone had been industriously letting them all out. Many of them had been eating and hunting each other, probably in desperation; others, maddened by years of starvation and darkness were simply hurtling about in frenzied agitation or lying, gasping wherever they fell when their energies ran out. Judging by the bones and entrails still recognisable there had been a lot of wyverns and cockatrix at one point, but the favourite dinner had been Yogg in various degrees of roasted, seared, flambéed and fricasseed. Side dishes of some kind of vegetable lifeform had been included, then discarded. Well, Ralas thought, that was salad for you. The leavings were slowly being digested by slowly roving globules of semi-sentient slime which were handily giving off the light they were using at the same time, so he had the pleasure of being filled equally with gratitude and repulsion. Other plant forms with black leaves and scarlet bark were growing in avid pleasure out of the blood and gore, tunnelling the walls with suckers and rootlets, forming black garlands and avenues perfumed with disgusting smelling flora mimicking the stench of various glands in order to lure whatever it was they were luring. Veils of easily broken tendrils hung from the roof in places and when crossed they stung horribly with an acidic burn. Barbs and thorns curved like scimitars, entirely blocking some ways. Huge rats with long faces lined in needle teeth skittered about. The only upshot was that everything that could run ran like stink as soon as it saw them coming. As Tricky explained, "Everything wants to live."

They came to the library. He could tell it was the library by the heaps of squelching paper residue and the greyish suppuration of glue and ink oozing out of it.

"Never figured him for a reader," Ralas said as they entered cautiously, Taedakh behind them and the shrieking terror-breath of Dr Catt providing a wheezy accompaniment to the plop and slurp of roving slimes.

"These weren't for reading. They were the accounts," Tricky said, stalking between heaps carefully. "The Meldi-slimes have collected these. They're digesting them."

"Into a readable short format?" Ralas suggested and found Dr Catt's wheezing starting to sputter with unexpected laughter.

"No, they're taking in the information and using it back at their main host—wherever that is. I think they're one of those things from the branching. The Kinslayer had a hole into a lot of other worlds. I wouldn't like to guess the purpose or even if purpose is a thing there. One thing I know. I came here before to try to find out what was this link between Lysandra and the damned *Book*. I didn't get much. It's all lost. I had hoped that Dr Catt would have better insight, having come to contact with so many things over the years. But time has got away from us now. Wanderer has his mission on the go."

"You say that like it's not your mission," Ralas said, picking his way, as a helldog, over a mound of scrolls. The parchment was slower to work on than the papers and had mostly survived intact so far.

"It's not my mission," Tricky said, stalking towards an area of racks and shelves. "I'll be honest with you, honey. I don't have a good feeling about this. Somewhere in here is the reason all of this started in the first place. Lysandra was part of his plan even if the Tzarkis did booby trap her, and she still is. If Wanderer takes her to the gods after they've been cut off—was that part of the deal or was it not? I just can't see the moves. I have to find out. I have to know if he is still playing me, because I'm damned if I did all the things I did for him to win from beyond the grave."

"You're after *The Book of All Things*," Dr Catt said, having gained enough ground to speak.

"No. I know where that is," she said offhandedly as though it was of no interest. Her hound form snuffled around the base of the shelves, looked sideways through its glowing, violet eye at the marks and scrolls remaining in place. "I'm after knowing what's happening to Taedakh's world, actually, because he says that if the two places become… what's the… if they kind of mix, then they're both finished and that means we're all done here, and so are the gods. Do you suppose that was the plan, or is it only a terrible accident? Because I've seen things in Vadakh—" She paused, listening, "—that have no answer here."

"By answer you mean—" Ralas began.

"I mean they're not defeatable, yes. Not even with a magic

sword." She shuffled around. "Something here made Reckoner change his ways." She sounded lost; she knew she wouldn't find it. Ralas started to see that she was in the grip of an obsession and his blood ran colder. He'd found her charming, he'd never thought about mad. Then Taedakh crouched low, folding up like a bundle of old broken spears. The furry mantle flowed down and along his arms and onto the mire of records. It broke up into individuals who scattered, with a speed that unnerved Ralas to the point of wanting to run away himself. They were over everything in seconds. Outside the room the screaming came, not far off.

"Just shut the door for a minute," Catt said quietly, going to do it himself. As it closed they heard the heavy wooden bar slide across, the locks clatter and whir. There was no sign of Dr Catt.

"He shut us in, didn't he?" Ralas said, wondering how he managed to feel surprise, but feeling it quite strongly.

"No doubt he got what he wanted and is hoping to get away," Tricky agreed, not bothered apparently. "Doesn't matter. No lock can hold me and the bar is on the inside. At least it buys a few minutes."

"These creatures are from Vadakh," Taedakh said. "The Kinslayer brought them here to do the job you speak of. It's their nature to cross worlds, using gaps none other can perceive. They memorise but only together as a group. They bring order as pattern. If they were here then they may remember what you want to know, but many of them have perished."

The creatures scurried, seemingly aimless, constantly regrouping and then scattering again, never following the same path twice. It looked as if they were trying to form a shape, but at the last moment they forgot their purpose, were driven off, then compelled back to try again.

"Who brought you from Vadakh? How were you on a piece of paper?" Ralas asked, realising that there might be more to the connections here than was obvious.

"I made him," Tricky said. "I wrote with charcoal ink, the ink of burned things, and I wrote him in the symbology of the Kelicerati, which is why he's like the burned things and like the Kelicae, a little. When I saw the portal to Vadakh and I first went in I knew there was no surviving it. It wears you away very fast, even if the creatures don't come. I had to have a protector, someone to ward off the things who was more powerful than they were. Vadakh is raw energy looking for form, so I gave it a form. But I wanted to hide him from the Kinslayer, just like I wanted to hide things in Vadakh, so I can put him on paper if I have to. See?"

"Oh, yes, when you put it like that it's obvious," Ralas said uneasily, trying to grasp the implications. "And these disguises?"

"Borrowed them from the bloody shadow dogs, didn't I? Might as well get some use out of the greedy bastards. Ah shit, that's it!" Dog Tricky stood with her hideous jaws open, oozing a bit of dark drool onto the undulating slime below her, her piggy little red eyes as wide as they would go in astonishment. "The *Book* is memories, not a written record. Written in flesh and bone. He destroyed the people and he destroyed the *Book*—they would never remember what he'd done to open Vadakh so it couldn't be undone. They knew how he cut off the gods. He took it from them. But now they're gone. All of them. Except Kula."

Ralas' jaw dropped too. He tasted a sudden astonishing taste, the sweet flavour of order, but it didn't knock out his amazement and horror. "But she's the one with Lysandra. And they're in Ilkand, maybe even left by now."

"Going to Wanderer's circle because it's the only way into Vadakh if you've got a body and want to keep it," Tricky said. "If you don't have the smarts to make yourself your own god."

"God?"

"Taedakh," she said proudly. "God of the underworld."

Ralas fished around in the leavings of his mind. "You made a god?"

"Well, what do you want to call him?"

"An imaginary friend?" He turned and looked at Taedakh, sitting in his own private gloom, a bundle of what could have been giant sticks, rather small now he was dwarfed by the library's arches of bioluminescent gloom. "But isn't that what the Tzarkomen were doing. With Lysandra? In their own way?"

Tricky turned to him and her face lit up. "You're right. All these silly words they used stopped me from seeing it. What they were doing. What he was doing. They were making their own god. Shit! A god of what, though?"

She studied the roving vholes and paused, her mercurial mind off on another tangent. "Ralas, you have to sing. These little things need structure, to be ordered, so they can focus. Sing them a work song. Something easy to remember."

He was already dreaming of the music he'd heard during their jump through the world, that strange symphony that was so vast and complex that he could only hear one thread at a time, though he knew the rest was there; but he picked the working song he'd heard Heno and Nedlam sing once, one without real words, because words got you killed. With his dog mouth words were out of the question anyway. It was hard to sit down in his dog form, but he managed it. It was harder still to sing and impossible to talk. The black mice, or vholes, or whatever they were—he didn't like the notion of a vole that was a hole or a hole that made itself into a vole or whatever so Ralas was sticking with mice—had briefly paused. He began the tune.

Within moments of finishing the first line the mice were attentive. Then they began to cluster. At the song's repetition the mice clustered and then formed themselves up into neat lines, then circles, then more complicated shapes, before clustering and bursting out time and time again to make increasingly complicated patterns before they swarmed back to Taedakh and reassumed their position as his living mantle.

"You are fortunate," Taedakh said, his long head stretching

up and seeming to lift him to a standing position. "The Kinslayer's Bride was meant to enter Vadakh at his command and to bring forth from it the power of eternity. Or power of creation. Or of destruction. The last part is unclear, but it is something comprehensively vast which he intended to use to claim what he considered the dues of the other races from the favoured humans. She would be the channel and the director of that power at his will."

Ralas was sitting in a pile of glop. A faintly happy notion of days long past was still with him in the turn and march of the song. "If you're the Lord of the Underworld, can't you find the gods?"

"They are falling," Taedakh said.

"Falling where?" Tricky asked, going to the door and standing on her hind legs to use her snout to push the bar back.

"Apart," came the reply.

"Shit," Tricky said and had to drop her dog form, suddenly reappearing small and busy, her fingers fiddling some magical patterns at the door. "Damn it, these locks are full of crap. Wait till I get my hands on that Catt." She struggled with lockpicks like fine hooked needles, slim but the same to Ralas' mind as those his grandmother used to crochet lace and thinking of her made him sentimental and watching Tricky made him even more so, until he felt like this was a new kind of torture.

"I..." he began without a clue as to what he was going to say. It wasn't, "Will we finish here and go out, back to Cinquetann? Are we to join Celestaine?" but that's what he came out with. In his mind he'd been going for something much more like "Can't we leave all this and escape? The world must be much larger than these concerns." But of course they wouldn't. And it wasn't.

She glanced at him and he saw with a sweet sense of—*yes, of all people ever to understand, you are the one*—that she knew exactly what was passing through him. "We're going to meet them in Vadakh. Get this sorted out, close the holes. Is what we're going to do."

But even if they were going back down all the way at least she was there and that made him happy for a moment, until he said, "Did you know this before? Is that why you brought me? For the music? So that I could fix these creatures?" Not for any other reason. Because he was simply useful. He couldn't believe it.

She glanced at him, a heavy clicking whirr betraying the undoing of the lock. The vault swung open. She smiled, a dazzling, victorious smile.

CHAPTER THIRTY-ONE

Kula wrapped her cloak tighter about her and tucked in her hands and feet. The brisk wind was cold and the spray from the sticky saltwater colder still. Surging through the waves, strengthened by the air, she felt she was so big. At the same time she could feel that she was only a mote against the mass of life that lay beneath them: down, down and down. She had never been above something so deep that was still filled with living beings. She was a small thing, cold, huddled on her rope, but she now knew that there was so much more to the world than she had seen or imagined. For this she loved the sea.

It was time to let go of the life she had borrowed. She could have kept it. She held it now, and felt its potency, waiting to be unfurled, like a seed within her mind. She didn't know how the magic of her people worked, only what it felt like. She had read the pattern of this beast, preserving it, and had taken out the life from it. Now she wanted to put it back in. For that she needed Lysandra. They had worked it out between them, with Horse's help, tested it on midges and ants and leaves and twigs and one of the riverboat's few remaining rats which had become cunning enough to navigate the galley without encountering any otters. It hadn't navigated Horse, however, who summoned it to her hand for Kula to witness.

Together they'd pored over the creature, but it actually wasn't as complicated as the midge pattern. Only when she sought to see this particular rat in all its individual, momentary detail—then it got complicated. She'd thought herself sitting a few minutes for the task, but hours had gone by and they were only lucky that the rest of the group had no interest in them or her stillness and fixity would have been noticed.

Under the cover of night they had crept off to the river-dragon's nest where it had laid its stillborn eggs. Guarded by Lysandra, she had studied the beast and they only made it back to the craft in time to pretend to wake up. The creature was strange but it wasn't the Ur-beasts of old, which had rivalled the gods for scale and ambition. She saw nothing unnatural in it. It wasn't even as interesting as the midge in some ways and that seemed a shame to her. So in the night of boring adult business out at the Widow Demadell's house, Kula had sat at one of the tables with the stone fruits and daydreamed about how it could be made better, more aware, more suited to this world, more great and impressive, more capable of being the thing she had wanted it to be—a creature of amazing powers.

Now she called Lysandra and handed over the dark little feather she had used to act as the anchor point for her work. Lysandra nodded to show she understood that they were going to complete their original plan to release the creature back into the wild where it was safe from idiot humans. They were sad that Horse was not there to see it, but Kula felt that she would find out soon and then she'd be pleased. That thought was exciting, so she hurried.

Lysandra leaned over on the leeward rail of the ship, the feather in her fingertips. Kula directed her to let it go. It was snatched away, down and down, onto the waters.

Kula closed her eyes and remembered the dragon of the river. It took shape in her mind with all the improvements: larger, better, its scale more glossy, its feather a deeper hue, its intelligence sharper and wiser with a vision that stretched into worlds beyond and wisdoms that only the oldest and greatest could reach, beyond Kula's tiny form and little span. To her it had something of the magnificence and mystery of the sea itself. Without an awareness of changing the pattern she was focused on this sense of power and majesty and limitless grace as Lysandra released the fire of life.

There was nothing to see. A girl sitting on a coil of rope. A woman leaning over the rail, holding back her hair so she could see the water, seabirds circling and calling above them as they made headway away from the land.

Then a huge spume of white foam erupted from the mild race of the wavelets in the open water where the feather had been. It was a short distance astern of them and went up in a geyser that fell to shattering on the deck even as the sailors sent up alarms and the helmsman spun the wheel to take them around and away in an avoidance manoeuvre. The ship tilted with alarming speed to one side. Kula screamed and gripped her rope. She heard Heno and Bukham yelling as their feet went out from under them on the deck.

Kula's rope was coiled on fixed pitons. It remained in place. Like most things on the ship she was battened fast in place. She reached out as the heavy form of Heno went slithering past her and a huge, rough hand grasped hers. The eyes that joined gaze with hers were the eyes of the mud-man, the Heart Taker. She could feel him resisting the urge to grab harder so he didn't break her fingers as the ship began to right itself. In that moment he was quite open, quite unexpecting. She read him, one mage to another, and she saw him know what she did. His life, in all its detail, was lightning in her bones. White fire crackled where they touched and in that second he also saw her.

The ship tilted back, coming to its new course. The crew were running, pointing at a huge shape below the surface which created a humped hill of water as it came alongside them before diving deep. Among them the two Ystachi dragonspeakers were ululating in shrill tones, singing some kind of song, most desperate to get the best view. Atop their scaled heads their frilled crests were rampant, their colours vivid. Unlike the human crew their clawed feet had no trouble keeping them upright on the deck. Kula let go of Heno as the deck levelled. She felt sad for him and as he let go and recovered himself she saw in his long face that he felt sad for her. Then crew and Celestaine ran between them, harpoons in hand, gestures sharp and sudden. Lysandra leant out, her arm flung wide in a clear instruction to the creature—go!

Kula wasn't worried. These people were too slow and too poorly equipped to hunt or defend against the creature. She felt their fear, intense, making their senses vivid, as they watched it go deep and then rise sharply, undulating in a single line from the wave to the deep. She felt them brace as they grabbed to whatever they could hold and held so tightly, holding to existence itself, as the dragon burst free of the water and powered up into the air, wings unfolding, riding currents of energy they could not see. It wound upwards into the sky a very different thing to its original form: shorter limbs, massive skull festooned with tentacles and weed-like vanes so that it seemed to swim there, circling them. Streams of water plummeted off its sides.

It circled them once, twice, the great crystal eye looking down. Kula put up her hand and waved.

Then it bent away to the east, over the water and rising, into the clouds there. A few jags of lightning, white like Heart Taker fire, crackled and lit the huge thunderheads from within as it passed on and away through them. They watched until minutes had passed and there was no more to see. She was pleased. She had made something that didn't belong into something that did.

HENO PICKED HIMSELF up slowly and sat down on the deck. He was only lightly wetted and ran his hands over his head to push back his rough hair and adjust his scarf against his ears. He took his time to gather himself after what had just happened. He waited as Lysandra helped Bukham regain his feet and the ship recovered its original course, tacking against the wind. He was a little seasick, truthfully, and it was good to stop trying to fight it and be still on the deck. Celestaine came back bloodied from hitting her head on a beam in the initial swerve, holding a cloth to her forehead. She sat with him. They watched as Bukham found that he had covered himself in mess from the chum bucket which had been prepared for deep sea angling, and the stink and the sight made him throw up. A big fuss took place involving buckets of seawater and brushes which gave them a moment of pause, knee to knee and shoulder to shoulder—well, to arm. He saw Celestaine watching Lysandra closely, amid the doings.

"What are we going to do with them?" she asked him quietly as the cleanup and chatter went on around them.

He knew she meant Lysandra and Kula. "Nothing," he said. "What can we do? You saw that."

"I don't know what I saw. What did you see?"

"The thing that was dead at the river just came out of the sea, bigger, faster and very much more than it was before."

"I didn't see them do anything," Celestaine said. "But imagine, if the Kinslayer had had that kind of power."

"Kula wanted it to have a good life," Heno said, taking down the cloth from Celestaine's forehead and looking at the wound just inside her hairline. "It's only a scratch. Just very bloody. It'll be all right." He let her hold it back in place.

"How do you know that?" Celestaine asked, keeping her voice low. She was shaken and her hand on the cloth trembled a bit.

"She stopped me sliding over the side and we had a moment," he said. "I think we should be grateful that whatever Lysandra is, Kula's got it covered."

"And if we piss her off one day and she has a temper tantrum is she going to throw dragons at us out of thin air?" Celestaine hissed in a whisper, really not wanting Lysandra to overhear from her place at the rail even though the wind was blowing vigorously and noisily, the sails snapping.

Heno shrugged. "Let's not piss her off."

"I'm starting to think they shouldn't be on this journey, should they? And she might see things like a child now but what about when she gets older? What about when all the compromises and the bad decisions and the obvious complete lack of control of anything and the temper and all of that kicks in?"

"What are you suggesting? Perhaps we should chain them up and put them in a mine under strict working conditions so they never think to do anything with themselves." It came out harsher than he intended.

Celestaine looked up at him, nodding circumspectly. "You're doing sarcasm now? A few more smiling lessons and you'll be a regular ladies' man." Then she winced, "Oh, my head aches."

"What's a ladies' man?" Nedlam asked coming to sit by them on the stashed barrels, Lady Wall carefully put by her. She was chewing a piece of sea tack, the sailors' biscuit, and offered some to them which they both declined.

"It's a man who has learned how to behave to impress genteel kinds of women," Celestaine said.

"It's a man who's not a man," Heno translated.

"Man who never gets any ladies. Right." Nedlam nodded with the same satisfaction as if she had discovered a lost continent. "Funny way of saying it. Heh, did you like that dragon little Kula made?"

"Yes, yeah, it was great. Terrific," Celestaine said. "Mmn hm."

"That's a good trick," Nedlam said. She chuckled. "Hey, if Kinslayer'd had that. Can you imagine?"

"No," Celestaine said. "Can't imagine. Can not. Imagine. Ned, d'you think they're dangerous?"

"Naw," Nedlam said, breaking off another chunk of indigestible stodge and starting to work it down.

"What makes you so sure?" Heno asked.

"Because. If they were we'd already be rowing this thing and eating shit like this." She spat the chunk out and then threw the lot over the rail into the sea. "I wish Buk wasn't sick all the time. Then he could make a new biscuit."

"Biscuits?" Murti edged closer to them and took a perch next to Nedlam, steadying himself with a foot hooked around some of the lashing that was holding the barrels steady. "Are there any?"

"Only if you want to kill someone," Nedlam said.

"I was just wondering what to do about—" Celestaine nodded in a significant way in the direction of Lysandra and Kula, who had also been given ship's biscuit and were throwing bits of it to the seagulls not far away.

"What makes you..."

"No," Celest interrupted him firmly. "You're not doing that again, the old throw the question back at me like I shouldn't even have a question thing. We're here because you wanted us here and I assume you wanted them here and maybe you even wanted Deffo here, wherever he is, so let's have a straight answer."

Murti blinked as if he was mildly befuddled. "Well, in that case there's a bit of a situation that requires people like—" he nodded in a copy of Celestaine's gesture, "—to get it fixed."

"How's that going to work?"

Murti shrugged. "I don't know. I gave you a sword, that worked out quite well. I was thinking that this may also resolve for the best without too much of a stranglehold."

Celestaine sighed and let the cloth drop into her hands. The bleeding had stopped and the wound was beginning to scab over. "So we're what? The guards?"

"In case of heavy lifting," Murti said. "Also, if you're here then Deffo isn't focused on trying to get me to promise to return the gods and restore him to glory."

"Who promised to return the gods?" Lysandra sat down breezily cheerful beside Celestaine. "When are they coming?" She looked about at the skies and the deck with eager anticipation as if they might pop up at any moment.

"They're um, not here right now," Celestaine said warily. "We're going to see what happened to them. Remember?"

Lysandra put her hands together in her lap. "Oh, yes. I don't suppose you know why all the biscuits are so horrible? Is it sabotage?" She kept a close eye on Kula who had her head through the deck railings so she could stare down the ship's side into the sea. Her accent, which had started out days ago as riddled with Tzarkish hard sibilants, was now almost a model of noble Forinthi intonation coupled with a bit of Ilkand society matriarch.

"I don't know about the biscuits, I think it's called preservation," Celest said, for the first time in her life feeling actually faint, and not all down to the head bashing. "Will you be making a lot of dragons, at all, while we're underway?"

"No!" Lysandra said as if that was a ludicrous question. "No, we were only putting that one back." She patted Celestaine's knee. "Don't worry so much. You'll give yourself grey hairs. Now, the wind is turning. If you want my advice we should avoid this hole the Ilkanders fear and head north with all speed. The hole is not something any of you could survive if you tried to use it as a way into Vadakh and you don't have the ability to close it from here. It will swallow you up and even if you only go to look it will delay us. If you want to stay alive on this journey, then it's as Wanderer says. We must go north, to the gate under the ice."

A long shadow fell across them all and they looked up to see Deffo, very pale and unsteady but with a dignified expression of well-borne suffering on his face, holding onto one of the decking cross ropes as he edged towards them. "There you all are." The ship tilted and he clung for dear life. "A messenger bird has come. It's brought this for you." He held out a narrow roll of parchment towards Celestaine who reached up and took it from him, unrolling it and holding it against her knees to read. "It's from Tricky. What does it say?"

Celestaine scanned it. "Everything's fine. She and Ralas got into a bit of trouble. They'll be delayed. Wish you were here. Haha." She was trying to close it quickly when Lysandra stopped her and leaned in.

"Ah, you forgot *this* bit," Lysandra said, pointing with her finger and reading aloud with dramatic flair. "The mazagal and the girl are probably part of the Kinslayer's plot to ensure total destruction of the human races and all of the Guardians. Proceed with extreme caution." She looked up at them and smiled radiantly, throwing her arms out wide with joy. "See? I can read!"

CHAPTER THIRTY-TWO

CELESTAINE READ THE note for the hundredth time and then balled it up. There was more on the back in Ralas' tiny, cramped script, detailing things. She contemplated tossing it in the sea but in the end stuffed it into her pocket. Nedlam continued to fish. Heno was dicing with the Kula. Lysandra was napping in one of the crew's hammocks below decks. Deffo and Murti had gone off somewhere and Bukham was being sick over the side for the umpteenth time.

Ralas could not reach them. He and the Guardian Celestaine least trusted, Tricky, were planning to rejoin them in the world that previously only gods and demigods could tread. It was probably a cunning trap.

Her mind was still full of the dragon. She had seen how it resembled the earlier, smaller beast of the river. There was no mistake in her mind—whatever Lysandra had done, she had taken something and remade it. That was a godly power. It exceeded, in one stroke, anything the Kinslayer had been able to manage. In comparison the dragon Celest had slain, Vermarod the Invincible, was a bumbling contraption. If they had deployed this new creature to slay all of Ilkand it would take a lot more than Celest and an army to stop it. The Shelliac had not even been prepared to cross the earlier version when it claimed a bit of a riverbank.

But much worse than was how difficult it was to replace her image of Lysandra as a subhuman monster with the intelligent person who had spoken to her minutes ago, who had done this magic, and who was now, subtly but distinctly, in charge of this expedition. That hurt. Being replaced so effortlessly, so easily. Until now she hadn't quite believed the story about the fire. She'd been able to get along with Lysandra as a dumb instrument, some kind of walking curiosity. Lysandra as a fresh power in the world was something she felt unequal to grasping and her impulse was to contain it—only she had no idea how to do that.

Scenarios ran through her mind in which she must act to stop Lysandra from doing something terrible and they all ended in failure. Only slaying her now seemed possible, as, at the rate she was changing, it was likely that within another day or two her intellect and her other abilities would outstrip all of them. If she didn't act now, she might never have another chance.

Kula had already lost so much. Lysandra was the product of an entire people's end if Ralas was right. And he had no idea of the Tzarkomen's vision for her either. She was a mystery. A potentially lethally dangerous, world-ending mystery.

She thought of talking to Murti but a great weight in her chest made her hesitate. She realised she didn't trust him either and wondered when that had happened. Ralas in Nydarrow—he might also be compromised. Tricky had been in cahoots with the Kinslayer a long time, before and during the war. Was anything she said or did remotely reliable?

She studied Kula, shaking the dice in her hand, blowing on them for luck like Heno did. She did not believe that the child was malign, though she had cause to be. Everything she had done, or Lysandra had done, had seemed to come out of a kind innocence. Yes, it was stupid and unworldly to throw a king's fortune around in a port town—Adondra was right about that. It would have ugly consequences as well as pleasant ones. But she watched Kula playing with her new, valueless dice, laughing as Heno tried blatantly to cheat to amuse her—and she didn't believe that there was an evil design at work there. Maybe the Kinslayer had not had an evil design either, for all it looked like it to her. That was too unbelievable to bear.

Her head hurt. At least there was one thing she could do, however. She went to find the Captain to request a change of course.

CHAPTER THIRTY-THREE

THE JOURNEY TOOK a week just to get them into the Guloss Archipelago proper. They made landfall at Calios, a large island at the tip of the whole Golden Isles chain which led like a handful of scattered grain one mote at a time all the way back to the mainland. It was the end of the true deep water and the last place that Captain Vakloz said he would be prepared to take them without further consideration of considerable danger fees.

"However," he added as he toasted them from the head of the table in the cramped seating below decks, "I will be handing your care over to a friend, well, an ally, who operates these waters."

"Another freebooter?" Nedlam asked. She was seated with the other larger-bodied amidships on their separate table but still had her knees around her ears as they ate fish stew and listened to a squall hammering the deck with rain that sounded like nails.

"Freebooters are pirates," Captain Vakloz said. "So no. But free traders. That we can call them. They're more used to dealing with the Varkadians." He gave a little shudder.

"And by dealing with you mean fighting," Celestaine said, taking a sip of the fortified wine gingerly. It was sweet, almost sickly, and was horrible with the fish but it was something all the crew apparently wouldn't eat without. They also drank it hot, mixed with some kind of warming spice which was considerably worse.

"I think that tends to be the case unless you want to be filleted," he replied. "On that note, do you have any words for me to convey back to Ilkand and beyond?"

"How should we signal you for a return journey?" Celest asked.

"I come by every six weeks until the winter. So I'll be back twice more. After that you'll be waiting a few months until the weather turns and if that happens you should stay on the central islands. They're larger and they have more shelter."

It was already cold and they had got used to wearing all their gear two days before, and never taking it off. The air below decks was fuggy and rank but it beat sitting outside. The wind could be raw and the rain made it painful on exposed skin. Celestaine already hated the north. "When will your ally be here?"

He glanced at the Ystachi who were seated together. A kind of glow of satisfaction had surrounded them since the appearance of Lysandra's creature. Their spiky scales glinted with fresh oil and they had repainted themselves daily with the bright coloured marks of their unfathomable faiths.

"Within the hour," the oldest one said. His scale was worn and had thinned off entirely in places but Celestaine had seen him climb foot and hand up a single rope to the top of the mizzenmast, so either age hadn't withered anything significant or they were all fearsomely agile. "I hear the songs."

"All this singing," Heno murmured to Celest. "They keep mentioning it. What are they talking about?"

"Something we can't hear, I assume," she said. "I've never met one before. I've no idea."

"It is in the water," the younger one informed them archly. She had a frill of raised scale above both eyes, pierced and riveted with small gold rings. Her hand on the cup was heavily webbed and her blunted claws tapped lightly against the wooden bowl.

"We favour southern weather but she will not allow the cold to stop her."

"She's Ystachi?" Celestaine asked, ready for anybody at this stage.

"One of the Seekers. Kalliendra," the young one said proudly and with a fierce admiration. "As if it is not enough she treats with the sea and its beasts, she has also mastered the northern ocean. She is a terrible heretic." She glanced at Murti, as though still somewhat unconvinced of his provenance but obviously well filled in on all their stories. "One of the Wanderer's chosen."

Celestaine turned to Murti. "Is there something I should know?"

"The difficulty of the task requires many hands," he said after a hesitation.

The Captain frowned. "I hadn't believed you were genuine about this mission until I saw that beast—did it come from the drowning pool? Should we fear more of them?"

Celestaine said nothing, didn't even look around. It was better that nobody knew if they didn't all want to go over the side or worse.

"If we can close the hole no more will come," Murti said, quietly, gently, as though it was a simple thing requiring only the kind of steady farmhand determination to gather and pile a few rocks and then spade down some earth.

All the hair on Celestaine's neck went up, slowly, as if it was trying to alarm her, but not too much. "Close it... you mean, from the other side?"

"That is the only side from which it can be done," he admitted.

Celestaine put down her fork and sat up straighter, connecting with the bulkhead on her sore spot. "So this jaunt to see the gods one more time, that was all a ruse?"

"No, I wouldn't call it that. We will see them if we manage to reach our destination."

Celestaine glanced at Lysandra, against her own will, and

saw that she and Kula were too busy counting fishbones and comparing who had found the most in their dinners to pay attention to the talk. The task seemed to thoroughly occupy them. Up on deck the rain was abating. A light patter, accompanied by various heavy percussion from drips and gulleys, was signalling the passing of the storm. The ship rolled softly against its anchor. The crew were deep in thought, the Ystachi muttering quietly in their own tongue, the rest focused on playing out their ration of the filthy brew to stretch their rest time as long as possible, and to stretch the present, lest it become a future full of unfortunate encounters with monsters.

"And after that we'll go home," Bukham said into the quiet. "Then I'm done, right? I can go back to Taib Post and this whole thing will be over." He hadn't kept anything down since they'd been aboard other than oats in water. He nursed a mug of it now.

"Yes," Celestaine said firmly before Murti could get in with some more cryptic nonsense that would be hiding the fact that going home was a very unlikely option indeed. "That's right."

"Home," Nedlam grunted, cramped and uncomfortable, head down because it was already touching the ceiling. "I've never understood the appeal."

"You've never been to the Post," Bukham offered.

"That's true," she said. "I'll go back with you and see it then. Though I doubt anywhere is as good as something to do."

Celestaine agreed with her. Home was always full of people who wanted things to stay the same. It was full of the past and it didn't want strange new things in it, like Heno. She couldn't imagine a place that did want them, but a trading post probably saw a lot of stranger things. It might almost be as free as the open road.

"Are you sure you want to be taking extra people with you?" the Captain asked, nodding slightly in the direction of Lysandra and Kula. His meaning was clear—women and children should not be going in the direction of danger. His gaze flitted briefly to

Bukham, the deadweight. He seemed mildly befuddled by their obvious unsuitability.

"They're with us," she said, for want of a better way of describing it. "Everyone comes as a package."

"Only, there's a high bounty on certain... types... of people right now."

Celestaine felt the atmosphere turn suddenly icy. She flexed her arms enough to feel Heno's stiffened form, Bukham's uneasy shrinking and absolutely no way out of the room, wedged in as they were cheek by jowl. "What types of people are you talking about?" Closest to the stair Nedlam had put down her bowl and was clenching her spoon in her hand.

The crew were looking calm but alert, which was the most disconcerting. All their weapons were on deck where now all rain had stopped, leaving enough space to be able to hear the soft tread of feet above them.

The Captain was looking at them all, each in the face, one at a time, patiently. "The types of people who played on the losing side of the war," he said. "Who else? Not you, of course, Slayer. For you there are other possibilities in places more exotic than mere Ilkand."

"I suppose offering you the last of our treasure in return for our freedom is out of the question?" She listened hard, figuring at least six moving above and guessing they were the friendly ally that he'd been discussing, and her own crew.

"You suppose right," he paused, another hesitation she didn't quite figure. He was waiting for something, filling in time. "It will be ours anyway." He kept his most acute looks for Murti. "Wanderer? Nothing to say? Your passivity was legendary, always. I counted on your lack of action and it seems you don't disappoint."

Celest glanced over Heno at the old man himself for a response. He was staring into the middle distance as if fuddled by drink. And then she realised. The food was drugged, but of course—then again, she felt perfectly well.

It was just at that moment that the older of the two Ystachi went down face first into the last of his grog.

"Very unlucky to get the bowls mixed up like that," Murti mumbled quietly, clearing his throat.

Two more of the crew, bold, brash Kellick and greasy Piperand went next, slumping sideways onto each other like drunks. The Captain's hand went to this throat, he started to gasp.

"And to get them *all* the wrong way round smacks of some kind of plot," Murti added. "Nedlam. Could you drag these fools out of the way? We have business awaiting us aloft, I fear."

Nedlam slammed the spoon down into the table and left it there, handle sticking up, bowl wedged halfway into the hardwood. She got up, bent nearly double, and began to haul unconscious bodies with her, two at a time, back into the half empty galley. As she moved out of the way of the galley door the cook was clearly visible as two feet pointing skywards, askew amid a basket of loose onions rolling gently back and forth with the swell.

The Captain's face now was purple, his lips turning blue.

"I didn't think we were going to kill them." Murti said, glancing at Lysandra.

"It's all right," she said calmly, looking up, fishbones dancing off her fingers down into her bowl as she discarded them. Beside her the Captain frothed and pounded the table with his hands, pulling at the silver gorget around his throat. She ignored him completely. "They meant to have Kula's head and mine for medicine. Tzarkomen cast long shadows in the worlds of dark magic. You and the boy they would merely murder. The rest were for other ends."

The Captain's gestures were weaker now. His eyes—staring wildly at Lysandra, baffled—began to soften their fury. His thumps turned to a grasp as he clutched at the table's gently swinging boards, and then he slid to the side and came to rest against the first mate, Ghar, the Yogg, who was in a deep sleep and beginning to snore. The Captain did not snore. A couple of bubbles popped at his lips and then he was quiet. Nobody had any doubt he was dead.

Lysandra looked across at Celestaine and Heno, gestured with a nod towards the stairs up to the deck. "Save the leader. She will be useful." Then she looked at Bukham who was staring at her, rigid with shock. "You can thank me later," and she smiled, a small and merciless smile.

Heno went first into the light, preparing the way with a blast of white lightning that scattered the expectant party awaiting the appearance of the Captain. They staggered back, hands to their eyes, and Celestaine and Nedlam came rushing up the gangway to Heno's sides, hoping to grab their weapons on the deck. But although they had an advantage the boarding crew were wily and used to fighting their way out of tight corners. They did not give ground, but stood, sabres and clubs at the ready, their sharp needle teeth bared. Long whiskers covered their cheeks and drooped down like sombre moustaches. They were part furred, with dark brown human faces stretched forwards into snouts, small ears tucked close to their heads and long, heavy tails held awkwardly aloft. They were...

"Valuti!" Bukham said from the back in astonishment, although there were some ordinary humans among the otter people, their various heritage stamped across features and in their skins, accessorised with a bizarre collection of beads, trinkets and tattoos. This ragtag motley unified them. And the colours they had chosen—blue and yellow—reflected the scale tones and the skin sheen of their obvious leader, the only Ystachi.

Scaled and crested like the two Ystachi crewmen they had grown used to seeing, this one was taller and leaner than they, her neck frills and head crests taller. They were coloured a most vivid and lustrous collection of blues and violets, which contrasted sharply with the white and yellow sand colours of her underbody and the middle of her face. Her large eyes were a reptilian green, rich in colour and texture, the central slit sharp as a shadow blade as she pushed past her flankers and came to meet them, swords raised in both hands. Her voice was throaty with fear and aggression but she held herself well, Celestaine noted, good enough to judge her a seasoned soldier. Her boots were cut off at the ankle, revealing long, clawed and webbed feet, the toes ringed in gold.

"Who in hell are you?"

"Celestaine of Fernreame." The title tripped out as if it meant something here. "Slayer," she added, and then, in the continued silence, "Kinslayer's end."

The Ystachi captain pulled her head back and cocked it in one move, so quick it was nearly comical. She blinked. "Reckoner's reckoning?" She chuckled. "You don't say." She didn't put up her blades though.

"It doesn't sound good no matter how you put it," Celestaine said. "But there it is. Surrender your weapons and stand down. The crew of this ship are not in a position to fulfil your bargains."

The Valuti bristled visibly, fur rising at their napes, crouching and brandishing their alarmingly sharp harpoons. Barbed hooks glinted in the weak sunlight. The human pirates stood fast.

"Don't speak of bargains," the Ystachi said. "Valuti cannot trade, only take or conquer. Are you not claiming this vessel, then, Reckoning? Or are you expecting Captain Vakloz to return?"

"He returns only if I say so," Lysandra appeared at Celestaine's shoulder, her ragged and dirty dress not much improved by its recent seawater baths. From its luxurious sleeving and skirts her arms and legs stuck out like twigs but there was nothing weak about her manner. At her side Kula looked out curiously without the faintest trace of concern.

"Deathmasters!" The shriek went up from one of the human boarders. "Kill them!" A hissing war ululation followed this, instantly taken up by all the pirates, immediately followed by an attack. Within seconds Celestaine, Heno and Nedlam had formed a kind of wall and were repelling a vicious assault of spears and blades. Although they were not taken off guard the ferocity of the attack was something not felt since the last true battle they had been in and their surprise added a sudden spurt of intensity which they all felt as one, a moment of joy that had not been evident this entire journey until now.

KULA FELT IT and clapped her hands to show her approval. A barbed lance from one of the Valuti sheared past Heno's leg and was knocked to the side, missing her by a hair's breadth. She felt the crackling agitation of his magic build and then the clear shock of it as it burned around the spear's shaft and back to the hand holding it.

The spear fell down, shivered to bits before it landed. Bukham was there suddenly, his enormous form blotting out the sky as he bent to pick her up and rush her below. She kicked crossly, not wanting to lose sight of the action, but then she felt the fall of a life ebbing away and let herself be carried, her ankle bashing the door frame for good measure.

In the dimness of the hold the pile of drugged crew were slumped all over one another, but none in danger of leaving life behind. Murti sat in the corner, the glow of his energy deceptively soft, like a fire behind an iron door that was never opened. She felt the furnace, though, and beyond that, a hint of the fire that fed it. She found herself staring at him and then the shift as he stared at her in return, the first time they had ever really examined one another, mage to mage.

Bukham bumbled about, attempting to tidy away the dinner's leavings as he recovered and organised every kitchen implement that was or could be considered a knife while the fighting went on upstairs, and between Kula and the Guardian a long pause stretched out.

His lips moved with talking and although she couldn't hear it she understood what he was asking—"What do you see?"

She put her finger to her lips in the way she'd seen them do when they weren't going to talk—*don't ask, not telling, it's a secret.*

He smiled. He had only meant to be friendly because he wasn't afraid of her or anything she might do. He was puzzled. He didn't understand what he had seen entirely and that didn't surprise her. In her family nobody had been sure what she was. She didn't know how to think of it herself, but now she knew him and, if she had to remember him, she would be able to do so well enough for Lysandra to make another. That was just how it was. But he didn't interest her.

His thoughts were preoccupied with the ever-thinning link to his life-force, trapped in the other world, and they soon regained all his attention as hers were taken up with dumping out the contents of one of the blue and white porcelain cups and hiding it away in her pocket because she really loved it and didn't want to leave it behind. It had a picture of a rabbit on it.

So that it was not stealing she took out a twig that Ned had whittled for her in the shape of a snail and put that in its place. It was more like a rock than snail to the untrained eye, but it would keep looking out for her and be lucky for whoever found it. Especially if they wondered where their cup had gone. She would have taken the Captain's but his was florid red and decorated with gold in the house mark of the bad Lady and she didn't care for it. She did like his little owl skull though. So she took out her knife when nobody was looking and cut that braid from his hair and put that in her pocket too. He would have approved, because he was a pirate and now she was one also and that felt good. If he had not tried to kill her she would have felt sorry he was gone.

She looked up at the deck above her. She felt Heno's pain, and Nedlam's concern, and Celestaine's thumping headache and the glee of a fight turning to the angry exhaustion of having to kill those who wouldn't see sense and back down.

She pulled a little on a certain vibrating line, with the skill of an expert fisherman.

"Hold, hold!" the Ysatchi captain called suddenly, feeling her death rise up to meet her unexpectedly, apropos of nothing, but certain and sure; an old carp from the depths coming to the surface of her, hideous and cold, breathless, unending. "Stop!"

Kula went to find if there was something nice to drink she could put into her rabbit cup and to help Bukham because he was afraid and might soon cut himself on the sharp things.

CELESTAINE LOOKED AROUND, her left foot braced against Heno's right, her sword ready to strike the crouched figure that had just released its grip on her leg where it had been attempting to gnaw through her mail. To her right Nedlam was pointing at her target, a big man with a huge sledge who was nearly her equal in size. His swing had gone wide and hers was ready to unleash but they had halted, awkwardly. A couple of bodies of the Valuti and other raiders lay at their feet. Blood ran freely out of Nedlam's nose and from a gouge on her arm. Celestaine felt Heno vibrating with too much adrenaline to feel pain, the white fire swarmed up his arms. Two Valuti were in a shivering, smoking heap a short way off. Harpoons studded the deck. The Ystachi woman who had issued the command stood tall, her short hook blade and longer scimitar raised high.

"Enough," she said. "I am beaten. Enough." She let both her blades fall out of her hands. They went clattering onto the deck and her hands remained high and visible. Her vibrant skin had gone a sickly shade of khaki, the paler parts grey.

"Whut?" Nedlam said thickly. "Why?" She straightened, lowering her hammer. Her opposite number let his thunk down and he turned to see what was going on. He looked as confused as she did. "You were winnin'. Nearly," Nedlam added and squinted through sweat and blood to Celestaine who nodded and waggled her hand—maybe.

Bit by bit they relaxed.

"Your Tzarkomen masters have won," the Ystachi said, humbly. "It was anyway a bit of a foolish gamble. Fug is an idiot anyway but once you start, you start. We surrender. Unconditional."

A couple of the Valuti hissed and chittered angrily but she said more insistently, "Surrender, damn you. Now is not the moment for your blood debts. Later. Later. Or all your debts will be paid out for you when you are tossed to the fishes."

They grumbled but obeyed, and went about to tend to the wounded.

Celestaine felt the deep ache of a gash in her leg starting to make itself known. She stepped back and looked for Lysandra, to find her right there, arms folded. In the slowly improving light she was the colour of a fully fledged bruise, the pale lustre on the surface of her skin giving her a pearly sheen so that she could have been undead herself.

"You must be the Captain Kalliendra noted in the ship's log," she said to the Ystachi. "These Cheriveni never can stop taking notes even when they're pirates. Whatever your deal was with Captain Vakloz here it is ended. Time is short so there will be a new bargain. Your crew and the remains of his will stay here and guard this vessel until we return when you will sail it where we wish to go." She made a gesture and the unhappy figure of Bukham appeared, waxy and pale even on his darker patches, sweating as he carried the body of the Captain up into the light. They stood aside and he set it down, weapons and bits of finery still attached.

"I will consider your treacheries paid out if you agree. And if you try to cross me you will feel that you are burning with the fire of a thousand suns until you return to my will. Whether this is agreeable to you or not is not important. Only that you understand."

"Tzarkan monsters!" The man who had first screamed out, did so again, this time accompanying his words with the cast of a harpoon directly at Lysandra. He had a good arm and it flew true, faster than Nedlam or Celestaine could have intercepted.

Heno was raising his arm, and moving—he may have got to deflect it—but before he could do so Lysandra made a gesture as if she was swatting a fly. The harpoon flared brilliant gold and then fell in blackened, smoking chunks to scatter around her feet and knees. The metal head, a melted lump, smacked into Heno's forearm guard and then onto his foot. At that moment the man who had cast it, Fug, made a sound like a soft thump and became a man who was made out of fire.

His scream didn't even make it beyond an intake of breath before his form had disintegrated to white ash as fine as powder. It skirled and scattered around before being blown out to sea by the breeze. There was a scorched indentation on the deck in the precise shape of his two boot soles, and no more.

"We could have dealt as friends," Lysandra said calmly as everyone stood in silent shock. "But you decided it could not be. I wish you no harm and there is no shame in being bested by a superior combatant. Only keep this ship safe."

Kalliendra swallowed hard, her throat bobbing and the shroud of skin there puffing half up and then down again as she mastered her desire to rebel. Slowly she let her hands come down to her sides. She blinked with both sets of eyelids, one pale and quick, one heavily scaled and armoured. Her natural colours began to return. "I never heard of any Deathmaster having friends. You said my crew, but what of me?"

"You will guide us through the islands to the mainland where the Wanderer's faithful have their settlement at the edge of the ice. You will wait there for our return. Did you bring your own ship?"

"I have a skiff. It is in the lee of this islet."

"Prepare it, we are leaving immediately. You may take whatever you wish from this ship's cargo. I care not."

That made Kalliendra's eyes widen again and her stance eased a little. She went to check her crew and Lysandra turned to Celestaine.

"I have no skill for mending the living. Are you well enough to travel?"

Celest looked at her and there was doubt in her face, mistrust vying with necessity to gain a foothold, but she nodded. "There must be supplies on the ship to deal with it. We will fix ourselves up."

"Maybe your Guardian master will help you." Lysandra's brow quirked upwards at one side, her smile gentle but distinctly mocking.

Celestaine opened her mouth but nothing came out. She closed it with a nod. "Maybe. Is the girl all right?"

"She is very well," Lysandra said, slightly mollified. "You three maintain order up here. I will see to what passes below. We leave as soon as you and this Captain Kalliendra are ready."

"Wait," Celestaine had her hand out, sword loosely held, point down in it. "I don't... what happened to you?" Her gaze was searching, puzzled beneath her sweaty fringes of hair that had sprung free from the braids attempting to rein it in, but regarding Lysandra as a person and an equal for the first time.

"You mean how did I move from being as mud to as I am now?"

"I guess..." Celest nodded and Heno, wincing with each movement, paid close attention. Only Nedlam unconcerned, moving to pick up her opponent's sledge by the grip and hand it back to him as they talked.

"I learned," Lysandra said. "From watching you."

"Hur hur hur." Nedlam was laughing although Celest didn't find it funny, at first. Then she saw Lysandra's face was holding back a smile.

"See," Nedlam said to Kalliendra as they all began to move

around one another with caution. "Tzarkomen have friends. Yorughan too. Let's go investigate what's on this ship. I fancy I smelled some ora. These little fishies and bunnies won't need that. And if it's free then it's twice as good."

"The other crew will wake up eventually," Heno said. "Then what?"

"It doesn't matter," Lysandra said. "They all mind the ship or they burn. Let them sort it out between them for something to do while we're gone." She turned and went below.

Celestaine looked at Heno. "I'm like that?"

Heno glanced up from examining his leg wound and grunted, "You're nicer about it."

"So yes."

"I like her," Nedlam said. "Gets to the point of things."

Celestaine looked around, making sure Lysandra was out of earshot. Under the moaning of the wounded she moved to the blackened spot in the deck and touched it with her foot. "She torched that guy. Pfft. Like he never was. Is that what she's going to do to us if we get on the wrong side of her?"

"Well, would you?" Heno asked.

"No," she said firmly, because incineration seemed very unfair to her and the unfairness sat unpleasantly. "But I'd want to. You don't use your magic lightly."

"I used it enough," he said and the groaning Valturi snarled at him, their burns raw.

"Shut up and be glad for your life," Kalliendra snarled at them. "Tifi, go for the medicines and bandages. Tufi, make some of that tea for the pain. Get moving."

They reluctantly obeyed and two of their fellows, a husky, silent human and a particularly small Valturi with a wizened hand, took the Captain's body by the feet and dragged it away behind the capstans to loot it.

CHAPTER THIRTY-FOUR

THE SKIFF THAT Kalliendra had brought was nothing like the ship the Captain had owned. It was a raft with a nearly invisible draft beneath the waterline and barely more than a bit of shape bent into its prow to show that this was the front. It rode easily on the water behind the two huge animals that pulled it. They were like nothing any of them had seen before, and only Murti knew what they were by a name; their strange long heads, their dragonish faces, their huge array of fins that looked like arcs and tufts of seaweed as they lifted and lowered them in the salt water, snorting and dipping their snouts not to drink but to breathe.

"Seahorses!" Kula was glued to the sight immediately, held back by Lysandra to prevent her plunging into the water to meet them.

They were beasts, but peaceful ones, and intelligent enough to recognise Kalliendra's return. She had a way of speaking with them which was perhaps not a surprise had they known anything about the Dragonspeakers, which they did not, other than that they had something somehow to do with dragons and these fish were a little like that. There was a rough hut at the centre of the skiff which provided a small amount of shelter, and a single mast towards the front with a tilted sail that was furled now. Ropes held everything together. The bulk of the thing was built from huge, reedy bunches and it looked much more precarious than the wooden ship but they all boarded and were able to stow their few possessions.

It was nearly nightfall, but the Ystachi captain assured them the dark was no trouble as her creatures knew the way, and in any case navigated by currents and tides. They found themselves sitting together as the stars came out, the water riffling past them, islands in the chain now visible as dark blots against the rose and metal coloured skies. It was beautiful, although it was cold. Bukham, left alone with the food, had mastered the potbellied stove with a little help from Kula and was cooking patties of crabmeat. Nedlam and Heno were chewing ora and looking at the sky. Celestaine was enjoying herself. Although it was far from true, it felt like they had left everything behind them, and that in doing so it had vanished. There was a lightness to that evening she would have kept on with, sailed on and on and not bothered doing any more things, if she'd had the guts for that; but it turned out she was convinced by Murti and Lysandra's stories and running away wasn't her kind of thing. She did enjoy thinking about it though.

As they wove slowly northward two more of the Valuti came swimming up from the darkness, fish baskets in tow, and joined them. After a bit of chatter they seemed to settle on the notion of what was going on and speared their catches to add to the day's roasting.

"We should have Ralas, for a song," Nedlam said and tried to sing until they all made her shut up.

"You're scaring the horses," Kalliendra said, and it was true, they had picked up a lot of speed.

Once the food was cooked enough they began to share it out and at this point the Valuti abandoned their apparent shyness and came forward to claim their shares. In the glow of light afforded by the open stove and the single deck lamp their features seemed much more human and less animal, although they were far less human than many and Celestaine did not know what to call them—they seemed as much otter as person. They talked, although they had a way of quickening through the words that made them hard to understand.

"Valuti own all archipelago, all lands and waters."

When asked about the hole in the sea they were thrilled and hateful at the same time, pouring curses on it and calling up the wrath of various named leviathans. "Signanush eat it up. We have offered things. It still there. Hate it. Hate it. Take all and give nothing. Sometime a creepy crawling come up and out, sometime go down. Shadows in the water. Shadows everywhere. Hungry. Nothing make it go. Badplace."

"And you don't know how it was made?"

"Big grey ones come," the female Valuti said, stabbing a blunt, clawed finger at Heno. "Like this. Onna ship bigship. Stole it thinks me, because smell all wrong. And purple people." She pointed at Lysandra and Kula and then proudly counted on her fingers. "One, two, three, four five of them, so."

"And what did they do?"

"Yah, not sure really but boat sink there, all on, all in, sink there. Pfoom! Down. Thing came big shadow took boat down. All gone. Finish. Like that. No more. Wrecksink. Gone."

"Were there any survivors?"

"Yah, no, swum away a bit. Drown. Few. Some reached islands but islands belong to us. Ettem. Notwaste. Ettem. You want bones I got bones big smalls. Heads. Hands. All medicine bones. Gottem. Trade good."

"All hands on deck, eh?"

They were all startled, but Celestaine the least, by the elegantly raddled older man coming out from behind her shoulder, his face a kindly and concerned picture to complete his wry words.

"Deffo," she said. "What brings you here?"

"Actually, I have a purpose not involving yourself," he said. "I've come for those fingerbones if you have them, Gurt."

"Esya gots my butter?" the Valuti said, her whiskers vibrating in anticipation.

"There is a barrel of butter, over on that main vessel which your Captain will soon have as her own," Deffo said.

"We already owns that butter, thissm said so," Gurt said with a little snarl, showing her needle teeth as she indicated Lysandra who was watching quietly as she made a comfortable spot for Kula to rest among the coiled ropes and the lashed crates at the wall of the hut. "What else?"

"I have dried riverfish."

"Yuksum." The Valuti spat in contempt.

Deffo looked at Celestaine. She shrugged at him and winced, her bound-up shoulder aching.

"Now really I have to get them. They're not for me you understand, they're for Fierce. For Tricky."

Gurt looked cross, her whiskers suddenly all at sharp angles, nose wrinkling. "I give two. Tell her no trick me. But you no trust you. I ax her when see her if you. If not I find fixwitch, send you good badtime. Wait." She dashed off and after a few strides leapt easily over the side and vanished beneath the surface of the sea.

Kalliendra came back from the prow, the seahorses swimming steadily. "More god bothersome interfering?" She looked at Deffo with disgust and then checked around to see where Murti and Lysandra had got to. "Get off my boat."

"I came for…"

"I said, get off my boat." She stepped across to where Deffo had appeared, cowering, and picked him up bodily, shoving past Celestaine and Nedlam before throwing him, kicking and yelling, over the side.

He splashed down and went briefly under before bobbing up in their wake, receding quickly.

"Gurt will find you easier in there," Kalliendra shouted after him, dusting off her hands. She cast a grim look at Celestaine. "What?"

"No, no," Celestaine held up her hands. "You carry on." She heard Nedlam and Heno chuckling with that deep rumble of mountainsides moving that adult Yorughan had and smiled.

Kalliendra pointed at her eyes and then at Murti. She threw her dislodged cap back around herself and went back to her driving.

CHAPTER THIRTY-FIVE

ATOP THE RAMPARTS of Nydarrow, amid the black and louring stoneworks where the untouched battlements ranged against the starry sky in defiance of all that was holy, a small cottage with warmly glowing windows was set, complete with a wagon outside and four sheep chewing amiably in a rickety bamboo pen. Inside the Bounteous Domicile of Hule Dr Catt sat in an armchair with his feet up by the fireside and opposite him, in another chair, sat Dr Fisher, his satchel and stave beside him.

"Lords, Fishy, I thought I'd never get out alive," Dr Catt was saying, adjusting his bread on the toasting fork to get a better angle for browning. "But it was worth it."

"I hope so," Fisher said, sniffing. "Where did you leave them?"

"Locked in her old study I believe," Catt said. "Not to worry. She'll get out of it. Then they'll go down and not up here, probably."

"No time to do otherwise," Fisher said gloomily. "Look what I found in Tzark." He undid the satchel flap and reached inside, drawing out an old clay tablet, broken off at one end, its face covered in the angled stylus marks of ancient Tzarkish. It predated the coffer and the language used on the coffer by a long way.

"Where was that?"

"Tomb of Xaxtaris II," Fisher said. "One of the first graves of the civilisation, upon which all others were modelled right up until..."

"But what does it say?" Catt put down his fork, propping it on the fireguard, and was reaching out although Fisher twitched it away, proudly, for a moment to give it a quick whisk with a horsehair brush. Fine sand pattered out of it all over the carpets.

"It says that all that is remembered shall live again and that the dead must not be forgotten."

Catt peered and then gasped with eagerness as Fisher let him have it. He rotated the tablet and studied the signs. "But... there isn't any magic here is there? I thought you would have brought something significant, some great..."

"Do you remember the Kinslayer, Catty?"

"What? Well, yes. Not personally. Not in detail. I... what are you getting at?"

"The Tzarkomen rituals are all about being and unbeing, memory and forgetting," Fisher said slowly. "Underneath Nydarrow there's a place that's opened up to Vadakh, the undoing, you say."

"Yes, I've seen it. Seen that creature from there."

"And the Kinslayer trashed *The Book of All Things*, which wasn't a book at all, it was memories inside living people's heads."

"Yes."

"And now Tricky, and whoever she's with, which includes at least one Slayer who probably does have quite a good memory of the Reckoner and a being made in Tzarkand who uses necromancers' magic, are going with Wanderer through the ice gate into Vadakh to find the gods."

"I still don't..." Dr Catt stopped and sat up. He looked down at the tablet. He looked up at Dr Fisher. "Oh I say, Fishy. That doesn't mean what I think it means, does it?"

"I'd say it's all up in the air," Fisher said. He leaned back and reached over to a little bookshelf upon which several gaming boards rested and took out a carved wooden trinket box, opening it up just enough that they heard the soft chime and whirr of a mechanism and then the sweet, distinctive sounds of a melody began to play.

"'The Gambler's Last Wager'," said Dr Catt, naming the song.

"Mmn, I'm going to need this," said Dr Fisher. He snapped it closed before any more of the distinctive, roistering tune could ring out, even though it was so quiet it was barely audible outside the Domicile. "You head back in the morning. I have business I must deal with elsewhere. I'll meet you at the shop in a few days' time."

"You will take care, won't you?" Dr Catt said anxiously as Fisher popped the box into his satchel and began to do up the straps.

Fisher looked back at him and grinned. "Straight home now. No dawdling for hawkers."

Catt showed a small gap between his finger and thumb to suggest he might dawdle a little bit if the hawkers were very good.

After the door had closed and he was alone again he recovered his toast and found it was burned along one edge. He looked at it from every angle but there were no secret runes there or anything to show what the future might hold.

"Damn," he said softly, and tossed it onto the coals. He got up and began to pack everything away as fast as he could. If he was quick enough and Tricky slow enough he could catch them up without them realising he had gone far. He wasn't going to let Fisher go into this alone. Not if the Kinslayer was going to bring himself back the hard way.

CHAPTER THIRTY-SIX

Even with the seahorses keeping a good pace it was the better part of a day twining around endless islets, which all looked the same to Kula, before they got near their destination. They spent the night skirting islands, following channels and negotiating with the complex currents which rushed between the shores. Once or twice they dampened lanterns and sat tight as the faintest gleams of other traffic reached them but by the time dawn came they had reached the shore of Galdinnion without being challenged. Kula had to spend most of that time below decks. The weather had turned noticeably and keeping warm was an art form made much easier without the wind. A small settlement of low buildings and sturdy moorings marked the water's edge. Two vessels of a strange, bulky design with two masts and fat, rounded hulls lay at dock in the lee of a curve of hills which functioned as the best harbour that could be achieved, slight as it was.

Kula managed to sneak up on the Captain at the front of the skiff, little by little, clinging tightly to the deck rail, a smile at the ready, so that she could enjoy the last moments of their arrival to the port. She wanted to see the seahorses again and would have asked if she could hold the reins but she was too shy so instead she settled for a good view which brought her close enough to overhear the Captain talking to the white warrior, as Kula thought of her, the hero who was brave enough to love a monster.

"Icebreakers," Kalliendra said to Celestaine, standing beside her on the driving plate. She indicated the other ships with obvious admiration. "They can't be nipped, like this skiff. If it all freezes up the boat goes up too, onto the ice, 'stead of sinking to the bottom." She hissed as she worked, not enjoying the temperature very much.

Celestaine nodded politely. As she looked ahead Kula followed her line of sight and saw that a dusting of snow and ice covered the roofs and blanketed the land where they were about to go ashore. The clouds had dropped and the air was still, so mercifully they were not frozen by the time they managed to turn the skiff and bring it up to the quay. Inside her mittens her hands were cosy though as she looked over the side she could see sludgy ice in the water. The swell was steady and the seahorses riding easily at rest, stretched out like eels just beneath the surface. A party, clearly expecting them, came to meet them, clad in furs and skins so thickly tied on that they were indistinguishable as to any individual features.

Kula watched as they brought food for the horses first, lowering baskets with long necks down into the water, the feelers of large shellfish poking out of the basket bellies. Then they assisted the unloading of the skiff. Kula went with Lysandra, Bukham with Murti, as their hosts, invisible within their fur-lined hoods, escorted all but Kalliendra and her crew to the shelter and warmth of the main hut where a door was quickly opened for them and shut after. As soon as they were safely within the building Kula nearly tripped up as Bukham threw himself down on the first clear space of rug and clutched the ground, weeping. After a minute she realised it was because he was so glad to be off the boat.

Inside it was so warm that the first few minutes for everyone was spent shucking outer clothing. As layers were discarded the identity of the people settling this place were revealed. They were humans, like Celestaine, but short and stocky with dark hair and pale skins. Broad features, flat faces—but nothing distinctive otherwise to mark them as special. Their grey eyes were friendly, men and women both bearded, though the women more lightly. A strong air of stolid confidence radiated from them all as they moved about in the small space, making it and all the conditions outside seem perfectly manageable. Their leader was a man, who introduced himself as Dern of Tesval.

"Tesval is this place," he said as they all were given bowls of hot, brackish tea with honey. "Tesval is also the worm. We are of Tesval, the worm and its lands. We are the wanderers of the ice."

Murti was greeted with particular care and celebration and Bukham, as his assistant and someone of a human-kind they hadn't seen for themselves, was equally feted. There was a quiet happiness here that was something Kula hadn't felt or seen since the day her people were taken away. Probably it was because they had avoided the Kinslayer. It wasn't her peace, but she recognised it, and immediately felt trust in the strange, pale folk with their hairy faces. That allowed her to forget where she was and the adult dealings that went on around her. She closed her eyes to explore the land here as she had explored the sea all night.

The land, she realised now, was living, in its soil, in a way she hadn't noticed before. Her sensitivity had grown, her refinement grown, and she felt a joy in expansion of her awareness of these things. The sea was living in all its depths—the volumes of it had bewitched her, seduced her, to a point of bliss she had never felt when she was aground. She had followed mites of life so small they were a dust in the water, and discovered hearts the size of towns, in whose chambers she could have set up house and lived. They had passed close to an empty place which she recognised as the thing the dragon had told her of. It was the strangest thing, more empty than anything she could think of. In comparison it made the whole world vibrant. She was glad she had seen it although it made her afraid to think of it there.

All things were swallowed there. Nothing could pass it. Even the dead were more present in several ways than this space. She had thought she knew what absence of life was but she had not known it.

Even here, in this place where the ground was frozen and ice and snow covered the land there was plenty of life, small and slow, but burning with the same purpose and presence as any living thing. She greeted it, shyly, as she had greeted the sea, and extended herself outwards, checking the people here, staying well away from the burning heart of Murti and the vortex that he concealed. Him she did not want to study further, purely on grounds that he was of the Kin that slew her kin and she felt instinctively that there was a part of him that could do much damage to her if he chose. They had decided to let another alone, for now, but it was very much a temporary state of affairs. She knew he had a purpose where they went, which included Lysandra, but other than that the details were unsure. Unlike the others whom she could have read as easily as books or the weather, he was opaque. She felt that there would be some tug of war over Lysandra in the future and she must be very careful because it was possible that there was no value at all in Kula to these people. Their thoughts and feelings rarely included her and if they did it was only to manage her, not to know her. Because she couldn't hear and kept to herself they assumed she didn't think much. She wasn't interested in them anyway, all their designs were of things she cared nothing about, but she knew they could be dangerous. They only lit up when they were involved with something dangerous or difficult. They had no peace in them. Except for Nedlam. She was at peace always, even in the midst of a brawl. Kula valued Nedlam highly. She could have been family.

Her meandering found nothing new among the people. Even the most odd of them in appearance, the Ystachi, was an ordinary life that she knew well the feel of. But a short distance away, below them, lay two huge beings, resting but perceptive. She fell asleep immersed in the strangeness of their world, in long lines and deep burrows and labyrinths far beneath the ice.

She didn't see them until the next day.

They were equipped and ready, a sense of expectation in the air that this was the day upon which something would happen. The Tesval led them on a short march through their huts and into a tunnel which had been dug out of the hill behind them. This was only two ordinary people wide and barely high enough for Nedlam to walk at all, even without a hat. They had to go single file, except for Kula and Lysandra, who were in the middle of the pack and able to enjoy the view of Heno's coat and a bit of floor for a quarter of a mile—although Kula didn't mind that as she was trying to decipher how far down life went here, and the answer was further than she had suspected, but not that far. The ice itself held life but it was slow, slow and old. She was so caught up in this sudden intensely aged presence hidden within the tiniest and coldest places that she walked right into Heno's back, and bumped her nose hard enough to make her eyes water when they stopped.

They had come to an opening where a platform stretched out into a wide underground cavern. A strange and spectral light lit the area with a dim blue gleam from two massive circular ports which headed out into the ice wall that made up the cavern's furthest end. As they emerged onto the wooden structure and one by one began to descend the staircase that ran against the rock, Kula strained to get a glimpse of the creatures she knew only by the focused mass of their living energies. She held Heno's coat tail for balance as they all paused at the sight of the giant furred worms that were coiled in the heart of the cave, their heads raised and marked out by special larger tufts of thick whiskery feelers that grew like a mass of droopy fringes and moustaches around the four petals of their mouths. They had a grey fur with regular masses of white bristles poking through at varying thicknesses and lengths, and one of them was busy being harnessed up with a huge apparatus of ropes and straps designed to hold carriers along its sides.

Lysandra paused to adjust Kula's furred hood and mittens, check the lacing on her coat and the position of her scarf, then they crossed the floor of the cavern towards the enormous worm and its handlers who were moving about purposefully. Kula saw quickly that they were a mixture of the Ystachi and the Tesval but then, as she got closer, she realised that the ones she had thought were Ystachi who had been clinging to the beast's head were living inside its skin, their entire bodies to the chest concealed within the fur so that only their arms and heads remained free. Although it was invisible to the eye she could feel how they were connected, that the Ystachi were not the humanoid type like Kalliendra, but another form whose lower bodies had mutated and grown into their worm host, sympathetically linking up to it so that they acted as extra eyes and ears and minds for what would otherwise have been a fairly simple beast.

She shared the insight with Lysandra and they both smiled, delighted to find new and strange things as wondrous as this. They privately agreed not to tell the others. Most people found the Kelicerati repellent, though Kula found them only interesting because they could share thoughts and that was similar to the way that her people had shared and now that they were gone, only she and Lysandra could do so.

She gripped Lysandra's hand very tightly as they went forwards and set foot onto a tiny hoisted platform which raised them up until they were able to install themselves into one of the ice worm's many howdahs. These seats were padded and just large enough for two to sit between bristle rows about a third of the way down the animal's flank.

A packet of food was given to them and instructions to hold onto it tightly by a free moving Tesval woman who climbed about over the harness and through the hairs even more quickly than Kula could have walked. Ahead of them Bukham and Murti were seated, and behind them Celest and the others. Along the length of the worm supply packages of various sizes were already tightly rigged. A warm, slightly musky or fungal odour rose from the thick fur and Kula sneaked off a mitten to touch it as she was on the inside and partly shrouded from lap to foot by the overhair. It was rough to the touch and damply matted, but deep beneath it there was a fine down that was exquisitely soft, even more so than the fur on her hood. They rocked slightly as the worm adjusted itself and then there were people moving with purpose. Through Lysandra she heard horns sounding a booming call throughout the cavern, suddenly answered by a vibrant bellow from the worm that carried them—so loud that the entire thing, even their seat, shivered with the sound.

From far off down the blue tunnels an answering call came echoing, faint but distinct, and then without warning they were speeding forwards suddenly, the shiver of the worm's rapid but million tiny movements a burr in their fingers and toes as they shot towards the leftmost tunnel. Bitterly cold air, sharp as knives, made Kula quickly pull her scarf right up over her nose and then they were inside and hurtling at a great rate with blue ice only a half-arm's length away from Lysandra's side, a mass of bristly, waving forest all around them and a roar that Kula could feel in the deepest of her bones that was the sound of every individual hair on the ice wall. Lysandra nudged her and she looked up. The light was sunlight, coming through thick, thick ice that streaked above them in pink and blue tones of breathtaking beauty. Lysandra pulled her glove off for a moment, and Kula's mitten, to trace something important into the palm of her hand with one finger. It took a minute but then she understood as they began to bend slowly rightwards into a long turn, the black, sudden maw of a cross-tunnel flashing by— they were entering the largest and most complex of labyrinths, a mandala created naturally by the worms, layered and shaped by their attendants into the fully worked symbol of the ultimate journey. Murti, the Wanderer, returns to the beginning.

Lysandra looked at her and carefully adjusted her scarf. "Where we are going is the origin and the end of all worlds," she told Kula. "You will see things there which are not yet, and which have been and are almost done. Don't fear the shades, but also, don't remember them. Stay quiet and I will take you home."

Kula nodded. "Will my family be there?"

Lysandra thought about it. "No. They are gone."

Kula nodded. She had thought so, but had to ask. Sometimes the things which she remembered didn't make sense to her, but when she gave them to Lysandra her mother was able to explain the meaning of them. They were the memories of her people, who had walked the worlds once long ago, like Murti did, but as women and men, sorcerers of great power who had been outlawed when the necromancers took power and forbade them from walking in the world any more. She wondered why they had been allowed to do that, but there was in Lysandra's making something by way of an apology. Lysandra did not walk a path. Lysandra was a path. A way out, perhaps, but come too late for the way intended. And too late for whatever the Kinslayer would have had. He had not even noticed that he had destroyed the thing he looked for because he had never recognised it for what it was.

The sad thoughts hurt her. She didn't want a world full of these things. So she thought about their river dragon, whom they had saved, and restored. She thought about Heno the Yorughan and how the love he felt for the blonde woman was changing him like a slow fire, making long forgotten moments live again, making the past change and darken as he changed and saw things in different lights. She wondered why they were here and now. She looked at Murti in the howdah ahead of them, the worm burring busily, the ice flashing past in darkening hues as they descended deeper into the glacier. She tugged Lysandra's hand.

"Where will you go when I die?"

Lysandra looked at her, eyes bright. "I don't know. You're not done making me yet. I'll go where you tell me."

Kula nodded, thoughtful, wanting to get matters right. "If the gods made the Guardians—did they just let them go?"

"I don't know. They had a purpose, once."

"Do you think they lived too long and when things didn't go as they wanted it to, that they lost their way?" She watched Murti and then Bukham, who was open like the sky, still thinking that this was only the extension to a delay before his life returned to the point he had left it. Like Celestaine, he was Murti's chosen. So even the Wanderer had a purpose of some sort.

Lysandra held Kula's hands fast, warming them in her own. "Each of them has a nature which is fixed. They can only be what they are and nothing else. No, they're not like people. They do what they know to do. They will not learn. They will not change. They were set to guard the human races and that's what they do."

"Well, why did the Reckoner want to kill us all? You said he had to do it to wake us up."

"I don't know. I am not the Reckoner. He must have had a reason. But even if you knew it, would it change anything?"

Kula thought about it. "I guess not. Maybe it would mean it wasn't his fault."

"Even if he could not help being as he was, he still was the one who acted and set so much in motion."

Kula thought of the Kinslayer and of the Tzarkomen necromancers who had enslaved her people. Caracu were a part of Tzarkand, but because of their unique ways they had been shut away from the world and kept in isolation by the other Tzarkomen clans. The clans had kept them to use and the Kinslayer had treated them that way too, as a resource, not a people. They were the same, in a way. They took power for themselves. "Why are the powerful ones so bad?" She was angry, but ashamed of her anger. It felt like it was the fuel that had lit the fires of the ones she hated and that it might be the cause. But she felt it anyway. She hadn't felt things much before now. She'd only been surviving, but now something else was happening to her. It was painful and difficult but that didn't stop her. She wanted to know the truth of how things were.

"Because they believe they know what is right to do, and they use their power to make people obey," Lysandra said. "They think they can fix the world."

"He wanted to make it all add up," Kula said. "Like me. I want it to make sense. I want the horrible things to stop. Forever. I want to fight and kill all those in the way. I want them to stop hurting people." She looked fearfully at Lysandra. "But that's what he wanted. To fight and kill. Will I be like him? Will I make you like him?"

Lysandra rubbed their hands together. "You have to choose," she said. "You have to do what must be done. But you cannot do nothing. That's what it means to be alive. Even if you sat your days away in a little house far from anything, that's still what you did, and that would change everything else in the world. So, you can be the warrior, the friend, the priest, the wanderer, the fool—any of those things. But I can't tell you. You have to feel the life in you and trust it to tell you what to do."

Kula smiled a little bit, to show she understood, even if she didn't like it. She wanted security, but there was only this moment and the way it flickered and dipped between them, the people and the worm. "Are we a monster?" she asked as they slowed down to make a tight turn, the path weaving them ever deeper into the darkness.

"Oh surely." Lysandra gripped her fingers so tightly that they hurt, their hands laced together, full of vivid energy and the exhilaration of the ride. "Yes. Yes!"

"Yes!" echoed Kula and then they threw their hands up in the air at arm's length and laughed, the frigid, dry air as making their eyes burn like fire.

CHAPTER THIRTY-SEVEN

BUKHAM TURNED AS he heard Kula laughing. He was so glad for the sound. The ride was terrifying and Murti had become so still beside him that he thought he might have died. He felt so far from home that it almost physically hurt. A part of him was exhilarated, and he tried to stick with that part and ignore the rest. At least that way he got to hold onto a shred of dignity and dry pants. The rigging creaked as they bent this way, that way, in huge sweeping curves. It was getting darker all the time as they went below the reach of light. He could barely see his hand in front of his face. He thought maybe through the forest of whiskers he could see Kula waving. He tried to wave but he wasn't able to let go of the leather straps that he was clutching for dear life. He smiled, but then a jolt and drop made him have to face forwards, heart in his mouth. They were now plunging down at a steep angle. He watched the wall slowly vanish and then there was only the tremendous sound and vibration of the worm and the heat radiating off it as they dived into absolute night, the icy air streaked in sharp pain across his cheeks.

Then just as he thought it would never end he felt the closeness of the tunnel break open into a huge space and at the same moment light showed him the grey shapes of his arms and hands, the fur of the worm and Murti, who was pulling off his gloves. The light was coming from his skin, a soft, golden gleam of distant sunlight, patched with the Oerni patterns in strange continental spots.

The worm was slowing to a leisurely pace, easing its way now across a flat plane and, as Murti's radiance increased to make much of it visible, his light acted like a beacon and new fires lit with the same glow, which suddenly became hurtfully bright as it refracted from a million tiny facets in the walls of the gigantic hall they had entered.

The creature had come to rest at the edge of a vast circle with a flat, smooth floor. The roof arched high up and came to a vertex way above them, a hill or a mountain high, Bukham would have said, but every bit of it was covered in a resplendent mass of crystals in purple and blue and white. The light, which glowed in sconces at the floor, ran up through these so that they all shone upon one another and gave the space a gentle, submarine light. At that moment of wonder the worm chose to shake itself, like a wet dog, and its handlers and all of the party were violently jostled with cries of alarm and reproach as the ripple went down the long length of the beast and nearly shivered them into all their constituent bits, or so it felt. A ripe stink issued from its fur afterwards. After that he was so glad to disembark the thing he nearly kissed the ground.

At the centre of this hall a stone circle stood, much like those he was used to visiting on the year's turn as they took the caravan in pursuit of the seasons of plenty. This one was not hewn but grown, however, and it had no cross pieces and no marks of human making. Crystals the size of walls stretched up, three of them making slender pillars all the way to the roof; the rest bluntly ended, the light inside them cloudy with billions of fractures. But they made an unmistakable Wanderer's Circle. A shape within them lay unmoving and ugly, at odds with the room. Once the worm had been soothed and set to rest Murti went out to approach it and Bukham followed him tentatively, not sure if he were doing so from curiosity or out of terror of leaving the old man's side.

It took them a minute of walking to get there, Bukham slipping a little on the smooth floor, trying not to put Murti directly in front but doing so anyway as if he was in the tracks of the master and not using the master as a deflecting shield. By glimpses he gathered that there was a creature before them, large and strange, made of some kind of crystal like the room. Murti sighed as he arrived and the last light of his skin went out.

"It's dead," he said, to Bukham since everyone else had remained at the edge by his command. "I feared that might be the case. Of course. He would have had to kill it. Or it died trying to stop him."

"What is it?" Bukham asked as Murti went forwards to the gigantic corpse of... whatever it was. Limbs of some kind were folded and possibly wings, although what you would do with wings down here was a strange thought. A long body was coiled up and the head hidden in the general jumble. A good many spines and spikes adorned it and had broken and fallen in pieces all around.

"It was the Guardian of this place," Murti said. "I made it long ago, to ensure I was never followed when I came this way out of the—"

"Out of the what?"

Murti turned and Bukham saw there were tears in his eyes and that he was struggling. "The other place. It doesn't have a name and it cannot be named. You'll know it when you see it. From there." He turned back and put his hand out to touch the gleaming, transparent shape. As soon as he was within a hair of it, it shattered suddenly and completely into a brilliant, glittering dust and fell to the floor. For a while it fell slowly in a great cloud and Bukham heard a sweet, distant ringing sound in it like many tiny bells. A tiny portion of it lingered, lit with a soft, blue glow that was fading as they watched.

"Goodbye," Murti said to it and it seemed to spin for a moment before it sped off and was gone. Upwards, Bukham thought, although it was also dissipating as it went so maybe it only seemed like up. He looked down, thinking he would be covered in it, but even the dust was evaporating as he looked and in a moment or two there was nothing left to see.

"Here is where we will go inside," Murti said and bent down to pick up the tiny handful of ash or grey earth that remained at his feet. "And here is where we will return. Bring the others. Tell them to be ready."

"Ready for what?"

"Ready," Murti said. "Really, didn't you learn anything in all this time?"

Bukham turned, feeling foolish and angry, but he went. The walk was long and when he reached the worm's side where a camp was being set up in the warm lee of its bulk he had got back to his normal self and realised that Murti was right. He was being stupid. He was here on this journey because he had never said no to it and now that it was getting to places he had never wanted to go, being interested only in staying with the caravan and the Posts and being a good Oerni, making his family proud, now he was finding that maybe he was interested to know what was going on with this divine being and the gods. He wanted to protect the little girl, because she had come to his stall and somehow that had expanded out into all this because she was involved with it in ways that he didn't understand. He wouldn't pretend he was ever going to understand it but he had buried the children on that farm and their fates were tied into this too—he felt it, but he could not express how it was. He hoped that he could do something to make that better than it was, or if that wasn't possible, that maybe he could come to a way of seeing it that didn't make him feel hateful and despairing and sad. He felt it was selfish, only wanting to feel better. It would be something greater to do as Celestaine did and try to make things actually better. He followed Murti because he believed, or, no, he had thought he believed, that Murti knew how to do this. But now there was a sensation he got off the old man that he was actually as he had always said, wandering, and he did not know any more than Bukham knew. He just had greater powers of winging it. This refusal to answer a question but instead make Bukham answer it was not because Murti had the answers and wouldn't share them. He didn't have answers any more than anyone else did. But perhaps that was the point. Bukham would always be a follower and a hoper and a dreamer until he was able to answer for himself and not even ask Murti's view any more. Bukham was lost, but he knew it for the first time, and there was a peace in that.

He found Celestaine, Heno and Nedlam waiting for him expectantly. He looked down at Celestaine's resolute face. "He says it's time to go."

"Go where?" Nedlam asked, looking at the entirely sealed cavern and the crystal circle.

"Wandering off," Bukham said and smiled, feeling how true and how unhelpful it was at the same time. "He'll take you where. I don't know how, so don't ask me."

"Where the Kinslayer went to cut off the gods, I assume," Celestaine said, adjusting the girdle that held her sword straight and hefting the shield on her back, testing how it was carried so that she could get at it easily. She looked up at Heno, to see how he was taking it.

The light was making everyone a corpselike shade, but Bukham fancied that Heno looked greyer than usual. "I have been there before. It's where the Heart Takers were sent to gain their... power." There was more, his expression said, but he was going to carry it by himself. He glanced across the top of Celestaine's head and Bukham saw Lysandra and Kula, tightly coated and booted against the cold. He waved at them and Lysandra tapped Kula to get her attention and then they came across to join the rest.

"We're going," Bukham said. "Do you have everything you need?"

Lysandra smiled and shrugged. "We are ready." She looked down dotingly on Kula, who was solemnly looking at each of their faces in turn.

Bukham studied them. He felt a deep resistance at the idea of taking a child into danger but he was too afraid of Lysandra to entirely believe that Kula was in that much danger. But looking at them they seemed a picture of a mother and child, entirely ordinary. The fire. The dragon. He swallowed awkwardly.

"Lead on," Celestaine said sharply.

"Oh." Flustered, he turned and made his way back across the room, slipping a little in the melting icewater from his own boots as he hurried, so glad he was not in charge of anything.

They reached the centre where Murti was standing alone. At this point the floor was a transparent sheet. Bukham looked down and almost fell over. They were standing on ice over a clear, deep lake. Its rocky-sided descent plunged down and down, defined by the crystal pillars that grew through towards the roof. They were suspended in mid-air.

"This place is somewhat grandly named the Lenses of the Mind," Murti said, his voice gentle and meandering in the manner of an old man beginning the telling of a lengthy fireside tale. "You will find that..."

The world flipped. One second they were in the cavern, listening to Wanderer, the next they were standing on a strange, dust-dry ground the colour of ash. Of the cavern there was no trace, other than the pillars which were revealed in a sepulchral light to be the trunks of petrified trees, black, their bark glinting with a constantly running coat of water that sank down into the sand and vanished among their roots. Leafless branches stretched up towards where sky ought to have been but when Bukham looked upwards he staggered and hunched with sudden fear.

Instead of space and air, the rippling surface of a lake stretched, inverted, as far as he could see in all directions. The grey light fed down through this water came from a long way above from some presumed distant sky. The trees were revealed not to be branching up there at all, but rooting, their reach mapping the depth of the water until murky gloom consumed them. The water barely moved, giving the light a constant soft and despairing quality, sometimes shifting just enough to create the illusions of movement here and there across the landscape they found themselves in, studded with lifeless stone trees, scattered with small rocks. In the distance hills were visible, and the broken towers and battlements of cities. The air, dry, and warm only in comparison to where they had come from, was motionless, odourless.

"...the transition is entirely unremarkable," Murti concluded and waited for them to gain their composure back. "This is where I believe the gods were sent."

"You couldn't come on your own and get them?" Nedlam asked, hefting Lady Wall onto her shoulder and turning to get a good look at everything.

"I could, but creatures roam here that are hungry for memory and I would likely fall victim to them faster than I found anything. That's what you're for," he looked at Celestaine, Heno and Nedlam. "Your business is to protect us so that we last long enough to find what remains."

Bukham saw a flicker at the edge of his vision and looked. Shadows, so faint as to be almost unseen, flowed over the nearest low hill. They were small, two or three of them, and it was difficult to be sure of them because of the occasional ripples of the lakelight.

"We're fighting shadows?" he asked, wondering.

"The shadows are something we must all resist," Murti said. "No, you are to fight the monsters who are what the shadows long to become. I think traditional means will suffice."

"All right," Celestaine said with determination. "Which way?"

"It really doesn't matter," Wanderer said. "The gods, if they still persist, will find us. Their hunger will lead them." He looked at Bukham with a gentle smile. "Pick a direction."

Bukham looked at the city far away. The walls at least promised some kind of protection. He pointed.

"So be it," Murti said, as though resigned to the walk as a needless expense.

They began to walk, their feet raising small puffs of grey-brown dust that settled behind them such that it left no trail at all.

"Why are you talking about the gods like they're already finished?" Heno asked, and the tone surprised Bukham and even made Celestaine look at him with concern because its major tone was one of fear, raw enough that he could not cover it up.

"Here the gods are prey for greater, stranger things," Murti said. "They are being hunted. As are we all. What remains depends on how savage they have been or if they have fallen. Those that have been consumed may have changed beyond recognition. It is what the Reckoner would have felt was a fitting adjustment, given that he could not kill them. He sent them here, to be eaten or dissolved and made again."

"And we're here to what?" Bukham asked, very quiet so as not to attract the attention of anything nearby—it was impossible to see with any conviction beyond a short distance. As they moved a certainty moved with them in a ring, but beyond the reach of easy seeing the few features that there were seemed to dissolve into a mystery, with only suggestions of form remaining. It wasn't that they couldn't see. It was that they could not know what it was that they were seeing.

"We're here to discover what has happened and, I think, we must close the ways that lead from here to our own plane, regardless of what we find"

"And the girl?" He had to know, not that he could stop anything. He just had to know.

"Oh, I've no idea, but since she led us this way to begin with I think there is probably a good reason for her to be here."

"Crazy," Nedlam said, but not in a way that suggested she was offended. "What about the other one?"

"I think she has a purpose here," Murti said. "In fact, I was rather counting on it."

Bukham heard Celestaine grinding her teeth. "Do you not think it might be wise to tell us your plans now while we still have time to hear them?" She had paused and was peering intently out to their left where something shimmered like a darker shape in the mirages, constantly returning from erasure with ever increasing frequency. She readied her shield and drew her sword, stepping in that direction as they continued to travel, slowly.

Murti nodded in agreement, wholehearted. "My dear, if I had a plan, you'd be the first to know."

Heno pushed Lysandra and Kula behind him. Bukham did his best to keep position at the front, though all his attention was on terrified glances to the left. Aside from the sounds of their own voices and movements there was a deep and utter silence.

"What is that?" It was the unstoppable question now and it came unbidden from Bukham's mouth as they all halted and grouped up to face what was coming.

The creature's slow, inevitable approach matched its growing clarity. Bukham saw with disbelief the corpse of a large human in the process of being preyed upon by three giant spiders. Each spider was made of web and visible inside their transparent bodies was a squirming goo filled with eyes—human, animal and insectoid—which rolled and blinked, looking in all directions. It approached them on all fours, walking like a bear. The goo, exposed to the air here and there through the holes in the webbed bodies, gave off a glowing miasma which trailed behind the thing like a rotting veil. Upon this veil a cluster of small, formless shadows dipped and settled, flew up and settled, like flies. As it got closer Bukham, his throat closed so tight he could barely breathe, expected to see the spiders more clearly but instead the distinction between spider and corpse became less and less obvious until he was forced to see that it was not a human preyed on by spiders at all, but something whole, as if it had naturally grown that way right from the start. When it was within a short distance the shadow swarm detached and drifted towards them. He felt their hunger as they came down and began to coat them as dapples of darkness.

Heno's cry startled him so much that, semi-paralysed by fear, he tripped over himself in his urge to flee and fell flat into the dust. The shout was accompanied by a burst of lightning that broke over them in a net of crackling white fire. Where the lightning touched the motes of darkness they immediately extinguished one another and, seeing his power, the swarm drew back and circled, lazily, awaiting the arrival of the creature's sluggish main body.

Nedlam had never liked waiting and her patience had been eroded to nonexistence by the sea voyage. She strode forwards, bracing the hammer back, balancing it finely for a good whack. In defence the spider-thing reared up to a height that matched her. Long limbs that had wrapped around its middle suddenly whipped out, their tips like blades. She dodged them, sent the hammer crashing in and down on the thing's shoulder area, its haft snapping off a couple of limbs on the way. The thing exploded in a snotty blurt of sickly green matter, a huge piece of it breaking free and revealing a core of soft, sponge over threads that hung and wiggled freely in the air once exposed.

It made no sound—it had no mouth or anything to make a sound with—but it staggered, giving Bukham a moment of hope, but then regained itself, the horrible, glowing veil drawing up and shivering as it raised it high. Like a fisherman it flung this blanket of gas out over Nedlam. The veil dropped, clinging and fouling her backswing. Bukham's view was obstructed as

Heno spun suddenly and another flaring web of white lightning shot across them. Moments had passed but it felt like years, Celestaine poised, looking for an opening, Bukham cowering, getting up off the sand, his awareness suddenly widening as he made it to his feet at last and he noticed, with a clench in his gut, that as they had been involved with this fight a number of larger ghostly forms had crept up on them. They hovered at the edge of the circle of clarity, crude and nebulous effigies of the most basic bodily forms, sending creepers along the ground where they seemed to gain strength in reaching desperately for a touch of the living. Only Heno's repeated blasts kept them at a respectful distance, but at the same time it seemed that the more often the fire struck them the more persistent they became.

Murti had noticed their resilience as well. His voice barely carried over the background duet of Nedlam, Celestaine and Heno: the sodden thunk of Lady Wall's weakening impacts and Nedlam's hoarse shouts of war fury, Celestaine's fierce exclamations as she hacked at the creature, Heno's buzzing magic. "We must move faster. Do not use the magic unless you must. Resist them by commanding them to obey you. Make your presence too real for them to touch. Those who have form here hold all the power. As long as we are beneath the Lenses you are strengthened."

Bukham glanced up to the lake water. Its surface with the soft ripples formed a billion lenses. He imagined himself stronger, then he pushed the vision into his body, as if he were Murti, a Divine Wanderer, as if it were true. He didn't know if it was him but someone had got the hang of it, for the circle of clarity widened sharply and the shadows slunk away. Now they had a better ground for themselves.

He looked around to check on the others and saw Nedlam tangled in webs of slime, struggling to breathe and having to fight a constant war to free her limbs enough to break it apart. Every time she snapped it open it simply grew back again, thickening in tough strings, binding her slowly more close to the main body. Above her head a long, fine black straw-like antennae with a needle tip was making fumbling stabs down towards her, each one closer and closer.

Celestaine ran up easily. Taking one foot onto Ned's bent knee and another onto her shoulder she launched herself into the air, shield held, sword fast and sliced off the needle limb before continuing over the monster's head, the sword point braced downward, her body in a crouch with the shield held under her left foot like a child's sled. He heard the solid sound of her impact on its back and then a slow, tearing rip followed by a massive splattering and a gush.

The net over Nedlam recoiled in agony. Loose whips of it writhed in unmistakable torment as it snaked back and began to wrap itself quickly around its own body like bandages, knitting itself back together. Freed, Nedlam strode forward and began to smash at the head of the thing with swift and massive swings of Lady Wall, one, two, one, two. If it had ever been human it was quickly turned to an unidentifiable grey pulp.

"Dis shit want to eat me!" she exclaimed and then, "No, NO, NO!" Every word with an added whump of Lady Wall's head. Grey globs of matter flew everywhere from the huge metal hammer, the smaller bits evaporating, the larger chunks landing with wet noises, immediately leapt upon and fought over by the lingering ghouls beyond the circle.

"Bukham, we must make your destination!" Murti's voice brought him back to himself. He looked up. "You are the only one who sees it. We must go before more things come."

He nodded and began to move, fearful but going because it was the only chance of safety and there was no cover in any direction. He thought he might have wet himself.

"We'll catch you up when we make sure this is dead!" Celestaine called, going to Nedlam's shoulder. "Go! Heno, stay with them!"

Bukham began to hurry, aware of Lysandra moving swiftly up to his side. There were low hills in the way, and plenty of ground to cover, some of which was already beginning to dance with odd shapes that came and went. From the corner of his eye he saw Kula turning slowly, her small coat skirt out flung as she spun around, dancing as she went. Her hands were free of their dangling mittens and stretched wide. Around her a tiny flurry of shadows was circling and she was leaping and dancing to catch them, one by one. As she spun she caught his eye and her smile was bright, a delight that was like a shot to the heart; it was so unexpected in this moment, at this place.

She snatched a shadow out of the air and then rubbed her palms together and cupped them. When she opened them to show him, a black bird flew out between her fingers and high up into the air. It arrowed away from them towards the crumbling towers and vaults of the ruins.

CHAPTER THIRTY-EIGHT

"RUINED WORLDS COLLIDE here," Taedakh said as they walked through the city. His voice was a necessary sustenance for Ralas, who listened as he watched Tricky scale walls and leap from roof to parapet, investigating, pausing to slay things here and there as she circled them, although Taedakh seemed to cut a wake through most beings that came near. Ralas walked just behind his shoulder in only the usual pain, his pleasure mostly unalloyed even by that, though the crumbling architecture was vast and dwarfed them all in a way that suggested none of them were worth time's considerations.

"All the things of this place strive to survive by eating the memories of the living. Vholes and my own kind are as the predators and the scavengers of your world. All that dies comes here and unless it is consumed quickly it is forgotten. It becomes dust. The ghost of memory. The dust you walk on is what remains of millions of years of living dreams from countless places."

Cheery, Ralas thought. Cheery with a side order of magnanimous. It was a great relief to know you didn't matter a jot. It left him feeling lightheaded with opportunities although he still missed his lute. Instead of focusing on that he hummed a little light wedding music from the operatic magnificence of the compositions of the Cheriveni's most famous and least appreciated domestic musician, Tarilas the bard. Once in a few generations you spawned someone like Tarilas who seemed to come out of nowhere, fully fledged, proficient as only a deity ought to be. Then as often as not they proved themselves human by dying a wretch's death and Tarilas had been no exception, dead by twenty-five from an outbreak of winter cough that left any number of lunk-headed nothings alive instead. Ralas felt briefly proud to have at least avoided that fate.

"Not all dust is equal though. Dust of Ages is here, in this place. Tricky searches for it now. Your companions will arrive soon and so will all they have sought. We need to find it by then."

"Dust of Ages? Sounds like something Dr Catt would like."

"It is something Dr Catt would like," said Catt, huffling as he made his way along behind Ralas, always pausing to have a little look and then a little hurry to catch up. Having resolved to find Fisher again he'd hurried back just in time to meet up with them as they descended beneath Taedakh's lake sky, all the way muttering about his terrible losses, the fate of the sheep chariot unattended for any old fool to meddle with and all the rest of his unique and valuable research gone to waste as the vaults of the Kinslayer were sacked by ignorant morons and unequivocally unqualified subspecies. "The Dust of Ages is the essence of memory—all of the structure and none of the contents. It is the only trap worth knowing about, for most of the terrible things lurking down here as they can't resist it, but as soon as they take it, it imprisons them, leaving them nicely harmless for collectors like myself to carry away for further examinations."

"Peachy," Ralas said. "Who were you hoping to get a last smidge of?"

"The gods of course," Catt said, coughing to clear his throat. "They are a few of the greater beings which had attempted to breach the Upper Realms by sheer force in ages past and so were seen as gods by the living already up there. They created worlds, we think, by bringing together scraps of memory and place. So they were the hyper-predators of this realm, successful over millennia of collection, curation and restoration. Master craftsmen, if you will." His enthusiasm gave him a little extra speed and he drew alongside Ralas, watching for Tricky as she zipped across their path from a collapsed townhouse into the tumbledown blocks of some mighty temple. She moved so quickly that they only really saw her hood and cloak in the vague greyness. It felt like even the light was being rendered down.

Taedakh spoke, as much like a living book as Ralas had ever encountered. "Those of whom you speak made every effort to preserve and to grow, but they fell prey to the dust in the end. The more of themselves the great spirits put into their works the less resistance they had to time's decay and they forgot things. They fled into the upper worlds to save themselves."

"And then the Reckoner threw them back here," Ralas said, feeling that he was due a high grade for his efforts at grasping the depth of their situation.

"It does seem." Taedakh plodded on, his long, clawed feet relentless, silently pacing along a dust filled avenue of broken cobblestones. They passed beneath precipitous arches supporting walkways that had once led to great chambers and now led nowhere.

"Is it the Dust of Ages that made me like I am?" Ralas asked, not with any hope of success.

"Maybe," Taedakh said, "but if so we can only get it out of you by making you back into dust."

"I'll pass for now." He shivered involuntarily and cleared his throat to renew his song, keeping it to a hum.

"The gods gather, and hunt here," Taedakh said. "Monuments are always the last to go. They are such strong shapes. They hold a lot. They make good caches."

"So... we're walking through their storehouse?" Ralas kept looking all over for any sign of the lute case. Ahead of him he saw Dr Catt also peering about, his hands anxiously washing themselves over and over in front of him as he trundled through the dust.

"We are. That is why we may find the Dust of Ages here. Anything they keep outside themselves will be hidden here or in a place like this one."

"How many places like this one are there?"

"An infinite number."

Ralas felt that the statement of this didn't fit with the apparent confidence in their ability to find the dust or Celestaine's party. "So how do you know we're in the right place for the others?"

"It was decided when they made it their destination."

Which was an answer and did make sense, in a way, if Taedakh was a god who could know when something had become significant—when it had taken on a meaning for someone in his domain. Ralas didn't feel like getting any more new about the gods. They didn't sound the way he had imagined them. He was foiled by Taedakh, who added, "My kind don't like the gods of your world. Here they are parasites. They hunt us to steal our ability to retain our form across all the planes of existence. We always kill them when we can."

"How is it that you're helping out this little Guardian, then?" Dr Catt asked as they crossed an open square and came to a place where six roads met, each leading to a less promising looking destination than the last, dark entryways and exits on all sides. 'Fishy?' he called out hopefully now and again in a plaintive little bleat like a constant accompaniment. 'Fishy? Are you there?'

"Because she gave me music." The god, or whatever he was, Taedakh, turned around to look at them and Ralas felt he was being smiled at, although the general hideousness of Taedakh's form didn't give much clue of that. "Your music," he said. "She brought me up to hear you sing while you were in the depth of Nydarrow."

Music, Ralas remembered, was what everything was made

of, knit, line and stitch. A stitch in time. A rhyme that binds. A glue and a thread. He felt abruptly humbled, and grateful, and scared, in case he was going to be asked to do something he couldn't but before he could articulate just what had got him bothered Taedakh stood up to his full, massive height and tilted his long head, scanning.

"They come," he said, slumping down again. "We cannot look any longer. We go to the gates. Come." He called out and Tricky came leaping down from a series of huge columns that were the end of a walkway for people who must have been a good deal larger than any people Ralas had ever seen.

"But she said she made you." The words were out before Ralas realised he was talking aloud.

The god ahead of him gestured for him to come along. "That could be." He was moving quickly now, so that he started to draw ahead of them.

"*How* could it be?" Ralas hissed at Dr Catt, looking at the Cheriveni's intent expression as they struggled to keep up in the dusty wake.

"I'm a collector, man, not a theologian," he replied between breaths.

Tricky appeared between them, her hand outstretched. She held a vial, stoppered with a silver stopper, and inside it a fine, golden powder could be seen, unremarkable except for its container. "Keep this for me," she said and handed it to Catt.

"Is it...?" he said, and paused to try to look but she was dragging them both by the sleeve now. They were slow and Ralas was trying to run and about to apologise for failing when a gigantic shape came bowling out between two buildings and took Taedakh down in a giant, tumbling destruction that knocked both of them into the vertiginous masses of a high tower and brought it down upon them as they smashed through what was left of a beautiful palace, something fine and delicate and quite out of place, Ralas thought, seeing it go up in clouds of dust like smoke as he ducked and Tricky yanked them the other way down a side street. They could hear detonations and blows in a muffled, slow series of booms and thuds.

"What..." Ralas began as the whole area darkened and something like a million strands of thread, utterly black and boiling together, flowed around them, trying to go through them but unable to because Tricky's cape was acting as a shield. Catt cowered into him and they had to run again as she tried to ward them from another direction as the threads left and a storm surrounded them, made of feather and bone and tiny bits of reeking flesh.

"The gods are here," she said.

CHAPTER THIRTY-NINE

HENÓ FELT HIS power beginning to wane.

Before he had never had to use it for long periods of time. Always there had been a few bursts, and then pauses, bought by defeats or by the surrender of those facing him. Among his cohorts in the armies of the Kinslayer he had fought at the melee and used it sparingly, as instructed. The reason for this was never clear, but he had never sought to know. When he had first come here he had been through to the underlake for moments only, enough to see the seizure of the child he had brought with him and the gift of its heart taken in by the roiling darkness of something he had never wanted to understand, or remember. But he remembered it now. With every draw of the fire and the light he felt himself tiring and his own heart had begun to feel a remorseless and debilitating ache.

Beside him the ghost of his cousin's child, Azu, was walking. He thought it was madness at first but then every one of his casts had caused the dust to cling to her more firmly, giving it the strength to adhere and join. As she grew more distinct so his power faded, little by little, and his heart ached more and more he had to recall that he had stolen her, on a promise to take her somewhere far from the war, somewhere that only he, a favoured soldier of the Kinslayer, could know. He had even believed it himself, right until the moment he stood before the portal and let them take her from him and push her through its seething black core. Then the portal master had caught his eye, this new, soon-to-be mage with so much power, the Kinslayer's elite—and the look of contempt and hate on that face had stuck with him and stuck with him in a baffling conundrum of the exchange of the girl for the power until he had been forced to sit down in the dark of the barracks and think it through. And from then on he'd never been able to stop thinking things through, questioning every story. The secret world far from the war. It was one way of saying dead.

At first he thought he imagined her as a figment of his private, well-deserved hell. After the first creature went down—they didn't know if it was dead and there were by then two more amalgams of horror bearing down so it didn't matter, only down mattered and that they could walk on, run on together—then he noticed her. But after the second and the third, when Nedlam was poisoned and began to stagger like a drunk, and Celestaine lost her shield to the crunching maw of something with bone blades for jaws, after that he saw that Kula looked back at them and she saw Azu too. As they ran Kula stretched out her hand to the ghostly girl. The ghost looked up at Heno, trustingly, if that was what that black emptiness meant in her eyes—and took the hand that was offered to her, instantly changed from transparent to solid, built of sand but alive and running, the details of her face and hair sharpening. At the same moment the storm of black, predatory motes gathered itself anew and fell, touching them with a little taste of death, licking away the thinnest layer of them at a time and hurtling off with it into the grey beyond. Heno had to call the fire, there was no choice. He called it, and then they all saw her. Azu grew with each cast. As they survived, as the darkness burned, so Azu became real.

Nedlam saw her. Gathering herself, she pointed, her eyes wide. She knew who it was. She remembered. The story of where the children had gone so that after the war there would be a safe, pleasant place to grow, to be untouched by adult nightmares, to walk under the sun as free women and men, to make the sacrifices of the parents mean something. This story was something they hadn't quite believed but they had all held it close as a hope—their only hope upon which to build a future. Nobody spoke of it but it was there in references, in chance shared looks. Yes, somewhere that land could be real, the children were safe, they were only waiting to be found. All Yorughan knew it. Now Nedlam was staring at the grey, dust-made Yorughan girl with her jaw loose in astonishment when a huge, snaking tentacle whipped out of the storm and lashed her flat, face-down in the powdery ground. She was rapidly coated in a clinging black snow.

"Hell, no!" Celestaine was rushing over to her, glaring at Heno, meaning *fire now, now!* And he had to call it down again and again until somehow Celest got Nedlam to her feet.

Bukham shouted out then, and there was something looming at them and over them out of the murk. It wasn't even bothering with a complex manifestation. This was a huge wave, rising higher and higher, the top starting to break and fall—and Heno realised it was a mass of the same black stuff, the hunger, as if every particle of it in the world had come together to swallow them whole so that it didn't matter about Celestaine's fight or Nedlam's strength or his power. Nothing could have stopped it. But he was the only one who had a hope of *stalling* it.

He looked towards Bukham, struggling to keep Murti upright as they pressed on, stopped now to look at the overarching hill of whatever it was about to crash on them. He looked at Lysandra, standing, her mouth ajar, staring up, at Kula, her hand holding tight to the hand of a Yorughan girl as the two of them stared, wide-eyed and the wave had teeth, mouths everywhere, filled with lacerating, working jaws, grinding, razor edges... and behind him Celestaine, getting off her knees, and Nedlam, barely on her feet with empty hands.

The surge stripped his bones. The fire swept upwards out of him, burning, burning him, and through its roots he felt how it ran, from him to them all, taking them and burning them to sustain its incredible force, feeding it upwards through the conduits of his nerves, moulded by his intent into the tree whose dazzling branches cauterised the falling waves, cut it into bits, made it into ash. Made them all into ash...

"No more!" Lysandra had stepped up to him, had got between him and Murti, seized him, seized the Guardian and used them both— the fire of heaven, so he'd heard the Kinslayer call it and laugh as he set the Draeyads ablaze in eternal torment. Now he felt it rip through him, cauterizing every fibre of him that had drawn the lightning, sealing it shut as it followed the path of least resistance through every jagged tendril and up into the plunging maws of the hunger. He saw the fire touch the black wave and, in an instant, transform it also into a thunderous, falling eternity of blinding white and yellow. The last thing he saw was Kula sweeping the Yorughan girl around into a tight clutch, enveloping her for protection in the heavy fur of her coat.

Celestaine saw Heno fall, collapsing in a cloud of grey beneath the falling wall of fire. She didn't move for she could never have reached him. She felt Nedlam's grasp on her arm tighten enough to break it as the warrior braced to face her death and she gripped back in return, feeling her hair singe and her forehead scald with the descending heat. She saw two girls, and Murti, his face aghast, his skin lucent, leaking light, Bukham trying to protect him with his cloak, standing in the way of the fall as the lightning vanished and Heno fell. Heno fell and she was not there. They were all falling and nothing she could do. Here, it had happened so fast. She was bewildered. This was hell. It was the moment in the room with the hand of the Reckoner falling at her strike and then the ravaging of the Guardian, but working against her favour this time, events out of hand, time ending.

She saw Lysandra step over Heno protectively, her arms raised to meet the fire she had lit into that thing, lit it up like a damn inferno, not with some internal spooky blaze but with a fire that ended all things and it was so big, she could see it now it was all fire—a mass of twisting ropes and threads, every part of its surface boiling with a sea of faces that came and went, faces of every kind of thing, every animal, every creature, every scrap of anything it had gleaned as it dwelt in the half-light of aeons.

Lysandra opened her mouth and a note came out of her, sung so pure and so bright for just one instant. The wave exploded. For one moment it was blown apart and then it ceased to exist utterly and there was a mighty thunderclap in its place so powerful that it knocked her down, Nedlam landing awkwardly across her legs and both of them sinking down into the deep, pale powder.

Then a hand came, helping her up. She was raised, coughing, into the dim gloom of that place she hated now above all other things, and she saw an old man peering anxiously at her and behind him another, with a long face she knew. "Deffo? Dr Fisher?"

"You must come away," Deffo was saying insistently although she was sure she had to stay, to find Heno. It was all she wanted.

"Get off me," she said, ungrateful.

"Mmn, off!" Nedlam said, shoving at Deffo and missing, throwing herself down on the ground again. Fisher sidestepped neatly.

"I'm afraid he is right. We should seek to evacuate as fast as possible," Fisher said.

She was not to be deflected. "Where's Heno?" She pushed past Deffo, sheathing her sword. There was a body on the ground in a dark coat. She made it there, fell on her knees to turn it over, bent close to press the fingers of her hand into his neck as she looked at his bald, burned head, tusks cracked and yellowed with the heat that had gone through him. "Come on," she whispered, feeling, hoping. "Come on, come on."

"We're tidying up loose ends, I think."

She turned, not able to believe her ears. Striding out of the fog of dust came a familiar figure, somewhat raddled and filthy, hobbling in a characteristic way, his long hair matted and his face pale and sickly. "Ralas?!"

"I see you made it," he said. "Capital effort, old friend. Not everyone survives both a Guardian and a God."

The sound of something enormous moving beyond the horizon. The tread of a god, dragging the corpses of a world behind it.

"Ah, dear," Deffo said behind her. "I believe the time has come for us to be more scarce."

And then she felt it, a flutter, and then a steady movement confirming that Heno lived, and the will to move came back to her in one moment more. "We can't leave him here." She saw Bukham bent over Murti a short distance away, as though trying to get him to stand.

"She's right." It was Lysandra that spoke, her voice carrying with a peculiar resonance that made it quite clear, as though it was coming from the land itself. "You have done enough. And you have done all that was asked of you to bring us here." She stood and faced the direction of the terrible sound, she looked back at Kula once and the girl nodded to her, firmly. Lysandra nodded back and smiled.

From the city, so near and still so far, a black bird was descending through the air. As it fell it tumbled and unravelled itself into the form of Tricky. Celestaine saw Ralas looking at her with the kind of expression she had never mastered—sheer, unbridled admiration. Tricky, the fourth Guardian now present, went to stand with Murti and Bukham. Bukham was taken aback by something. Then Fisher and Catt blocked her line of sight as they hugged one another and began to gabble, both at once, about being hunted by lorebeasts and vhermin and greater spirits and of all the treasures that must be here, lost in the sands and...

She bent down, to feel that heartbeat again, and under her other hand, placed on the ground, she felt the tremor of a much larger approaching dread. Someone sat down beside her in a puff of dry grey. She glanced over and saw Kula, sitting with her to look at Heno's face. The girl was dirty but otherwise seemed fine. Celest tried to smile but it wasn't in her at that moment enough to make it onto her face.

"Stand aside." It was Wanderer's voice.

Celestaine looked up as Fisher and Catt stepped back.

Wanderer didn't look the same. He was grey, only the shape of a person but without features save a mouth. The light that glowed out of him was the soft planelight. He had a sword in his hand, made out of the same grey that he was, the shape of the blade familiar to her as the one that the Kinslayer had worn and never wielded, every part of him covered over so that he was erased, remade. She realised, looking at him, that he meant to kill her. She was first, Nedlam second, Heno third. "What?" she said. "You can't be serious. It's not even possible!"

She felt Kula take her hand. Behind Wanderer Deffo was standing, and Tricky, engaged in some kind of argument which was immediately a fight, Deffo getting beaten down, Tricky furiously striking, searching him, tearing at his garments as they rolled in the dust and were lost to sight.

Then the grey brown nothing behind them began to form shapes of its own. They were made up of nightmare collections of features, masses of this and that, the leavings and traces of a million years of life's rise and fall, their wings storms of cloudy shadows, arching to block the lake overhead. The hunger storm skirled around them in its deadly dance, gathering at their backs.

"This was always your purpose on the journey," Lysandra said to her, confidential. "Mortals cannot survive here, but your demise would feed an army of revenants, enough to distract them while the gods were recovered."

"I told you it was wrong! Now you must give up!" This

scream came in Tricky's voice, her limbs and Deffo's lit by flickering blades of light as they fought one another and—to Celestaine's appalled amazement—their bodies began to come off, breaking free in shards and plates, a clay that was brittle now and falling away, revealing a strange, viscous, luminous core to each of them. She thought that Deffo glowed pale, white and blue, while Tricky was every hue imaginable, smaller, more liquid. Their shapes came and went as they tangled. It was beautiful, but savage to see and she looked to Lysandra again, seeing her dark figure illumined in a thousand shades, the most solid thing. Her anger focused and she turned to Lysandra.

"What? How do you know this all of a sudden?"

"I have always known it," she said. "I am of the Tzarkomen. We sacrificed our being to become the dealers with this place, the arbiters of the dead. Anything not here as a sorcerer is here as a sacrifice. All of us came here in the end, in order to survive him, the Kinslayer, and here they all are now." She touched her own chest to indicate that she was referring to herself. "As they fight, the gods possess their vessel. He cannot help it. His nature is to be the way." Lysandra gestured with her arm to where Bukham and Murti had been.

Celestaine looked past Wanderer's grey form and saw Bukham on his knees. The dust had fallen enough to reveal that the young Oerni had not been taken aback. He had been stabbed by the old man. As she watched he toppled over and from behind him came flowing massive dark shapes; the shreds and tatters of what had once been unimaginably mighty beings. They were clustering around him, veiling him from sight. As they neared the fallen body they began to reform, little by little, a hand here, a foot there—as if trying them on for size. And from the midst of them suddenly there came a figure in grey, unmistakable, his overgrown form huge, like a walking statue, both hands restored and sword raised.

Celestaine said, "I don't believe it. He was the one who

brought them here to die."

"He knew you would come," Lysandra said, pointing at Wanderer, or what was once Wanderer but was now the gateway for the Kinslayer's return, so that Celestaine realised she actually meant the Kinslayer. Her head was high, her gaze contemptuous. "He counted on you bringing some of the Guardians with you. People with godly strengths, who remembered him so very well" She gestured at Tricky and Deffo. "And here you are, walking someone else's path, warrior, into the trap. Doesn't suit you."

Tricky was blurred suddenly, shimmering. For a moment she was there, with Deffo, a rainbow smear. Then at the same time she was in her woman form, beside Kula, pressing something into the child's hand. Then gone. Celestaine looked down into Kula's small palm to see what Tricky had given her.

"It's a trick!" the little Guardian whispered in the midst of her incredible speed, in two places at once. She said it to Kula, in hand sign and with her voice. "Quick, be not the book, be the blank slate, unbind them!" Brown bones there, fingerbones, the kind that necromancers used to tell fortunes. A shiver went through Celestaine from head to toe, all wounds and woes forgotten. It could not be...

Wanderer's new, impressively featureless head jerked around to her. He didn't look much like the Kinslayer, but then, he didn't look like Wanderer. He was a blurred, in-between thing, not one or the other, sluggish as if animated by two conflicted wills. He raised his sword, but Lysandra was in his way. The sword slashed down, but missed. Lysandra was to the side of the mark. He had missed. A roar, soft, from a throat full of sand, blasted a wave of furious particles over Lysandra as she stood and—yes—straightened up her dress and adjusted the thick matted mane of her hair as though in preparation for a ceremony of importance. She didn't seem perturbed as the sword became metallic, sharpened and was drawn back for another swing.

Celestaine stared at the things Kula was holding.

"Are you telling me those are *his* bones from *his* hand that I...?"

Kula's fist closed around them, tight shut. Her eyes sharpened, intensified, reading what nobody else could see in swift moves back and forth. At the same time she thrust her free hand down, into the sand. She looked at Celestaine, met her eye and for a moment Celestaine saw him, knew that gaze anywhere, the cold judgement of it, the absolute knowledge, the condemnation and utter contempt. There was no mistaking such a pure hatred.

She groped for her sword in the powdery muck, flapping about. In the darkness and distance Bukham toppled over.

"No, no, you shits, what have you done?" She was grappling around, couldn't find it, couldn't find anything. He could not come back. He could not make all that death and suffering into nothing. It must not, could not happen. Then she focused on Kula's fist upheld right before her face. It was turned upright, thumb closed on top, and from it a grainy dust was falling. The girl opened her mouth and her odd, awkward voice came out, so seldom used it cracked as she spoke the words clumsily, croaking.

"Forgotten," she said, and smiled into Celestaine's desperate face. "All gone." She opened her hand and showed her empty palm.

The figure that had been Wanderer and was trying to be the Kinslayer stopped in his tracks motionless, empty as a statue to a king from millennia past, waiting for time to grind it to nothing. The blade of the sword, frozen mid-stroke, just brushed the top of Lysandra's head and gently tangled her hair as she turned back to her daughter.

"Well done."

Celestaine gawped. He was gone. Just like that. He was gone. She slumped, relief and hope making her want to laugh, exhaustion suddenly making itself known now the worst seemed past.

Kula glowed with pride. Behind her the gods' revenants circled, hungry, the black storm at their backs like an honour guard, only waiting for a fresh opportunity. The gods were terrifying, fermented brews of every kind of imagined power and form, surging, starving, little morsels of command slipping out in snatches of sound.

'...feed the pure...'

'...smite the wicked...'

'...cleanse the unworthy...'

'...worship me....'

'...bring help to those who... to those who... to those who...'

'...be kind to each other...'

'...slay the evil doer... let none remain...'

Lysandra looked down at Celestaine and Kula and smiled, a gentle smile, as soft as spring rain on new grass. The decorations in her hair, the golden wire, the flickers of silk, gleamed faintly. Her face was veiled with pale dust. She looked at the statue of the Kinslayer-thing. "Come, my dear, let us be wed." She made a pulling motion with her outstretched hand, as if yanking on a chain.

A streak of boiling grey and white flame shot out of the core of the Guardian's statue as if he had been pierced from behind by a blade that extended all the way to her palm. It was a flame that was gabbling as it went, explaining, protesting, words and prayers flying with it, in scraps and gibbers so garbled they could not be made out. As it fled, the veil of thick dust it wore fell away and revealed Wanderer's previous body, an old Oerni wayfarer, tired, collapsing. As he sank to his knees and then to his side he looked up at her. "Help Bukham. Help my student," he whispered and Lysandra nodded.

Meanwhile, in their own tangle of wills Deffo and Tricky were still fighting, "I can't let you end them," Deffo was saying, weakly, unconvinced, now in the form of a young man with mussed hair and a dandy's clothes from a long-ago era, perhaps the way he had first appeared in the world. He was trapped under Tricky, her coat become feathered wings, her hands around his throat. He was buckling visibly in terror as he choked. "It was always my duty. You don't understand. We all had a duty. Except you of course. But I am supposed to prevent..." And then he was hit by a form surging out of the sand but very definitely not made out of it, a form that smothered and hid both of the Guardians with its massive, feral mass of teeth and claws and wolflike monstrosity.

Fury had weighed in, but for whom and for what it was impossible to say. The three of them became a blur of fighting shapes.

Where Bukham had been the gods had gathered and were now seething. Celestaine could make them out now, one by one, empty outlines of them anyway, as they had been shown in their temples and their devotional paintings, outlines that were gradually filling up as they gained structure and sense from Bukham's memories of them. As he died so they expanded, legends and prayers, dreams and hopes, fears and loathings all combining to remake them in his images. Celestaine was horrified, but also awed, as she saw them begin to manifest. She was witnessing the birth of gods.

"I don't think so." Lysandra put out her hand and opened her palm to the gods.

In an unstoppable, rapid torrent the huge, trailing sails and rags of what was about to be mighty beings rushed to her like water down a mountainside, helpless, thundering to the point of contact with her palm. Within two seconds they were gone, entirely.

Lysandra grinned at Kula and bobbed a tiny, playful curtsey. She was impish, so pleased with herself. She raised her hands up and did a little jiggle, saying in a childish singsong. "I've won!"

The mass of Guardian war became a still, exhausted tangle of limbs and fur and feathers, After a second a large badger huffed, puffed and struggled its way out from the pack and lay on the ground, panting.

On the sandy ground Bukham lay still.

"...endings," the badger gasped. "Duty... prevent... endings."

Celestaine saw the waiting creatures of the plane begin to lumber off, rather hastily and with the distinct air of tails between their legs although only a couple had anything like tails. Only one remained, a tower of black wood and claws, its long head low and tilted, some kind of shield suggesting eyes tipped in their direction as if it listened closely to all that transpired. At its back the black storm remained and around its feet and hands tiny creatures like dark mice darted and ran in mazes.

Lysandra shook the piles of grey ash out of her dress. She looked at Deffo-the-badger and smiled. "Nothing ever really ends, it only changes form," she said. "So—job done."

"What just happened?" Nedlam slurred from her hands and knees, trying to shake the grogginess out of her head. She sat back on her heels, holding her forehead with both hands as if she were trying to keep it on.

"Lysandra ate the gods," Celestaine said, hoarse, brushing dust away from Heno's nose and mouth. Bending to blow it off, to feel whether or not he was breathing.

"Hope they tasted better than this filthy muck," Nedlam spat and coughed. "It's like those ship biscuits, only worse."

The light from the lake-sky was growing. The creatures that had remained on the periphery—revenants, ghosts, shades, the jackals of the deserts—were fading away, recoiling and withdrawing to hunt the plains again in search of something to cling to, some way to keep existing. One tentacle snaked out in an attempt to snag Lysandra's ankle.

"Ah-ah-ah," she said reprovingly and it shrivelled up into a tiny rag of shame and blew away in a sudden gust of wind, the first that place had ever felt.

Tricky and Deffo were looking at each other. Deffo shrugged.

Tricky shrugged and then she grinned. "That's what I like to call a Long Game. Outplayed the bastard, at last! Now, admit you were wrong. Bringing them back was a terrible idea."

"But I had to," Deffo whined. "I was made for that. Don't you see? We are all…"

"Tricky? I think I'm dying…"

Celestaine looked around, trying to figure out who was speaking, and saw Ralas a few yards away, nearly buried in sand.

Tricky looked around, sudden terror on her face. "Plucky?"

CHAPTER FORTY

"OH, NOT TODAY," Lysandra said with the air of someone who has had quite enough trouble and is on the verge of losing their temper. She reached down to where Wanderer had sunk to the ground and picked up what looked like an old sack—as it came up it was unmistakably his skin and clothing, somehow together as if they had both been only a suit he wore. She shook it hard and it disintegrated, eroding with the usual speed Vadakh offered to anything untethered by the living. Dusting off her fingers she made a peremptory gesture with both hands, one in the direction of Ralas and one in the direction of Bukham who lay as he had fallen, a short distance from Deffo.

A bolt of vivid golden fire shot from each of her movements. They struck the hearts of her targets silently and the storm of dark motes that had covered half the sky boiled backwards like waves receding from the shore on an outward tide.

"Actually, I may have overstated the case," Ralas said, wonderingly as he sat up from where he'd fallen. The horrid sensations of his flesh reknitting itself came again, working through his body on every broken bone and tendon but this time there was no stopping. His crooked toes realigned. His ribs straightened. "I... appear to be all right. Really, actually, all right."

Tricky, kneeling beside him, smiled her dazzling, crooked smile. "Look, I found this!" She produced the lute from inside her pocket.

"But, where was it?"

"Lying around some old mansion over in the city," she said. "I saw it when I was looking for that dust stuff."

"Wait, does this mean… can I… die?" He looked at Lysandra, who was bending down to brush the dirt off Kula's legs as the girl stood up from where she had been sitting at Heno's side, comforting the big Yogg with little pats.

Lysandra looked at Ralas, straightened, tucked her wild, long hair back behind her ears. "I thought I should leave that for now, seeing as you've got so many wedding plans, and all. Would be unfair to give a mouldy old man to an ever-youthful bride. She can kill you when you've both had enough."

Tricky blinked in surprise and Nedlam laughed. "Ah, you had me goin' until the end bit. Dead romantic, that is." She was holding her head and laughing, obviously hurt, but she managed to rise to her feet and pick up the worn and sludge-drenched haft of Lady Wall. She staggered over to where Bukham lay as he had before, beaten to it by an eager Dr Fisher—now returned to his less terrifying form—who was waving a jar of something under Bukham's nose.

"Salts of Micka," he said enthusiastically. "Proven to raise all but the absolutely long dead."

"Not too much, Fishy," Catt called out. "Too much makes them…"

Bukham sat up and promptly vomited all over the sand. They had eaten long ago so this wasn't much of a trouble. Wiping his mouth off he got sand all over himself and then managed to clean with the help of a handkerchief that Dr Catt reluctantly passed to him with many assurances he need never, ever give it back. "What… something's different… Did something happen to me?" He stood up. He was glowing faintly all over, the coloured piebald of his skin like some strange cowhide lamp that he'd once seen on a market stall.

Deffo looked at him, mouth ajar. He looked at Lysandra,

questioningly. "Oh that's... Did you put the old man into him? Is Wanderer...?"

"Lost and Found," she said. "I liked them. We liked them."

Kula nodded up at her, smiling and jumped up and down once, in happiness. She worked her mouth with difficulty, her speech as awkward as ever, but distinct. "Thanks. Ma"

Then the dark creature got up from its place and the roiling dark of mice and motes surged to its back. "You should leave here. I can't hold them back much longer." His vermin mantle swirled around him, swarmed up his limbs to deliver all the morsels they had scoured from the dust.

"Oh, what?" Deffo said, looking at him with a wrinkled nose and then at Tricky. "It was holding them back? I thought it was preparing to kill us all."

"You would think that," Celestaine said, trying hard to be happy, trying hard not to ask the inevitable question as Heno remained still. "Not all ugly things are out to get you. We only wish they were. But... " She looked up at Lysandra in appeal.

Lysandra looked at Kula as if for permission. Kula nodded solemnly.

Lysandra twitched her fingers.

Heno took a breath.

Dr Catt turned, holding his returned handkerchief between forefinger and thumb at arm's length. He dropped it and it disintegrated before it hit the ground, a storm of grey shadows swirling to grab its fading threads. "So, old girl," he looked at Lysandra. "What was it exactly the Kinslayer would have had you do here, if you'd come on his ticket, so to speak?"

Lysandra looked around and then shrugged. "But I didn't," she said and held up her hand and flipped the world inside out.

CELESTAINE LOOKED AROUND. They were on a blustery headland, wind very much in the face, soggy grass under them, within a circle of trees that reached like pillars from earth to the sky and seemed to hold it up on huge canopies of green. Through the long avenue of wild growth that led down the hill they could see the shape of Roherich's Tower and the white gleam of Ilkand Temple below them. Of Deffo, Tricky, Ralas and Drs Catt and Fisher there was no sign. Lysandra stood beside Kula, who was holding hands with a taller, stronger girl, a Yorughan girl in a tunic and short trousers, with a grey skin and just the beginnings of new tusks pushing out her lower lip. Nedlam was still holding her head, staring around her, puzzlement on her face. Heno was getting up, looking in bewilderment as they were circled by the bronze and gold form of Horse, cantering in excitement as she went around and around the Wanderer's Circle she had grown, brandishing her silver spear, shouting, "It worked!"

"What...?" Celestaine was asking when Heno jumped up, almost knocking her over, his gaze on the children.

"Azu?" he said, and his voice was shaking, his knees were shaking. He called on his power of the white fire, and nothing happened. He felt nothing, nothing at all where it used to be, not even a whisper.

"Heno," the girl said in obvious relief, sagging suddenly. "You came back for me. I knew you would." She let go of Kula's hand and rushed over into Heno's embrace and they hugged one another tightly, Nedlam rushing towards them to see if it was true and not a trick of some kind.

Lysandra was looking at Celestaine watching them. Celestaine shook her head, thinking she'd ask later, now not the right time. Instead of the question about the girl, she looked hard at Lysandra. "Could you bring them all back. All the ones who made you?"

Lysandra shook her head. "Fire burns everything up—flesh, memory, form—until only the energy remains. I have been made in fire. They're gone forever, just like the gods."

"And are you a god?"

"I think it would be a very bad idea," Lysandra said as Horse slowed down and turned in, out of breath, her javelin twined with living flowers whose scent trailed a sweet fragrance across the grass towards them.

Celestaine got up, feeling left out. She looked at Heno and at the girl, obviously related to him now she looked closely. She asked silently as he looked at her—*is it?*

"My cousins' girl," he said. "Azu." Tears were running down his craggy face. He held out his arm.

Later, she thought. *Later, I'll ask.* She hurried to join the hug.

Kula was already riding around on Horse's back, her mouth open in excitement, eyes wide as she held on. They stayed there long enough to regain their bearings.

"What about Deffo?" Celest asked once they'd checked themselves over and recovered.

"I thought he could take the boat," Lysandra said. "Tricky and Ralas have their own ways with Taedakh, um, I mean with the big dark evil-looking Vadakhi of the Storm. And Catt and Fisher wanted to see the City before it was ruined so it's up to them whether they can tear themselves away in time."

"Where's Bukham?" Nedlam asked. "And that hole in the sea thing. Did we close it?"

"Bukham," Lysandra said. "I think he will find his way back—otherwise I've made a big mistake. As for the hole in the sea—that one will fade. It's the one under Nydarrow that's going to be harder to deal with." She shrugged with that eloquent move that said she'd done her bit, she was over it. "But now Kula and I are both hungry. I don't know what all of you are going to do with yourselves—" she reached out and plucked Kula off Horse's back and set her on her feet, "—but we are going back to town for another one of those pies."

"But—" Celestaine started to say, but Lysandra shook her head and held her finger up to her lips.

"Do you think we should go with them?" Nedlam asked

as they watched the two of them heading down the avenue together, hand in hand.

"No, I think they'll be all right on their own actually," Celestaine said, sadly. She was already starting to miss them. "After all, a kid and a woman that can unmake and remake the world. What trouble could they possibly get in that needs three crocked has-beens?"

"Speak for yerself," Nedlam said with a huff, but she was grinning. "Oi, Horsie. What about a lift?"

"You've got legs," the centaur said. "But I'll walk with you if you like."

"I want pie," Azu said. "Kula said there was pie."

"She did say that," Celestaine agreed, longing to go. "Oh, what are we waiting here for?" And she took Azu's hand in her own, not even sure she was going to until she did, and then they were running down the hill after, until Kula turned and saw them and then she and Lysandra picked up their skirts and started to run too, away, and they were racing, racing fast as they could, jumping down through the wet grass, the hooves of Horse a merry thunder in the back, and it was nearly, nearly like flying.

CHAPTER FORTY-ONE

RALAS DUNWIN OF Forinth, scion of the noble but minor house of Parsleymaine, bard to the courts of Ilkand, was married to Gwenthyn, orphan of Tredyllant, which is somewhere far far to the South of Cinquetann on a nameless bend of river, at Cinquetann Temple. The happy couple were received at a modest roadside tavern and celebrated with a feast that went on for several days in which guests, at first few, then many as the word spread, stayed to eat and drink until they passed out only to wake later and find a silver polly in every pocket—though on the third day the Dunwins were nowhere to be found. Not that anyone minded.

As well as paying for their stay they had managed to leave behind a rather worn leather wallet which, when the lady of the house checked it, had but one copper scit in it but later, when she had decided to give it away to her nephew he found it had one scit in it and thereafter whenever he opened it to play with it he found it always had one scit in it no matter how many times you took one out and, unfortunately on one occasion, no matter how many pollys you put in.

ACKNOWLEDGEMENTS

ONE DAY EVERYONE will realise that my works are all a rehash of 1980s classic animations, fairytales and the skiffy and fanty collection of the Leeds City Libraries 1978-1988 running on the Star Wars/Labyrinth engine. However, until such a time occurs and some academic punts out the critical paper proving it beyond all doubt I'd like to thank not only those things mentioned above but the following people for enabling me to become a very happy recombiner algorithm.

This book is dedicated to my son, Daniel, who is 16 this week (June 2018). All my children have changed my outlook on humanity and the meaning of life enormously but since he was the first he did the most damage to my previously oblivious state so a great debt of thanks to him. Also to Ben and Alice: I'm sure you have many revelations yet to offer and books dedicated to you will be along in due course.

Secondly I'm going to thank Adrian Tchaikovsky in whose sagely footsteps I have trod in creating this story. Not only did I tread on his footsteps and stamp on his characters and expand his world with wild and poorly-geographically understood extensions, I have also scribbled on his map and mucked around with all his toys. They were such great toys! In addition to that I would never have been able to write for Rebellion on this project if we hadn't been standing at the pub carvery counter together one day and Adrian said, 'I'm writing this fun little book for a project. I think they might be looking for other writers to...' and I bit his hand off. They should have served that turkey a lot faster.

Third I am thanking my editor Michael Rowley, who did a fantastic and thorough job. His instincts for pace and his meticulous help with continuity issues (arising from the fact that Adrian writes a beautiful rich history in every sentence and I seemingly forget every bit of it and then misremember the bits I do recall) were invaluable.

Thanks to my husband for helping me stay relatively sane—not only when I'm prey to writing pitfalls but also at all other times.

Thank you to my patrons at Patreon for their cheerleading and just for being there at all. It means a lot every day.

Finally thanks to my mother and her constant and unwavering support, both emotional and financial, which has enabled me to have any kind of writing career at all.

ABOUT THE AUTHOR

JUSTINA ROBSON WAS born in Yorkshire, England in 1968. After completing school she dropped out of Art College, then studied Philosophy and Linguistics at York University. She sold her first novel in 1999 which also won the 2000 amazon.co.uk Writers' Bursary Award.

She has been a student (1992) and a teacher (2002, 2006) at The Arvon Foundation, in the UK, (a centre for the development and promotion of all kinds of creative writing). She was a student at Clarion West, the US bootcamp for SF and Fantasy writers, in 1996.

Her books have been shortlisted for most major genre awards. An anthology of her short fiction, "Heliotrope", was published in 2012 and she continues to write a couple of short pieces a year. In 2004 Justina was a judge for the Arthur C Clarke Award on behalf of The Science Fiction Foundation.

Her novels and stories range widely over SF and Fantasy, often combining the two and often featuring AIs and machines who aren't exactly what they seem.

She is also the proud author of "The Covenant of Primus" (2013) beckermeyer USA—the Hasbro-authorised history and 'bible' of The Transformers.

DISCOVER NEW WORLDS

2018 marks the launch of Solaris's boldest new project. We've invited your favourite writers to explore new worlds *together*, weaving new legends and laying the groundwork for years to come.

THE AFTERMATH: A hundred years after asteroid strikes wiped out civilisation, the new communities rising from the ashes struggle to survive.

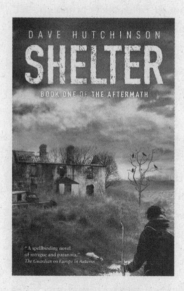

SHELTER
Dave Hutchinson
June 2018

HAVEN
Adam Roberts
August 2018

AFTER THE WAR: The Armies of Light gathered, and after a long, bitter war, the Dark Lord was slain. But glory is easy; true peace is hard, and bitter.

REDEMPTION'S BLADE

Adrian Tchaikovsky

July 2018

SALVATION'S FIRE

Justina Robson

September 2018

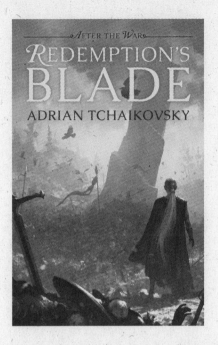

AFTER THE WAR

REDEMPTION'S BLADE

ADRIAN TCHAIKOVSKY

Ten years ago, the Kinslayer returned from the darkness. His brutal Yorughan armies issued from the pits of the earth, crushing all resistance, leaving burnt earth and corruption behind. Thrones toppled and cities fell.

And then he died.

Celestaine—one of the heroes that destroyed him—has tasked herself with correcting the worst excesses of the Kinslayer's brief reign, bringing light back to a broken world. With two Yorughan companions, she faces fanatics, war criminals and the Kinslayer's former minions, as the fragile alliances of the War break down into feuding and greed.

The Kinslayer may be gone, but he cast a long shadow: one from which she may never truly escape.

 WWW.SOLARISBOOKS.COM

Follow us on Twitter! www.twitter.com/solarisbooks

FIND US ONLINE!

www.rebellionpublishing.com

/rebellionpub /rebellionpublishing /rebellionpub

SIGN UP TO OUR NEWSLETTER!

rebellionpublishing.com/sign-up

YOUR REVIEWS MATTER!

Enjoy this book? Got something to say?

Leave a review on Amazon, GoodReads or with your
favourite bookseller and let the world know!